PEN]

The Ow

Crosbie Garstin (1887-1930) was the eldest child of Norman Garstin, an Irishman who settled in Penzance and became one of the leading lights of the Newlyn School of Art.

Crosbie Garstin's short life was as dramatic as any. Following education in Penzance, Cheltenham and Bedford, he travelled to the United States and Canada where he worked as a horse breaker on ranches, in threshing gangs, as a sawyer in lumber camps and as a Pacific coast miner. Subsequently, he travelled to Africa where he became manager of a cattle ranch.

At the start of World War I he returned to Cornwall and enlisted as a trooper in the 1st King Edward's Horse regiment. Commissioned in the field, he also served as an intelligence officer in Ireland following the 1916 Easter Rising before returning to the Western Front.

Whilst at the front, his poetry that had previously been published in Punch and other magazines was issued as *Vagabond Verses*, followed by *The Mud Larks*, a series of sketches from the front for Punch magazine. He then embarked on a short, but prolific literary career that included the three Ortho Penhale books—*The Owls' House*, *High Noon* and *The West Wind*—as well as further novels, poetry and travel writing (*The Sunshine Settlers*, *The Coasts of Romance*, and *The Dragon and the Lotus*). Crosbie Garstin lived at Lamorna in west Cornwall.

His final novel, *China Seas*, was made into a Hollywood movie starring Clark Gable in 1935, but Crosbie didn't live to see his work on screen. Following an early morning boating accident off Salcombe, Devon in April 1930, Crosbie Garstin disappeared, presumed drowned, although no body was ever found.

* * *

Spencer Smart dug up his roots in rural East Anglia, put them in the back of an old Volvo, then planted them by a sandy beach in west Cornwall. He has worked as a technical author, marketing consultant and part-time writer since the late 1980s.

Spencer's first thriller *No Regrets* introduced Dutch detective Pieter van Es, who fled Amsterdam for a not-so-peaceful new life in Penzance. *A Statement Of Intent*, the second in the series is set for publication by Literary Nation in 2015. He is also working on a fictional 'what-if?' biography of Crosbie Garstin for future publication.

Crosbie Garstin Bibliography

Vagabond Verses

The Mud Larks

The Mud Larks Again

The Sunshine Settlers

The Black Knight (with Mrs Alfred Sidgwick)

The Ballad of the Royal Ann

The Coasts of Romance

The Owls' House

Samuel Kelly, an Eighteenth Century Seaman (as editor)

High Noon

The West Wind

The Dragon and the Lotus

Houp-la!

China Seas

Also by Spencer Smart

No Regrets

CROSBIE GARSTIN

PENHALE
The Owls' House

Edited and revised by
SPENCER SMART

LITERARY
NATION

Literary Nation
North Street, Marazion
Cornwall TR17 0EA

www.literarynation.com
www.crosbiegarstin.com

First published in the United Kingdom in 1923

Fully revised edition with introduction,
published by Literary Nation, 2015. Reprinted with amendments, 2017.

A CIP catalogue record for this book is available from the British Library

ISBN 978-0-9933131-0-3

LITERARY
NATION

Introduction

ON A windy spring evening, looking out towards the English Channel from the rocky shore of Lamorna Cove, it's easy to see how Crosbie Garstin imagined the adventures of the characters in this novel. Tales of smuggling handed down from generation to generation. Stories of shipwrecks; of piracy; and of day-to-day life in 18th century west Cornwall. All human life, as they say, could once be found here, in this little cove.

I only discovered Crosbie Garstin's work a few years ago. A friend lent me copies of the books that make up the Penhale trilogy—*The Owls' House*, *High Noon* and *The West Wind*—and I was captivated. So much so, that I've dedicated a huge amount of time to edit and republish new editions of the books, in order to bring Crosbie Garstin to a new audience.

After much soul-searching on whether to publish the novels in their original format or to revise them for a 21st century audience, I took the latter route and hope that I have made the right decision.

I have laid a light touch over these works in the editing process: using an early edition of the texts, I have corrected mistakes and pla-cenames, adapted hyphenation and spellings to make it an easier read (to-day becomes today, etc.) and brought consistency to the style and format of the three novels. Finally, I purged the books of outdated words that were considered normal in a country that still had its grip on an empire when originally written. The gripping drama, the romance, the language and the exploits of the Penhale family remain unchanged. If you are reading this book for the first time, you will be none the wiser. Only a Garstin enthusiast with a minuscule eye for detail will notice the changes.

Crosbie Garstin himself, remains an enigma. Following a dec-ade-long professional writing career, he disappeared from a rowing boat in Salcombe harbour in April 1930. Whilst his companions survived by swimming to shore or clinging to a nearby boat, Crosbie

Garstin, the strong swimmer, the adventurer, disappeared and despite the efforts to find him or his body, he was never seen again.

According to newspaper reports at the time, the rowing boat was discovered near Castle Rocks, upturned with its oars nearby. Did Crosbie Garstin drown in the early hours of that fateful April morning? Or did the eternal adventurer seize the opportunity to escape from his settled, married life in Lamorna and begin afresh in another village, another city, another country?

To learn more about Crosbie Garstin, you must get a copy of *The Witty Vagabond – A Biography of Crosbie Garstin (1887-1930)*. Comprehensively researched and written by David Tovey, a leading Cornish art historian, *The Witty Vagabond* offers a thorough and excellent insight into his life and times. Find out more information about this biography at www.stivesart.info.

I hope you enjoy this new edition of *The Owls' House* as much as I have enjoyed immersing myself in the 18th century and bringing Ortho Penhale (and Crosbie Garstin!) back from their undeserved obscurity.

Spencer Smart
Cornwall
August, 2017

Chapter I

IT WAS late evening when John Penhale left the Helston lawyer's office. A fine drizzle was blowing down Coinage Hall Street; thin beams of light pierced the chinks of house shutters and curtains, barred the blue dusk with misty orange rays, touched the street puddles with alchemic fingers, turning them to gold. A chaise clattered uphill, the horses' steam hanging round them in a kind of lamplit nimbus, the postboy's head bent against the rain.

Outside an inn an old soldier with a wooden leg, and very drunk, stood wailing a street ballad, both eyes shut, impervious to the fact that his audience had long since left him. Penhale turned into the Angel, went on straight into the dining room, and sat down in the far corner with the right side of his face to the wall. He did so from habit. A trio of squireens in mud-bespattered riding-coats sat near the door and made considerable noise. They had been hare hunting and were rosy with sharp air and hard riding. They greeted every appearance of the ripe serving maid with loud whoops, and passed her from arm to arm. She protested and giggled. Opposite them a local shopkeeper was entertaining a creditor from Plymouth to the best bottle the town afforded. The company was made up by a very young Ensign of Light Dragoons, bound to Winchester to join his regiment for the first time, painfully self-conscious and aloof in his new scarlet. Penhale beat on the table with his knife. The maid escaped from the festive sportsmen and brought him a plate of boiled beef and onions. As she was about to set the plate before him, one of the hare hunters lost his balance and fell to the ground with a loud crash of his chair and a yell of delight from his companions.

The noise caused Penhale to turn his head. The girl emitted an "ach" of horror, dropped the plate on the table, and recoiled as though someone had struck her. Penhale pulled the plate towards him, picked up his knife and fork, and quietly began to eat. He was quite used to these displays. The girl backed away, staring in a sort of dreadful fascination. A squireen caught at her wrist, calling her his "sweet slut," but she wrenched herself free and ran out of the door.

She did not come near Penhale again; the tapster brought him the rest of his meal. Penhale went on eating, outwardly unmoved; he had been subject to these outbursts, off and on, for eighteen years.

Eighteen years previously myriads of birds had been driven south by the hard winter up country. One early morning, after a particularly bitter snap, a hind had run in to say that the pond on Polmenna Downs, above the farm, was covered with wild duck. Penhale took an old flintlock fowling-piece of his father's which had been hanging neglected over the fireplace for years, and made for Polmenna, loading as he went. He had to wriggle on his stomach round boulders and clumps of sedge for some two hundred yards, but came to the pool's edge without disturbing the quarry.

As the hind had said, the pool was covered with duck. Penhale crouched under cover of some willows, brought the five-foot gun to his shoulder, and blazed into the brown.

An hour later a fisherman, setting rabbit snares in a hedge above the Luddra, saw what he described as "a red man" fighting through the scrub and bramble that fringed the cliff. It was John Penhale. The gun had exploded, blowing half his face away. Penhale had no intention of throwing himself over the Luddra. He was blind with blood and pain. The fisherman led him home with difficulty, and then, being of a practical mind, returned to the pond to pick up the duck.

An old crone, who had the reputation of being a "white witch," was summoned to Bosula, and managed to stop the bleeding by means of incantations, cobwebs, and dung—principally dung. The hind was sent on horseback to Penzance to fetch Doctor Spargo.

Doctor Spargo had been making a night of it with his friend the Collector of Customs and a stray ship Captain who was peculiarly gifted in the brewing of rum toddies. The doctor was put to bed at dawn by his household staff, and when he was knocked up again at eleven he was not the best pleased. He bade his housekeeper tell the Bosula messenger that he was out, called out to a confinement in

Morvah parish and was not expected back till evening and turned over on his pillow.

The housekeeper returned, agitated, to say that the messenger refused to move. He knew the doctor was in, he said; the groom had told him so. Furthermore, if Spargo did not come to his master's assistance without further ado, he would smash every bone in his body. Doctor Spargo rolled out of bed, and, opening the window, treated the messenger to samples from a vocabulary enriched by a decade of army life. The messenger listened to the tirade unmoved, and as Doctor Spargo cursed it was borne in on him that he had seen this outrageous fellow before. Presently he remembered when; he had seen him at St Gwithian Feast, a canvas jacket on, tossing parish stalwarts as a terrier tosses rats. The messenger was Bohenna the wrestler. Doctor Spargo closed both the tirade and the window abruptly and bawled for his boots.

The pair rode westwards, the truculent hind cantering on the heels of the physician's cob, laying into it with an ash plant whenever it showed symptoms of flagging. The cob tripped over a stone in Bucca's Pass and shied at a goat near Trewoofe, on each occasion putting its master neatly over its head. By the time Spargo arrived at Bosula he was shaking worse than ever. He demanded more rum to steady his hand, but there was none. He pulled himself together as best he could and set to work, trembling and wheezing.

Spargo was a retired army surgeon; he had served his apprenticeship in the shambles of Oudenarde and Malplaquet among soldiers who had no option but to submit to his ministrations. His idea was to patch men up so that they might fight another day, but without regard to their appearance. He sewed the tatters of John Penhale's face together securely but roughly, pocketed his fee, and rode home, gasping, to his toddies.

John Penhale was of fine frame and hearty. In a week or two he was out and about; in a month he had resumed the full business of the farm; but his face was not a pleasant sight. The left side was merely marked with a silvery burn on the cheekbone, but the right might have been dragged by a harrow; it was ragged scars from brow to chin.

The eye had gone and part of an ear, the broken jaw had set concave, and his cheek had split into a long harelip, revealing a perpetual snarl of teeth underneath. He hid the eye socket with a black patch, but the lower part of his face he could not mask.

Three months after his accident he rode into Penzance Market. If one woman squeaked at the sight of him, so did a dozen, and children ran to their mothers blubbering that the devil had come for them. Even the men, though sympathetic, would not look him in the face, but stared at their boots while they talked, and were plainly relieved when he moved away. John never went in again unless driven by the direst necessity, and then hurried out the moment his affairs were transacted. For, despite his bulk and stoic bearing, he was supersensitive, and the horror his appearance awoke cut him to the raw. Thus at the age of twenty-three he became a bitter recluse, a prisoner within the bounds of his farm Bosula, cared for by a widow and her idiot daughter, mixing only with his few hinds and odd farmers and fishermen that chance drove his way.

He had come to Helston on business, to hear the terms of his aunt Selina's will, and now that he had heard them he was eager to be quit of the place. The serving girl's behaviour had stung him like a whiplash, and the brawling of the drunken squires jarred on his every nerve. He could have tossed the three of them out of the window if he liked, but he quailed at the thought of their possible mockery. They put their heads together and whispered, hiccuping and sniggering. They were, as a fact, planning a descent on a certain lady in Pigs Street, but John Penhale was convinced that they were laughing at him. The baby Ensign had a derisive curl in his lip, John was sure. . . . He could feel the two shopkeepers' eyes turned his way. . . . It was unbearable.

Sneers, jeers, laughter. . . . He hated them all, everybody. He would get out, go home to Bosula, to sanctuary. He had a sudden longing for Bosula, still and lonely among the folding hills . . . his own place. He drank off his ale, paid the score, and went out to see what the weather was like.

The wind had chopped round easterly and the rain had stopped. The moon was up, breasting through flying ridges of cloud like a naked white swimmer in the run of surf. Penhale found an ostler asleep on a pile of straw, roused him and told him to saddle his horse, mounted, and rode westwards out of town.

He passed a lone pedestrian near Antron and a string of pack-horses under Breage church, but for the rest he had the road to himself. He ambled gently, considering the terms of his aunt's will. She had left him her strong farm of Tregors, in the Kerrier Hundred, lock, stock, and barrel, on the one condition that he married within twelve months. In default of his marrying it was to pass to her late husband's cousin, Carveth Donnithorne, ship chandler, of Falmouth.

John Penhale paid silent tribute to his aunt's cleverness. She disliked the smug and infallible Donnithorne intensely, and in making him her next heir had passed over four nearer connections with whom she was on good terms. Her reasons for this curious conduct were that she was a Penhale by birth, with intense family pride, and John was the last of her line. A trivial dispute between John and Carveth, over a coursing match, she had fostered with all the cunning that was in her till the men's dislike of each other amounted to plain hatred. She knew John would do anything in his power to keep Donnithorne out of the Tregors rents. She would drive him into matrimony, and then, with reasonable luck, the line would go on and Penhales rule at Bosula for ever and ever.

John laughed grimly at the thought of his aunt, sly old devil! She had married and left home before he was born, and he had not seen her a score of times in his life; but she was a vivid memory. He could see her now, riding into Bosula a-pillion behind one of her farm hands, her cold blue eyes taking in every detail of the yard, and hear her first words of greeting to her brother after a year's separation.

'Jan, thou mazed fool, the trash wants cutting back down to Long Meadow, and there's a cow coughing. Bring her in to once and I'll physick her!'

The cow came in at once. Everybody obeyed Selina without question or delay, both at Bosula and Tregors. Her husband, Jabez Donnithorne, was the merest cipher whose existence she barely acknowledged.

On one occasion Jabez, returning very drunk from Helston Market, having neglected to buy the heifers he was sent after, Selina personally chastised him with a broom handle and bolted him in the pigsty for the night, where he was overlaid by a sow and suffered many indignities. That cured Jabez.

Selina never stopped long at Bosula—three days at the most. But in that time she would have inspected the place from bound to bound, set everybody to rights, and dictated the policy of the farm for twelve months to come. As she had ruled her brother in boyhood, she ruled him to the day of his death. She was fond of him, but only because he was head of the family. His wife she looked on merely as a machine for producing male Penhales. She would see to it that on her death Tregors fell to her family, and then, doubly endowed, the Penhales of Bosula would be squires and gentlefolk in the land.

When after many years John remained the only child, Selina bit back her disappointment and concentrated on the boy. She insisted on his being sent to Helston Grammar School, paid half the cost of his education, kept him in plentiful pocket money, and saw that his clothes were of the best. He was a handsome, upstanding lad, and did her credit. She was more than satisfied. He would go far, she told herself, make a great match. Then came John's accident. Selina made no move until he was out and about again, and then rode over to assess the damage. She stalked suddenly into the kitchen one morning, surveyed the ruins of her nephew's comely face, outwardly unmoved, and then stalked out again without a word of consolation or regret, barked instructions that her horse was to be baited and ready in two hours, and turned up the hill.

Up the hill she strode, over Polmenna Downs and on to that haunt of her girlhood, the Luddra Head. Perched high on its stone brows, the west wind in her cloak and hair, she stared, rigid and unseeing, over the glitter of the Channel. She was back in the two hours, but her eyelids were red. For the last time in her life Selina had been crying.

She slept at the Angel at Helston that night, visited a certain disreputable attorney next morning, and left his office with the Tregellas mortgage in her pocket.

Mr Hugh Tregellas, of Tregellas, had four daughters and a mania for gambling. He did not fling his substance away on horse racing, cock or man fights; indeed, he lifted up his voice loudly against the immorality of these pursuits. He took shares in companies formed to extract gold from seawater, in expeditions to discover the kingdom of Prester John, and such like. Any rogue with an oiled tongue and a project sufficiently preposterous could win a hearing from the squire. But though much money went out, few ships came home, and the four Miss Tregellases sat in the parlour, their dowries dwindling to nothing, and waited for the suitors who did not come.

All this was well known to their neighbour, Selina Donnithorne. She knew that when the four Miss Tregellases were not in the parlour playing at ladies they were down on their kneebones scrubbing floors. She even had it on sound authority that the two youngest forked out the cow-byre every morning.

She called on the squire one afternoon, going to Tregellas in state, dressed in her best, and driving in a cabriolet she had purchased dirt cheap from a broken-down roisterer at Bodmin Assizes. She saw Mr Tregellas in his gunless gunroom and came to the point at once. She wanted his youngest daughter for John Penhale. Mr Tregellas flushed with anger and opened his mouth to reply, but Selina gave him no opportunity. Her nephew was already a man of moderate means, she said, living on his own good farm in the Penwith Hundred, with an income of nearly one hundred pounds per annum into the bargain. When she died he would have Tregors also. He was well educated, a fine figure of a man, and sound in wind and limb, if a trifle cut about one side of the face—one side only. But then, after all these wars, who was not?

Here Mr Tregellas managed to interpose a spluttering refusal. Selina nodded amiably. She ventured to remind Mr Tregellas that since Arethusina's dowry had sunk off Cape St Vincent with the Fowey privateer *God's Providence*, her chances of a distinguished marriage were negligible; also that she, Selina, was now mortgagee of Tregellas and the mortgage fell due at Michaelmas.

A gambler is fundamentally an optimist *ad absurdum*, a believer that the one chance shall prevail over the ninety-and-nine, in short, an upholder of miracles. Mr Tregellas was a gambler. As long as there was one chance left to him, no matter how long, the future was radiant. He laughed at Selina. He had large interests in a company for trading with the King of certain South Sea atolls, he said, the lagoons of which were paved with pearl. It had been estimated that this enterprise could not fail to enrich him at a rate of less than eleven hundred and fifty-three per year. A ship bearing the first fruits was expected in Bristol almost any day now; was, in fact, overdue, but these nor'-easterly headwinds. . . . Mr Tregellas saw Selina to the door, his good humour restored, promising her that long before Michaelmas he would not only be paying off the mortgage on Tregellas, but offering her a price for Tregors as well.

Selina rocked home in her cabriolet no whit perturbed by the squire's optimism. Nor'-easterly headwinds indeed! . . .

Three months from that date Mr Tregellas returned the call. Selina was feeding ducks in the yard when he came. She emptied her apron, led the squire into the kitchen, and gave him a glass of cowslip wine, which he needed.

'Come to offer me a price for Tregors?' she asked.

The old gambler winked his weak eyes pathetically, like a child blinking back tears, and buried his face in his hands. Selina did not twit him further. There was no need; she had him where she wanted him. She smiled to herself. So the pearl ship had gone the deep road of the Fowey privateer and all the other ventures. She clicked her tongue, "Tchuc–tchuc" and offered him another glass of wine.

'I'll send for John Penhale tomorrow,' said she. 'I'll tell him that if he don't take your maid he shan't have Tregors. You tell your maid if she don't take my John I'll put you all out on the road come Michaelmas. Now get along wid 'ee.'

Arethusina came over to Tregors to pay Mrs Donnithorne a week's visit, and John was angled from his retreat by the bait of a roan colt he had long coveted and which his aunt suddenly expressed herself willing to sell.

The sun was down when he reached the farm; Selina met him in the yard, and leading him swiftly into the stables explained the lay of the land while he unsaddled his horse; but she did not tell him what pressure had been brought to bear on the youngest Miss Tregellas.

John was amazed and delighted. Mr Hugh Tregellas's daughter willing to marry him, a common farmer! Pretty, too; he had seen her once, before his accident, sitting in the family pew in Cury church—plump, fluffy little thing with round blue eyes, like a kitten. This was incredible luck!

He was young then and hot-blooded, sick of the loneliness of Bosula and the haphazard ministrations of the two slatterns. He was for dashing into the house and starting his lovemaking there and then, but Selina held him, haggling like a fishwife over the price of the roan. When he at length got away from her it was thick dusk. It was dark in the kitchen, except for the feeble glow of the turf fire, Selina explaining that she had unaccountably run out of tallow dips, the boy should fetch some from Helston on the morrow.

Arethusina came downstairs dressed in her eldest sister's bombazine dress, borrowed for the occasion. She was not embarrassed; she, like John, was eager for change, weary of the threadbare existence and unending struggle at home, of watching her sisters grow warped and bitter. She saw ahead, saw four grey old women, dried kernels rattling in the echoing shell of Tregellas's house, never speaking, hating each other and all things, doddering on to the blank end—four grey nuns cloistered by granite pride. Anything were better than that. She would sob off to sleep swearing to take any chance rather than come to that, and here was a chance. John Penhale stood for life full and flowing in place of want and decay. He might only be a yeoman, but he would have two big farms and could keep her in comfort. She would have children, she hoped, silk dresses, and a little lapdog. Some day she might even visit London.

She entered the kitchen in good heart and saw John standing before the fire, a vague but imposing silhouette. A fine figure of a man, she thought, and her heart lifted still higher. She dropped him a mischievous curtsey. He took her hand laughing, a deep, pleasant laugh. They sat on the settle at the back of the kitchen and got on famously.

John had barely spoken to any sort of woman for a year, leave alone a pretty woman; he thought her wonderful. Arethusina had not seen a presentable man for double that period; all her stored coquetry bubbled out. John was only twenty-four, the girl but nineteen; they were like two starved children, sitting down to a square meal.

The brass-studded grandfather clock tick-tocked in its corner; the yellow house-cat lay crouched on the hearth watching the furze kindling, for mice; Selina nodded in her rocker before the fire, sub-consciously keeping time with the beats of the clock. A whinny of treble laughter came from the settle, followed by John's rumbling bass, then whisperings.

Selina beamed at her *vis-à-vis*, the yellow cat. She was elated at the success of her plans. It had been a good idea to let the girl get to know John before she could see him. The blow would be softened when morning came. In Selina's experience, obstacles that appeared insurmountable at night dwindled to nothing in the morning light; one came at them with a fresh heart. She was pleased with Arethusina. The girl was healthy, practical, and ambitious — above all, ambitious. She might not be able to do much with John, marred as he was, but their children would get all the advantages of the mother's birth, Selina was sure. The chariot of the Penhales would roll onwards, steered by small, strong hands.

She glanced triumphantly at the pair on the settle and curled her thin lips. Then she rose quietly and slipped off to bed. The yellow cat remained, waiting its prey. Arethusina and John did not notice Selina's departure; they were engrossed in each other. The girl had the farmer at her finger-ends and enjoyed the experience; she played on his senses as on a keyboard. He loomed above her on the settle, big, eager, boyish, with a passionate break in his laughter. She kept him guessing, yielded and retreated in turn, thrilled to feel how easily he responded to her flying moods. What simpletons men were and what fun!

John shifted nearer up the settle, his great hot hand closed timorously over hers. She snatched it free and drew herself up.

'La! Sir, you forget yourself, I think. I will beg you to remember I am none of your farm wenches! I—I . . .' She shook with indignation.

John trembled. He had offended, lost her. . . . O fool! He tried to apologise and stuttered ridiculously. He had lost her! The prospect of facing a lifetime without this delectable creature, on whom he had not bestowed a moment's thought three hours before, suddenly became intolerable. He bit his nails with rage at his impetuosity. So close beside him, yet gone for ever! Had she gone already? Melted into air? . . . a dream after all? He glanced sideways. No, she was still there. He could see the dim pallor of her face and neck against the darkness, the folds of the bombazine dress billowing out over the edge of the settle like a great flower.

A faint, sweet waft of perfume touched his nostrils. Something stirred beside him. He looked down. Her hand . . . her hand was creeping back up the settle towards him! He heard a sound and looked up again. She was crying! . . . Stay! *Was* she crying? No, by the Lord in heaven she was not. She was *laughing!* In a flash he was on his feet, had crushed her in his arms, as though to grasp the dear dream before it could fade, and hold it to him for ever. He showered kisses on her mouth, throat, forehead—anywhere. She did not resist, but turned her soft face up to his, laughing still. Tregors and Bosula were safe, safe for both of them and all time.

At that moment the yellow cat sprang, and in so doing toppled a clump of furze kindling over the embers. The dry bush caught and flared, roaring, up the chimney. The kitchen turned in a second from black to red, and John felt the youngest Miss Tregellas go suddenly rigid in his arms, her blue eyes stared at him big with horror, her full lips were drawn tight and colourless across her clenched teeth. He kissed her once more, but it was like kissing the dead.

Then she came to life, struggled frantically, battered at his mouth with both fists, giving little "Oh! Ohs!" like a trapped animal mad with pain. He let her go, amazed.

She fled across the kitchen, crashing against a table in her blind hurry, whipped round, stared at him again, and then ran upstairs panting and sobbing. He heard the bolt of her door click, and then noises, as though she was piling furniture against it.

John turned about, still amazed, and jumped back startled. Who was that, that ghoul's mask lit by flickers of red flame, snarling across the room? Then he remembered it was himself, of course, himself in the old round mirror. After his accident he had smashed every looking glass at home and had forgotten what he looked like . . . During the few hours of fool's paradise he had forgotten about his face altogether . . . supposed the girl knew . . . had been told. The fatal furze bush burnt out, leaving him in merciful darkness.

John opened the door, stumbled across to the stable, saddled his horse, and, riding hard, was at Bosula with dawn.

When the farm girl went to call Arethusina next morning she found the room empty and the bed had not been slept in. Selina sent to the squire at once, but the youngest Miss Tregellas had not returned. They discovered her eventually in an old rab pit halfway between the two houses, her neck broken. She had fallen over the edge in the dark. It was supposed she was trying to find her way home.

Chapter II

SINCE THAT night, seventeen years before, John Penhale had done no lovemaking, nor had he again visited Tregors. The Tregellas affair had broken his nerve, but it had not impaired that of his aunt in the slightest degree; and he was frightened of her, being assured that, did he give her a chance, she would try again.

And now the old lady was dead, and in dying had tried again. John pictured her casting her final noose sitting up, gaunt and tall, in her four-poster bed, dictating her last will and testament to the Helston attorney, awed farm hands waiting to fix their marks, sunset staining the west window, and the black bull roaring in the yard below. And it was a shrewd cast she had made. John could feel its toils tightening about him. He had always been given to understand that Tregors was as good as his, and now it was as good as Carveth Donnithorne's. Carveth Donnithorne! John gritted his teeth at the thought of the suave and ever-prospering ship chandler. Tregors had always been a strong farm, but in the last seventeen years Selina had increased the acreage by a third, by one hundred acres of sweet upland grazing lopped from the Tregellas estate. There were new buildings, too, built of moor granite to stand for ever, and the stock was without match locally. John's yeoman heart yearned to it. Oh, the clever old woman! John pictured Carveth Donnithorne taking possession, Carveth Donnithorne with his condescending airs, patronising wife, and school of chubby little boys. Had not Carveth goods enough in this world but that he must have Tregors as well?

John swore he should not have Tregors as well, not if he could stop it. How could he stop it? He puzzled his wits, but returned inevitably to the one answer he was trying to evade: "Marry within twelve months! Marry within twelve months!" His aunt had made a sure throw, he admitted with grim admiration, the cunning old devil! It was all very well saying "marry," but who would marry a man that even the rough fisher girls avoided and children hid from. He would have no more force or subterfuge. If any woman consented to marry him, it must be in full knowledge of what she was doing and of her own free will. There should be no repetition of that night seventeen years before. He shuddered. 'No, by the Lord, no more of that! Rather let Tregors go to Carveth.'

In imagination he saw the squire's daughter as he was always seeing her in the dark nights when he was alone, stricken numb in his arms, glazed horror in her eyes — saw her running across the blind country, sobbing, panting, stumbling in furrows, torn by brambles, trying to get home away from him, the terror. He shut his eyes, as though to shut out the vision, and rode on past Germoe to Kenneggy Downs.

The moon was flying through clouds like a circus girl through hoops; the road was swept by winged shadows. Puddles seemed to brim with milk at one moment, ink the next. At one moment the surrounding country was visible, agleam as with hoar frost, and then was blotted out in darkness; it was a night of complete and startling transformations. The shadow of a bare oak leapt upon them suddenly, flinging unsubstantial arms at man and horse as though to grasp them, a phantom octopus. Penhale's mare shied, nearly unseating him. He came out of his sombre thoughts, kicked spurs into her, and drove her on at a smart trot. She swung forward trembling and uneasy, nostrils swelling, ears twitching, as though she sensed uncanny presences abroad. They reached the high ground above Perranuthnoe — waste, gorse-covered downs. To the south the great indent of Mount's Bay gloomed and glittered under cloud and moonshine; westwards Paul Hill rose like a wall, a galaxy of ship's riding lights pricking the shadow at its base. The track began to drop downhill, the moors gave over to fields with high banks. An old packhorse track, choked with undergrowth, broke into the road from the seaward side. The mare cocked her ears towards it, snorted, and checked. Penhale laid into her with his whip. She bounded forward and shied again, but with such violence this time that John came out of the saddle altogether. He saw a shadow rush across the road, heard something thwack on the mare's rump as she swerved from under him, and he fell, not on the road as he expected, but on top of a man, bearing him to the ground. As John fell he knew exactly what he had to deal with. Highwaymen! The mare's swerve had saved him a stunning blow on the head. He grappled with the assailant as they went down, and they rolled over and over on the ground feeling for strangleholds. John was no tyro at the game; he was muscled like a bull, and had been taught many a trick by his hind Bohenna, the champion. But this thief was strong also, and marvellously elusive. He buckled and twisted under the farmer's weight, finally slipped out of his clutch altogether, and leapt to his feet. John scrambled up just in time to kick the heavy oak cudgel from the man's reach and close with him again. John cross-buttocked and back-heeled him repeatedly, but on each occasion the man miraculously regained his feet. John tried sheer strength—hugged the man to him, straining to break his back. The man bent and sprang as resilient as a willow wand. John hugged him closer, trying to crush his ribs. The man made his teeth meet in the farmer's ear and slipped away again.

Once more John was just in time to stop him from picking up the club. He kicked it into the ditch and set to work with his knuckles. But he could not land a blow. Wherever he planted his fists the fellow was not, eluding them by a fraction of an inch, by a lightning sidestep or a shake of the head. The man went dancing backwards and sideways, hands down; bobbing his head, bending, swaying, bouncing as though made of rubber. He began to laugh. The laugh sent a shiver through John Penhale. The footpad thought he had him in his hands, and unless help came from somewhere the farmer knew such was the case. It was only a question of time, and not much time. He was out of trim and cooked to a finish already, while the other was skipping like a dancing master, had breath to spare for laughter.

At that time of night nobody would be on the road, and help was not likely to drop from Heaven. He had only himself to look to. He thought over the manifold tricks he had seen in the wrestling ring, thought swift and desperately; hit out with his left and followed with an upward kick of his right foot—Devon style. His fist missed, as he expected, but his boot caught the thief a tip under the kneecap as he sidestepped. The man doubled up, and John flung himself at him.

15

The footpad butted him in the pit of the stomach with his head and skipped clear, shouting savagely in Romany, but limping. John did not know the language, but it told him there was a companion to reckon with, a fresh man. The struggle was hopeless. Nevertheless, he turned and ran for the club. He was not fast enough, not fast enough by half; three yards from the ditch the lamed thief was on him. John heard the quick hop-skip of feet behind him and dropped on one knee as the man sprang for his back. The footpad, not expecting the drop, went too high; he landed across John's shoulders, one arm dropping across the farmer's chest. In a flash John had him by the wrist and jerked upright, at the same time dragging down on the wrist. It was an adaptation of the Cornish master throw "The Flying Mare." The man went over John's shoulders like a rocket, made a wonderful effort to save himself by a back somersault, but the tug on his wrist was too much, and he crashed on his side in the road. John kicked him on the head till he lay still, and, picking up the club, whirled to face the next comer. Nobody came on. John was perplexed. To whom had the fellow been shouting, if not to a confederate?

Perhaps the cur had taken fright and was skulking in the gorse. Very well, he would drub him out. He was flushed with victory and had the club in his hands now. He was stepping towards the furze when he heard a slight scrunching sound to his left, and, turning, saw a dark figure squatting on the bank at the roadside. John stood still, breathing hard, his cudgel ready. The mysterious figure did not stir. John stepped nearer, brandishing his club. Still the figure made no move. John stepped nearer yet, and at that moment the moon broke clear of a mesh of clouds, flooding the road with ghostly light, and John, to his astonishment, saw that the confederate was a girl, a girl in a tattered cloak and tarnished tumbler finery, munching a turnip. Strolling acrobats! That explained the man's uncanny agility.

'What are you doing here?' he demanded.

'Nothing, sir,' said the girl, chawing a lump of the root.

'I'll have him hung and you transported for this,' John thundered.

'I did you no harm,' said the girl calmly.

That was true enough. John wondered why she had not come to the assistance of her man. Tribe law was strong with these outcasts, he understood. He asked her.

The girl shrugged her shoulders. 'He beat me yesterday. I wanted to see him beat. You done it. Good.'

She thrust a bare, well-moulded arm in John's face. It was bruised from elbow to shoulder. She spat at the unconscious tumbler.

'What is he to you?' John asked. 'Nothing,' she retorted; 'muck!' and took another wolfish bite at the turnip. She appeared ravenous.

John turned his back on her. He had no intention of proceeding with the matter, since to do so meant carrying a stunned footpad, twelve stone at least, a mile into Market Jew and later standing the publicity of the Assizes. He was not a little elated at the success of his Flying Mare and in a mood to be generous. After all, he had lost nothing but a little skin. He would let the matter drop. He picked the man up and slung him off the road into the gorse of the pack track. Now for his horse. He walked past the munching girl in silence, halted, felt in his pocket, found a florin, and jerked it to her.

'Here,' he said, 'get yourself an honest meal.'

The florin fell in the ditch. The girl dropped off the bank on to it as he had seen a hawk drop on a field vole.

'Good God!' he muttered, 'she must be starved' and walked on.

He would knock up the inn in Market Jew and spend the remainder of the night there, he decided. He would look for his horse in the morning, but he expected it would trot home.

A hundred yards short of the St Hilary turning he came upon the mare. She was standing quietly, a forefoot planted on a broken rein, holding herself nose to the ground. He freed her, knotted the rein, and, mounting, clattered down the single street and out on the beach road on the other side. Since he had his horse, he would push straight through after all; if he stopped he would have to concoct some story to account for his battered state, which would be difficult. He went at a walk, pondering over the events of the night. On his left hand the black mass of St Michael's Mount loomed out of the moon-silvered bay like some basking sea monster; before him lay Penzance, with the spire of St Mary's rising above the masts of the coasters, spearing at the stars.

At Ponsandane River the mare picked up a stone. John jumped off, hooked it out, and was preparing to remount when he noticed that she had got her head round and was staring back down the road, ears pricked. There *was* someone behind them. He waited a full minute, but could neither see nor hear anything, so went on again, through Penzance, over Newlyn Green and up the hill. The wind had died away; it was the still hour that outrides dawn; the east was already paling. In the farms about Paul, John could hear the cocks bugling to each other; hidden birds in the blackthorns gave sleepy twitters; a colt whinnied "good morning" from a nearby field and cantered along the hedge shaking the dew from its mane. Everything was very quiet, very peaceful, yet John could not rid him of the idea that he was being followed. He pulled up again and listened, but, hearing nothing, rode on, calling himself a fool.

He dropped down into Trevelloe Bottoms, gave the mare a drink in Lamorna Stream, and climbed Boleigh. A wall-eyed sheepdog came out of a cottage near the Pipers and flew yelping at the horse's heels. He cursed it roundly, and it retired whence it came, tail between its legs. As he turned the bend in the road he heard the cur break into a fresh frenzy of barking.

There *was* somebody behind him after all, somebody who went softly and stopped when he did. It was as he had suspected; the tumbler had come to and was trailing him home to get his revenge, to fire stacks or rip a cow — an old gypsy trick. John swung the mare into a cattle track, tied her to a blackthorn, pulled a heavy stone out of the mud, and waited, crouched against the bank, hidden in the furze. He would settle this rogue once and for all. Every yeoman instinct aroused, he would have faced forty such in defence of his stock, his place.

Dawn was lifting her golden head over the long arm of the Lizard. A chain of little pink clouds floated above her like adoring cherubs. Morning mists drifted up from the switchbacked hills to the north, white as steam. Over St Gwithian tower the moon hung, haggard and deathly pale, an old siren giving place to a rosy debutante. In the bushes birds twittered and cheeped, tuning their voices against the day. John Penhale waited, bent double, the heavy stone ready in his hands. The footpad was a long time coming. John wondered if he had taken the wrong turning; but that was improbable; the mare's tracks were plain. Someone might have come out of the cottage and forced the fellow into hiding, or he might have sensed the ambush. John was just straightening his back to peer over the furze when he heard the soft thud of bare feet on the road, heard them hesitate and then turn towards him, following the hoof prints. He held his breath, judged the time and distance, and sprang up, the stone poised in both hands above his head. He lowered it slowly and let it drop in the mud. It was the girl!

She looked at the stone, then at John, and her mouth twitched with the flicker of a smile. John felt foolish and consequently angry. He stepped out of the bushes.

'Why are you following me?' he demanded.

She looked down at her bare feet, then up at him out of the corner of her deep dark eyes, but made no answer.

John grasped her by an arm and shook her. 'Can't you speak? Why are you following me?'

She did not reply, but winced slightly, and John saw that he was gripping one of the cruel bruises. He released her, instantly contrite.

'I did not mean to do that,' he said; then, hardening again: 'But look you, I'll have no more of this. I'll have none of your kind round here burning ricks. If I catch you near my farm I'll hand you over to the law for . . . for what you are and you'll be whipped. Do you hear me?'

The girl remained silent, leaning up against the bank, pouting, looking up at John under her long lashes. She was handsome in a sulky, outlandish way, he admitted. She had a short nose, high cheek-bones, and very dark eyes with odd lights in them; her bare head was covered with crisp black curls, and she wore big brass earrings. A little guitar was tucked under one arm. The tattered cloak was drawn

19

tight about her, showing the thin but graceful lines of her figure. A handsome trollop.

'If you won't speak you won't . . . but remember, I have warned you,' said John, but with less heat, and untied his horse and mounted. As he turned the corner he glanced furtively back and met the girl's eyes full. He put spurs to the mare, flushing hotly.

A quarter of an hour later he reined up in his yard. He had been away rather less than twenty-four hours, but it seemed like as many days. It was good to be home. A twist of blue smoke at a chimney told him Martha was stirring and he would get breakfast soon. He heard the blatter of calves in their shed and the deep, answering moo of cows from the byre, the splash and babble of the stream. In the elms the rooks had already begun to quarrel. Familiar voices.

He found Bohenna in the stable wisping a horse and singing his one song, "I Seen a Ram at Hereford Fair," turned the mare over to him, and sought the yard again.

It was good to be home . . . and yet, and yet . . . things moved briskly outside. One found adventures out in the world, adventures that set the blood racing. He was boyishly pleased with his tussle with the vagabond; had tricked him rather neatly, he thought. He must tell Bohenna about that. Then the girl. She had not winced at the sight of his face; not a quiver; had smiled at him even. He wondered if she were still standing in the cow track, the blue cloak drawn about her, squelching mud through her bare toes; or was she ranging the fields after more turnips — turnips! She was no better than an animal, but a handsome animal for all that, if somewhat thin. Oh, well, she had gone now. He had scared her off, would never see her again.

He turned to walk into the house and saw the girl again. She was leaning against the gatepost, looking up at him under her lashes. He stood stock still for a moment, amazed as at a vision, and then flung at her:

'You — you . . . Didn't you hear what I said?'

She neither stirred nor spoke.

John halted. He felt his fury going from him like wind from a pricked bladder. In a second he would be no longer master of himself.

In the glow of morning she was handsomer than ever; she was young, just a little more than twenty, there was a blue gloss on the black curls, the brass earrings glinted among them; her skin had a golden sunburnt tint, and her eyes smouldered with curious lights.

'What do you want?' John stammered, suddenly husky.

The girl smiled up at him, a slow, full-lipped smile.

'You won me . . . so I came,' she said.

John's heart leapt with old pagan pride. To the victor the spoils! Ay, verily! He caught the girl by the shoulders and whirled her round so that his own face came full to the sunrise.

'Do you see this?' he cried. 'Look well! Look well!'

The girl stared at him steadily without a tremor, without the flick of an eyelid, and then, bending, rubbed her forehead, cat-like, against his shoulder.

'Marry,' she purred. 'I've seen worse than that where I came from.'

For answer John caught her up in his arms and marched, shouting with rough laughter, into the house, the tumbler girl clasped tight to his breast, her arms about his neck.

To the victor the spoils!

Chapter III

BOSULA—"The Owls' House"—lay in the Keigwin valley, about six miles south-west of Penzance. The valley drained the peninsula's bare backbone of tors, ran almost due south until within a mile and a half of the sea, formed a sharp angle, ran straight again, and met the English Channel at Monk's Cove. A stream threaded its entire length, its source a holy well on Bartinny Downs, the water of which, taken at the first of the moon, was reputed a cure for chest complaints. Towards the river's source the valley was a shallow swamp, a wide bed of tussocks, flags, willow, and thorn, the haunt of snipe and woodcock in season; but as it neared Bosula it grew narrower and deeper until it emptied into the sea, pinched to a sharp gorge between precipitous cliffs.

It was a surprising valley. You came from the west over the storm-swept, treeless table-land that drives into the Atlantic like a wedge and is beaten upon by three seas, came with clamorous salt gales buffeting you this way and that, pelting you with black showers of rain; came suddenly to the valley rim and dropped downhill into a different climate, a serene, warm place of trees, with nothing to break the peace but the gentle chatter of the stream. When the wind set roundabouts of south it was not so quiet. The covemen had a saw:

> 'When the river calls the sea,
> Fishing there will be.
> When the sea calls the river,
> 'War'e foul weather.'

Bosula stood at the apex of the angle, guarded on all sides; but when the wind, set southerly and strong, the boom of the breakers on the Twelve Apostles Reef came echoing up the valley in deep, tremendous organ peals. So clear did they sound that one would imagine the sea had broken inland and that inundation was imminent.

The founder of the family was a tin streamer from Crowan, who, noting that the old men had got their claws into every inch of payable dirt in the parish, loaded his implements on a donkey and

went westwards looking for a stream of his own. In due course he
and his ass meandered down Keigwin valley and pitched camp in the
elbow. On the fourth day Penhale the First, soil-stained and unkempt,
approached the lord of the manor and proposed washing the stream
on tribute. He held out no hopes, but was willing to give it a try, being
out of work. The lord of the manor knew nothing of tin or tinners,
regarded the tatterdemalion with casual contempt, and let him draw
up almost what terms he liked. In fifteen years Penhale had taken a
small fortune out of the valley, bought surrounding land, and built a
house on the site of his original camp. From thenceforth the Penhales
were farmers, and each in his turn added something—a field, a bit of
moorland, a room to the house.

When John Penhale took possession the estate held three hundred
acres of arable land, to say nothing of stretches of adjoining bog and
heather, useful for grazing cattle. The buildings formed a square with
the yard in the centre, the house on the north and the stream enclos-
ing the whole on three sides, so that the place was serenaded with
eternal music—the song of running water tinkling among boulders,
purling over shallows, splashing over falls.

Penhale the tinner built a two-storied house of four rooms, but his
successor had seven children, and an Elizabethan, attuning himself
to a prolific age, thirteen. The first of these added a couple of rooms,
the second four. Since building forwards encroached on the yard and
building backwards would bring them into the stream, they perforce
extended sideways and westwards. In John Penhale's time the house
was five rooms long and one thick, with the front door stranded at
the east end and the thatch coming down so low the upper windows
had the appearance of old men's eyes peering out under arched and
shaggy brows. There was little distinctive about the house save the
chimneys, which were inordinately high, and the doorway, which
was carved. Penhale the First, who knew something of smelting and
had ideas about draught, had set the standard in chimney pots, but
the Elizabethan was responsible for the doorway. He pulled a half-
drowned sailor out of the cove one dawn, brought him home, fed
and clothed him. The castaway, a foreigner of some sort, being unable

to express gratitude in words, picked up a hammer and stone chisel and decorated his rescuer's doorway—until then three plain slabs of granite. He carved the date on the lintel and a pattern of interwoven snakes on the uprights, culminating in two comic little heads, one on either side of the door, intended by the artist as portraits of his host and hostess, but which they, unflattered, and doubtless prompted by the pattern below, had passed down to posterity as Adam and Eve.

The first Penhale was a squat, burly man, and built his habitation to fit himself, but the succeeding generations ran to height and were in constant danger of braining themselves against the ceilings. They could sit erect, but never rose without glancing aloft, and when they stood up their heads well-nigh disappeared among the deep beams. This had inculcated in them the habit of stooping instinctively on stepping through any door. A dean of St Gwithian used to swear that the Penhale family entered his spacious church bent double.

The first Penhale, being of small stature, made his few windows low down. The subsequent Penhales had to squat to see out of them. Not that the Penhales needed windows to look out of; they were an open air breed who only came indoors to eat and sleep. The ugly, cramped old house served their needs well. They came home from the uplands or the bottoms at the fall of night, came in from ploughing, shooting, hedging, or driving cattle, came, mud-plastered, lashed by the winter rains, saw Bosula lights twinkling between the sheltering trees, bowed their tall heads between Adam and Eve, and, entering the warm kitchen, sat down to mighty meals of good beef and good vegetables, stretched their legs before the open hearth, grunting with full-fed content, and yawned off to bed and immediate sleep, lulled by the croon of the brook and the whisper of the wind in the tree-tops, Gales might skim roofs off down in the cove, ships batter to matchwood on the Twelve Apostles, upland ricks be scattered over the parish, the Penhales of Bosula slept sound in the lap of the hills, snug behind three-foot walls.

In winter, looking down from the hills, you could barely see Bosula for trees; in summer not at all. They filled the valley from side to side and for half a mile above and below the house. Oak, ash, elm, and sycamore, with an undergrowth of hazel and thorn. Near the house the stream narrowed to a few feet, ran between banks of boulders piled up by the first Penhale and his tinners. They had rooted up boulders everywhere and left them lying anyhow, on their ends or sides, great uneven blocks of granite, now covered with an emerald velvet of moss or furred with grey and yellow lichen. Between these blocks the trees thrust, flourishing on their own leaf mould. The ashes and elms went straight up till they met the wind leaping from hill to hill, and then stopped, nipped to an even height, as a box hedge is trimmed by shears; but the thorns and hazels started crooked and grew crooked all the way, their branches writhing and tangling into fantastic clumps and shapes, to be overgrown and smothered in toils of ivy and honeysuckle.

In spring the tanglewood valley was a nursery of birds. Wrens, thrushes, chiffchaffs, greenfinches, and chaffinches built their nests in scented thickets of hawthorn and may; blue and oxeye tits kept house in holes in the apple and oak trees. These added their songs to that of the brook. In spring the bridal woods about Bosula rippled and thrilled with liquid and debonair melody. But it was the owls that were the feature of the spot. Winter or summer they sat on their boughs and hooted to each other across the valley, waking the woods with startling and eerie screams. 'To-whoo, whe-ee, who-hoo!' they would go, amber eyes burning, and then launch themselves heavily from their perches and beat, grey and ghostly, across the moon. 'Whoo, wha-hoo!'

Young lovers straying up the valley were apt to clasp each other the tighter and whisper of men murdered and evil hauntings when they heard the owls, but the first Penhale in his day camped with his ass in the crook of the stream, took their banshee salutes as a good omen. He lay on his back in the leaves listening to them and wondering at their number.

'Bos hula enweer ew'n teller na,' said he in Cornish as he rolled over to sleep. 'Truly this is the owls' house.'

Chapter IV

WHEN JOHN Penhale carried the gypsy girl into Bosula he thought she would be off again in a fortnight, or a month at most. On the contrary, she curled up as snug as a dormouse, apparently prepared to stay for ever. At first she followed him wherever he went about the farm, but after a week she gave that up and remained at Bosula absorbed in the preparation of food. The number of really satisfying meals the girl Teresa had had in her time could be counted on her fingers and toes almost. Life had been maintained by a crust here and a bone there. She was only half gypsy; her mother had been an itinerant herbalist, her father a Basque bear-leader, and she was born at Blyth Fair. Her twenty-two years had been spent on the highways, singing and dancing from tavern to tavern, harried by the law on one side and hunger on the other. She had no love for the open road; her feet were sore from trudging it, and she knew it led nowhere but to starvation. Her mother had died in a ditch and her father had been hanged. For years she had been waiting a chance to get out of the dust, and when John came along, knocked out the tumbler and jerked her a florin, she saw that possible chance.

A sober farmer who tossed silver so freely should be a bachelor, she argued; and a man who could fight like that must have a good deal of the lusty animal about him. She knew the type, and of all men they were the easiest to handle. She followed up the clue hotfoot, and now here she was in a land of plenty. She had no intention of leaving in a fortnight, a month, or ever, if she could help it; no desire to exchange three meat meals daily, smoking hot, for turnips, or a soft bed for the lee of a haystack. She would sit on the floor after supper, basking at the roaring hearth, her back propped against John's knees, and listen to the drip of the eaves, the sough of the treetops, the echoed organ crashes of the sea, snuggle closer to the farmer and laugh.

When he asked her why she did that she shrugged her shoulders. But she laughed to think of what she was escaping, laughed to think that the tumbler was out in it. But for that flung florin and the pricking of her thumbs she would have been out in it too, crouched under a hedge, maybe, soaked and shivering. Penhale need have had no fears she would leave him. On the contrary, she was afraid he would tire of her, and strove by every means to bind him to her irrevocably. She practised all her wiles on John, ran to him when he came in, fondled and kissed him, rubbed her head on his shoulder, swore he didn't care for her, pretended to cry—any excuse to get taken in his arms. Once there she had him in her power. The quarter-strain of *Gitano* came uppermost then, the blood of generations of ardent Southern women, professional charmers all, raced in her veins and prompted her, showed her how and when. It was all instinctive and quite irresistible; the simple Northern yeoman was a clod in her hands.

Martha had found Teresa some drugget clothes, rummaging in chests that lay under the dust of twenty years in the neglected west wing—oak chests and mahogany, with curious iron clasps and hinges, the spoil of a score of foundered ships. Teresa had been close behind the woman when the selection was made, and she had glimpsed many things that were not drugget. When she gave up following John abroad she took to spending most of her time, between meals, in the west wing, bolting the doors behind her so that Martha could not see what she was doing.

John was lurching home down the valley one autumn evening, when, as he neared Bosula, he heard singing and the tinkling of melodious wires. There was a small grove of ashes close ahead, encircling an open patch of ground supposed to be a fairy ring—in May a purple pool of bluebells, but then carpeted with russet and yellow leaves. He stepped nearer, peered round an oak bole, and saw a sight which made him stagger and swear himself bewitched. There was a marvellous lady dancing in the circlet, and as she danced she sang, twanging an accompaniment on a little guitar:

> 'Then, Lovely Boy, bring hither
> The Chaplet, e'er it wither,
> Steep'd in the various Juices
> The Cluster'd Vine produces,
> The Cluster'd Vine produces.'

She was dressed in a straight-laced bodice, stitched with silver and low cut, leaving her shoulders bare; flowing daffodil sleeves caught up at the elbows, and a cream-coloured skirt sprigged with blue flowers and propped out at the hips on monstrous farthingales. On her head she wore a lace fantail, but her feet were bare. She swept round and round in a circle, very slow and stately, swaying, turning, curtseying to the solemn audience of trees.

> 'So mix't with sweet and sour,
> Life's not unlike the flower;
> Its Sweets unpluck'd will languish,
> And gather'd 'tis with anguish,
> And gather'd 'tis with anguish.'

The glare of sunset shot through gaps in the wood in quivering golden shafts, fell on the smooth trunks of the ashes, transforming them into pillars of gold. In this dazzle of gold the primrose lady danced, in and out of the beams, now glimmering, now in haze and delicate shadow. A puff of wind shook a shower of pale leaves upon her; they drifted about her like confetti; her bare feet rustled among them, softly, softly.

> 'This, round my moistened tresses,
> The use of Life expresses.
> Wine blunts the thorn of Sorrow.
> Our Rose may fade tomorrow,
> Our Rose — may — fade — to — morrow.'

The sun went down behind the hill; twilight, powder-blue, swept through the wood, quenching the symphony in yellows. The lady made a final fritter of strings, bowed to the biggest ash, and faded among the trees towards Bosula. John clung to his oak, stupefied. Despite his grammar school education, he half believed in the crones' stories of piskies and "the old men," and if this was not a supernatural being, what was it? A fine lady dancing in Bosula woods at sundown — and in the fairy circle too! If not a sprite, where did she come from? There was not her match in the parish, or Hundred even. He did not like it at all. He would go home by circling over the hill. He hesitated. That was a long détour; he was tired, and his own orchard was not a furlong distant. His common sense returned. Damme! He would push straight home; he was big and strong enough whatever betide.

He walked boldly through the woods, whistling away his fears, snapping twigs beneath his boots.

He came to a dense clump of hollies at the edge of the orchard and heard the *tinkle-tinkle* again, right in front of him. He froze solid and stared ahead. It was thick dusk among the bushes; he could see nothing. *Tinkle-tinkle*—from the right this time. He turned slowly, his flesh prickling. Nothing. A faint rustle of leaves behind his back and the tinkle of music once more. John began to sweat. He was piskie-led for certain—and only fifty yards from his own door. If one listened to this sort of thing, one was presently charmed and lost for ever, he had heard. He would make a dash for it. He burst desperately through the hollies and saw the primrose lady standing directly in front of him on the orchard fringe. He stopped. She curtsied low.

'Oh, Jan, Jan,' she laughed. 'Jan, come here and kiss me.'

'Teresa!'

She pressed close against him and held up her full, tempting mouth. He kissed her over and over.

'Where did you get these—these clothes?' he asked.

'Out of the old chests,' said she. 'You like me thus? . . . Love me?'

For answer he hugged her to him, and they went on into the kitchen, linked arm in arm. Martha in her astonishment let the cauldron spill all over the floor, and the idiot daughter threw a fit.

The drugget dress disappeared after that. Teresa rifled the chests and got some marvellous results. The chests held the hoardings of a century, samples of every fashion, washed in from wrecks on the Twelve Apostles, wardrobes of officers' mistresses bound for the garrison at Tangier, of proud ladies that went down with Indiamen, packet ships, and vessels sailing for the Virginia Colony. Jackdaw pickings that generations of Penhale women had been too modest to wear and too feminine to part with. Gowns, undergowns, bodices, smocks and stomachers of silk, taffeta, sarsnet, and satin of all hues and shapes, quilted, brocaded, embroidered, pleated, scalloped, and slashed; cambric and holland ruffs, collars, bands, kerchiefs, and lappets; scarves, trifles of lace, pointed and gadrooned; odd gloves of cordovan leather, heavily fringed; vamped single shoes, red-heeled; ribbons, knots; spangled garters; feathers and fans.

The clothes were torn and faded in patches, eaten by moth, soiled and rusted by salt water, but Teresa cared little; they were treasure trove to her, the starveling. She put them all on in turn (as the Penhale wives had done before her, but in secret) without regard to fit, appropriateness, or period, and with the delight of a child dressing up for a masquerade. She dressed herself differently every evening, even wearing articles with showy linings inside out, aiming only at a blaze of colour, and spending hours in the selection.

The management of the house she left entirely to Martha, which was wise enough, seeing she knew nothing of houses. John, coming in of an evening, never knew what was in store for him. It gave life an added savour. He approached Adam and Eve his heart aflutter—what would she be like this time?—opened the low door and stepped within. And there she would be, standing before the hearth waiting for him, mischievous and radiant, brass earrings winking, a knot of ribbons in her raven curls, dressed in scarlet, cream, purple or blue, cloth of gold or silver lace—all worn and torn if you came to examine closely, but, in the leaping firelight, gorgeous.

Sometimes she would spend the evening wooing him, sidling into his arms, rubbing with her cheek and purring in her cat fashion; and sometimes she would take her guitar and, sitting cross-legged before the hearth, sing the songs by which she had made her living. Pretty, innocent twitters for the most part, laments to cruel Chloes, Phyllises, and Celias, in which despairing Colins and Strephons sang of their broken hearts in tripping, tuneful measures; morris and country airs she gave also and patriotic staves:

> 'Tho' the Spaniards invade
> Our int'rest and trade,
> And often our merchantmen plunder,
> Give us but command
> Their force to withstand,
> We'll soon make the slaves truckle under.'

Such stuff stirred John—as the lyrics lulled him. He would inflate his chest and tap his toe on the flags in time with the tune, very manful.

All this heady stuff intoxicated the recluse. He felt a spell on the place, could scarcely believe it was the same dark kitchen in which he had sat alone for seventeen years listening to the stream, the rain, and the wind. It was like living in a droll-teller's story where charcoal-burners fell asleep on enchanted barrows and woke in fairyland, or immortals put on mortal flesh and sojourned in the homes of men. Reared on superstition among a race that placed balls on their roofs and hung rags about holy wells to keep off witches, he almost smelt magic now. At times he wondered if this strange creature he had met on the high moors under the moon were what she held to be, if one day she would not get a summons back to her own people, the earth gape open for her, and he would be alone again. There had been an authentic case in Zennor parish. His own grandmother had seen the forsaken husband. He would glance at Teresa half fearfully, see her squatting before the blaze, lozenges of white skin showing through the rips in her finery, strong fingers plucking the guitar strings, round throat swelling as she sang—

> 'I saw fair Clara walk alone.
> The feathered snow came softly down.'

—and scout his suspicions. She was human enough, and even if she were not, sufficient for the day. . . .

As for the girl, with the unstinted feeding she put on flesh and good looks. Her bones and angles disappeared, her figure took on bountiful curves, her mouth lost its defiant pout. She had more than even she wanted to eat, a warm bed, plenty of colourful kickshaws, and a lover who fell prostrate before her easiest artifices. She was content—or very nearly so. One thing remained, and that was to put this idyllic state of affairs on a permanent basis. That accomplished, her cup of happiness would brim, she told herself. How to do it? She fancied it was more than half done already, and that, unless she read him wrong, she would presently have such a grip on the farmer he would never throw her off. By January she was sure of herself and laid her cards on the table.

According to her surmise, John took her forthwith into St Gwithian, a-pillion on the bay mare, and married her, and on the third of July a boy was born. It was a great day at Bosula. All the employees, including Martha, got blind drunk, while John spent a delightful afternoon laboriously scratching a letter to Carveth Donnithorne apprising him of the happy event.

Upstairs, undisturbed by the professional chatter of wise women, Teresa lay quietly sleeping, a fluffy small head in the crook of her arm, a tired smile on her lips. She was in out of the rain for good.

It is to be presumed that in the Donnithorne vault of Cury church the dust of old Selina at length lay quiet. The Penhales would go on and on.

Chapter V

THE FIRST boy was born in 1754, and was followed in 1756 by another. They christened the eldest Ortho, a family name, and the second Eli.

When his younger son was three months old, John died. He got wet extricating a horse from a bog hole, and took no heed, having been wet through a hundred times before. A chill seized him; he still took no notice. The chill developed into pneumonia, but he struggled on, saying nothing. Then Bohenna found him prostrate in the muck of the stable. He had been trying to yoke the oxen, with the intention of going out to plough.

Bohenna carried him, protesting, up to bed. Only when he was dying would he admit he was ill. He was puzzled and angry. Why should he be sick now who had never felt a qualm before? What was a wetting, i' faith? For forty odd winters he had seldom been dry. It was ridiculous. He tried to lift himself, exhorting the splendid loyal body that had never yet failed him to have done with this folly and bear him outside to the sunshine and the day's work. It did not respond—might have been so much lead. He fell back, betrayed, helpless, frightened, and went off into a delirium. The end was close. He came to his senses once again about ten o'clock at night and saw Teresa bending over him, the new son in her arms. She was crying, and had a tender look in her tear-bright eyes he had never seen before. He tried to smile at her. Nothing to cry about. He'd be all right in the morning—after a night's sleep—go ploughing—everything came right in the morning. Towards midnight, Martha, who was watching, set up a dreadful screech. It was all over. As if awaiting the signal, came a hooting from the woods about the house: 'Too-whee-wha-ho-oo-oo!' The Bosula owls lamenting the passing of its master.

* * *

Fate, in cutting down John Penhale in his prime, did him no disservice. He went into oblivion, knowing Teresa only as a thing

33

of beauty, half magical, wholly adorable. He was spared the years of disillusionment which would have pained him sorely, for he was a sensitive man.

Teresa mourned for her husband with a passion which was natural to her and which was very highly considered in the neighbourhood. At the funeral she flung herself on the coffin and refused to be loosened from it for a quarter of an hour, moaning and tearing at the lid with her fingers. Venerable dames, who had attended every local interment for half a century, wagged their bonnets and admitted they had never seen a widow display a prettier spirit.

Teresa was quite genuine in her way. John had treated her with a gentleness and generosity she had not suspected was to be found on this earth, and now this kindly cornucopia had been snatched from her—and just when she had made so sure of him too! She blubbered in good earnest. But after the lawyer's business was over she cheered up.

In the first flush of becoming a father, John had ridden into Penzance and made a will; but since Eli's birth he had made no second. There was plenty of time, he thought, years and years of it. Consequently everything fell to Ortho when he came of age, and in the meanwhile Teresa was sole guardian. That meant she was mistress of Bosula and had the handling of the hundred and twenty pounds invested income, to say nothing of the Tregors rents, fifty pounds per annum. One hundred and seventy pounds a year to spend! The sum staggered her. She had hardly made that amount of money in her whole life. She sat up that night long after the rest of the household had gone to bed, wrapped in delicious dreams of how she would spend that annual fortune. She soon began to learn. Martha hinted that in a lady of her station the wearing of black was considered proper as a tribute to the memory of the deceased, so, finding nothing dark in the chests, she mounted a horse behind Bohenna and jogged into town.

A raw farmer's wife, clutching a bag of silver and demanding only to be dressed in black, is a gift to any shopman. The Penzance draper called up his seamstresses, took Teresa's measure for a silk dress (nothing but silk would be fitting, he averred; the greater the cost the greater the tribute), added every sombre accessory that he could think of, separated her from thirteen pounds six shillings and fourpence of her hoard, and bowed her out, promising to send the articles by carrier within three days. Teresa went through the ordeal like one in a trance, too awed to protest or speak even. On the way home she sought to console herself with the thought that her extravagance was on John's, dear John's behalf. Still, thirteen pounds six shillings and fourpence! More than Bohenna's wages for a year gone in a finger snap! Ruin stared her in the face.

The black dress, cap, flounced petticoat, stiff stays, stockings, apron, cloak of Spanish cloth, and high-heeled shoes arrived to date and set the household agog. Teresa, its devastating price forgotten, peacocked round the house and yard all day, swelling with pride, the rustle of the silk atoning for the agony she was suffering from the stays and shoes. As the sensation died down she yearned for fresh conquests, so, mounting the pillion afresh, made a tour through the parish, paying special attention to St Gwithian churchtown and Monk's Cove.

The tour was a triumph. Women rushed to their cottage doors and stared after her, goggling. At Pridden a party of hedgers left work and raced across a field to see her go by. Near Tregadgwith a farmer fell off his horse from sheer astonishment. She was the sole topic of the district for a week or more. John's memory was duly honoured.

In a month Teresa was tired of the black dress; her fancy did not run to black. The crisp and shining new silk had given her a distaste for the old silks, the soiled and tattered salvage of wrecks. She stuffed the motley rags back in the chests and slammed the lids on them. She had seen some breathtaking rolls of material in that shop in Penzance—orange, emerald, turquoise, coral, and lilac. She shut her eyes and imagined herself in a flowing furbelowed dress of each of these colours in turn, or one combining a little of everything. O rapture!

She consulted Martha in the matter. Martha was shocked. It was unheard of. She must continue to wear black in public for a year at least. This intelligence depressed Teresa, but she was determined to be correct, as she had now a position to maintain, was next thing to a lady. Eleven months more to wait, heigh-ho!

Then, drawn by the magnet of the shops, she went in Penzance again. Penzance had become something more than a mere tin and pilchard port; visitors, attracted by its mild climate, came in by every packet; there was a good inn, the Ship and Castle, and in 1752 a coffee house had been opened and the road to Land's End made possible for carriages. Many fine ladies were to be seen fanning themselves at windows in Chapel Street or strolling on the Green, and Teresa wanted to study their costumes with a view to her own.

She dismounted at the Market Cross, moved about among the booths, and peeped furtively in at the shops. They were most attractive, displaying glorious things to wear and marvellous things to eat—tarts, cakes, Dutch biscuits, gingerbreads shaped like animals, oranges, plum-and-sugar candy. Sly old women wheedled her to buy, enlarging ecstatically on the excellence and cheapness of their wares. Teresa wavered, and reflected that though she might not be able to buy a new dress for a year, there was no law against her purchasing other things. The bag of silver burnt her fingers, and she fell. She bought some gingerbread animals at four for a farthing, tasted them, thought them ambrosia, and bought six penn'orth to take with her, also lollipops. She went home trembling at her extravagance, but when she came to count up what she had spent it seemed to have made no impression on the bag of silver. In six weeks she went in again, bought a basketful of edibles, and replaced her brass earrings with large gold half-moons. When these were paid for the bag was badly drained. Teresa took fright and visited town no more for the year, but as a matter of fact she had spent less than twenty pounds in all. But she had got in the way of spending now.

The tinworks in which John's money was invested paid up at the end of the year—one hundred and twenty-six pounds seventeen shillings and eightpence on this occasion—and Tregors rent came in on the same day. It seemed to Teresa that the heavens had opened up and showered uncounted gold upon her.

She went into Penzance next morning as fast as the bay mare could carry her and ordered a dress bordered with real lace and combining all the hues of the rainbow. She was off. Never having had any money, she had not the slightest idea of its value, and was milched accordingly. In the third year of widowhood she spent the last penny of her income.

The farm she left to Bohenna, the house to Martha, the children to look after themselves, and rode in to Penzance Market and all over the Hundred to parish feasts, races, and hurling matches; a notable figure with her flaming dresses, raven hair, and huge earrings, laying the odds, singing songs and standing drinks in alehouses, like any squire.

When John died she was at her zenith. The early bloom of her race began to fade soon after, accelerated by gross living. She still ate enormously, as though the hunger of twenty-two lean years was not yet appeased. She was like an animal at table, seizing bones in her hands and tearing the meat off with her teeth, grunting the while like a famished dog, or stuffing the pastries she bought in Penzance into her mouth two at a time. She hastened from girlish to buxom, from buxom to stout. The bay mare began to feel the increasing weight on the pillion; Bohenna was left at home, and Teresa rode alone, sitting sideways on a pad, or astraddle when no one was looking. Yet she was still comely in a large way, and had admirers aplenty. Sundry impecunious gentlemen, hoping to mend their fortunes, paid court to the lavish widow, but Teresa saw through their blandishments, and, after getting all possible sport out of them, sent them packing.

With the curate-in-charge of St Gwithian it was the other way about: Teresa made the running. She went to church in the first place because it struck her as an opportunity to flaunt her superior finery in public and make other women feel sick. She went a second time to gaze at the parson. This gentleman was an anaemic young man with fair hair, pale-blue eyes, long hands, and a face refined through partial starvation—the absentee beneficiary allowed him eighteen pounds a year. Obeying the law of opposites, the heavy, dark gypsy woman was vaguely attracted by him at once, and the attraction strengthened.

37

He was something quite new to her. Among the clumsy-limbed country-folk he appeared so slim, so delicate, almost ethereal. Also, unable to read or write herself, and surrounded by people as ignorant as she, his easy familiarity with books and the verbose phrasing of his sermons filled her with admiration. On Easter Sunday he delivered himself of a particularly flowery effort. Teresa understood not a word of it, but nevertheless thought it beautiful, and wept audibly. She thought the preacher looked beautiful too, with his clear skin, veined temples, and blue eyes. A shaft of sunlight pierced the south window and fell upon his fair head as though an expression of Divine benediction. Teresa thought he looked like a saint. Perhaps he was a saint.

She rode home slowly, so wrapped in meditation that she was late for dinner—an unprecedented occurrence. She would marry that young man. If she were going to marry again, it must be to someone she could handle, since the law would make him master of herself and her possessions. The curate would serve admirably; he would make a pretty pet and no more. He could keep her accounts too. She was always in a muddle with money. The method she had devised of keeping tally by means of notched sticks was most untrustworthy. And, incidentally, if he really were a saint her hereafter was assured. God could never condemn the wedded wife of a saint and clergyman to hell; it wouldn't be decent. She would marry that young man.

She began the assault next day by paying her overdue tithes and throwing in a duck as makeweight. Two days later she was up again with a gift of a goose, and on the following Sunday she presented the astonished clerk with eight penn'orth of gingerbreads. Since eating was the occupation nearest to the widow's heart, she sought to touch the curate's by showering food upon him. Something edible went to the deanery at least twice a week, occasionally by a hind, but more often Teresa took it herself. A fortnight before Whitsuntide, Teresa, in chasing an errant boar out of the yard, kicked too violently, snapped her leg, and was laid up for three months. Temporarily unable to reduce the curate by her personal charms, she determined to let her gifts speak for her; doubled the offerings; the eggs, fowls, butter, cheese, and hams passed from the farm to the deanery in a constant stream. Lying in bed with nothing to do, the invalid's thoughts ran largely upon the clerk. She remembered him standing in the pulpit that Easter Sunday uttering lovely if unintelligible words; slim and delicate, the benedictory beam on his flaxen poll. The more she pictured him, the more ethereally beautiful did he become. He would make a charming toy.

As soon as she could hobble about she put on her best dress—cherry satin—and, taking the bull by the horns, invited her intended to dinner. She would settle matters without further ado. The young man obeyed the summons with feelings divided between fear and determination. He knew perfectly well what he was in for. Nobody but an utter fool could have mistaken the meaning of the sighs and glances the big widow had thrown when visiting him before her accident. There was no finesse about Teresa. She wanted to marry him, and prudence told him to let her. Two farms and four hundred pounds a year, so rumour had it. The catch of the district; and he only a poor clerk. He was sick of poverty. Teresa's bounty had shown him what it was to live well, and he dreaded returning to the old way of things. Moreover, he admired her; she was so bold, so luscious, so darkly handsome, possessed of every physical quality he lacked. But he was afraid of her for all that. If she ever got really angry with him, good Lord!

It took every ounce of determination he owned to drive his feet down the hill to Bosula. Twice he stopped and turned to go back. He was a timid young man. His procrastination made him late for dinner. When he reached the farm the meal had already been served. His hostess was hard at work; she would not have delayed five minutes for King George himself. She had a mutton bone in her hands when the curate entered. She did not notice him for the moment so engrossed was she, but tore off the last shred of meat, scrunched the bone with her teeth, and bit out the marrow. The curate reeled against the doorpost, emitting an involuntary groan. Teresa glanced up and stared at him, her black eyebrows meeting.

Who was this stranger wobbling about in her doorway, his watery eyes popping out of his podgy face, his fleshy knees knocking together, his dingy coat stretched tightly across his protruding stomach? A lost innkeeper? A strayed tallow chandler? No; by his cloth he was a clerk. Slowly she recognised him. He was *her* curate, ecod! Her pretty toy! Her slim, transparent saint developed into this corpulent earthling! *Fat*, ye gods! She hurled the bone at his head, which was unreasonable, seeing it was she had fattened him.

The metamorphosed curate turned and bolted out of the house, through the yard, and back up the hill for home.

'My God,' he panted as he ran, 'biting bones up with her teeth—with her teeth! My God, it might have been *me!*'

That was the end of that.

Chapter VI

I N THE meanwhile the Penhale brothers grew and grew. Martha took a sketchy charge of their infancy, but as soon as they could toddle they made use of their legs to gain the out-o'-doors and freedom. At first Martha basted them generously when they came in for meals, but they soon put a stop to that by not showing up at the fixed feeding times, watching her movements from coigns of vantage in the yard, and robbing the larder when her back was turned. Martha thereupon postponed the whippings till they came in to bed. Once more they defeated her by not coming in to bed; when trouble loomed they spent the night in the loft, curled up like puppies in the hay. Martha could not reach them there; she dared not trust herself on the crazy ladder, and Bohenna would give her no assistance; he was hired to tend stock, he said, not children.

For all that, the woman caught the little savages now and again, and when she did she dressed them faithfully with a birch of her own making. But she did not long maintain her physical advantage.

One afternoon, when Ortho was eight and Eli six, she caught them red-handed. The pair had been out all the morning sailing cork boats and mudlarking in the marshes. They had had no dinner. Martha knew they would be homing wolfish hungry some time during the afternoon and that a raid was indicated. There were two big apple pasties on the hearth waiting the mistress's supper, and Martha was prepared to sell her life for them, since it was she that got the blame if anything ran short, and had suffered severely of late.

At about three o'clock she heard the old sheepdog lift up its voice in asthmatic excitement and then cease abruptly. It had recognised friends. The raiders were at hand. She hid behind the settle, near the door. Presently she saw a dark patch slide across the east doorpost. The shadow of Ortho's head. The shadow slid on until she knew he was peering into the kitchen. Ortho entered the kitchen, stepping delicately, on bare, grimy toes. He paused and glanced round the room. His eye lit on the pasties and sparkled. He moved a chair carefully so that his line of retreat might be clear, beckoned to the invisible Eli, and went straight for the mark. As his hands closed on the loot, Martha broke cover. Ortho did not look frightened or even surprised; he did not drop the pasty. He grinned, dodged behind the table, and shouted to his brother, who took station in the doorway.

Martha, squalling horrid threats, hobbled halfway round the table after Ortho, who skipped in the opposite direction and nearly escaped her. She just cut him off in time, but she could not save the pasty. He slung it under her arm to his confederate and dodged behind the table again. Eli was fat and short-legged. Martha could have caught him with ease, but she did not try, knowing that if she did Ortho would have the second pasty. As it was, Ortho was hopelessly cornered. He should suffer for both. Ortho was behind the table again and difficult to reach. She thought of the broom, but it was at the other side of the kitchen; did she turn to get it, Ortho would slip away.

Eli reappeared in the doorway, lumpish and stolid. He had hidden the booty and come back to see the fun. Martha considered, pushed the table against the wall and upturned it. Ortho sprang for the door, almost gained it, but not quite. Martha grasped him by the tail of his smock, drew him to her, and laid in. But Ortho, instead of squirming and whimpering as was his wont, put up a fight. He fought like a little wildcat, wriggling and snarling, scratching with toes and fingernails. Martha had all she could do to hold him, but hold him she did, dragged him across the floor to the peg where hung her birch—a bunch of hazel twigs—and gave him a couple of vicious slices across the seat of his pants. She was about to administer a third when an excruciating pain nipped her behind her bare left ankle. She yelled, dropped Ortho and the birch as if white-hot, and grabbed her leg. In the skin of the tendon was imprinted a semicircle of red dents—Eli's little sharp teeth marks. She limped round the kitchen for some minutes, vowing dreadful vengeance on the brothers; who in the meanwhile were sitting astride the yard gate munching the pasty.

The pair slept in the barn for a couple of nights, and then, judging the dame's wrath to have passed, slipped in on the third. But Martha was waiting for Eli, birch in hand, determined to carry out her vengeance. It did not come off. She caught Eli, but Ortho flew to the rescue this time. The two little fiends hung on her like weasels, biting, clawing, squealing with fury, all but dragging the clothes off her. She appealed to Teresa for help, but the big woman would do nothing but laugh. It was as good as a bear-bait. Martha shook the brothers off somehow and lowered her flag for good. Next day Ortho burnt the birch with fitting ceremony, and for some years the brothers ran entirely wild.

If Martha failed to inspire any respect in the young Penhales, they stood in certain awe of her daughter Wany, on account of her connection with the supernatural. In the first place, she was a change-ling herself. In the second, Providence, having denied her wits, had bequeathed her an odd sense. She was weather-wise; she felt heat, frost, rain, or wind, days in advance; her veins might have run with mercury. In the third place, and this was far more attractive to the boys — she knew the movements of all the "small people" in the valley; the cows told her.

The cows were Wany's special province. She could not be trusted with any housework, however simple, because she could not bring her mind to it for a minute. She had no control over her mind at all; it was for ever wandering over the hills and far away in dark, enchanted places.

But cows she could manage, and every morning the cows told her what had passed in the half-world the night before.

There were two tribes of small people in the Keigwin valley — buccas and piskies. In the buccas there was no harm. They were poor foreign-ers, the souls of the first miners, condemned for their malpractices to perpetual slavery underground. They inhabited a round knoll formed of rocks and rubble, thrown up by the original Penhale, and were seldom seen, even by the cows, for they had no leisure, and their work lay out of sight in the earth's dark, dripping tunnels. Once or twice the cows had glimpsed a swarthy, hook-nosed old face, caked in red ore and seamed with sweat, gazing wistfully through a crack in the rocks — but that was all. Sometimes, if under Wany's direction you set your ear to the knoll and listened intently, you could hear a faint thump and scrape far underground—the Bucca's picks at work. Bohenna declared these sounds emanated from badgers, but Bohenna was of the earth earthy, a clod of clods.

The piskies lived by day among the tree roots at the north end of Bosula woods, a sprightly but vindictive people. At night they issued from a hollow oak stump, danced in their green ballrooms, paid visits to distant kinsfolk, or made expeditions against offending mortals. The cows, lying out all night in the marshes, saw them going and coming. There were hundreds of them, the cows said. They wore green jerkins and red caps, and rode rabbits, all but the king and queen, who were mounted on white hares. They blew on horns as they galloped, and the noise of them was like a flock of small birds singing. On moonless nights a cloud of fireflies sped above them to light the way. The cows heard them making their plans as they rode afield, laughing and boasting as they returned, and reported to Wany, who passed it on to the spellbound brothers.

But this did not exhaust the nightlife in the valley. According to Wany, other supernaturals haunted the neighbourhood—spectres, ghosts, men who had sold their souls to the Devil, folk who had died with curses on them or been murdered and could not rest. There was a demon huntsman who rode a great black stallion behind baying hellhounds; a woman who sat by Red Pool trying to wash the blood off her fingers; a baby who was heard crying but never seen. Even the grey Druid stones she invested with periodic life. On such-and-such a night the tall Pipers stalked across the fields and played to the Merry Maidens, who danced round thrice; the Mên-an-Tol whistled; the Logan rocked; up on misty hills, barrows opened and old Cornish giants stepped out and dined hugely, with the cromlechs for tables and the stars for tapers.

These stories had one virtue—namely, that they brought the young Penhales home punctually at set of sun. The wild valley they roamed so fearlessly by day assumed a different aspect when the enchanted hours of night drew on; inanimate objects stirred and drew breath, rocks took on the look of old men's faces, thorn bushes changed into witches, shadows harboured nameless crouching things. The creak of a bough sent chills down their spines, the hoot of an owl made them jump, a patch of moonlight on a tree trunk sent them huddling together thinking of the ghost lady; the bark of a fox and a cow crashing through undergrowth set their hearts thumping for fear of the demon huntsman. If caught by dusk, they turned their coats inside out and religiously observed all the rites recommended by Wany as charms against evil spirits. If they were not brought up in the love of God, they were at least taught to respect the Devil.

With the exception of this spiritual concession the Penhale brothers knew no restraint; they ran as wild as stoats. They arose with the sun, stuffed odds and ends of food in their pockets, and were seen no more while daylight lasted.

In spring there was plenty of birds' nesting to be done up the valley. Every other tree held a nest of some sort, if you only knew where to look: up in the forks of the ashes and elms, in hollow boles and rock crevices, cunningly hidden in dense ivy clumps, or snug behind barbed entanglements of thorn. Bohenna, a predatory naturalist, marked down special nests for them, taught them to set bird and rabbit snares and how to tickle trout.

In spring they hunted gulls' eggs as well, round the Luddra Head, swarming perpendicular cliffs with prehensile toes and fingers hooked into cracks, wriggling on their stomachs along dizzy foot-wide shelves, leaping black crevices with the assurance of chamois. It was an exciting pursuit with the sheer drop of two hundred feet or so below one, a sheer drop to jagged rock ledges over which the green rollers poured with the thunder of heavy artillery and then poured back, a boil of white water and seething foam. An exciting pursuit with the backdraught of a south-westerly gale doing its utmost to scoop you off the cliffside, and gull-mothers diving and shrieking in your face — a clamorous snowstorm — trying to shock you off your balance by the whirr of their wings and the piercing suddenness of their cries.

The brothers spent most of the summer at Monk's Cove playing with the fisherchildren, bathing and scrambling along the coast. The tide, ebbing, left many pools, big and little, among the rocks, clear basins enamelled with white and pink sea lichen, studded with limpets, yellow snails, ruby and emerald anemones. Delicate fronds of coloured weed grew in these saltwater gardens, tiny green crabs scuttered along the bottom, gravel-hued bull-cod darted from shadow to shadow. They spent tense if fruitless hours angling for the bull-cod with bent pins, limpet baited. In the largest pool they learnt to swim. When they were sure of themselves they took to the sea itself.

Their favourite spot was a narrow funnel between two low promontories, up which gulf the rollers raced to explode a white puff of spray through a blowhole at the end. At the mouth of the funnel stood a rock they called "The Chimney," the top standing eight feet above low-water level. This made an ideal diving place. You stood on the "Chimney Pot," looked down through glitters and glints of reflected sunshine, down through four fathoms of bottle green water, down to where fantastic pennants of bronze and purple weed rippled and furled and smooth pale boulders gleamed in the swaying light—banners and skulls of drowned armies. You dived, pierced cleanly through the green deeps, a white shooting star trailing silver bubbles. Down you went, down till your fingers touched the weed banners, curved, and came up, saw the water changing from green to amber as you rose, burst into the blaze and glitter of sunlight with the hiss of a breaker in your ears, saw it curving over you, turned and went shorewards shouting, slung by giant arms, wallowing in milky foam, plumed with diamond spray. Then a quick dash sideways out of the sparkling turmoil into a quiet eddy and ashore at your leisure to bask on the rocks and watch the eternal surf beating on the Twelve Apostles and the rainbows glimmering in the haze of spindrift that hung above them.

Porpoises went by, skimming the surface with beautiful lazy curves; solitary cormorants paddled past, popping under and reappearing fifty yards away, with suspicious lumps in the throat. Now and then a shoal of pilchards crawled along the coast, a purple stain in the blue, with a cloud of vociferous gannets hanging over it, diving like stones, rising and poising, glimmering in the sun like silver tinsel. Sometimes a brown seal cruised along, sleek, round-headed and big-eyed.

There was the Channel traffic to watch as well—smacks, schooners, ketches, and snows; all manner of rigs and craft; Tyne collier brigs, grimy as chimney sweeps; smart Falmouth packets carrying mail to and from the world's ends; an East Indiaman maybe, nine months from the Hooghly, wallowing leisurely home, her quarters aglitter of "gingerbread work", her hold redolent with spices; and sometimes a great First-Rate with triple rows of gun ports, an Admiral's flag flying, and studding sails set, rolling a mighty bow wave before her.

Early one summer morning they heard the boom of guns, and round Black Carn came a big Breton lugger under a tremendous press of sail, leaping the short seas like a greyhound. On her weather quarter hung a King's cutter, gaff-topsail, and ring-tail set, a tower of swollen canvas. A tongue of flame darted from the Breton's counter, followed by a mushroom of smoke and a dull crash. A jet of white water leapt thirty feet in the air on the cutter's starboard bow, then another astern of her, and another and another. She seemed to have run among a school of spouting whales, but in reality it was the ricochets of a single round shot. The cutter's bow chaser replied, and jets spouted all round the lugger. The King's ship was trying to crowd the Breton ashore, and looked in a fair way to do so. To the excited boys it appeared that the lugger must inevitably strike the Twelve Apostles did she hold her course. She held on, passed into the drag of the big seas as they gathered to hurl themselves on the reef. Every moment the watchers expected to see her caught and crashed to splinters on the jagged anvil. She rose on a roaring wave crest, hung poised above the reef for a breathless second, and clawed by, shaking the water from her scuppers.

The Cove boys cheered the lugger as she raced by, waving strips of seaweed and dancing with joy. They were not so much for the French as against the Preventive. A Revenue cutter was their hereditary foe, a spoke in the wheel of fortune.

'Up, the Froggy!' they yelled. 'Up, Johnny Roscoff! Give him salt-petre soup, Moosoo! Hurrah! Hooroo!'

The two ships foamed out of sight behind the next headland, the boom of their pieces sounding fainter and fainter.

* * *

Those were good days for the Penhale brothers, the days of early boyhood.

Chapter VII

ORTHO AND Wany were in Penzance looking for cows that had been taken by the press gang, when they met the Pope of Rome wearing a plumed hat and Teresa's second-best dress. He had an iron walking stick in his hand with a shrunken head carved at the top and an ivory ferrule, and every time he tapped the road it rang under him.

'Hollow, you see,' said His Holiness. 'Eaten away by miners and Buccas. Scandalous! One more convulsion like the Lisbon earthquake of 'fifty-five and we shall all fall in. Everything is hollow when you come to think of it—cups, kegs, cannon, ships, churches, crowns, and heads—everything. We shall not only fall in, but inside out. If you don't believe me, listen.'

Whereupon he gathered his skirts and ran up Market Jew Street, laying about him with the iron stick, hitting the ground, the houses, and bystanders on the head; and everything he touched rumbled like a big or little gong in proportion to its size. Finally he hit the Market House. It exploded, and Ortho woke up.

There was a full gale blowing from the south-west, and the noise of the sea was rolling up the valley in roaring waves. The Bosula trees creaked and strained. A shower of broken twigs hit the window, and the wind thudded on the pane like a fist. Ortho turned over on his other side and was just burying his head under the pillow when he heard the explosion again. It was a different note from the boom of the breakers; sharper. He had heard something like that before. Where? Then he remembered the Breton with the cutter in chase. Guns! A chair fell over in his mother's room. She was up. A door slammed below, boots thumped upstairs, Bohenna shouted something through his mother's door and clumped down hurriedly. Ortho could not hear all he said, but he caught two essential words, "wreck" and "cove." More noise on the stairs, and again the house door slammed. His mother had gone. He shook Eli awake.

'There's a ship ashore down to Cove,' he said. 'Banging off guns she was. Mother and Ned's gone. Come on.'

Eli was not anxious to leave his bed; he was comfortable and sleepy. 'We couldn't do nothing,' he protested.

'Might see some foreigners drowned,' said Ortho optimistically. 'She might be a pirate like was sunk in Newlyn last year, full of Turks.'

'They'd kill and eat us,' said Eli.

Ortho shook his head. 'They'll be drowned first; and if they ain't, Ned'll wrastle 'em.'

In settlement of further argument he placed his foot in the small of his brother's back and projected him on to the floor. They dressed in the dark, fumbled their way downstairs, and set off down the valley. In the shelter of the Bosula woods they made good progress; it was comparatively calm there, though the treetops were a-toss and a rotten bough hurtled to earth a few feet behind them. Once round the elbow and clear of the timber the gale bent them double; it rushed shrieking up the funnel of the hills, pushed them round and back-wards. Walking against it was like wading against a strong current. The road was the merest track, not four feet at its widest, littered with rough boulders, punctuated with deep holes. The brothers knew every twist and trick of the path, but in the dark one can blunder in one's own bedroom; moreover, the wind was distorting everything. They tripped and stumbled, were slashed across the face by flying whip thongs of bramble, torn by lunging thorn boughs, pricked by dancing gorse bushes. Things, suddenly invested with malignant animation, bobbed out of the dark, hit or scratched you, and bobbed back again. The night was full of mad terror.

Halfway to the cove, Ortho stubbed his toe for the third time, got a slap in the eye from a blackthorn, and fell into a puddle. He wished he hadn't come, and proposed that they should return. But Eli wouldn't hear of it. He wasn't enjoying himself any more than his brother, but he was going through with it. He made no explanation, but waddled on. Ortho let him get well ahead and then called him back, but Eli did not reply. Ortho wavered. The thought of returning through those creaking woods all alone frightened him. He thought of all the things that went by night, of hellhounds, horsemen, and witches. The air was full of witches on broomsticks and demons on black stallions stampeding up the valley on a dreadful hunt. He could hear their blood-freezing halloos, the blare of horns, the baying of hounds. He wailed to Eli to stop, and trotted, shivering, after him.

The pair crawled into Monk's Cove at last, plastered with mud, their clothes torn to rags. A feeble pilchard-oil "chill" burnt in one or two windows, but the cottages were deserted. Spindrift, mingled with clots of foam, was driving over the roofs in sheets. The wind pressed like a hand on one's mouth; it was scarcely possible to breathe facing it. Several times the boys were forced down on all fours to avoid being blown over backwards. The roar of the sea was deafening, appalling. Gleaming hills of surf hove out of the void in quick succession, toppled, smashed, flooded the beach with foam, and ran back, sucking away the sands.

The small beach was thronged with people; all the Covers were there — men, women, and children, also a few farm folk, drawn by the guns. They sheltered behind boulders, peered seawards, and shouted in each other's ears.

'Spanisher, or else Portingal,' Ortho heard a man bellow.

'Jacky's George seen she off Cribba at sundown. Burnt a tar barrel and fired signals south-west of Apostles — dragging by her lights. She'll bring up presently and then part — no cables won't stand this. The Minstrel'll have her.'

'No, the Carracks, with this set,' growled a second. 'Carracks for a hundred poun'. They'll crack she like a nut.'

'Carracks, Minstrel, or Shark's Fin, she's *ours*,' said the first. 'Hearken!'

Came a crash from the thick darkness seawards; followed a grinding noise and second crash. The watchers hung silent for a moment as though awed, and then sprang up shouting.

'Struck!'

'Carracks have got her!'

'Please God a general cargo!'

'Shan't be long now, my dears. Pickin's for one and all.'

50

Men tied ropes round their waists, gave the ends to their women-folk, and crouched like runners awaiting the signal.

A dark object was tossed high on the crest of a breaker, dropped on the beach, dragged back, and rolled up again.

Half a dozen men scampered towards it and dragged it in: a ship's pinnace smashed to splinters. Part of a carved rail came ashore, a poop ladder, a litter of spars, and a man with no head.

These also were hauled above the surf line. The wreckers wanted a clear beach. Women set to work on the spars, slashing off tackle, quarrelling over the possession of valuable ropes and blocks. A second batch of spars washed in with three more bodies tangled amongst them, battered out of shape. Then a mass of planking, timbers, barrel-staves, some bedding, and, miraculously, a live dog. Suddenly the surf went black with bobbing objects. The cargo was coming in—barrels.

A sea that will play bowls with half-ton rocks will toss wine casks airily. The breakers flung them on the beach, they trundled back down the slope, and were spat up again. The men rushed at them whooping; rushed right into the surf up to their waists, laid hold of a prize and clung on; were knocked over, sucked under, thrown up, and finally dragged out by the women and ancients pulling like horses on the lifelines. A couple of tar barrels came ashore among the others. Teresa, who was much in evidence, immediately claimed them, and with the help of some old ladies piled the loose planking on the wreck of the pinnace, saturated the whole with tar, and set it afire to light the good work. In a few minutes the gale had fanned up a royal blaze. That done, she knotted a salvaged halyard about Bohenna, and with Davy, the second farmhand, Teresa, and the two boys holding on to the shore end, he went into the scramble with the rest.

Barrels were spewed up by every wave, the majority stove in, but many intact. The fisherfolk fastened on them like bulldogs, careless of risk. One man was stunned, another had his leg broken. An old widow, having nobody to work for her and maddened at the sight of all this treasure trove going to others, suddenly threw sanity to the winds, dashed into the surf, butted a man aside, and flung herself on a cask. The cask rolled out with the backdrag, the good dame with it. A breaker burst over them, and they went out of sight in a boil of sand, gravel, and foam. Bohenna plunged after them, was twice swept off his feet, turned head over heels and bumped along the bottom, choking, the sand stinging his face like small shot. He groped out blindly, grasped something solid, and clung on. Teresa, feeling more than she could handle on her line, yelled for help. A dozen sprang to her assistance, and with a tug they got Bohenna out—Bohenna clinging to the old woman, she still clinging to her barrel. She lay on the sand, her arms about her prize, three-parts drowned, spitting saltwater at her saviour.

He laughed 'All right, mother; shan't snatch it from 'ee; 'tis your plunder sure 'nough,' took breath, and plunged back into the surf. The flow of cargo stopped; beams still came in, a topmast, more shattered bodies, some lengths of cable, bedding, splinters of cabin panelling, and a broken chest, valueless odds and ends. The wreckers set about disposing of the sound casks: men staggered off carrying them on rough stretchers, women and children rolled others up the beach, the coils of rope disappeared. Davy, it turned out, had brought three farm horses and left them tied up in a pilchard-press. These were led down to the beach now, loaded—two barrels a horse—and taken home by the men.

Teresa still had a cask in hand. Bohenna could hardly make a second journey before dawn. Moreover, it was leaking, so she stove the head in with a stone and invited everybody to help themselves. Some ran to the houses for cups and jugs, but others could not wait, took off their sodden shoes and baled out the contents greedily. It was overproof Oporto wine, and went to their unaccustomed heads in no time. Teresa, imbibing in her wholesale fashion, was among the first to feel the effects. She began to sing. She sang "Prithee Jack, prithee Tom, pass the can around" and a selection of sottish ditties which had found favour in Portsmouth taverns, suiting her actions to the words. From singing she passed to dancing, uttering sharp "Ai-ees" and "Ah-has" and waving and thumping her detached shoe as though it were a tambourine. She infected the others. They sang the first thing that came into their heads and postured and staggered in an endeavour to imitate her; hoarse-throated men, dripping with seawater; shrill young women; gnarled beldames, dribbling at the mouth; loose-jointed striplings; cracked-voiced ancients contracted with rheumatism; squeaky boys and girls. Drink inspired them to strange cries, extravagant steps and gesticulations. They capered round the barrel, dipping as they passed, drank and capered again, each according to his or her own fashion. Teresa, the presiding genius, lolled over the cask, panting, shrieking with laughter, whooping her victims on to fresh excesses. They hopped and staggered round and round, chanting and shouting, swaying in the wind which swelled their smocks with grotesque protuberances, tore the women's hair loose and set their blue cloaks flapping. Some tumbled and rose again, others lay where they fell. They danced in a mist of flying spindrift and sand with the black cliffs for background, the blazing wreckage for light, the fifes and drums of the gale for orchestra. It might have been a scene from an infernal ballet, a dance of witches and devils, firelit, clamorous, abandoned.

The eight drowned seamen, providers of this good cheer, lay in a row apart, their dog nosing miserably from one to the other, wondering why they were so indifferent when all this merriment was toward, and barking at anyone who approached them.

When the Preventive men arrived with dawn they thought at first it was not a single ship that had foundered, but a fleet, so thick was the beach with barrel-staves and bodies; but even as they stared some corpses revived, sat up, rose unsteadily, and made snake-tracks for the cottages. They were merely the victims of Teresa's bounty. Teresa herself was fast asleep behind a rock when the Preventive came, but she woke up as the sun rose in her eyes, and spent a pleasant hour watching their fruitless hunt for liquor and offering helpful suggestions.

Hunger gnawing her, she whistled her two sons as if they had been dogs, and made for home, tacking from side to side of the path like a ship beating to windward, and cursing every time she stumbled. The frightened boys kept fifty yards in rear.

In return for Teresa's insults the Preventive paid Bosula a visit later in the day. Teresa, refreshed by some hours' sleep, followed the searchers round the steading, jeering at them while they prodded sticks into haystacks and patches of newly-dug ground, or rapped floors and walls for hollow places. She knew they would never find those kegs; they were half a mile away, sunk in a muddy pool further obscured by willows. Bohenna had walked the horses upstream and down so that there should be no telltale tracks. The Preventive were drawing a blank cover. It entertained Teresa to see them getting angrier and angrier. She was prodigal with jibes and personalities. The Riding Officer retired at dusk, informing the widow that it would give him great pleasure to tear her tongue out and fry it for breakfast. Teresa was highly amused. Her good humour recovered, and that evening she broached a cask, hired a fiddler, and gave a dance in the kitchen.

Chapter VIII

THE PENHALE brothers grew and grew, put off childish things and began to seek the company of men, worshipfully and with emulation as puppies imitate grown dogs. Ortho's first hero was a fisherman whose real name was George Baragwanath, but who was invariably referred to as "Jacky's George," although his father, the possessive Jacky, was long dead and forgotten, and had been nothing worth mentioning when alive.

Jacky's George was a remarkable man. At the age of seventeen, while gathering driftwood below Pedn Boar, he had seen an intact ship's pinnace floating in. The weather was moderate, but there was sufficient swell on to stave the boat did it strike the outer rocks; and it was a good boat. The only way to save it was to swim off, but Jacky's George, like most fishermen, could not swim. He badly wanted that boat; it would make him independent of Jacky, whose methods were too slow to catch a cold, leave alone fish. Moreover, there was a girl involved. He stripped off his clothes, gathered the bundle of drift-wood in his arms, flopped into the backwash of a roller, and kicked out frog fashion, knowing full well that his chances of reaching the boat were slight and that if he did not reach it he would surely drown.

He reached the boat, however, scrambled up over the stern, and found three men asleep on the bottom. His heart fell like lead. He had risked his life for nothing; he'd still have to go fishing with the timorous Jacky, and the girl must wait.

'Here,' said he wearily to the nearest sleeper. 'Here, rouse up; you'm close ashore . . . be scat in a minute.'

The sleeper did not stir. Jacky's George kicked him none too gently. Still the man did not move. He then saw that he was dead; they were all dead. The boat was his after all! He got the oars out and brought the boat safely into Monk's Cove. Quite a sensation it made, Jacky's George, stark naked, pulling in out of the sea fog with a cargo of dead men. He married that girl forthwith, was a father at eighteen, a grandfather at thirty-five. In the interval he got nipped by the press gang in a Falmouth grog shop, and sent round the world with Anson in the *Centurion*, rising to the rank of quarter-gunner. One of the two hundred survivors of that lucrative voyage, he was paid off with a goodly lump of prize money, and, returning to his native cove, opened an inn with a florid cock-hatted portrait of his old commander for sign.

Jacky's George, however, was not inclined to a life of bibulous ease ashore. He handed the inn over to his wife and went to sea again as gunner in a small Falmouth privateer mounting sixteen pieces. Off Ushant one February evening they were chased by a Maloman of twice their weight of metal, which was overhauling them hand over fist when her foremast went by the board and up she went in the wind. Jacky's George was responsible for the shot that disabled the Breton, but her parting broadside disabled Jacky's George; he lost an arm.

He was reported to have called for rum, hot tar, and an axe. These having been brought, he gulped the rum, chopped off the wreckage of his forearm, soused the spurting stump in tar, and fainted. He recovered rapidly, fitted a boathook head to the stump, and was at work again in no time; but the accident made a longshoreman of him; he went no more a-roving in letters of marque, but fished offshore with his swarm of sons, Ortho Penhale occasionally going with him.

Physically Jacky's George was a sad disappointment. Of all the Covers he was the least like what he ought to have been, the last man you would have picked out as the desperado who had belted the globe, sacked towns and treasure ships, been master gunner of a privateer, and killed several times his own weight in hand-to-hand combats. He was not above five feet three inches in height, a chubby, chirpy, red-headed, cock robin of a man who drank little, swore less, smiled perpetually, and whistled wherever he went, even, it was said, at the graveside of his own father—in a moment of abstraction, of course.

His wife, who ran the Admiral Anson (better known as the Kiddlywink), was a heavy, dark woman, twice his size, and very downright in her opinions. She would roar down a roomful of tipsy mariners with ease and gusto, but the least word of her smiling little husband she obeyed swiftly and in silence. It was the same with his children. There were nine of them, two daughters and seven sons, all red-headed and freckled like himself, a turbulent, independent tribe, paying no man respect—but their father.

Ortho could not fathom the nature of the little man's power over them; he was so boyish himself, took such childish delight in their tales of mischief, seemed in all that boatload of boys the youngest and most carefree. Then one evening he had a glimpse of the cock robin's other side. They were just in from sea, were lurching up from the slip, when they were greeted by ominous noises issuing from the Kiddlywink, the crash of woodwork, hoarse oaths, a thump, and then growlings as of a giant dog worrying a bone. Jacky's George broke into a run, and at the same moment his wife, terrified, appeared at the door and cried out, 'Quick! Quick do 'ee! Murder!'

Jacky's George dived past her into the house; Ortho, agog for any form of excitement, close behind him.

The table was lying over on its side, one bench was broken and the other tossed, end on, into a corner. On the wet floor among chips of shattered mugs two men struggled, locked together, a big man on top, a small man underneath. The former had the latter by the throat, rapidly throttling him. The victim's eyeballs seemed on the point of bursting, his tongue was sticking out.

'Tinners,' wailed Mrs Baragwanath. 'Been drinkin' all day—gert stinkin' toads!'

Jacky's George did not waste time in wordy remonstrance; he got the giant's chin in the crook of his sound arm and tried to wrench it up. Useless; the maddened brute was too strong and too heavy. The man underneath gave a ghastly clicking choke. In another second there would have been murder done in the Admiral Anson and a blight would fall on that prosperous establishment, killing trade. That would never do. Without hesitation its landlord settled the matter, drove his stump hook into the giant's face, gaffed him through the cheek as he would a fish.

'Come off,' said he.

The man came off.

'Come on.' He backed out, leading the man by the hook.

'Lift a hand or struggle, and I'll drag your face inside out,' said Jacky's George. 'This way, if you please.'

The man followed, bent double, murder in his eyes, hands twitching, but at his sides.

At the end of the hamlet Jacky's George halted. 'You owe me your neck, mate, but I don't s'pose you'll thank me; tedd'n in human nature you would,' said he sadly, as though pained at the ingratitude of mortal man. 'Go on up that there road till you'm out of this place an' don't you never come back.'

He freed the hook deftly and jumped clear. 'Now crowd all canvas, do 'ee.'

The great tinner put a hand to his bleeding cheek, glared at the smiling cock robin, clenched his fists and teeth, and took a step forward—one only. A stone struck him in the chest, another missed his head by an inch. He ducked to avoid a third, and was hit in the back and thigh, started to retreat at a walk, broke into a run, and went cursing and stumbling up the track, his arms above his head to protect it from the rain of stones. Goliath pursued by seven red-headed little Davids, and all the covewomen standing on their doorsteps jeering.

'Two mugs an' a bench scat,' Jacky's George commented as he watched his sons speeding the parting guest. 'Have to make t'other poor soul pay for 'em, I s'pose.' He turned back into the Kiddlywink whistling "Strawberry leaves make maidens fair."

Ortho enjoyed going to sea with the Baragwanath family; they put such zest into all they did; no slovenliness was permitted. Falls and cables were neatly coiled or looped over pins, sail was stowed properly, oars tossed man-o'-war fashion, everything went with a snap. Furthermore, they took chances; for them no humdrum harbour-hugging; they went far and wide after the fish, and sank their crab pots under dangerous ledges no other boat would tackle. In anything like reasonable weather they dropped a tier or two seaward of the Twelve Apostles. Even on the calmest of days there was a heavy swell on to the south of the reef, especially with the tide making. It was shallow there, and the Atlantic flood came rolling over the shoal in great shining hills. At one moment you were up in the air and could see the brown coast with its purple indentations for miles, the patchwork fields, scattered grey farmhouses, the smoke of furze fires, and lazy clouds rolling along the high moors. At the next moment you were in the lap of a turquoise valley, shut out from everything by rushing cliffs of water. There were oars, sheets, halyards, backropes and lines to be pulled on, fighting fish to be hauled aboard, clubbed, and gaffed. And always there was Jacky's George whistling like a canary, pointing out the various rigs of passing vessels, spinning yarns of privateer days and of Anson's wonderful voyage, of the taking of Paita City and the great Plate ship *Nuestra Señora de Covadonga*. And there was the racing.

Very jealous of his craft's reputation was Jacky's George. A hint of defiance from another boat, and he was after the challenger instanter, even though it took him out of his course. Many a good spin did Ortho get coming in from the Carn Base, Wolf, and other outer fishing grounds, backed against the weather-side with the Baragwanath boys, living ballast, while the gig, trembling from end to end, went leaping and swooping over the blue-and-white hillocks on the trail of an ambitious Penberth or Porthgwarraman. Sheets and weather-stays humming in the blast, taut and vibrant as guitar strings; sails rigid as though carved from wood, lee gunnel all but dipping under; dollops of spray bursting aboard over the weather-bow. Tense work, culminating in exultation as they crept up on the chase, drew to her quarter, came broad abeam, and, with derisive cheers, passed her. Speed was a mania with the cock robin. He was in perpetual danger of sailing the *Game Cock* under; on one occasion he very nearly did.

They were tearing close-hauled through the Runnelstone Passage after an impudent Mouseholeman when a cross sea suddenly rose out of nowhere and popped aboard over the low lee gunnel. In a second the boat was full of water, only her gunnels and thwarts were visible. It seemed to Ortho that he was standing up to his knees in the sea.

'Luff!' shouted Jacky's George.

His eldest son jammed the helm hard down, but the boat wouldn't answer. The way was off her; she lay as dead as a log.

'Leggo sheets,' shouted the father. 'Aft all hands!'

Ortho tumbled aft with the Baragwanath boys and watched Jacky's George in a stupor of fright. The little man could not be said to move; he flickered, grabbed up an oar, wrenched the boat's head round, broke the crest of an oncoming wave by launching the oar blade at it, and took the remainder in his back.

'Heave the ballast out an' bale,' he yelled gleefully, sitting in the bows, forming a living bulwark against the waves. 'Bale till your backs break, my jollies.'

They baled like furies, baled with the first things to hand—line-tubs, caps, boots, anything—in the meanwhile drifting rapidly towards the towering cliffs of Tol-Pedn-Penwith. The crash of the breakers on the ledges struck terror through Ortho. They sounded like a host of ravenous great beasts roaring for their prey—him. If the boat did not settle under them they would be dashed to pieces on those rocks; death was inevitable one way or the other. He remembered the Portuguese seamen washed in from the Twelve Apostles without heads. He would be like that in a few minutes—no head. Ugh!

Jacky's George, jockeying the bows, improvising a weather-cloth from a spare jib, was singing "Hey boys, up we go!" This levity in the jaws of destruction enraged Ortho. The prospect of imminent death might amuse Jacky's George, who had eaten a rich slice of life, but Ortho had not and was terrified. He felt he was too young to die; it was unfair to snatch a mere boy like himself. Moreover, it was far too sudden—no warning at all. At one moment they were bowling along in the sunshine, laughing and happy, and at the next up to their waists in water, to all intents dead, cold, headless, eaten by crabs. Ugh! He thought of Eli up the valley, flintlock in hand, dry, happy, safe for years and years of fun; thought of the Owls' House bathed in the noon glow, the old dog asleep in the sun, pigeons strutting on the thatch, copper pans shining in the kitchen; thought of his home, symbol of all things comfortable and secure, and promised God that if he got out of the mess he would never set foot in a boat again.

The roar of the breakers grew louder, and he felt cold and sick with fear, but nevertheless baled with the best, baled for dear life, realising for the first time how inexpressibly precious life may be. Jacky's George whistled, cracked jokes, and sang "The Bold British Tar." He made such a din as to drown the noise of the surf—the "British Tar" had brave words and a good rousing chorus; the boys joined in as they baled. Presently. Ortho found himself singing too.

Six lads toiling might and main can shift a quantity of water. The gig began to brisk in her movements, to ride easier. Fifty yards off the foam-draped Hella Rock, Jacky's George laid her to her course again, but the Mouseholeman was out of sight.

No Dundee harpooner, home from a five years' cruise, had a more moving story of perils on the deep to tell than did Ortho that night. He staggered about the kitchen affecting a sea-roll, spat over his shoulder, and told and retold the tale till his mother boxed his ears and drove him up to bed. Even then he kept Eli awake for two hours baling that boat out over and over again. He had enjoyed every moment of it, he said. Nevertheless, he did not go fishing for a month, but the Baragwanath family were dodging off St Clement's Isle before sunup next day, waiting for that Mousehole boat to come out of port. When she did they led her down to the fishing grounds and then led her home again, a tow rope trailing derisively over the *Game Cock's* stern. They were an indomitable breed.

Ortho recovered from his experience off Tol-Pedn, and, despite his promise to his Maker, went to sea occasionally. But that phase of his education was nearing its close. Winter and its gales were approaching, and even the fearless cock robin seldom ventured out. When he did go he took only his four eldest boys, departed without ostentation, was gone a week or even two, and returned quietly in the dead of night.

"Scilly—to visit his sister" was given by Mrs Baragwanath as his destination and object, but it was noted that these demonstrations of brotherly affection invariably occurred when the Admiral Anson's stock of liquor was getting low. The wise drew their own conclusions. Ortho pleaded to be taken on one of these mysterious trips, but

Jacky's George was adamant, so he had perforce to stop at home and follow the *Game Cock* in imagination across the wintry Channel to Guernsey and back again through the patrolling frigates, loaded to the bends with ankers of gin and brandy.

Cut off from Jacky's George, he looked about for a fresh hero to worship, and lit upon Pyramus Herne.

Chapter IX

PYRAMUS HERNE was the head of a family of gypsy horse dealers that toured the south and west of England, appearing regularly in the Land's End district on the heels of the New Year. They came not particularly to do business, but to feed their horses up for the spring fairs. The climate was mild, and Pyramus knew that to keep a beast warm is to go halfway towards fattening it.

He would arrive with a chain of broken-down skeletons, tied head to tail, file their teeth, blister and fire their game legs, and turn them loose in the sheltered bottoms for a rest cure. At the end of three months, when the bloom was on their new coats, he would trim their feet, pull manes and tails, give an artistic touch here and there with the shears, paint out blemishes, make old teeth look like new, and depart with a string of apparently gamesome youngsters frolicking in his tracks.

It was his practice to pitch his winter camp in a small coppice about two and a half miles north of Bosula. It was No-Man's-Land, sheltered by a wall of rocks from the north and east, water was plentiful, and the trees provided fuel. Moreover, it was secluded—a weighty consideration, for the gypsy dealt in other things besides horses, in the handling of which privacy was of the first import. In short, he was a receiver of stolen goods and valuable articles of salvage. He gave a better price than the junk dealers in Penzance because his travels opened a wider market, and also he had a reputation of never "peaching," of betraying a customer for reward—a reputation far from deserved, be it said. But he peached always in secret and with consummate discretion.

He did lucrative business in salvages in the West, but the traffic in stolen goods was slight because there were no big towns and no professional thieves. The few furtive people who crept by night into the little wood seeking the gypsy were mainly thieves by accident, victims of sudden overwhelming temptations. They seldom bargained with Pyramus, but agreed to the first price offered, thrust the stolen articles upon him as if red-hot, and were gone, radiant with relief, frequently forgetting to take the money.

'I am like their Christ,' said Pyramus; 'they come to me to be relieved of their sins.'

In England of those days gypsies were regarded with well-merited suspicion and hunted from pillar to post. Pyramus was the exception. He passed unmolested up and down his trade routes, for he was at particular pains to ingratiate himself with the two ruling classes, the law officers and the gentry, and, being a clever man, succeeded.

The former liked him because, once "King" Herne joined a fair, there would be no trouble with the Romanies; also he gave them reliable information from time to time. Captain Rudolph, the notorious Bath Road highwayman, owed his capture and subsequent hanging to Pyramus, as did also a score of lesser tobymen. Pyramus made no money out of footpads, so he threw them as a sop to Justice.

The gentry Pyramus fawned on with the oily cunning of his race. Every man has a joint in his harness, magistrates no less. Pyramus made these little weaknesses of the great his special study. One influential landowner collected snuffboxes, another firearms. Pyramus in his traffickings up and down the world kept his eyes skinned for snuffboxes and firearms, and, having exceptional opportunities, usually managed to bring something for each when he passed their way—an exquisite casket of tortoiseshell and paste, a pair of silver-mounted pistols with Toledo barrels. Some men had to be reached by other means.

Lord James Thynne was partial to coursing. Pyramus kept an eye lifted for greyhounds, bought a dog from the widow of a Somersetshire poacher (hung the day before), and Lord James won ten matches running with it. The Herne tribe were welcome to camp on his waste lands for ever.

But his greatest triumph was with Mr Hugo Lorimer, J.P., of Stane, in the county of Hampshire. Mr Lorimer was death on gypsies, maintaining against all reason that they hailed from Palestine and were responsible for the Crucifixion. He harried them unmercifully. He was not otherwise a devout man; the persecution of the Romanies was his sole form of religious observance. Even the astute Pyramus could not melt him, charm he never so wisely.

This worried King Herne, the more so because Mr Lorimer's one passion was horses—his own line of business—and he could not reach him through it.

He could not win the truculent J.P. by selling him a good nag cheap; because he bred his own and would tolerate no other breed. He could not even convey a good racing tip to the gentleman, because he did not bet. The Justice was adamant, Pyramus baffled.

Then one day a change came in the situation. The pride of the stud, the crack stallion Stane Emperor, went down with fever, and, despite all ministrations, passed rapidly from bad to worse. All hope was abandoned. Mr Lorimer, infinitely more perturbed than if his entire family had been in a like condition, sat on an upturned bucket in the horse's box and wept.

To him entered Pyramus, pushing past the grooms, fawning, obsequiously sympathetic, white with dust. He had heard the dire news at Downton, and come instanter, spurring.

Might he humbly crave a peep at the noble sufferer? . . . Perhaps his poor skill might effect something . . . had been with horses all his life . . . had succeeded with many cases abandoned by others more learned . . . it was his business and livelihood . . . would his Worship graciously permit? . . .

His Worship ungraciously grunted an affirmative. Gypsy horse-coper full of tricks as a dog of fleas . . . at all events could make the precious horse no worse. . . . Go ahead!

Pyramus bolted himself in with the animal, and in two hours it was standing up lipping bran mash from his hand, sweaty, shaking, but saved.

Mr Hugo Lorimer, all gratitude, his one soft spot touched at last. Pyramus must name his own reward. Pyramus, both palms upraised in protest, would hear of no reward, honoured to have been of any service to *such a* gentleman.

Departed, bowing and smirking, the poison he had blown through a grating into the horse's manger the night before in one pocket, the antidote in the other.

Henceforward the Herne family plied their trade undisturbed within the bounds of Mr Lorimer's magistracy, to the exclusion of all other gypsies, and throve mightily in consequence.

He had been at pains to commend himself to Teresa Penhale, but had only partly succeeded. She was the principal landowner in the valley where he wintered, and it was necessary to keep on her right side.

The difficulty with Teresa was that, being of gypsy blood herself, she was proof against gypsy trickery and exceedingly suspicious of her, own kind. He tried to present her with a pair of barbaric gold earrings, by way of throwing bread upon the waters, but she asked him how much he wanted for them, and he made the fatal mistake of saying 'Nothing.'

'Nothing today and my skin tomorrow?' she sneered. 'Outside with you!'

Pyramus went on the other tack—pretended not to recognise her as a Romni, addressed her in English, treated her with extravagant deference, and saw to it that his family did the same.

It worked. Teresa rather fancied herself as a "lady," though she could never go to the trouble of behaving like one, and it pleased her to find somebody who treated her as such. It pleased her to have the great King Herne back his horse out of her road and remain, hat in hand, till she had passed by, to have his women drop curtsies and his bantlings bob. It worked—temporarily. Pyramus had touched her abundant conceit, lulled the Christian half of her with flattery; but he knew that the gypsy half was awake and on guard. The situation was too nicely balanced for comfort; he looked about for fresh weight to throw into his side of the scale.

One day he met Eli wandering up the valley alone, flintlock in hand, on the outlook for woodcock.

Pyramus could be fascinating when he chose; it lubricated the wheels of commerce. He laid himself out to charm Eli, told him where he had seen a brace of cock and also some snipe, complimented him on his villainous old blunderbuss, was all gleaming teeth, geniality, and oil. He could not have made a greater mistake. Eli was not used to charm and had an instinctive distrust of the unfamiliar. He had been reared among boors who said their say in the fewest words, and therefore distrusted a talker. Further, he was his father's son, a Penhale of Bosula on his own soil, and this fellow was an Egyptian, a foreigner, and he had an instinctive distrust of foreigners. He growled something incoherent, scowled at the beaming Pyramus, shouldered his unwieldy cannon, and marched off in the opposite direction.

Pyramus bit his fleshy lip. Nothing to be done with that truculent bear cub. But what about the brother, the handsome dark boy? What about him—eh?

He looked out for Ortho, met him once or twice in company with other lads, made no overtures beyond a smile, but heeled his mare and set her caracoling showily.

He did not glance round, but he knew the boy's eyes were following him. A couple of evenings after the last meeting he came home to learn that young Penhale had been hanging about the camp that afternoon.

The eldest Herne son, Lussha, had invited him in, but Ortho declined, saying he had come up to look at some badger diggings. Pyramus smiled into his curly beard. The badger holes had been untenanted for years. Ortho came up to carry out a further examination of the badger earths the very next day.

Pyramus saw him, high up among the rocks of the carn, his back to the diggings, gazing wistfully down on the camp, its tents, fires, and horses. He did not ask the boy in, but sent out a scout with orders to bring word when young Penhale went home.

The scout returned at about three o'clock. Ortho, he reported, had worked stealthily down from the carn top and had been lying in the bracken at the edge of the encampment for the last hour, imagining himself invisible. He had now gone off towards Bosula. Pyramus called for his mare to be saddled, brushed his breeches, put on his best coat, mounted, and pursued. He came up with the boy a mile or so above the farm, and brought his mount alongside, caracoling and curvetting. Ortho's expressing eyes devoured her.

'Good day to you, young gentleman,' Pyramus called, showing his fine teeth. Ortho grinned in return.

'Wind gone back to the east; we shall have a spell of dry weather, I think,' said the gypsy, making the mare do a right pass, pivot on her hocks, and pass to the left.

'Yeh,' said Ortho, his mouth wide with admiration.

King Herne and his steed were enough to take any boy's fancy; they were dressed to that end. The gypsy had masses of inky hair, curled moustaches, and an Assyrian beard, which frame of black served to enhance the brightness of his glance, the white brilliance of his smile. He was dressed in the coat he wore when calling on the gentry, dark blue frogged with silver lace and buff spatterdashes. He sat as though bolted to the saddle from the thighs down; the upper half of him, hinged at the hips, balanced gracefully to every motion of his mount, lithe as a panther for all his forty-eight years.

And the mare, she was his pride and delight, black like himself, three-quarter Arab, mettlesome, fine-boned, pointed of muzzle, arched of neck. Unlike her mates, she was assiduously groomed and kept rugged in winter, so that her coat had not grown shaggy. Her long mane rippled like silken threads, her tail streamed behind her like a banner. The late sunshine twinkled on the silver mountings of her bridle and rippled over her hide till she gleamed like satin. She bounded and pirouetted along beside Ortho, light on her feet as a ballerina, tossed her mane, pricked her crescent ears, showed the whites of her eyes, clicked the bit in her young teeth, a thing of steel and swansdown, passion and docility.

Ortho's eyes devoured her. Pyramus noted it, laughed, and patted the glossy neck.

'You like my little sweet—eh? She is of blood royal. Her sire was given to the Chevalier Lombez Muret by the Basha of Oran in exchange for three pieces of siege ordnance and a chiming clock. The dam of that sire sprang from the sacred mares of the Prophet Mahomet, the mares that, though dying of thirst, left the life-giving stream and galloped to the trumpet call. There is the blood of queens in her.'

'She is a queen herself,' said Ortho warmly.

Pyramus nodded. 'Well said. I see you have an eye for a horse, young Squire. You can ride, doubtless?'

'Yes, but only packhorses.'

'So? Only packhorses, farm drudges? That is doleful travelling. See here! Mount my Rriena, and drink the wind.' He dropped the reins, vaulted off over the mare's rump, and held out his hand for Ortho's knee.

'Me! I . . . I ride her?' The boy stuttered, astounded.

The gypsy smiled his dazzling, genial smile. 'Surely—an' you will. There is nothing to fear; she is playful only—the heart of a dove. Take hold of the reins. . . . Your knee. . . . Up you go!'

He hove the boy high and lowered him gently into the saddle.

'Stirrups too long? Put your feet in the leathers—so. An easy hand on her mouth; a touch will serve. Ready? Then away, my chicken.'

He let go the bridle and clapped his palms. The mare bounded into the air. Ortho, frightened, clutched the pommel, but she landed again light as a feather, never shifting him in the saddle. Smoothly she caracoled, switching her plumy tail, tossing her head, snatching playfully at the bit. There was no pitch, no jar, just an easy, airy rocking. Ortho let her gambol on for a hundred yards or so, and then, thinking he'd better turn, fingered his off rein. He no more than fingered the rein, but the mare responded as though she divined his thoughts, circled smoothly, and rocked back towards Pyramus.

'Round again,' shouted the gypsy, 'and give her rein; there's a stretch of turf before you.'

Again the mare circled. Ortho tapped her with his heels. A tremble ran through her, an electric thrill. She sprang into a canter, from a canter to a gallop, and swept down the turf all out. It was flight—no less; winged flight, skimming the earth. The turf streamed under them like a green river; bushes, trees, boulders flickered backwards, blurred, reeling. The wind tore Ortho's cap off, ran fingers through his hair, whipped tears to his eyes, blew jubilant bugles in his ears, drowning the drum of hoofs, filled his open mouth, sharp, intoxicating, the heady wine of speed. He was one with clouds, birds, arrows, all things free and flying. He wanted to sing, and did so, a wordless, crazy carolling. They swept on, drunk with the glory of it. A barrier of thorn stood across the way, and Ortho came to his senses. They would be into it in a minute unless he stopped the mare. He braced himself for a pull, but there was no need; she felt him stiffen and sit back, sat back herself, and came to a full stop within ten lengths. Ortho wiped the happy tears from his eyes, patted her shoulder, turned, and went back at the same pace, speed-drunk again. They met the gypsy walking towards them, the dropped cap in hand. He called to the mare; she stopped beside him and rubbed her soft muzzle against his chest. He looked at the flushed, enraptured boy.

'She can gallop, my little Rriena?'

'Gallop! Why, yes. Gallop! I . . . I never knew . . . never saw. . . . I . . .' Words failed Ortho.

Pyramus laughed. 'No, there is not her match in the country. But, mark ye, she will not give her best to anybody. She felt the virtue in you, knew you for her master. You need experience, polish; but you are a horseman born, flat in the thigh, slim-waisted, with light, strong hands.' The gypsy's voice pulsed with enthusiasm, his dark eyes glowed. 'Tcha! I wish I had the schooling of you. I'd make you a wizard with horses.'

'Oh, I wish you would. Will you? Will you?' cried Ortho.

Pyramus made a gesture with his expressive hands.

'I would willingly. I love a bold boy, but . . .'

'Yes?'

Pyramus shrugged his shoulders. 'The lady, your mother, has no liking for me. She is right, doubtless. You are Christian gentry, I but a poor Rom. . . . Still, I mean no harm.'

'She shall never know—never,' said Ortho eagerly. 'Oh, I would give anything if you would.'

Pyramus shook his head reprovingly. 'You must honour your parents, Squire; it is so written . . . and yet I am loath to let your gifts lie fallow. A prince of jockeys I could make you.'

He bit his fingernails as though wrestling with temptation. 'See here! Get your mother's leave and then come; come and a thousand welcomes. I have a chestnut pony, a red flame of a pony that would carry you as my beauty carries me.'

He vaulted into the saddle, jumped the mare over a furze bush, whirled about, waved his hat, and was gone up the valley, scattering clods. Ortho watched the flying pair until they were out of sight, and then turned homewards, his heart pounding, new avenues of delight opening before him.

Out of sight, Pyramus eased Rriena to a walk and, leaning forward, pulled her ears affectionately. 'Did he roll all over you and tug your mouth, my sweetmeat?' he purred. 'Well, never again. But we have him now. In a year or two he'll be master here, and I'll graze fifty nags where I grazed twenty. We will fatten on that boy.'

Ortho reported at the gypsy camp shortly after sunup next morning. He was wasting no time. Questioned, he swore he had Teresa's leave, which was a lie, as Pyramus knew it to be. But he had covered himself; did trouble arise he could declare he understood the boy had got his mother's permission.

Ortho did not expect to be discovered. Teresa was used to him being out day and night with either Bohenna or Jacky's George, and would not be curious. The gypsies had the head of the valley to themselves; nobody ever came that way except the cow-girl Wany, and she had no eyes for anything but the supernatural.

The riding lessons began straightaway on Lussha's red pony Cherry. The chestnut was by no means as perfect a mount as the black mare, but for all that a creditable performer, well schooled, speedy and eager, a refreshing contrast to the stiff-jointed, iron-mouthed farm horses. Pyramus took pains with his pupil. Half of what he had said was true: the boy was shaped to fit a saddle, and his hands were sensitive. There was a good deal of the artist in King Herne; it pleased him to handle promising material for its own sake; but above all he sought to infect the boy with horse-fever to his own material gain.

Ortho made good progress. He was intelligent, and in his admiration for his master implicitly obedient. He learnt to keep his head up, his heels and hands low, to steer with his legs and weight, to vault in and out of the saddle. He learnt to jump, and took a fall or two, but the country was soft with winter rains, and he came to no harm thereby. He rode all over the moors with Pyramus and went out herding with the gypsy lads. Good fun this, bringing the strays in at full speed, hallooing and singing, splashing through streams and mudholes, crashing through thorn brakes, leaping, spring-heeled, over boulders and gorse bushes.

The gypsy camp saw him early and late. He returned to Bosula only to sleep and fill his pockets with food. Food in wasteful plenty lay about everywhere in that slipshod establishment, the door was never bolted. He would creep home through the orchard, silence the dogs with a word, take off his shoes in the kitchen, listen to Teresa's hearty snores in the room above, drive the cats off the remains of supper, help himself, and tiptoe up to bed. Nobody except Eli knew where he spent his days; nobody cared.

The gypsies attracted him for the same reason that they repelled his brother; they were something new, something he did not understand.

Ortho did not find anything very elusive about the males; they were much like other men, if quicker witted and more suave. It was the women who intrigued and, at the same time, awed him. He had watched them at work with the cards, bent over the palm of a trembling servant girl or farm woman. What did they know? What didn't they know? What virtue was in them that they should be the chosen mouthpieces of Destiny? He would furtively watch them about their domestic duties, stirring the black pots or nursing their half-naked brats, and wonder what secrets the fates were even then whispering into their ringed ears, what enigmas were being made plain to those brooding eyes. He felt his soul laid bare to those omniscient eyes.

But it was solely his own imagination that troubled him; the women gave him no cause. They cast none but the gentlest glances at the dark boy. Sometimes of an evening they would sing, not the green English ballads and folk songs that were their stock-in-trade, but epics of Romany heroes, threnodies and canzonets.

Pyramus was the principal soloist. He had a pliant, tuneful voice, and accompanied himself on a Spanish guitar.

He would squat before the fire, the women in a row opposite him, toss a verse across to them, and they would toss back the refrain, rocking to the time as though strung on a single wire.

The scene stirred Ortho—the gloomy wood, the overhanging rocks, the gypsy king, guitar across his knees, trumpeting his wild songs of love and knavery, and the women and girls in their filthy colourful rags, seen through a film of wood smoke, swaying to and fro, to and fro, bright eyes and barbaric brass ornaments glinting in the firelight. On the outer circle children and men lay listening in the leaf-mould, and beyond them invisible horses stamped and shifted at their pickets, an owl hooted, a dog barked.

The scene stirred Ortho; it was so strange and yet somehow so familiar. He had a feeling that sometime, somewhere, he had seen it all before; long ago and far away he had sat in a camp like this and heard women singing. He liked the boastful stormy songs, "Invocation to Timour," "The Master Thief," "The Valiant Tailor," but the dirges carried him off—one especially. It was very sweet and sad. It had only four verses, and the women sang each refrain more softly than the one before, so that the last was hardly above a whisper and dwindled into silence like the wind dying away—'aïë, aïë; aïë, aïë.' Ortho did not understand what it was about—its name even—but when he heard it he lost himself, became someone else, someone else who understood perfectly crept inside his body, forced his tears, made him sway and feel queer. Then the gypsy women across the fire would glance at him and nudge each other quietly. 'See,' they would whisper, 'his Rom grandfather looking out of his eyes.'

Chapter X

ONE EVENING in late February there was mullet pie for supper, which was so much to Teresa's taste that she ate more than even her heroic digestive organs could cope with, rent the stilly night with lamentations, and did not get up for breakfast. Towards nine o'clock she felt better, at eleven was herself again, and, remembering it was Paul Feast, dressed in her finery and rode off to see the sport.

She arrived to witness what appeared to be a fratricidal war between the seafaring stalwarts of the parish and the farmhands. A mob of boys and men surged about a field, battling claw and hoof for the possession of a cowhide ball which occasionally lobbed into view, but more often lay buried under a pile of writhing bodies.

Teresa was very fond of these rough sports, and journeyed far and wide to see them, but what held her interest most that afternoon was a party of gentry who had ridden from Penzance to watch the barbarians at play. Two ladies and three gentlemen there were, the elder woman riding pillion, the younger side-saddle. They were very exquisite and superior, watched the uncouth mob through quizzing glasses, and made witty remarks, after the manner of visitors at a menagerie commenting on near-human antics of the monkeys. The younger woman chattered incessantly—a thinly, pretty creature, wearing a gold-braided cocked hat and long brown coat cut in the masculine mode.

'Eliza, Eliza, I beseech you look at that woman's stomacher! . . . and that wench's farthingale! Elizabethan, I declare. One would imagine oneself at a Vauxhall masquerade. Mr Borlase, I felicitate you on your entertainment.' She waved her whip towards the mob. 'Bear pits are tedious by comparison. I must pen my experiences for the *Spectator*—"Elegantia inter Barbaros; or, A Lady's Adventures Among the Wild Cornish." Tell me, pray, when it is all over do they devour the dead? We must go before that takes place. I should positively expire of fright. Though my cousin Venables, who has voyaged the South Seas, tells me cannibals are as a rule an amiable and loving people, vastly preferable to Tories. Captain Angus, I have dropped my kerchief. . . . You neglect me, sir! My God, Eliza, there's a handsome boy! . . . behind you . . . the gypsy boy on the sorrel pony. What a pretty young rogue!'

The whole party turned their heads to look at the Romany Apollo. Teresa followed their example, and behold, it was Ortho! Under the delusion that his mother was abed and, judging by the noise she made, at death's door, he had ventured afield in company with four young Hernes. He wore no cap, his sleeve was ripped from shoulder to cuff, and he was much splashed all down his back and legs. He did not see his mother; he was absorbed in the game. Teresa shut her teeth and drew a long deep breath through them.

The battle suddenly turned against the fishermen; the farmhands, uttering triumphant howls, began to force them rapidly backwards towards the churchtown. Ortho and his ragged companions wheeled their mounts and ambled downhill to see the finish. Teresa did not follow them; she found her horse, mounted, and rode straight home.

'The gypsy boy on the sorrel pony—the *gypsy* boy!'

People were taking her Ortho, Ortho Penhale of Bosula and Tregors, for a vagabond Rom were they?

She was furious, but admitted they had cause—dressed like a scarecrow and mixed up with a crowd of young horse thieves! Teresa swore so savagely that her horse started. Anyhow, she would stop it at once! She'd settle all this gypsy business. *Gypsy!* Time after time she had vowed to send Ortho to school, but she was always hard up when it came to the point, and year after year slipped by. He must be somewhere about sixteen now—fifteen, sixteen, or seventeen. She wasn't sure and it didn't matter to a year or so. She would look it up in the parish registers if need be. He should go to Helston like his father and learn to be a gentleman, and, incidentally, learn to keep accounts. It would be invaluable to have someone who could handle figures. Then the damned tradesmen wouldn't swindle her, and she'd have money again.

'The gypsy boy! . . .' The words stung her afresh. Had she risen out of the muck of vagrancy to have her son slip back into it? Never! She'd settle all that. Not for a moment did she doubt her ability to cope with Ortho. What must John in heaven be thinking of her stewardship? She wept with mingled anger and contrition. Tomorrow she'd open a clean page. Ortho should go to school at once. *Gypsy!* She'd show them!

She was heavily in debt, but the money should be found somehow. All the way home she was planning ways and means.

Ortho returned late that night and went to bed unconscious that he had been found out. Next morning he was informed that he was to go with his mother to Penzance. This was good tidings. He liked going to town with Teresa; she bought all kinds of eatables, and one saw life, ladies and gentlemen, a soldier or two sometimes, blue-water seamen drunk as lords, and big windbound ships at anchor. He saddled the dun pony and jogged alongside her big roan, prattling cheerfully all the way.

She watched him, her interest aroused. He certainly was good looking with his slim uprightness, eager expression, and quick, graceful movements. He had luminous dark eyes, a short nose, round chin, and crisp black curls—like her own. He was like her in many ways, so many ways! Good company too. He told her several amusing stories and laughed heartily at hers. A debonair, attractive boy, very different from his brother. She felt suddenly drawn towards him. He would make a good companion when he came back from school. His looks would stir up trouble in sundry dovecotes later on, she thought, and promised herself much amusement, having no sympathy for doves.

It was not until they arrived in Penzance that she broke the news that he was going to school. Ortho was a trifle staggered at first, but, to her surprise, took it very calmly, making no objections. In the first place, it was something new, and the prospect of mixing with a herd of other boys struck him as rather jolly; secondly, he was fancying himself enormously in the fine clothes, with which Teresa was loading him. He had never had anything before but the roughest of homespuns stitched together by Martha and speedily reduced to shreds. He put the best suit on there and then and strutted Market Jew Street like a young peacock ogling its first hen.

They left Penzance in the early afternoon, spare kit stuffed in the saddlebags. In the ordinary way Teresa would have gone straight to the Angel at Helston and ordered the best, but now, in keeping with her new vow of economy, she sought a free night's lodging at Tregors; also she wanted to raise some of the rent in advance.

Ortho was entered at his father's old school next day.

Teresa rode home pleasantly conscious of duty done, and Ortho plunged into the new world convinced that he had only to smile and conquer. In which he erred. He was no longer a Penhale in his own parish, prospective squire of the Keigwin valley, but an unsophisticated young animal thrust into a den of sophisticated young animals, and therefore a heaven-sent butt for their superior humour. Rising seventeen, and set to learn his ABC in the lowest form among the babies! This gave the wits an admirable opening. That he could ride, sail a boat, and shoot anything flying or running, weighed as nothing against his ignorance of Latin declensions.

He sought to win some admiration or even tolerance for himself by telling of his adventures with Pyramus and Jacky's George, but it had the opposite effect. His tormentors (sons of prosperous landowners and tradesmen) declared that anyone who associated with gypsies and fishermen must be of low caste himself and taunted him unmercifully. They would put their hands to their mouths and halloo, after the manner of fish hawkers: 'Mack-erel! Fresh mack-erel! . . . Say, Penhale, what's the price of pilchards today?'

Or 'Hello, Penhale; there's one of your Pharaoh mates at the gate. Better go and have a clunk over old-times.'

Baiting Penhale became a fashionable pastime. Following the example of their elders, the small boys took up the ragging. This was more than Ortho could stand; he knocked some heads together, whereby earning the reputation of a bully.

A bulky freckled lad named Burnadick, set on by friends, and professing himself champion of the oppressed, challenged Ortho to fight.

Ortho had not the slightest desire to fight the reluctant champion, but the non-combatants (as is the way with non-combatants) gave him no option. They formed a ring round the pair and pulled the coats off them.

For a moment or two it looked as if Ortho would win. An opening punch took him under the nose and stung him to such a pitch of fury that he tumbled on top of the freckled one, whirling like a windmill, fairly smothering him. But the freckled one was an old warrior; he dodged and sidestepped and propped straight lefts to the head whenever he got a chance, well knowing that Ortho could not last the crazy pace.

Ortho could not, or any mortal man. In a couple of minutes he was puffing and grunting, swinging wildly, giving openings everywhere. The heart was clean out of him. He had not wanted to fight in the first place, and the popular voice was against him. Everybody cheered Burnadick; not a single whoop for him. He ended tamely—dropped his fists and gave Burnadick best. The mob jeered and hooted and crowded round the victor, who shook them off and walked away licking his raw knuckles. He had an idea of following Penhale and shaking hands with him . . . hardly knew what the fight had been about . . . wished the other fellows weren't always arranging quarrels for him. They never gave his knuckles time to heal. He'd have a chat with Penhale one of these days . . . tomorrow perhaps . . .

His amiable intentions never bore fruit, for on the morrow his mother was taken ill and he was summoned home, and nobody else had any kindly feelings for Ortho. He wrestled with incomprehensible primers among tittering infants during school hours; out of school he slunk about alone always, cold-shouldered everywhere. His sociable soul grew sick within him. He rebelled at the sparse feeding, hated the irritable, sarcastic ushers, the bewildering tasks, the boys, the confinement, everything. At night in bed he wept hot tears of misery.

A spell of premature spring weather touched the land. Incautious buds popped out in the Helston back gardens; the hedgerow gorse was gilt-edged; the warm scent of pushing greenery blew in from the hillsides. Armadas of shining clouds cruised down the blue. Ortho, laboriously spelling C-A-T cat, R-A-T rat, in a drowsy classroom, was troubled with dreams. He saw the Baragwanath family painting the *Game Cock* on the Monk's Cove slip, getting her summer suit out of store; saw the rainbows glimmering over the Twelve Apostles, the green and silver glitter of the Channel beyond; smelt seaweed; heard the lisp of the tide. He dreamt of Pyramus Herne wandering northwards with Lussha, and the other boys behind bringing up the horses, wandering over hill and dale, new country out-reeling before him every day. He bowed over the desk and buried his face in the crook of his arm.

A fly explored the spreading ear of "Rusty Rufus," the junior usher. He woke out of his drowse, one little pig eye at a time, and glanced stealthily round his class. Two young gentlemen were playing noughts and crosses, two more were flipping pellets at each other, a fifth was making chalk marks on the back of a sixth, who in turn was absorbed in cutting initials on the desk; a seventh appeared to be asleep. Rufus, having slumbered himself, passed over the first six and fell upon his imitator.

'Penhale, come here,' he rumbled, and reached for his stick.

Ortho obeyed. The usher usually indulged in much laboured sarcasm at the boy's expense, but he was too lazy that afternoon.

'Hand,' he growled.

Ortho held out his hand; Rufus swung back the stick and measured the distance with a puckered eye. Ortho hated him. He was a loathly sight, lying back in his chair, shapeless legs straddled out before him, fat jowl bristling with the rusty stubble from which he got his name, protuberant waistcoat stained with beer and snuff. A hateful creature! An icy glitter of cruelty, a flicker as of lightning reflected on a stagnant pool, suddenly lit the indolent eyes of the junior usher, and down came the cane, whistling. But Ortho's hand was not there to receive it. How it came about he never knew. He was frightened by the revealing blaze in Rufus's eyes, but he did not mean to shirk the stick; his hand withdrew itself of its own accord, without orders from his brain—a muscular twitch. However, it happened, the results were fruitful. Rufus cut himself along the inside of his right leg with all his might. He dropped the stick, bounded out of his chair, and hopped about the class cursing horribly, yelping with pain. Ortho stood transfixed, horrified at what he had done. A small boy, his eyes round with admiration, hissed at him from behind his hand:

'Run, you fool—he'll kill you!'

Ortho came to his senses and bolted for the door.

But Rufus was too quick for him. He bounded across the room, choking, spluttering, apoplectic, dirty fat hands clawing the air. He caught Ortho by the hair and collar and dragged him to him. Ortho hit out blindly, panicked. He was too frightened to think. He thought Rufus was going to kill him, and fought for his life with the desperation of a cornered rat. He shut his eyes and teeth, rammed Rufus in the only part of him he could reach—namely, the stomach. One, two, three, four, five, six, seven—it was like hitting a jelly. At the fourth blow he felt the usher's grip on him loosen, at the fifth he was free, the sixth sent the man to the floor, the seventh was wasted.

Rufus lay on the boards, clutching his stomach, making the most dreadful retching noises. The small boys leapt up on their desks cheering and exhorting Ortho to run. He ran. Out of the door, across the court, out of the gates, up the street and out into the country. Ran on and on without looking where he was going; on and on.

It was fully an hour later before it occurred to him that he was running north, but he did not change direction.

* * *

Teresa was informed of Ortho's sensational departure two days later. The school authorities sent to Bosula, expecting to find the boy had returned home, and were surprised that he had not. Where had he got to? Teresa had an idea that he was hiding somewhere in the district, and combed it thoroughly, but Ortho was not forthcoming. The gypsy camp was long deserted, and Jacky's George had gone to visit his Scillonian sister by the somewhat circuitous route of Guernsey.

It occurred to her that he might be lying up in the valley, surreptitiously fed by Eli, and put Bohenna on to beat it out, but the old hind drew blank. She then determined that he was with the tinners around St Just (a sanctuary for many a wanted Cornishman), and since there was no hope of extricating him from their underground labyrinths, the only thing to do was to wait. He'd come home in time, she said, and promised the boy a warm reception when he did.

Then came a letter from Pyramus Herne, dictated to a public letter writer. Pyramus was at Ashburton buying Dartmoor ponies, and Ortho was with him. Pyramus was profuse with regrets and disclaimed all responsibility. Ortho had caught up with him at Launceston, footsore, ragged, starving, terrified—but adamant. He (Pyramus) had chided him, begged him to return, even offered to lend him a horse to carry him back to Helston or Bosula, but Ortho absolutely refused to do either, declaring that rather than return he would kill himself. What was to be done? He could not turn a friendless and innocent boy adrift to starve or be maltreated by the beggars, snatch-purses, and loose women who swarmed into the roads at that season of the year. What was he to do? He respectfully awaited Teresa's instructions, assuring her that in the meanwhile Ortho should have the best his poor establishment afforded, and remained her ladyship's obedient and worshipful servant, etc.

Teresa took the letter to the St Gwithian parish clerk to be read, and bit her lip when she learnt the contents. The clerk asked her if she wanted a reply written, but she shook her head and went home. Ortho could not be brought back from Devon handcuffed and kept chained in his room. There was nothing to be done.

So her son had reverted to type. She did not think it would last long. The Hernes were prosperous for gypsies. Ortho would not go short of actual food and head-cover, but there would be days of trudging against the wind and rain, soaked and trickling from head to heel, beds in wet grass; nights of thunder with horses breaking loose and tumbling over the tents; shuddering dawns chilling the very marrow; parched noons choked with dust; riots at fairs, cudgels going and stones flying; filth, blows, bestiality, hard work and hard weather, hand to mouth all the way. Ortho was no glutton for punishment. He would return to the warm Owls' House ere long, curl up gratefully before the fire, cured of his wanderlust. All was for the best doubtless, Teresa considered, but she packed Eli off to school in his place. The zest for duty was still strong in her, and, furthermore, she must have somebody who could keep accounts.

Chapter XI

ELI WENT to school prepared for a bad time. Ortho had not run away for nothing; he was no bulldog for unprofitable endurance. Lessons had been irksome, no doubt, but he should have been in his element among a horde of boys. He liked having plenty of his own kind about him and naturally dominated them. He had won over the surly St Gwithian farmboys with ease; the turbulent Monk's Cove fisherlads looked to him as chief; and even those wild hawks, the young Hernes, followed him unquestioning into all sorts of mischief. Yet Ortho had fled school as from torment.

If the brilliant and popular brother had come to grief, how much more trouble was in store for him, the dullard? Eli set his jaw. Come what might, he would see it through; he would stick at school, willy-nilly, until he got what he wanted out of it—namely, the three R's. It had been suddenly borne in on Eli that education had its uses.

Chance had taken him to the neighbouring farm of Roswarva, which bounded Polmenna Moors on the west. There was a new farmer in possession, a widower by the name of Penaluna, come from the north of the Duchy with a thirteen-year old daughter, an inarticulate child, leggy as a foal.

Eli, scrambling about the Luddra Head, had discovered an otter's holt, and then and there lit a smoke fire to test if the tenant were at home or not. The otter was at home and came out with a rush. Eli attempted to tail it, but his foot slipped on the dry thrift, and he sprawled on top of the beast, which bit him in three places. He managed to drop a stone on it as it slid away over the rocks, but he could hardly walk. Penaluna met him limping across a field, dragging his victim by the tail, and took him to Roswarva to have his wounds tied up.

Eli had not been to Roswarva since the days of its previous owners, a beachcombing, shiftless crew, and he barely recognised the place. The kitchen was creamy with whitewash; the cupboards freshly painted; the table scrubbed spotless; the ranked pans gleamed like copper moons; all along the mantelshelf were china dogs with gilt collars, and ladies and gentlemen on prancing horses, hawks perched a-wrist. In the corner was an oak grandfather clock with a bright brass face engraved with the signs of the zodiac and the cautionary words:

> 'I mark ye hours, but cannot stay their race;
> Nor priest nor king may buy a moment's grace.
> Prepare to meet thy Maker face to face.'

Sunlight poured into the white kitchen through the south window, setting everything a-shine and a-twinkle—a contrast to unkempt Bosula, redolent of cooking and stale food, buzzing with flies, incessantly invaded by pigs and poultry. Outside Roswarva all was in the same good shape; the erst-littered yard cleared up, the tumbledown sheds rebuilt and thatched. Eli limped home over trim hedges, fields cultivated up to the last inch and plentifully manured, and came upon his own land—crumbling banks broken down by cattle and grown to three times their proper breadth with thorn and brambles; fields thick with weed; windfalls lying where they had dropped; bracken encroaching from every point.

He had never before remarked anything amiss with Bosula, but coming straight from Roswarva the contrast struck him in the face. He thought about it for two days and then marched over to Roswarva. He found Simeon Penaluna on the cliffside rooting out slabs of granite with a crowbar and piling them into a wall. A vain pursuit, Eli thought, clearing a cliff only fit for donkeys and goats.

'What are you doing that for?' he asked.

'Potatoes,' said Simeon.

'Why here, when you got proper fields?'

'Open to sun all day, and sea'll keep 'em warm at night. No frost. I'll get taties here two weeks earlier than up-along.'

'How do you know?'

'Read it. Growers in Jersey has been doin' it these years.'

Eli digested this information and leaned against the wall watching Penaluna at work.

Eli liked the man's air of patient power, also his economy of speech. He decided he was to be trusted. 'You're a good farmer, aren't you?'

'Yes,' said Penaluna truthfully.

'What's wrong with our place—Bosula?' Eli inquired.

'Undermanned,' said Penaluna. 'Your father had two men besides himself, and he worked like a bullock and was clever, I've heard tell. Now you've got but two and not a head between 'em. Place is going back. Come three years the trash'll strangle 'e in your beds.'

Eli took the warning calmly. 'We'll stop that,' he announced.

Penaluna subjected him to a hard scrutiny, spat on his palms, worked the crowbar into a crevice, and tried his weight on it.

'Hum! Maybe. But you'd best start soon.'

Eli nodded and considered again. 'Are you clever?'

Penaluna swung his bar from left to right, the rock stirred in its bed.

'No, but I can read.'

Eli's eyes opened. That was the second time reading had been mentioned. What had that schoolmastering business to do with real work like farming?

'Went to free school at Truro,' Simeon explained. 'There's clever ones that writes off books, and I reads 'em. There's smart notions in books—sometimes, got six books on farming—six brains.'

'Um-m,' muttered Eli, the idea slowly taking hold.

In return for advice given he helped the farmer pile walls until sunset, and not another word was interchanged. When he got home it was to learn that Ortho was in Devon with Pyramus and that he was to go to school in his stead.

Eli's feelings were mixed. If Ortho had had a bad time, he would undoubtedly have worse; but on the other hand he would learn to read and could pick other people's brains—like Penaluna. He rode to Helston with his mother, grimly silent all the way, steeling himself to bear the rods for Bosula's sake. But Ortho, by the dramatic manner of his exit, had achieved popularity when it was no longer of any use to him. Eli stepped in at the right moment to receive the goodly heritage.

Was he not own brother to the hero who had tricked Rufus into slicing himself across the leg and followed up this triumph by pommelling seven bells out of the detested usher and flooring him in his own classroom? The story had lost nothing in the mouths of the spectators. A half-minute scramble between a sodden hulk of a man and a terrified boy had swollen into a Homeric contest as full of incident as the Seven Years' War, lasting half an hour and ending in Rufus lying on the floor spitting blood and imploring mercy. Eli entered the school surrounded by a warm nimbus of reflected glory and took Ortho's place at the bottom of the lowest form.

That he was the criminal's brother did not endear him to Rufus, who gave him the benefit of his acid tongue from early morn to dewy eve; but beyond abuse the usher did not go. Eli was not tall, but he was exceptionally sturdy, and Rufus had not forgotten a certain affair. He was chary of these Penhales—little better than savages—reared amongst smugglers and moormen—utterly undisciplined . . . no saying what they might do . . . murder one even. He kept his stick for the disciplined smaller fry and pickled his tongue for Eli. Eli did not mind the sarcasm in the least. His mental hide was far too thick to feel the prick, and anyhow it was only talk.

One half-holiday, bird nesting in Penrose Woods, he came upon the redoubtable Burnadick similarly engaged, and they compared eggs. In the midst of the discussion a bailiff appeared on the scene and they had to run for it. The bailiff produced dogs, and the pair were forced to make a wide detour via Praze and Lanner Vean. Returning by Helston Mill, they met with a party of town louts who, having no love for the "grammar scholards," threw stones. A brush ensued, Eli acquitting himself with credit. The upshot of all this was that they reached school seven minutes late for roll call and were rewarded with a thrashing. Drawn together by common pain and adventure, the two were henceforth inseparable, forming a combination which no boy or party of boys dare gainsay. With Rufus's sting drawn and the great Burnadick his ally, Eli found school life tolerable. He did not enjoy it; the food was insufficient, the restraint burdensome; but it was by no means as bad as he had expected. By constant repetition he was getting a parrot-like fluency with his tables, and he seldom made a bad mistake in spelling—providing the word was not of more than one syllable.

* * *

At the Owls' House in the meanwhile economy was still the rage. Teresa's first step was to send the cattle off to market. In vain did Bohenna expostulate, pointing out that the stock had not yet come to condition, and, further, there was no market. It was useless. Teresa would not listen to reason. Into Penzance they went and were sold for a song. After them she pitched pigs, poultry, goats, and the dun pony. Her second step was to discharge the second hind, Davy. Once more Bohenna protested. He could hardly keep the place going as it was, he said. The moor was creeping in to right and left, the barn thatch tumbling, the banks were down, the gates falling to pieces. He could not be expected to be in more than two places at once. Teresa replied with more sound than sense, and a shouting match ensued, ending in Teresa screaming that she was mistress and that if Bohenna didn't shut his mouth and obey orders she'd pack him after Davy.

But if Teresa bore hard on others she sacrificed herself as well. Not a single new dress did she order that year, and even went to the length of selling two brooches, her second-best cloak, and her third-best pair of earrings. Parish feasts, races, bull-baitings and cockfights she resolutely eschewed; an occasional stroll down the Cove and a pot of ale at the Kiddlywink was all the relaxation she allowed herself. By these self-denying ordinances she was able to foot Eli's school bills and pay interest on her debts, but her temper frayed to rags. She railed at Martha morning, noon, and night, threw plates at Wany, and became so unbearable that Bohenna carried all his meals afield with him.

Eli came home for a few days' holiday at midsummer, but spent most of his waking hours at Roswarva.

On his last evening he went ferreting with Bohenna. The banks were riddled with rabbit-sets, but so overgrown were they it was almost impossible to work the fitchets. Their tiny bells tinkled here and there, thither and hither in the dense undergrowth, invisible and elusive as the clappers of derisive sprites. They gambolled about, rejoicing in their freedom, treating the quest of fur as a secondary matter. Bohenna pursued them through the thorns, shattering the holy hush of evening with blasphemies.

'This ought to be cut back—rooted out,' Eli observed.

The old hind took it as a personal criticism and turned on him, a bramble scratch reddening his cheek, voice shaking with long-suppressed resentment. 'Rooted out, saith a'! Cut back! Who's goin' do et, then? Me, s'pose.'

He held out his knotted fists, a resigned ferret swinging in each.

'Look you! How many hands have I got? Two edden a'? Two only. But your ma do think each o' my fingers is a hand, I b'lieve. Youp! Comin' through!'

A rabbit shot out of a burrow on the far side of the hedge, the great flintlock bellowed, and it turned somersaults as neatly as a circus clown.

'There'll be three of us here when I've done schooling next midsummer and Ortho comes home,' said Eli calmly, ramming down a fresh charge. 'We'll clear the trash and put the whole place in crop.'

Bohenna glanced up surprised. 'Oh, will us? An' where's cattle goin'?'

'Sell 'em off—all but what can feed themselves on the bottoms. Crops'll fetch more to the acre than stock.'

'My dear soul, hearken to young Solomon! . . . Who's been tellin' you all this?'

'Couple of strong farmers I've talked with on half-holidays near Helston—and Penaluna.'

Bohenna bristled. Wisdom in foreign worthies he might admit, but a neighbour . . .

'What's Simeon Penaluna been sayin'? Best keep his long nose on his own place. I'll give it a brear wrench if I catch it sniffing over here! What'd he say?'

'Said he wondered you didn't break your heart.'

'Humph!' Bohenna was mollified, pleased that someone appreciated his efforts. This Penaluna at least sniffed with discernment. He listened quietly while Eli recounted their neighbour's suggestions.

They talked farming all the way home, and it was a revelation to him how much the boy had picked up. He had no idea Eli was at all interested in it; had imagined, from his being sent to school, that he was destined for a clerk or something bookish. He had looked forward to fighting a losing battle for John's sake and Bosula's sake, single-handed to the end; saw himself, a silver ancient, dropping dead at the ploughtail and the triumphant bracken pouring over him like a sea. But now the prospect had changed. Here was a true Penhale coming back to tend the land of his sires. With young blood at his back they would yet save the place. He knew that Eli, once he set his face forward, would never look back. His brain was too small to hold more than one idea. He gloated over the boy's promising shoulders, thick neck, and sturdy legs. He would root out the big boulders as his father had done, swing an axe or scythe from cockcrow to owl light without flag, toss a sick calf across his shoulders and stride for miles, be at once the master and lover of his land, the right husbandman. But of Ortho, the black gypsy son, Bohenna was not so sure. Nevertheless, hope dawned afresh as he went home to his crib among the rocks singing "I Seen a Ram at Hereford Fair" for the first time in six months.

* * *

Eli was back again a few days before Christmas, and on Christmas Eve Ortho appeared. There was nothing of the chastened prodigal about him; he rode into the yard on a showy chestnut gelding (borrowed from Pyramus), ragged as a scarecrow, but shouting and singing. He slapped Bohenna on the back, hugged Eli affectionately, pinned his mother against the doorpost and kissed her on both cheeks and her nose, chucked old Martha under the chin, and even tossed a genial word at the halfwit Wany.

With the exception of Eli no one was particularly elated to see him back. They remembered him only as an unfailing fount of mischief, but from Ortho's manner one would have concluded he was restoring the light of their lives. He did not give them time to close their front. They hardly knew he had arrived before he had embraced them all. The warmth of his greeting melted their restraint. Bohenna's hairy face split athwart in a yellow-toothed grin, Martha broke into bird-like twitters, Wany blushed, and Teresa said weakly 'So you're back.'

She had not forgiven him for his school escapade, and had intended to make his return the occasion of a demonstration as to who ruled the roost at Bosula. But now she thought she'd postpone it. He had foiled her for the moment—kissed her. . . . She couldn't very well pitch into him immediately after that . . . not immediately. Besides, deep in her heart she felt a cold drop of doubt. A new Ortho had come back, very different from the callow, pliant child who had ridden babbling to Helston beside her ten months previously. Ortho had grown up. He was copper-coloured with exposure, sported a downy haze on his upper lip, and was full two inches taller. But the change was not so much physical as spiritual. His good looks were, if anything, emphasised; but he had hardened; innocence was gone from his eyes; there was the faintest edge to his mirth. She had not wanted to be kissed, had struggled against it, but he had taken her by surprise, handled her with dispatch and assurance that could only come of practice. Master Ortho had not been idle on his travels. An idea occurred to her that she had been forestalled; it was Ortho who had made the demonstration. Their eyes met, crossed like bayonets, and dropped. It was all over in the fraction of a second, but they had felt each other's steel.

Teresa was not alarmed by the sudden development of her first-born. She was only forty-one, weighed fourteen stone, radiated rude health, and feared no living thing. Since John's death she had not seen a man she would have stood a word from—a great measure of her affection for her husband sprang from the knowledge that he could have beaten her. She apprised Ortho's slim figure and mentally promised him a bellyful of trouble did he demand it, but for the moment she concluded to let bygones be—just for the moment.

Ortho flipped some crumbs playfully over Wany, assured Martha she had not aged a day, told Bohenna they'd have a great time after woodcock, threw his arm around Eli's neck and led him out into the yard.

'See here what I've got for you, my old heart,' said he, fishing in his pocket. 'Bought it in Portsmouth.'

He placed a little brass box in Eli's hand. It had a picture of a seventy-four under full sail chased on the lid and the comfortable words "Let jealous foes no hearts dismay; Vernon our hope is, God our stay." Inside was coiled a flint, steel, and fuse. Eli was profoundly touched. Ortho's toes were showing through one boot, his collarbones had chafed holes in his shirt, and his coat was in ribbons. The late frost must have nipped him severely, yet he had not spent his few poor pence in getting himself patched up, but bought a present for him. As a matter of fact, the little box had cost Ortho no small self-denial.

Eli stammered his thanks, which Ortho laughed aside, and the brothers went uphill towards Polmenna Down, arms about shoulders, talking, talking. Eli furnished news of Helston. Burnadick was sorry about that row he had had with Ortho—the other fellows pushed him on. He was a splendid fellow really, knew all about hare hunting and longdogs. Eli only wished he could have seen Ortho ironing Rufus out. It must have been a glorious set-to. Everybody was still talking about it. Rufus had never been the same since—quaking and shaking. Dirty big jellyfish! Always swilling in pothouses and stalking serving maids. The whole town had laughed over his discomfiture.

Ortho was surprised to learn of his posthumous popularity at Helston. Eli's version of the affair hardly coincided with his recollection in a single particular. All he remembered was being horribly frightened and hitting out blindly, with results that astonished him even more than his victim. Still, since legend had chosen to elevate him to the pinnacle of a St George, slayer of dragons, he saw no reason to disprove it.

They passed on to other subjects. How had Ortho got on with the Romanies? Oh, famously! Wonderful time. Had enjoyed every moment of it. Eli would never believe the things he had seen. Mountains twice, three, four times as high as Chapel Carn Brea or Sancreed Beacon; rivers with ships sailing on them as at sea; great houses as big as Penzance in themselves; lords and ladies driving in six-horse carriages; regiments of soldiers drilling behind slave drummers; and fairs with millions of people collected and all the world's marvels on view: Italian midgets no higher than your knee, Irish giants taller than chimneys, two-headed calves and six-legged lambs, contortionists who knotted their legs round their necks, conjurers who magicked glass balls out of country boys' ears, dancing bears, trained wolves, and an Araby camel that required but one drink a month. Prizefights he had seen also; tinker women battling for a purse, in a ring like men; and fellows that carried live rats in their shirt-bosoms and killed them with their teeth at a penny a time. And cities! . . . Such cities! Huge enough to cover St Gwithian parish, with streets so packed and people so elegant you thought every day must be market day.

London? No-o, he had not been quite to London. But travellers told him that some of the places he had seen—Exeter, Salisbury, Plymouth, Winchester—were every bit as good; in some ways better. London, in the opinion of many, was overrated. Oh, by the way, in Salisbury he had seen the cream of the lot—two men hanged for sheep-stealing. They kicked and jerked in the most comical fashion. A wonderful time!

The recital had a conflicting effect on Eli. To him Ortho's story was as breathtaking as that of some swart mariner returned from fabulous spice islands and steamy Indian seas. But at the same time he was perturbed. Was it likely that his brother, having seen the great world and all its wonders, would be content to settle down to the humdrum life at Bosula and dour struggle with the wilderness? Most improbable! Ortho would go adventuring again, and he and Bohenna would have to face the problem alone. Bohenna was not getting any younger. His rosy hopes clouded over. He must try to get Ortho to see the danger. After all, Bosula would come to Ortho some day; it was his affair. He began forthwith; pointed out the weedy state of the fields, the littered windfalls, the invasion of the moor. To his surprise, Ortho was immediately interested—and indignant.

What had that lazy lubber Bohenna been up to? . . . and Davy? By Gad, it was a shame! He'd let 'em know. . . .

Eli explained that Davy had been turned off and Bohenna was doing his best. 'In father's time there were three of 'em here, and it was all they could manage, working like bullocks,' said he, quoting Penaluna.

'Then why haven't we three men now?'

'Mother says we've got no money to hire 'em.'

Ortho's jaw dropped. 'No money! *We?* . . . Good God! Where's it all gone to?'

Eli didn't know, but he did know that if someone didn't get busy soon they'd have no farm left. 'It's been going back ever since father died,' he added.

Ortho strode up and down, black-browed, biting his lip. Then he suddenly laughed. 'Hell's bells!' he cried. 'What are we fretting about? There are three of us still, ain't there? . . . You, me, 'n Ned. I warrant we're a match for a passel of old brambles, heh? I warrant we are.'

Eli was amazed and delighted. Did Ortho really mean what he said?

'Then—then you're not going gypsying again?' he asked.

Ortho spat. 'My Lord, no! Done with that. It's a dog's life, kicked from common to heath, living on hedgehogs, sleeping under bushes, never dry. Mind you, I enjoyed it all. But I've had all I want. No, boy' —once more he hugged his brother to him—'I'm going to stop home long o' thee. Us'll make our old place the best in the Hundred—in the Duchy—and be big rosy yeomen, full of good beef and cider. . . . Eh, look at that!'

The sun had dipped. Cirrus dappled the afterglow with drifts of smouldering crimson feathers. It was as though monster golden eagles were battling in the upper air, dropping showers of lustrous, blood-stained plumes. Away to the north the switchbacked tors rolled against the sky, wine-dark against pale primrose. Mist brimmed the valleys, dusk, empurpled, shrouded the hills. The primrose faded, a star outrider blinked boldly in the east, then the green eve suddenly quivered with the glint of a million, million spearheads. Night's silver cohorts advancing. So still was it that the brothers on the hilltop could plainly hear the babble and cluck of the hidden stream below them, the thump of young rabbits romping in nearby fields, and the bark of a dog at Boskennel being answered by another dog at Trevider. From Bosula yard came the creak and bang of a door, the clank of a pail—Bohenna's voice singing.

> ' "I seen a ram at Hereford Fair,
> The biggest gert ram I did ever behold." '

Ortho laughed, and took up the familiar song, sent his pleasant, tuneful voice ringing out over the darkling valley:

> ' "His fleece were that heavy it stretched to the ground,
> His hoofs and his horns they was shodden wi' gold." '

Below them sounded a gruff crow of mirth from Bohenna, and the second verse:

> ' "His horns they was curled like to the thorn tree,
> His fleece was as white as the blossom o' thorn;
> He stamped like a stallion an' roared like a bull,
> An' the gert yeller eyes of en sparkled wi' scorn." '

Among the bare trees a light winked, a friendly beckoning wink —the kitchen window.

Ortho drew a deep breath and waved his hand. 'Think I'd change this—this lew lil' place I was born in for a gypsy tilt, do 'ee? No, no, my dear! Not for all the King's money and all the King's gems! I've seen's much of the cold world as I do want—and more.' He linked his arm with Eli's. 'Come on; let's be getting down along.'

* * *

That night the brothers slept together in the same big bed as of old. Eli tumbled to sleep at once, but Ortho lay awake. Towards ten o'clock he heard what he had been listening for, the 'Te-whoo-whee-wha-ha' of the brown owls calling to each other. He grunted contentedly, turned over, and went to sleep.

Chapter XII

CHRISTMAS PASSED merrily at Bosula that year. Martha was an authority on "feasten" rites and delicacies, and Christmas was the culmination. Under her direction the brothers festooned the kitchen with ropes of holly and ivy, and hung the "kissing-bush"—two barrel hoops swathed in evergreens—from the middle beam.

Supper was the principal event of the day, a prodigious spread; goose giblet pie, squab pie made of mutton, raisins and onions, and queer-shaped saffron cakes, the whole washed down with draughts of "eggy-hot," an inspiring compound of eggs, hot beer, sugar, and rum, poured from jug to jug till it frothed over.

The Bosula household sat down at one board and gorged themselves till they could barely breathe. Upon them in this state came the St Gwithian choir, accompanied by the parish fiddler, "Jiggy" Dan, and a score or so of hangers-on. They sang the sweet and simple old "curls" of the West Country, "I Saw Three Ships Come Sailing In," "Come and I Will Sing You," "The First Good Joy That Mary Had," and—

> 'Go the wayst out, Child Jesus,
> Go the wayst out to play;
> Down by God's Holy Well
> I see three pretty children
> As ever tongue can tell.'

Part-singing is a natural art in Cornwall. The St Gwithian choir sang well, reverently, and without strain. Teresa, full-fed after long moderation, was in melting mood. The carols made her feel pleasantly tearful and religious. She had not been to church since the unfortunate affair with the curate, but determined she would go the very next Sunday and make a rule of it.

She gave the choir leader a silver crown and ordered eggy-hot to be served round. The choir's eyes glistened. Eggy-hot seldom came their way; usually they had to be content with cider.

Martha rounded up the company. The apple trees must be honoured, or they would withhold their fruit in the coming year. Everybody adjourned to the orchard, Martha carrying a jug of cider, Bohenna armed with the flintlock loaded nearly as full as himself. Wany alone was absent ; she was slipping up the valley to the great barrow to hear the Spriggans, the gnome-miners, sing their sad carols, as was the custom of a Christmas night.

The Bosula host grouped, lantern-lit, round the king tree of the orchard. Martha dashed the jug against the trunk and pronounced her incantation:

> 'Health to thee, good apple tree!
> Hats full, packs full, great bushel bags full!
> Hurrah and fire off the gun.'

Everybody cheered. Bohenna steadied himself and pulled the trigger. There was a deafening roar, a yard long tongue of flame spurted from the muzzle. Bohenna tumbled over backwards, and Jiggy Dan, uttering an appalling shriek, fell on his face and lay still.

The scared spectators stooped over the fiddler.

'Dead is 'a?'

' 'Ess, dead sure 'nough; dead as last year, pore soul.'

Panegyrics on the deceased were delivered.

'A brilliant old drinker, 'a was.'

' 'Ess, an' a clean lively one to touch the strings.'

'Shan't see his like no more.'

'His spotty sow coming to her time too—an' a brearly loved roast sucking-pig, the pretty old boy.'

Bohenna sat up in the grass and sniffed.

'There's a brear strong smell o' burning, seem me.'

The company turned on him reproachfully. 'Thou'st shotten Jiggy Dan. Shot en dead an' a-cold. Didst put slugs in gun by mistake, Ned?'

Bohenna scratched his head. 'Couldn't say rightly this time o' night . . . Maybe I did . . . But look 'ee, there wasn't no offence meant; 'twas done in good part, as you might say.' He sniffed again and stared at the corpse of his victim.

'Slugs or no, seem me the poor angel's more hot than cold. Lord love, he's afire! . . . The wad's catched in his coat!'

That such was the case became painfully apparent to the deceased at the same moment. He sprang to his feet and bounded round and round the group, uttering ghastly howls and belabouring himself behind in a fruitless endeavour to extinguish the smouldering cloth. The onlookers were helpless with laughter; they leaned against each other and sobbed. Teresa in particular shook so violently it hurt her.

Somebody suggested a bucket of water, between chokes, but nobody volunteered to fetch it. To do so would be to miss the fun.

'The stream,' hiccuped Bohenna, holding his sides. 'Sit 'ee down in stream, Dan, my old beauty, an' quench thyself.'

A loud splash in the further darkness announced that the unhappy musician had taken his advice.

The apple trees fully secured for twelve months, the party returned to the kitchen, but the incident of Dan had dissipated the somewhat pious tone of the preceding events. Teresa, tears trickling down her cheeks, set going a fresh round of eggy-hot. Ortho pounced on Tamsin Eva, the prettiest girl in the room, carried her bodily under the kissing-bush, and saluted her again and again. Other men and boys followed suit. The girls fled round the kitchen in mock consternation, pursued by flushed swains, were captured and embraced, giggling and sighing. Jiggy Dan, sniffing hot liquor as a pointer sniffs game, limped, dripping, in from the stream, was given an old petticoat of Martha's to cover his deficiencies, a pot of rum, propped up in a corner, and told to fiddle for dear life. The men, headed by Ortho, cleared the kitchen of furniture, and then everybody danced old heel-and-toe country dances, skipped, bowed, sidled, passed up and down the middle, and twirled around till the sweat shone like varnish on their scarlet faces.

The St Gwithian choir flung themselves into it heart and soul. They were expected at Monk's Cove to sing carols, were overdue by some hours, but they had forgotten all about that.

Teresa danced with the best, with grace and agility extraordinary in a woman of her bulk. She danced one partner off his feet and all but stunned another against the corner of the dresser, bringing most of the crockery crashing to earth. She then produced that relic of her vagabondage, the guitar, and joined forces with Jiggy Dan.

The fun became furious. The girls shook the tumbled hair from their eyes, laughed roguishly; the men whooped, and thumped the floor with their heavy boots. Jiggy Dan, constantly primed with rum by the attentive Martha, scraped and sawed at his fiddle, beating time with his toe. Teresa plucked at the guitar till it droned and buzzed like a hive of melodious bees. Occasionally she sang ribald snatches. She was in high feather, the reaction from nine months' abstinence. The kitchen, lit by a pile of dry furze blazing in the open hearth, grew hotter and hotter.

The dancers stepped and circled in a haze of dust, steaming like overdriven cattle. Eli alone was out of tune with his surroundings. The first effects of the drink had worn off, leaving him with a sour mouth and slightly dizzy. The warmer grew the others, the colder he became.

He scowled at the junketeers from his priggish altitude and blundered bedward, to find it already occupied by the St Gwithian blacksmith, who, dark with the transferable stains of his toil, lay sprawled across it, boots where his head should have been. Eli rolled the unconscious artificer to the floor (an act which in no way disturbed that worthy's slumbers) and turned in sick and sulky.

With Ortho, on the other hand, things were never better. He had not drunk enough to cloud him, and he was getting a lot of fun out of Tamsin Eva and her "shiner." Tamsin, daughter of the parish clerk, was a bronze-haired, slender creature with a skin like cream and roses and a pretty timid manner. Ortho, satiated with swarthy gypsy charmers, thought her lovely, and insisted upon dancing with her for the evening. That her betrothed was present and violently jealous only added piquancy to the affair. The girl was not happy; Ortho frightened her, but she had not enough strength of mind to resist him. She shot appealing glances at her swain, but the boy was too slow in his movements and fuddled with unaccustomed rum. The sober and sprightly Ortho cut the girl out from under his nose time and time again. Teresa, extracting appalling discords from the guitar, noted this by-play with gratification. This tiger cub of hers promised good sport.

Towards one o'clock, the supply of spirituous impulse having given out, the pace slackened down. Chastened husbands were led home by their wives. Single men tottered out of doors to get a breath of fresh air and did not return, were discovered at dawn peacefully slumbering under mangers, in hen-roosts, and out of the way corners. Tamsin Eva's betrothed was one of these. He was entering the house, fired with the intention of wresting his lass from Ortho and taking her home, when something hit him hard on the point of the jaw and all the lights went out. He woke up next morning far from clear as to whether he had blundered into the stone doorpost or somebody's ready fist. At all events, it was Ortho who took Tamsin home.

Teresa fell into a doze and had an uncomfortable dream. All the people she disliked came and made faces at her, people she had forgotten ages ago, and who in all decency should have forgotten her. They flickered out of the mists, distorted but recognisable, clutched at her with hooked fingers, pressed closer and closer, leering malevolently. Teresa was dismayed. Not a friend anywhere! She lolled forward moaning 'John! Oh, Jan!' Jiggy Dan's elbow hit her cheek, and she woke up to an otherwise empty kitchen, filled with the reek of burnt pilchard-oil, a dead hearth, and cold night air pouring in through the open door. She shuddered, rubbed her sleepy lids, and staggered, yawning, to bed.

Jiggy Dan, propped up in the corner, fiddled on, eyes sealed, mind oblivious, arm sawing mechanically.

They found him in the morning on the yard muckheap, Martha's petticoat over his head, fiddle clasped to his bosom, back-to-back with a snoring sow.

* * *

The Christmas festivities terminated on Twelfth Night with the visit of geese-dancers from Monk's Cove, the central figure of whom was a lad wearing the hide and horns of a bullock, attended by other boys dressed in female attire. Horseplay and crude buffoonery was the feature rather than dancing, and Teresa got some more of her crockery smashed.

Next morning Eli went to Helston for his last term, and Ortho took off his coat.

When Eli came home at midsummer he could hardly credit his eyes. Ortho had performed miracles. Very wisely he had not attempted to fight back the moor everywhere, but had concentrated, and the fields he had put in crop were done thoroughly, deep-ploughed, well manured, and evenly sown. Penaluna could not make a better show.

The brothers walked over the land on the evening of Eli's return. Everywhere the young crops stood up thick and healthy, pushing forwards to fruition. Ortho glowed with justifiable pride, talked farming eagerly. He and Ned had given the old place a hammering, he said. By the Holy they had! Mended the buildings, whitewashed the orchard trees, grubbed, ploughed, packed ore-weed and sea-sand, harrowed and hoed from dawn-blink to star-wink, day in, day out—Sundays included. But they'd get it all back. Oh, ay, and a hundredfold.

Eli had been in the right. Agriculture was the thing—the good old soil! You put in a handful and picked up a bushel in a few months. Cattle—pah! One cow produced but one calf per annum, and that was not marketable for three or four years. No; wheat, barley, and oats for ever!

Now Eli was home they could hold all they'd got and reclaim a field or so a year. In next to no time they'd have the whole place waving yellow from bound to bound. Ortho even had designs on the original moor, saw no reason why they should not do their own milling in time; they had ample water power. He glowed with enthusiasm. Eli's cautious mind discounted much of these grandiose schemes, but his heart went out to Ortho. The mellowing fields before him had not been lightly won.

Ortho was as lean as a herring bone, sweated down to bare muscle and sinew. His fingernails were broken off short, his hands scarred and calloused, his face was torn with brambles and leathern with exposure. He had fought a good fight and was burning for more. O splendid brother!

99

Ned Bohenna was loud in Ortho's praise. He was a marvel. He was quicker in the uptake than even John had been, and no work was too hard for him. The old hind was most optimistic. They had seeded a fine area, and crops were looking famous. Come three years at this pace the farm would be back where it was at John's death, the pick of the parish.

For the rest there was not much news. Martha had been having the cramps severely of late, and Wany was getting whishter than ever. Said she was betrothed to a Spriggan Earl who lived in the big barrow. He had promised to marry her as soon as he could get his place enlarged. He, he!

There had been a sea battle fought with gaffs and oars off the Gazells, between Jacky's George and a couple of Porthgwarra boats. Both sides accused each other of poaching lobster pots. Jacky's George sank a Porthgwarra boat by dropping a lump of ballast through her, and then rescued the crew. They had seen a lot of Pyramus Herne, altogether too much of Pyramus Herne. He had come down with a bigger mob of horses and donkeys than usual and grazed them all over the farm — after dark. Seeing the way he had befriended Ortho, they could not well say much to him, especially as they had grass to spare at present; but it could not go on like that.

Eli buckled to beside the others. They got the hay in, and while waiting for the crops to ripen pulled down a bank (throwing two small fields into one), rebuilt a couple more, cleaned out the orchard, hoed the potatoes, and put a new roof on the stables. They were out of bed at five every morning and into it at eight of an evening, deadbeat, soiled with earth and sweat, stained with sun and wind. They worked like horses, ate like wolves, and slept like sloths.

Ortho led everywhere. He was first afoot in the morning, last to bed at night. His quick mind discerned the easiest way through difficulties, but when hard labour was inevitable he sprang at it with a cheer. His voice rang like a bugle round Bosula, imperious yet merry. He was at once a captain and a comrade.

Under long days of sunshine and gentle drenches of rain the crops went on from strength to strength. It would be a bumper year.

Then came the deluge. Wany, her uncanny weather senses prick-ling, prophesied it two days in advance. Bohenna was uneasy, but Ortho, pointing to the serene sky, laughed at their fears. The next day the heat became oppressive, and he was not so sure. He woke at ten o'clock that night to a terrific clap of thunder, sat up in bed, and watched the little room flashing from black to white from the winks of lightning, his own shadow leaping gigantic across the illuminated wall; heard the rain come up the valley, roaring through the treetops like surf, break in a cataract over the Owls' House, and sweep on. 'This'll stamp us out . . . beat us flat,' he muttered, and lay wondering what he should do, if there was anything to do, and, as he wondered, merciful sleep came upon him, weary body dragging the spirit down with it into oblivion.

The rain continued with scarcely less violence for a week, held off for two days, and came down again. August crept out blear-eyed and draggle-tailed.

The Penhales saved a few potatoes and about one-fifth of the cereals—not enough to provide them with daily bread; they would actually have to buy meal in the coming year. Bohenna, old child of the soil, took the calamity with utter calm; he was inured to these bitter caprices of nature. Ortho shrugged his shoulders and laughed. It was nobody's fault, he said; they had done all they could; Penaluna had fared no better. The only course was to whistle and go at it again. That sort of thing could hardly happen twice running. He whistled and went at it again at once, breaking stone out of a field towards Polmenna, but Eli knew that for all his brave talk the heart was out of him, there was a lassitude in his movements, he was merely making a show of courage.

Gradually he slowed down. He began to visit the Kiddlywink of a night and lay abed long after sunrise.

At the end of October a fresh bolt fell out of the blue. The Crowan tinworks in which the Penhale money was invested suddenly closed down. It turned out that they had been running at a loss for the last eight months in the hope of striking a new lode, a debt of three hundred pounds had been incurred, the two other shareholders were without assets, so, under the old cost-book system current in Cornish mining, Teresa was liable for the whole sum.

She was at first aghast, then furious; swore she'd have the law of the defaulters, and hastened straightaway into Penzance to set her lawyer at them. Fortunately her lawyer was honest; she had no case, and he told her so. When she returned home she was confronted by her sons. They demanded to know how they stood. She turned sulky and refused details, but they managed to discover that there was not five pounds in the house, that there would be no more till the Tregors rent came in, and even then was pledged to moneylenders and shopkeepers. But as to the extent of her liabilities they could not find out. She damned them as a pair of ungrateful whelps and went to bed as black as thunder.

Ortho had a rough idea as to the houses Teresa patronised, so next day the brothers went to town, and, after a door to door visitation, discovered that she owed not much less than four hundred pounds! Four plus three made seven. Seven hundred pounds! Where was it to come from? The Penhales had no notion. By selling off all their stock they might possibly raise two hundred. Two hundred! What was that? A great deal less than half. Their mother would spend the rest of her life in a debtors' prison. O unutterable shame!

They doddered about Penzance, sunk in misery. Then it occurred to Ortho to consult the lawyer. These quill-driving devils were as cunning as dog foxes; what they couldn't get round or over they'd wriggle through.

The lawyer put them at their ease at once. Mortgage Bosula or Tregors. . . . Nothing simpler. Both strong farms, should produce the required sum—and more. He explained the system, joined his fingertips, and beamed at the pair over the top.

The brothers shifted on their chairs and pronounced for Tregors simultaneously. The lawyer nodded. Very well, then. As soon as he got their mother's sanction be would set to work. Ortho promised to settle his mother, and the two left.

Ortho had no difficulty with Teresa. He successfully used the hollow threat of a debtor's prison to her, for she had been in a lock-up several times during her roving youth and had no wish to return.

Besides, she was sick of debt, of being pestered for money, here, there, and everywhere.

She gave her consent readily enough, and within a fortnight was called upon to sign.

Carveth Donnithorne, the ever-prospering ship chandler of Falmouth, was the mortgagee. Nine hundred and fifty pounds was the sum he paid, and very good value it was.

Teresa settled the Crowan liabilities with the lawyer, and, parading round the town, squared all her other accounts in a single afternoon. She did it in style, swept into the premises of those who had pressed her, planked her money down, damned them for a pack of thieves and leeches, swore that was the end of her custom, and stamped majestically out.

She finished up in a high state of elation. She had told a number of her enemies exactly what she thought of them, was free of debt, and had a large sum of ready money in hand again—two hundred and fifty pounds in three canvas bags, the whole contained in a saddle wallet.

Opposite the Market Cross she met an old crony, a retired ship captain by the name of Jeremiah Gish, and told him in detail what she had said to the shopkeepers. The old gentleman listened with all his ears. He admired Teresa immensely. He admired her big buxom style, her strength, her fire; but most of all he revered her for her language. Never in forty years' seafaring had he met with such a flow of vituperation as Teresa could loose when roused—such range, such spontaneity, such blistering invention. It drew him like music. He caught her affectionately by the arm, led her to a tavern, treated her to a pot of ale, and begged her to repeat what she had said to the shopkeepers.

Teresa, nothing loath, obliged. The old tarpaulin listened rapt, nodded his bald head in approval, an expression on his face of one who hears the chiming of celestial spheres.

A brace of squires jingled in and hallooed to Teresa. Where had she been hiding all this time? The feasten sports had been nothing without her. She ought to have been at Ponsandane the week before. They had a black bull in a field tied to a ship's anchor. The ring parted, and the bull went loose in the crowd with two dogs hanging on him. Such a screeching and rushing you never did see. Old women running like two-year-olds, and young women climbing like squirrels and showing leg. . . . Oh, mercy! The squire hid his face in his hands and gulped.

Teresa guffawed, took a pound out of one of the bags, strapped up the wallet again and sat on it. Then she called the potboy and ordered a round of drinks. To blazes with economy for that one evening!

The company drank to her everlasting good health, to her matchless eyes and cherry lips. One squire kissed her. She boxed his ears — not too hard. He saluted the hand that smote him. His friend passed his arm round her waist. She let it linger.

Jerry Gish leaned forward and tapped her on the knee. 'Tell 'em what you said to that draper, my blossom. Ecod, yes, and to the jeweller! . . . Tell 'em!'

Once more Teresa obliged. The company applauded. Very apt; that was the way to talk to the snivelling swine! But her throat must be dry as a brick. They banged their pots. 'Hey, boy! Another round, damme!'

Other admirers drifted in and greeted Teresa with warmth. Where had she been all this time? They had missed her sorely. There was much rejoicing among the unjust over one sinner returned.

Teresa's soul expanded as a sunflower to the sun. They were all old friends, and she was glad to be with them again. Twice more for the benefit of newcomers did Captain Gish prevail on her to repeat what she had said to her creditors, and by general request she sang three songs. The potboy ran his legs off that night.

Towards eleven p.m. she shook one snoring admirer from her shoulder, removed the head of another from her lap, dropped an ironical curtsey to the prostrate gentlemen about her, and, grasping the precious wallet, rocked unsteadily into the yard. She had to rouse a hostler to girth her horse up for her, and her first attempts at mounting met with disaster; but she got into the saddle at last, and once there nothing short of gunpowder could dislodge her. Her lids were like lead, drowsiness was crushing her; she kept more or less awake until Bucca's Pass was behind, but after that she abandoned the struggle, and sleep swallowed her whole.

She was aroused at Bosula gate by the barking of her own dogs, unstrapped the wallet, turned the roan into the stable as it stood and staggered upstairs. Five minutes later she was shouting at the top of her lungs. She had been robbed; one of the hundred-pound bags was missing!

The household ran to her call. When had she missed it? Who had she been with? Where had she dropped it? Teresa was not clear about anything. She might have dropped it anywhere between Penzance and home, or, again, she might have been robbed in the tavern or the streets. The point was that she had lost one hundred pounds, and they had got to find it—now, at once! They were to take the road back, ransack the town, inform the magistrates. Out with them! Away!

Having delivered herself, she turned over, and was immediately asleep.

Ortho went back to bed. He would go to Penzance if necessary, he said, but it was useless before dawn. Let the others look close at home first.

Wany and Martha took a lantern and prodded about in the yard, clucking like hens. Eli lit a second lantern and went to the stable. Perhaps his mother had dropped the bag dismounting. He found the roan horse standing in its stall, unsaddled it, felt in the remaining wallet, turned over the litter. Nothing! As he came out he noticed that the second horse was soaking wet. Somebody had been riding hard, could only have just got in before Teresa. Ortho, of course. He wondered what his brother was up to. After some girl probably. . . . He had heard rumours.

Martha reported the yard bare, so he followed the hooftracks up the lane some way. Nothing!

Ortho was up at dawn, ready to go into town; but Teresa whose recuperative powers were little short of marvellous, was up before him and went in herself. She found nothing on the road and got small consolation from the magistrates.

People who mixed their drinks and their company when in possession of large sums of ready money should not complain if they lost it. She ought to be thankful she had not been relieved of the lot. They would make inquiries, of course, but held out no hope. There was an officer with a string of recruits in town, an Irish privateer and two foreign ships in the port, to say nothing of the Guernsey smugglers; the place was seething with covetous and desperate characters. They wagged their wigs and doubted if she would ever see her money again.

She never did.

Chapter XIII

SOME THREE weeks after Teresa's loss Eli found his brother in the yard fitting a fork head to a new haft.

'Saw William John Prowse up to churchtown,' said he. 'He told me to tell you that you must take the two horses over to once because he's got to go away.'

Ortho frowned. Under his breath he consigned William John Prowse to eternal discomfort. Then his face cleared.

'I've been buying a horse or two for Pyramus,' he remarked casually. 'He'll be down along next week.'

Eli gave him a curious glance. Ortho looked up, and their eyes met.

'What's the matter?'

'It was you stole that hundred pounds from mother, I suppose.'

Ortho started and then stared. 'Me! My Lord, what next! Me steal that? . . . Well I be damned! Think I'd turn Toby and rob my own family, do you? Pick my right pocket to fill my left? God's wrath! You're a sweet brother!'

'I do think so, anyhow,' said Eli doggedly.

'How? Why?'

' 'Cos King Herne can do his own buying, and because on the night mother was robbed you were out.'

Ortho laughed again. 'Smart as a gauger, aren't you? Well now, I'll tell you. William John let me have the horses on trust, and as for being out, I'm out 'most every night. I'd been to churchtown. I've got a sweetheart there, if you must know. So now, young clever!'

Eli shrugged his shoulders and turned away.

'Don't you believe me?' Ortho called.

'No.'

'Why not?'

' 'Cos 'tis well known William John Prowse wouldn't trust his father with a turnip, and that Polly mare hadn't brought you two miles from Gwithian. She'd come three times that distance and hard. She was as wet as an eel; I felt her.'

Ortho bit his lip. 'So ho, steady!' he called softly. 'Come round here a minute.'

He led the way round the corner of the barn, and Eli followed. Ortho leaned against the wall, all smiles again.

'See here, old son,' said he in a whisper, 'you're right. I did it. But I did it for you, for your sake, mind that.'

'Me!'

Ortho nodded. 'Surely. Look you, in less than two years Tregors and this here place fall to me, don't they?'

'Yes,' said Eli.

Ortho tapped him on the chest. 'Well, the minute I get possession I'm going to give you Tregors, lock, stock, and barrel. That's the way father meant it, I take it—only he didn't have time to put it in writing. But now Tregors is in the bag, and how are we going to get it out if mother will play chuck-guinea like she does?'

'So that's why you stole the money?'

'That's why. And harkee, don't shout "stole" so loud. It ain't stealing to take your own, is it?' Ortho whistled. 'My Lord, I sweated, Eli! I thought someone would have it before I did. The whole of Penzance knew she'd been about town all day with a bag of money, squaring her debts and lashing it about. To finish up she was in a room at the Star with a dozen of bucks, all of 'em three sheets in the wind and roaring. I seen them through a chink in the shutters, and I tell you I sweated blood. But she's cunning. When she sat down she sat on the wallet and stopped there. It would have taken a block and tackle to pull her off. I went into the Star passage all muffled up about the face like as if I had jaw ache. The potboy came along with a round of drinks for the crowd inside. "Here, drop those a minute and fetch me a dash of brandy for God Almighty's sake!" says I, mumbling and talking like an up-countryman. "I'm torn to pieces with this tooth. Here's a silver shilling, and you can keep the change if you're quick. Oh, whew! Ouch!"

'I tossed him the shilling—the last I'd got—and he dropped the pots there and then and dived after the brandy. I gave the pots a good dusting with a powder Pyramus uses on rogue horses to keep 'em quiet while he's selling 'em. Then the boy came back. I drank the brandy and went outside again and kept watch through the shutters. It worked pretty quick; what with the mixed drinks they'd had and the powder, the whole crew was stretched snoring in a quarter-hour. But not she. She's as strong as a yoke of bulls. She yawned a bit, but when the others went down she got up and went after her horse, taking the wallet along. I watched her mount from behind the rain barrel in the yard, and a pretty job she made of it. The hostler had to heave her up, and the first time she went clean over—up one side and down t'other. Second time she saved herself by clawing the hostler's hair, and near clawed his scalp off; he screeched like a slit pig.

'I watched that hostler as well, watched in case he might chance his fingers in the wallet; but he didn't. She was still half awake, and would have brained him if he'd tried it on. A couple of men, stranded seamen, I think, came out of an alley by the Abbey and dogged her as far as Lariggan, closing up all the time; but when they saw me behind they gave over and hid in under the riverbank. She kept awake through Newlyn, nodding double. I knew she couldn't last much longer; the wonder was she had lasted so long. On top of Paul Hill I closed up as near as I dared and then went round her, across country as hard as I could flog, by Chywoone and Rosvale.

'A dirty ride, boy, black as pitch and crossed with banks and soft bottoms. Polly fell down and threw me over her head twice ... thought my neck was broke. We came out on the road again at Trevelloe. I tied Polly to a tree and walked back to meet 'em. They came along at a walk, the old horse bringing his cargo home like he's done scores of times.

'I called his name softly and stepped out of the bushes. He stopped quiet as a lamb. Mother never moved; she was dead gone, but glued to the saddle. She's a wonder. I got the wallet open, put my hand in, and had just grabbed hold of a bag when Prince whinnied. He'd winded his mate Polly down the road. You know how it is when a horse whinnies; he shakes all through. Hey, but it gave me a start. It was a still night, and the old brute sounded like a squad of trumpets shouting "Ha!" like they do in the Bible. "Ha, ha, ha, he, he, he!"

'I jumped back my own length, and mother lolled over towards me and said, soft-like: "Pass the can around."'

'That's part of a song she sings,' said Eli, 'a drinking song.'

Ortho nodded. 'I know, but it made me jump when she said it, she said it so soft-like, I thought the horse had shaken her awake, and I ran for dear life. Before I'd gone fifty yards I knew I was running for nothing, but I couldn't go back. It was the first time I'd sto . . . I'd done anything like that, and I was scared of Prince whinnying again. I ran down the road, with the old horse coming along clop-clop behind me, jumped on Polly and galloped home without looking back. I wasn't long in before her as it was.' He drew a deep breath. 'But I kept the bag, and I've got it buried where she won't find it.' He smiled at his own cleverness.

'What are you going to do with the money?' Eli asked.

'Buy horses cheap and sell 'em dear. I learnt a trick or two when I was away with Pyramus, and I'm going to use 'em. There's nothing like it. I've seen him buy a nag for a pound and sell it for ten next week. I'm going to make Pyramus take my horses along with his. They'll be bought as his, so that people won't wonder where I got the money, and they'll go up-country and be sold with his—see? I've got it all thought out.'

'But will Pyramus do it?'

Ortho clicked his even white teeth. 'Ay, I reckon he will . . . if he wants to winter here again. How many two-pound horses can I buy for a hundred pounds?'

'Fifty.'

'And fifty sold at ten pounds each, how much is that?'

'Five hundred pounds.'

'How long will it take me to pay off the mortgage at that rate?'

'Two years . . . at that rate. But there's the interest too, and . . .'

Ortho smote him on the back. 'Oh, cheerily, old long-face, all's well! The rent'll pay the interest, as thou thyself sayest, and I'll fetch

110

in the money somehow. We'll harvest a mighty crop next season, and the horses'll pay bagfuls. In two years' time I'll put my boot under that fat cheese weevil Carveth, and you shall ride into Tregors like a king. If only I could have got hold of that second hundred! You don't know where mother hides her money, do you?'

'No.'

'No more do I . . . but I will. I'll sit over her like a puss at a mouse-hole. I'll have some more of it yet.'

'Leave it alone,' said Eli. 'She's sure to find out, and then there'll be the devil to pay. Besides, whatever you say about it being our money, it don't seem right. Leave it be.'

Ortho threw an arm about his neck and laughed at him.

* * *

Pyramus Herne arrived on New Year's Eve, and was not best pleased when Ortho announced his project. He had no wish to be bothered with extra horses that brought no direct profit to himself, but he speedily recognised that he had a new host to deal with, that young Penhale had cut his wisdom teeth, and that if he wanted the run of the upper Keigwin valley he'd have to pay for it. So he smiled his flashing smile and consented, on the understanding that he accepted no responsibility for any mishap and that Ortho found his own custom. The boy agreed to this and set about buying.

He picked up a horse here and there, but mainly he bought broken-down pack-mules from the mines round St Just. He bought wisely. His purchases were a ragged lot, yet never so ragged but that they could be patched up. When not out looking for mules, he spent practically all his time in the gypsy camp, firing, blistering, trimming misshapen hoofs, shotting roarers, filing and bishoping teeth. The farm hardly saw him; Eli and Bohenna put the seed in.

Pyramus left with February, driving the biggest herd be had ever taken north. This, of course, included Ortho's lot, but the boy had not got fifty beasts for his hundred pounds; he had got thirty-three only. But he was still certain of making his four hundred per cent, he told Eli. Mules were in demand, being hardy, long-lived, and frugal, and his string were in fine fettle. With a few finishing touches, their blemishes stained out, a touch of the clippers here and there, a pinch of ginger to give them life, some grooming, and a sleek over with an oil-rag, there would be no holding the public back from them. He would be home for harvest, his pockets dribbling gold.

He went one morning before dawn without telling Teresa he was going; jingled out of the yard, dressed in his best, astride one of Pyramus' showiest colts. His tirade against gypsy life and his eulogy of the delights of home, delivered to Eli on his return from his first trip with Pyramus, had been perfectly honest. He had had a rough experience and was played out.

But he was tired no longer. He rode to join Pyramus, singing the Helston Furry Song:

> '"Where are those Span-i-ards
> That made so brave a boast—O?
> They shall eat the grey goose feather
> And we will eat the roast—O."'

Eli, leaning over the gate, listened to the voice dwindling away up the valley and then turned with a sigh.

Dawn was breaking, the mists were rolling up, the hills loomed gigantic in the half-light, studded with granite escarpments, patch-worked with clumps of gorse, thorn, and bracken—his battlefield.

Ortho had gone again, gone singing to try his fortune in the great world among foreign multitudes. For him the dour grapple with the wilderness. And he was glad of it. He disliked foreigners, disliked taking chances. Here was something definite, something to lock his teeth in, something to be subdued by sheer dogged tenacity. He broke the news that Ortho had gone gypsying again that evening at supper.

Teresa exploded like a charge of gunpowder. She announced her intention of starting after her son at once, dragging him home, and having Pyramus arrested for kidnapping. Then she ramped up and down the kitchen cursing everybody present for not informing her of Ortho's intentions. When they protested that they had been as ignorant as herself, she damned them for answering her back.

Eli, who came in for most of her abuse, slipped out and over the hill to Roswarva, had a long farming talk with Penaluna, and bor-rowed a pamphlet on the prevention of wheat diseases.

The leggy girl Mary sat in a corner sewing by the light of a pilchard chill and saying never a word. Just before Eli left she brought him a mug of cider, but beyond drinking the stuff he hardly noticed the act, and even forgot to thank her. He found Teresa sitting up for him. She had her notched sticks and the two remaining money-bags on the table in front of her. She looked worried.

'Here,' she growled as her younger son entered, 'count this.'

Eli counted. There was a round hundred pounds in the one bag and thirty-one pounds ten shillings and fourpence in the other. He told her.

'There was fifty,' said she. 'How much have I spent, then?'

'Eighteen pounds ten shillings and eightpence.' Eli made a demonstration on his fingers.

Teresa's black eyebrows first rose and then crumpled together ominously.

'Eighteen!' she echoed, and began to tick off items on her own fingers, mumbling *sotto voce*. She paused at the ninth finger, racked her brains for forgotten expenditures, and began the count over again.

Eli sat down before the hearth and pulled his boots off. He could feel his mother's suspicious eyes on him. Twice she cleared her throat as if to speak, but thought better of it. He went to bed, leaving her still bent over the table twiddling her notched stick. Her eyes followed him up the stairs, perplexed, angry, with a hot gleam in them like a spark in coal.

So Ortho had found her hiding place after all, and had robbed her so cleverly that she was not perfectly sure she had been robbed. Eli tumbled into bed wishing his brother were not quite so clever. He fell asleep and had a dream, in which he saw his brother hanging in chains which creaked as they swung in the night winds.

Scared by the loss of her money, Teresa had another attack of extravagant economy, during which the Tregors lease fell in. She promptly put up the rent. The old tenant refused to carry on, and a new one had to be found. An unknown hind from Budock Water, near Falmouth, accepted the terms. Teresa congratulated herself on a bright stoke of business, and all went on as before.

Eli and Bohenna worked out early and late. The weather could not have been bettered, and the crops promised wonders. Eli, surveying the propitious fields, was relieved to think Ortho would be back for harvest, else he did not know how they would get it home.

No word had come from the wanderer; none was expected. But he was sure to be back for August; he had sworn to be. Ortho was back on the fourth of July.

Eli came in from work and, to his surprise, found him sitting in the kitchen relating the story of his adventures. He had a musical voice, a Gallic trick of gesticulation, and no compunction whatever about laughing at his own jokes. His recital was most vivacious.

Even Teresa guffawed—in spite of herself. She had intended to haul Master Ortho over an exceedingly hot bed of coals when he returned, but for the moment she could not bring herself to it. He had started talking before she could, and his talk was extremely diverting; she did not want to interrupt it. Moreover, he looked handsomer than ever, tall, graceful, darkly sparkling. She was proud of him; her mother sense stirred. He was very like herself.

From hints dropped here and there she guessed he had met with not a few gallant episodes on his travels, and determined to sit up after the others had gone to bed and get details out of him. They would make spicy hearing. Such a boy must be irresistible. The more women he had ruined the better she would be pleased, the greater the tribute to her offspring. She was a predatory animal herself, and this was her own cub. As for the wigging, that could wait until they fell out about something else and she was worked up; fly at him in cold blood she could not, not for the moment.

Ortho jumped out of his chair when Eli entered and embracing him with great warmth, commented on his growth, thumped the boy's deep chest, pinched his biceps, and called to Bohenna to behold the coming champion.

'My Lord, but here's a chicken that'll claw the breast feathers out o' thee before long, old fighting cock—thee or any other in Devon or Cornwall—eh, then?'

Bohenna grinned and nodded his grizzled poll.

'Stap me, little brother, I'd best keep a civil tongue before thee, seem me. Well, as I was saying—'

He sat down and continued his narrative.

Eli leaned against the settle listening and looking at Ortho. He was evidently in the highest spirits, but he had not the appearance of a man with five hundred pounds in his possession. He wore the same suit of clothes in which he had departed, and it was in an advanced state of dilapidation; the braid edging hung in strings, one elbow was barbarously patched with a square of sailcloth, and the other was out altogether. His high wool stockings were a mere network, and his boots lamentable. However, that was no criterion; gypsying was a rough life, and it would be foolish to spoil good clothes on it. Ortho himself looked worn and thin, he had a nasty livid cut running the length of his right cheekbone, and the gesticulating palms were raw with open blisters, but his infectious laugh rang through the kitchen, melodious, inspiring; he bore the air of success. All was well doubtless.

Eli fell to making calculations. Ortho had five hundred pounds; Teresa still had a hundred. That made six. Ortho would require a hundred as capital for next year, and then, if he could repeat his success, they would be out of the trap. He felt a rush of affection for his brother, ragged and worn from his gallant battle with the world—all for his sake. Tregors mattered comparatively little to Ortho, since he was giving it up and was fully provided for with Bosula. Ortho's generosity overwhelmed him. There was nobody like Ortho.

The gentleman in question finished an anecdote with a clap of laughter, sprang to his feet, pinned his temporarily doting mother in her chair and kissed her, twitched Martha's bonnet-strings loose, punched Bohenna playfully in the chest, caught Eli by the arm and swung him into the yard.

'Come across to the stable, my old dear; I've got something to show you.'

'Horse?'

'Lord, no! I've got no horse. Walked from Padstow.'

'You—walked!'

'Yes, heel and toe . . . two days. God, my feet are sore!'

'How did you come to get to Padstow?'

'Collier brig from Cardiff. Had to work my passage at that; my hands are like raw meat from hauling on those damned braces. Look! Slept in a cowshed at Illogan last night and milked the cows for breakfast. I'll warrant the farmer wondered why they were dry this morning. Ha, ha! Never mind, that's all over. What do you think of this?'

He reached inside the stable door and brought out a new fowling-piece.

'Bought this for you in Gloucester,' said he. 'Thought of you the minute I saw it. It's pounds lighter than father's old blunderbuss, and look here . . . this catch holds the priming and keeps it dry; pull the trigger, down comes the hammer, knocks the catch up, and bang. See? Clever, ain't it? Take hold.'

Eli took hold of the gun like a man in a dream. Beautiful weapon though it was, he did not even look at it.

'But why . . . why did you work your passage?' he asked.

'Because they wouldn't carry me for nothing, wood-head.'

'Were you trying to save money?'

'Eh? Er—ye-es.'

'Have you done as well as you expected, Ortho?'

'N-o, not quite. I've had the most damnable luck, old boy'—he took Eli's arm—'and none of it my fault. I sold a few mules at first at good prices, but the money went. A man must eat as he goes, you know; and then there was that gun, it cost a pretty penny. Then trouble began. I lost three beasts at Tewkesbury. They got scared in the night. One broke a shoulder and two went over a quarry. But at Hereford . . . Oh, my God!'

'What happened?'

'Glanders. They went like flies. Pyramus saw what it was right off, and we ran for it, south, selling horses to the first bid—that is, we tried to, but they were too sick, and word went faster than we. The crowd got ugly, swore we'd infected the country and they'd hang us. They would have, too, if we'd waited. They very nearly had me, boy—very nearly.'

'Did they mark your face like that?'

'They did, with a lump of slate. And that isn't all; I've got half a dozen more like it scattered about.' He laughed. 'But no matter, they didn't get me, and I'm safe home again, thank God!'

'And the horses?'

'They killed every one of 'em to stop the infection.'

'Then you haven't got any money?'

Ortho shook his head. 'Not a penny.'

Chapter XIV

MISFORTUNE DID not daunt Ortho for long; the promising state of the home fields put fresh heart in him. He plunged at the work chanting a paean in praise of agriculture, tore through obstacles, and swept up his tasks with a speed and thoroughness which left Eli and Bohenna standing amazed.

The Penhale brothers harvested a record crop that season; but so did everybody else. The market was glutted and prices negligible. Except that their own staple needs were provided for, they were no better off than previously. Eli did not greatly care. He had done what he had set out to do—bring a good crop home. But Ortho fell into a state of profound gloom, for it was money that he wanted.

It seemed to make little difference in agriculture whether you harvested a bumper yield or none at all. He had no capital to start in the secondhand horse trade, even did he wish to, and he had no knowledge of any other business. He was on the desperate point of enlisting in the army on the chance of being sent abroad and gathering in a little loot, when opportunity rapped loudly on his door.

He had run down towards Tol-Pedn-Penwith with Jacky's George one afternoon in late September. It was a fine afternoon with a smooth sea, and all the coves between Merther Point and Carn Scathe were full of whitebait. They crowded close inshore in dense shoals, hiding from the mackerel. When the mackerel charged them they stampeded in panic, fritting the surface like wind-flaws. The gig's crew attacked the attackers, and did so well that they did not notice the passage of time.

Jacky's George came to his senses as the sun slipped under and clapped on all sail for home. He appeared in a hurry. By the time they were abreast of the Gamper the wind, which had been hacking all the afternoon, was a dead-muzzler. Jacky's George did what he was seldom known to do: he blasphemed, ported his helm, and ran on a long leg out to sea. By ten o'clock they had levelled Boscawen Point, but the wind fell away altogether, and they were becalmed three miles out in the Channel. Jacky's George blasphemed again and ordered oars out. The gig was heavy and the tide against them. It took Ortho and three young Baragwanaths an hour and a half to open Monk's Cove.

Ortho could not see the reason of it, of wrenching one's arms out when in an hour or two the tide would carry them in. However, he knew better than to question Jacky's George's orders. Even when Monk's Cove was reached the little man did not go in, but pointed across for Black Carn. As they paddled under the lee of the cape there came a peculiar whistle from the gloom ahead, to which the bow-oar responded, and Ortho made out a boat riding to a kedge. They pulled alongside and made fast. It was the second Baragwanath gig, with the eldest son, Anson, and the remainder of the brothers aboard.

'Who's that you got wid 'e?' came the hushed voice of Anson.

'Ortho Penhale,' his father replied; 'hadn't time to put 'en ashore—becalmed way out. Has 'a showed up yet?'

'Naw, 'a's late.'

' 'Ess. Wind's felled away. All quiet in Cove?'

' 'Ess, sure. Every road's watched, and ma's got a furze stacked up to touch off if she gets warning.'

'All right. . . . Well, keep your eye peeled for his signal.'

Light suddenly broke on Ortho. There was a run on and he was in it. Thrilling! He leaned towards Jacky's George and whispered: 'Who's coming? Roscoff boat?'

Jacky's George uttered two words which sent an electric quiver through him:

'King Nick.'

"King Nick!" Captain Nicholas Buzza, Prince of Free Traders, the man who had made more runs than all the rest put together, who owned a fleet of armed smugglers and cheated the Revenue of thousands a year; who had fooled the riding officers times out of number and beaten off the militia; who had put to sea after a big privateer sent to suppress him, fought a running fight from Godrevy to Trevose and sent her diving down the deep sea. The mercurial, daredevil King Nick, who was said to be unable to sleep comfortably unless there was a price on his head; who had raided Penzance by the light of the moon and recaptured a lost cargo; who had been surprised by the gaugers off Cawsand, chopped to bits with cutlasses, left for dead, and then swam ashore; who was reported to walk through Peter Port with all the Guernsey merchants bowing low before him, was called "Duc de Roscoff" in Brittany, and commanded more deference in Schiedam than its own Burgomaster. King Nick, the romantic idol of every West Country boy, coming to Monk's Cove that very night—even then moving towards them through the dark. Ortho felt as if be were about to enter the presence of Almighty God.

'Is it a big run?' he whispered to Jacky's George, trembling with excitement.

'Naw, main run was at Porthleven last night. This is but the leavings. A few trifles for the Kiddlywink to oblige me.'

'Is King Nick a friend of yours, then?' said Ortho, wide-eyed.

'Lord save you, yes! We was privateering together years ago.'

Ortho regarded the fisherman with added veneration.

'If 'a don't come soon 'a'll miss tide,' Anson hissed from the other boat.

'He'll come, tide or no tide,' snapped his father.

'Hold tongue, will 'e. Dost want whole world to hear?'

Anson subsided.

There was a faint mist clouding the sea, but overhead rode a splendour of stars, an illimitable glitter of silver dust. Nothing was to be heard but the occasional scrape of sea-boots as one cramped boy or other shifted position, the wail of a disturbed seabird from the looming rookeries above them, the everlasting beat of surf on the Twelve Apostles a mile away to the south-west, and the splash and sigh of some tired ninth wave heaving itself over the ledges below Black Carn.

An hour went by. Ashore a cock crowed, and a fisherman's donkey tethered high up the cliffside, roared asthmatically in reply. The boats swung round as the tide slackened and made. The night freshened. Ripples lapped the bows. The land wind was blowing. Ortho lay face down on the stroke thwart and yawned. Adventure—if adventure there was to be—was a long time coming. He was getting cold. The rhythmic lift and droop of the gig, the lisp and chuckle of the water-voices, had a hypnotic effect on him. He pillowed his cheek on his forearms and drowsed, dreamt he was swaying in gloomy space, disembodied, unsubstantial, a wraith dipping and soaring over a bottomless void. Clouds rolled by him as big as continents. He saw the sun and moon below him, no bigger than pins' heads, and world upon glittering world strewn across the dark like grains of sand. He could not have long lain thus, could not have fallen fully asleep, for Anson's first low call set him wide awake.

'Sail ho!'

Both boat's crews sat up as one man.

'Where away?'

'Sou'-east.'

Ortho's eyes bored into the hollow murk seawards, but could distinguish nothing for the moment. Then, as he stared, it seemed to him that the dark smudge that was the corner of the Carn was expanding westwards. It stretched and stretched until finally a piece detached itself altogether, and he knew it was a big cutter creeping close inshore under full sail. Never a wink of light did the stranger show.

'Hast lantern ready?' hissed Jacky's George.

'Ay,' from Anson.

'Cast off there, hoist killick, and stand by.'

'Ay, ay.'

The blur that was the cutter crept on, silent as a shadow, almost indistinguishable against the further dark, a black moth on black velvet. All eyes watched her. Suddenly a green light glowed amidships, stabbing the inky waters with an emerald dagger, glowed steadily, blinked out, glowed again, and vanished. Ortho felt his heart bound into his throat.

'Now,' snapped Jacky's George, 'show lantern . . . four times, remember.'

Anson stood up and did as he was bid.

The green lantern replied, the cutter rounded up in the wind and drifted towards them, tide-borne.

'Out oars and pull.' said Jacky's George.

They swept within forty yards of the cutter.

' 'Vast pulling,' came a voice from her bows.

'Back water all,' Jacky's George commanded.

'Is that George Baragwanath?' came the voice again, a high-pitched, kindly voice, marvellously clear.

'Ay, ay.'

'What's the word then, my dear?'

'Hosannah.'

'What's that there boat astern of 'e? '

'Mine—my second boat.'

'Well, tell him to keep off a cable's length till I've seen to 'e,' the amiable voice continued. 'If he closes 'fore I tell 'en, I'll blow him outer the water as God is my salvation! No offence meant, but we can't take chances, you understand. Come ahead, you.'

The gig's crew gave way and brought their craft alongside the smuggler.

'One at a time,' said the voice somewhere in the darkness above them, mild as a ringdove. 'George, my dear soul, step up alone, will 'e, please?'

Jacky's George went over the rail and out of sight.

Ortho heard the voice greet him affectionately and then attend to the helmsman.

'Back forsail, Zebedee; she'll jam 'tween wind and tide. No call to anchor. We'll have this little deckload off in ten minutes, please God, amen! There it is all before you, George: low Holland's proof, brandy, sugar, and a snatch of snuff. Tally it, will you, please? We're late, I'm afraid. I was addressing a few earnest seekers after grace at Rosudgeon this afternoon, and the word of the Lord came upon me and I spake over-long, I fear, trembling and sweating in my unworthiness—and then the wind fell very slight. I had to sweep her along till, by God's infinite mercy, I picked up this shore-draught. Whistle up your second boat, and we'll load 'em both sides to once. You haven't been washed in the blood of the Lamb as yet, have you, George? Ah, that it might be vouchsafed this unworthy vessel to purge you with hyssop! I must have a quiet talk with you. Steady with them tubs, Harry; you'll drop 'em through the gig.'

For the next quarter of an hour Ortho was busy stowing casks lowered by the cutter's crew, but all the time the sweet voice went on. It seemed to be trying to persuade Jacky's George into something he would not do. He could hear the pair tramping the deck above him side by side—one, two, three, four, and roundabout; one, two, three, four, and roundabout—the voice purling like a melodious brook; Jacky's George's gruff negatives, and the brook purling on again unruffled. Nobody else on the cutter uttered a sound; it might have been manned by a company of mutes.

Anson called from the port side that he was loaded. Jacky's George broke off his conversation and crossed over.

'Pull in, then. Soon's you've got 'em stowed, show a spark and I'll follow.'

Anson's gig disappeared shorewards, wallowing deep. Jacky's George gripped a stay with his hook and swung over the rail into his own boat.

'I can't do it, cap'n,' he called. 'Good night, and thank 'e kindly all the same. Cast off!'

They were away. It burst upon Ortho that he had not seen his hero, that he never would. In a minute the tall cutter would be fading away seawards as mysteriously as she had come, and that the great King Nick would be never anything to him but a voice. He could have cried out with disappointment.

'Push off,' said Jacky's George.

Ortho leant on his oar and pushed, and as he did so somebody sprang from the cutter's rail, landed on the piled casks behind him as lightly as a cat, steadied himself with a band on his shoulder, and dropped into the sternsheets beside the fisherman.

'Coming ashore wid 'e, George,' said the voice, 'and by God's grace I persuade 'e yet.'

King Nick was in the boat!

'Mind what I bade 'e, Zebedee,' he hailed the cutter. 'Take she round to once, and I'll be off tomorrow night by God's providence and loving-kindness.' The cutter swung slowly on her heel, drifted beam-on to the lapping tide, felt her helm, and was gone, blotted out, swallowed up, might never have been.

But King Nick was in the boat. Ortho could not see him, he was merely a smudged silhouette, but he was in the sternsheets not a yard distant. Their calves were actually rubbing! Could such things be?

They paddled in and hung a couple of cables' lengths offshore, waiting Anson's signal. The smuggler began his argument again, and this time Ortho heard all—he couldn't help it.

'Think of the money in it, George. You've got a growing family. Think o' your duty to them.'

'I reckon they won't starve. Why won't the Bay men do 'e?'

' 'Cos there's a new collector coming to Penzance and a regiment of dragoons, and you know what they rogues are—"their mouth is full of cursing and bitterness, their feet are swift to shed blood"—nothing like they poor lambs the militia. Won't be able to move a packhorse between Mousehole and Marazion wid they lawless scum about. God ha' mercy on 'em and pardon 'em!'

'Who told 'e new collector and sojjers is coming?'

'The old collector, Mr Hawkesby. Took him a pin o' crafty old Jamaica with my respects only last Tuesday, and he showed me the letter signed and sealed. An honourable Christian gentleman is Mr Hawkesby. Many a holy discourse have I had with him. He wouldn't deceive me. No, George, "Strangers are risen up against me and tyrants." . . . "Lo, the ungodly bend their bow."'

'Umph! Well, why don't 'e run it straight on north coast handy to market?'

King Nick's voice took on a slightly pained tone. 'George, George, my dear life, ponder, will 'e? Consider where between St Ives and Sennen can I run a cargo. And how many days a week in winter can I land at Sennen—eh? Not one. Not one in a month hardly. "He gathereth the waters of the sea together as it was upon a heap:" Psalm thirty-three. And it's in winter that the notable hard drinking's done, as thou well knowest. What else is the poor dear souls to do in the long bitter evenings? Think o' they poor St Just tinners down in the damp and dark all day. 'Tis the duty of any man professing Christian love and charity to assist they poor souls to get a drop of warm liquor cheap. What saith the Book? "Blessed is he that considereth the poor and needy." Think on that, George.' There were tears in the melodious brook.

Jacky's George grunted. 'Dunno as I've got any turrible love for tinners. The last pair o' they mucky toads as comed here pretty nigh clawed my house down. Why not Porthgwarra or Penberth?'

' 'Cos there aren't a man there I'd trust, George. I wouldn't put my trust en nobody but you—"The faithful are minished from among the sons o' men." You run a bit for yourself. Why can't 'e run a bit more and make a fortune? What's come over 'e, my old and bold? 'Fraid, are 'e, all to once? What for? You've got a snug landing and a straight track over the moors, wid never a soul to see 'e pass. Riders can't rush 'e here in this little crack o' the rocks; they'd break their stiff necks. "Let their way be dark and slippery and let the angel of the Lord persecute them: and we shall wash our footsteps in the blood of the ungodly." What makes 'e hold back, old shipmate?'

'Horses,' said Jacky's George. 'Lookee, Cap'n Nick, the money's good and I do respect it as much as the next man. I aren't 'fraid of riders nor anything else—save tumours—and if it were only a matter of landing, why I'd land s' much stuff as you've a mind to. But carry goods to St Just for 'e I won't, for that means horses, and horses means farmers. I'm bred to the sea myself, and I can't abide farmers. I've tried it before, and there's always trouble. It do take a week walking round the earth collecting 'em, and then some do show up and some don't, and where are we then? Why, where the cat was—in the tar barrel. Paul farmers won't mix wid Gwithian, and Sancreed can't stomach neither. And what is more, they do eat up all your profits—five shillings here, ten shillings there—and that ain't the end of it. When you think you've done paying a farmer, slit me! You've only just begun. I won't be plagued wid 'em, so that's the finish.'

'Listen to me a minute,' King Nick purled on, quite undeterred. 'I'll tell 'e. . . .'

'T'eddn no manner of use, cap'n,' said Jacky's George, standing up. 'There's the light showing. Way all! Bend to it!'

The gig shot shorewards for the slip.

The manner in which the Baragwanath family disposed of a run contained the elements of magic; it was a conjuring trick, no less—"now you see it, now you don't." At one moment the slip head was chock-a-block with bales and barrels, at the next it was bare. They swooped purposefully out of nowhere, fell upon the goods, and spirited themselves back into nowhere, leaving the slip wiped clean.

Including one son and two daughters-in-law, the tribe mustered fourteen in all, and in the handling of illicit merchandise the ladies were as gifted as the gentlemen. Ortho was laboriously trundling a cask up the slip when he encountered one of the Miss Baragwanaths, who gave him a push and took the matter out of his hands. By the time he had recovered his balance, she had gone and so had the cask. It was too dark to see which way she went. Not that he was interested; on the contrary, he wanted to think. He had a plan forming in his head, a moneymaking plan.

He strode up and down the bare strip by the boat capstan getting the details clear. It did not take him long, being simplicity itself. He hitched his belt and marched up the little hamlet, hot with inspiration.

Subdued mysterious sounds came from the surrounding darkness—whisperings, thuds, shovel scrapings, sighs as of men heaving heavy weights. A shed suddenly exploded with the clamour of startled hens. In another a sow protested vocally against the disturbance of her bed. There was a big bank running beside the stream in front of the Admiral Anson. As Ortho passed by, the great mass of earth and boulders became articulate. A voice deep within its core said softly: 'Shift 'em a bit further up, Zack; there's three more to come.'

Ortho saw a thin chink of light between two of the boulders, grinned, and strode into the kitchen of the Kiddlywink. There was a chill burning on the table and a kettle humming on the hearth. Jacky's George sat before the fire stirring a mug of grog which he held between his knees. Opposite him sat a tall old man dressed in unrelieved black from neck to toe. A wreath of snowy hair circled his bald pate like a halo. A pair of tortoiseshell spectacles jockeyed the extreme tip of his nose; he regarded Jacky's George over their rims with an expression benign but pained.

Jacky's George looked up at Ortho's entrance.

'Hallo, what is it?'

'Where's King Nick? I want to see him.'

The tortoiseshell spectacles turned slowly in his direction.

'There is but one King, my son, omnipotent and all-merciful. One King—on High . . . but my name is certainly Nicholas.'

Ortho staggered. This the master smuggler, the swashbuckling devil-may-care hero of song and story! This rook-coated, bespectacled, white-headed old Canorum local preacher King Nick! His senses reeled. It could never be! And yet he knew it was. It was the same voice, the voice that had blandly informed Anson he would blow him out of the water if he pulled another stroke. He felt for the doorpost and leaned against it goggling.

'Well?'

Ortho licked his lips.

'Well? I eddn no fiery dragon to eat 'e, boy. Say thy say.'

Ortho drew a long breath, hesitated, and let it out with a rush:

'I can find the horses you're wanting. I can find thirty horses a night any time after Twelfth Night, and land your goods in St Just under four hours.'

King Nick screwed round in his chair, turning the other side of his face to the light, and Ortho saw, with a shock of revulsion, that the ear had been sheared off and his face furrowed across and across with two terrible scars—relics of the Cawsand affair. It was as though the old man was revealing the other side of him, spiritual as well as physical.

'Come nearer, lad. How do 'e knaw I want horses?'

'I heard you. I was pulling stroke in boat.'

'Son o' yourn, George? He don't favour 'e, seem me.'

'Naw. Young Squire Penhale from Bosula up valley.'

'You knaw 'em?'

'Since he were weaned.'

'Ah, ha! Ah, ah!' The smuggler's blue eyes rested on Ortho, benevolent yet probing. 'And where can you find thirty horses, my son? 'Tis a brear passel.'

'Gypsy Herne rests on my land over winter; he has plenty.'

'An Egyptian! An idolater! A worshipper after false gods! Put not thy trust in such, boy—though I do hear many of the young ones is baptised and coming to the Way of Light. Hum! Ha! . . . But how do 'e knaw he'll do it?'

' 'Cos he wants the money bad. He lost three parts of his stock in Wales this summer. I was with 'en.'

'Oh, wid 'en, were 'e? So you knawn 'en well. And horse-leaders?'

'There's seven Romanys and three of us up to farm.'

'You knaw the country, s'pose?'

'Day or night, like my own yard.'

King Nick turned on Jacky's George, a faint smile curling the corners of his mouth. 'What do 'e say now, George? Can this young man find the horses, think you?'

' 'Ess, s'pose.'

'Do 'e trust 'en?'

A nod.

'Then what more 'ave 'e got to say, my dear?'

The fisherman scratched his head, breathed heavily through his nostrils, and said, 'All right.'

King Nick rose to his feet, rubbing his hands together. ' "Now let Jacob rejoice and Israel be glad." That's settled. Welcome back to the fold, George, my old soul! "This is my brother that was dead but is alive again." Soon's you give me word the Romany is agreeable I'll slip 'e the cargoes; so shall the poor tinner be comforted at a reasonable price and the Lord be praised with cymbals, yea, with trumpets also and shawms. Gather in all the young men and maidens, George, that we may ask a blessing on our labours. Fetch 'em in to once, for I can feel the word of the Lord descending upon me!'

* * *

Dawn, peering through the bottle-panes of Jacky's George's Kiddlywink, saw the entire Baragwanath family packed shoulder to shoulder singing lustily, while before them on a chair stood a benevolent old gentleman in black, beating time with one of John Wesley's hymnals, white hair wreathing his head like a silver glory.

'Chant, my dear beauties!' he cried. 'Oh, be cheerful, be jubilant! Lift up your voices unto the Lord! "Awake up my glory, awake lute and harp!" Now altogether:

> '"When passing through the watery deep
> I ask in faith His promised aid;
> The waves an awful distance keep
> And shrink from my devoted head.'"

Chapter XV

PYRAMUS CAME down earlier than usual that year; the tenth of December saw his smoke-grimed wigwams erected in the little wood, the cloaks and scarves of the Romany women making bright blots of colour among the sombre trees, bronze babies rolling among bronze leaves.

Ortho was right; the gypsy chief had been hard hit, and was open to any scheme for recouping his fortunes. After considerable haggling he consented to a fee of six shillings per horse per run—leaders thrown in—which was a shilling more than Ortho had intended to give him and two shillings more than he would have taken if pressed. The cavalry had not arrived as yet, and Ortho did not think it politic to inform Pyramus they were expected. There were the makings in him of a good business man.

The first run was dated for the night of January the third, but the heavy groundswell was rolling in, and the lugger lay off until the evening of the fifth. King Nick arrived on the morning of the third, stepped quietly into the kitchen of the Admiral Anson as the Baragwanath family were sitting down to breakfast, having walked by night from Germoe. The meal finished, he gave melodious thanks to Heaven, sent for Ortho, asked what arrangements had been made for the landing, condemned them root and branch, and substituted an entirely fresh lot. That done, he rode off to St Just to survey the proposed pack route, taking Ortho with him.

He was back again by eight o'clock at night, and immediately held a prayer meeting in the Kiddlywink, preaching on "Lo, he thirsteth even as a hart thirsteth after the water-brooks"—a vindication of the gin traffic—and passing on to describe the pains of hell with such graphic detail that one Cove woman fainted and another had hysterics.

The run came off without a hitch two nights later. Ortho had his horses loaded up and away by nine o'clock. At one-thirty a crowd of enthusiastic diggers (all armed with clubs) were stripping his load and secreting it in an old mine working on the outskirts of St Just. He was home in bed before dawn. Fifty-six casks of mixed gin, claret, and brandy they carried that night, not to mention five hundredweight of tea.

On January the seventeenth he carried forty-three casks, a bale of silk, and a hundredweight of tea to Pendeen, dumping some odds and ends outside St Gwithian as he passed by. And so it went on.

The consumption of cheap spirits among the miners was enormous. John Wesley, to whose credit can be placed almost the whole moral regeneration of the Cornish tinner, describes them as "those who feared not God nor regarded man," accuses them of wrecking ships and murdering the survivors, and of taking their pleasure in "hurling, at which limbs are often broken, fighting, drinking, and all other manner of wickedness."

In winter their pastimes were restricted to fighting and drinking—principally drinking, in furtherance of which Ortho did a roaring trade. Between the beginning of January and the end of March he ran an average of five landings a month without anyone so much as wagging a finger at him. The dragoons arrived at Christmas, but instead of a regiment, two troops only appeared, and they speedily declared a policy of "live and let live." Their commanding officer, Captain Hambro, had not returned to his native land after years of hard campaigning to spend his nights galloping down blind byways at the behest of a civilian riding officer.

He had some regard for his horses' legs and more for his own comfort. He preferred playing whist with the local gentry who had fair daughters, and who were the soul of hospitality. He temporised good-humouredly with the collector, danced quadrilles with the fair daughters at the Ship and Castle, and toasted their bright eyes in excellent port and claret—the knowledge that it had not paid a penny of duty in nowise detracting from its flavour. Occasionally, when he had no other appointment and the weather was passable, he mounted his stalwarts and made a spectacular drive. This as a sop to the collector. But he never came westwards; the going was too rough, and besides, St Just was but small potatoes compared with big mining districts to the east.

For every cask landed at Monk's Cove, King Nick and his merry men landed twenty, either at Prussia Cove, Porthleven, Hayle, or Portreath—sometimes at all four places simultaneously. Whenever Captain Hambro's troopers climbed into their saddles and took the road to Long Rock a simple but effective system of signals flashed ahead of them, so that they found very little. There was one nasty affair on Marazion beach. Owing to a misunderstanding, the cavalry came upon a swarm of tinners in process of making a landing. The tinners, who had broached a cask and were full of spirit in more senses than one, foolishly opened hostilities. The result was two troopers wounded, six miners killed—bearing out King Nick's warning that the soldiers might easily be fooled but they were by no means so easily frightened. The trade absorbed this lesson, and there were no more regrettable incidents that season.

Ortho was satisfied with his winter's work beyond all expectations. It was a common tenet among free traders of those days that one cargo saved would pay for two lost, and Ortho, so far from losing a single cargo, had only lost five tubs in all—three stove in transhipping and two when the mule carrying them fell into a pit. Everybody was satisfied. The district was flooded with cheap liquor. All the Covers in turn assisted in the boat work and so picked up money in the off season when they needed it most. Pyramus, with his animals in constant employment, did so well that he delayed his northern trip for a month.

The only person (with the exception of His Majesty's Collector of Customs) who was not entirely pleased was Eli. In defrauding the Revenue he had no scruples whatever, but it interfered with his farming. This smuggling was all very fine and remunerative, but it was a mere sideline. Bosula was his lifework, his being. If he and Bohenna had to be up all night horse-leading, they could not be awake all day. The bracken was creeping in again. However, they were making money, heaps of it; there was no denying that.

With the instinctive dislike of a seaman for a landsman and *vice versa*, neither Jacky's George nor Pyramus would trust each other. The amphibious Ortho was the necessary link between them, and, as such, paid out more or less what he thought fit—as has been the way with middlemen since the birthday of the world. He paid Jacky's George one shilling and sixpence per cask for landing and Pyramus three shillings for racking (they went two to a horse), making a profit of ten shillings clear himself. Eli, the only person in the valley who could read, write, or handle figures, kept the accounts, and knew that at the end of March they were three hundred and forty pounds to the good. He asked Ortho where the money was.

'Hid up the valley,' said his brother. 'Put away where the devil himself wouldn't find it.'

'What are you hiding it like that for?' Eli asked.

'Mother,' said Ortho. 'That last rip-roar she had must have nigh baled her bank dry, and now she's looking for more. I think she've got a notion who bubbled her last year, and she's aiming to get a bit of her own back. She knows I've got money, and she's spying on me all the time. I'd tell you where it is only I'm afeard you'd let it out without meaning to. I'm too sly for her, but you, you're like a pane of glass.'

Wholesale smuggling finished with the advent of spring. The shortening nights did not provide sufficient cover for big enterprises. Dragoons and Preventive men had not the same objections to being out of their beds in summer as in winter, and, moreover, the demand for liquor had fallen to a minimum.

This was an immense relief to Eli, who now gave himself heart and soul to the farm, haling Bohenna with him; but two disastrous seasons had impaired Ortho's vaunted enthusiasm for "the good old soil," and he was absent most of the week working up connections for next winter's cargo-running—so he told Eli—but it was noticeable that his business appointments usually coincided with any sporting events held in the Hundred; and at hurling matches, bull-baitings, cockfights, and pony races he became almost as familiar a figure as his mother had been, backing his fancy freely and with not infallible judgement. However, he paid his debts scrupulously and with good grace, and though he drank but little himself was most generous in providing gratis refreshment for others. He achieved strong local popularity, a priceless asset to a man who lives by flaunting the law.

The money was not all misspent.

He developed in other ways, began to be particular about his person in imitation of the better-class squires, visited a Penzance tailor of fashion, and was henceforth to be seen on public occasions in a wide-skirted suit of black broadcloth frogged with silver lace, high stockings to match, and silver buckled shoes; very handsome altogether.

He had his mother's blue-black hair, curling, bull-like, all over his head, sparkling eyes, and strong white teeth. When he was fifteen she had put small gold rings in his ears—to improve his sight, so she said. At twenty he was six feet tall, slim and springy, moving among the boorish crowds like a rapier among bludgeons. His laugh was ready, and he had a princely way with his money. Women turned their eyes his way, sighing—and he was not insensible.

Rumours of his brother's amorous affairs drifted home to Eli from time to time. He had cast off the parish clerk's daughter, Tamsin Eva, and was after a farmer's young widow in St Levan. Now he had quarrelled with the widow and was to be seen in Trewellard courting a mine captain's daughter. Again, he had put the miner's daughter by, and St Ives gossips were coupling his name with that of the wife of a local preacher and making a great hoity-toity about it. And so on. It was impossible to keep track of Ortho's activities in the game of hearts.

He came home one morning limping from a slight gunshot wound in the thigh, and on another occasion brought his horse in nearly galloped to death; but he made no mention of how either of these things came about. Though his work on the farm was negligible, be spent a busy summer, one way and another.

Pyramus was down by the eighth of November, and on the night of the fourteenth the ball was opened with a heavy run of goods, all of which were safely delivered. From then on till Christmas cargo after cargo was slipped through without mishap, but on St Stephen's

Day the weather broke up, the wind bustled round to the south-east and blew great guns, sending the big seas piling into Monk's Cove in foaming hills. The covemen drew their boats well up, took down snares and antique blunderbusses, and staggered inland rabbiting.

Eli turned back to his farm work with delight, but prosaic hard labour had no further attraction for Ortho. He put in a couple of days sawing up windfalls, a couple more ferreting with Bohenna, then he went up to churchtown and saw Tamsin Eva again.

It was at a dance in the long room of the Lamb and Flag tavern, and she was looking her best, dressed in blue flounced out at the hips, with a close-fitting bodice. She was what is known in West Cornwall as a "red Dane"; masses of bright auburn hair she had, and a soft white skin. Ortho, whose last three little affairs had been pronounced brunettes, turned to her with a refreshened eye, wondering what had made him leave her. She was dancing a square dance with her faithful swain Tom Trevaskis when Ortho entered, circling and curtseying happily to the music of four fiddles led by Jiggy Dan.

The mine captain's daughter glowed as rosy as a pippin—too rosy; the preacher's spouse was an olive lady, almost swarthy. Tamsin Eva's slender neck might have been carved from milk-ivory, and she was tinted like a camellia. Ortho's dark eyes glittered. But it was her hair that fascinated him most. The room was lit by dips lashed to decorated barrel-hoops suspended from the rafters, and as Tamsin in her billowy blue dress swept and sidled under these the candlelight played tricks with her burnished copper head, flicked red and amber lights over and into it, crowned her with living gold. The black Penhale felt his heart leap. She was most lovely! Why on earth had he ever dropped her? Why?

Deep down he knew it was because, for all her physical attractions, she wearied him utterly, seemed numbed in his presence and had not a word to say. That Trewellard wench at least had a tongue in her head, and the widow had spirit; he could still almost feel his cheek tingle where she had hit him. But that queenly crown of hair! He had an overmastering desire to pull it down and bury his face in the shining golden torrent. He would too, ecod! Dull she might have been, but that was two years ago; she'd grown since then, and so had he, and learnt a thing or two; a score of women had been at pains to teach him. He hadn't gone far with Tamsin previously, she'd been too damned soft, but he would now. He'd stir her up. Apparently shallow women were often deep as the sea, deep enough to drown one. He'd take the risk of drowning; he fed on risks. That the girl was formally betrothed to Trevaskis did not deter him in the slightest. There was no point in the game in which he could not outmanoeuvre the slovenly yokel.

He waited till the heated boy went to get himself a drink, and then shouldered through the press and claimed Tamsin for the next dance, claiming her smiling, inevitably, as though she was his private property and there had not been a moment's break between them. The girl's eyes went blank with dismay; she tried to decline. He didn't seem to hear, but took her hand. She hung back weakly. There was no weakness in Ortho's grip; he led her out in spite of herself. She couldn't resist him, she never had been able to resist him. Fortunately for her, he had never demanded much. Poor Tamsin! Two years had not matured her mentally. She had no mind to mature: she was merely a pretty chattel, the property of the strongest claimant. Ortho was stronger than Trevaskis, so he got her.

When the boy returned she was dancing with the tall free trader. The golden head drooped, the life had gone out of her movements, but she was dancing with him. Trevaskis tried to get to her at every pause, but always Ortho's back interposed. The farmer went outside and strode up and down the yard, glaring from time to time through the windows. Always Tamsin was dancing with Penhale. Trevaskis ground his teeth. Two years ago he had been jockeyed in the same way. Was this swart gypsy's whelp, whose amorous philanderings were common talk, to have first call on his bright girl whenever he deigned to want her? Trevaskis swore he should not, but how to frustrate him he did not know. Plainly Tamsin was bewitched, was incapable of resistance; she had admitted as much, weeping. Thrash Ortho to a standstill he could not; he was not a brave man, and he dared not risk a maul with the smuggler. Had Penhale been a "foreigner" he could have roused local feeling against him. But Penhale was no stranger; he was the squire of Bosula, and, moreover, most popular—far more popular than he was himself. He had a wild idea of trying a shot over a bank in the dark—and abandoned it shuddering. Supposing he missed! What would Penhale do to him? What wouldn't he do to him? Trevaskis hadn't courage enough even for that. He strode up and down, oblivious of the rain-gusts, trying to discover a chink in the interloper's armour.

As for Ortho, he went on dancing with Tamsin, and when it was over took her home. He buried his face in that golden torrent. He was up at churchtown the very next night, and the next night, and every night till the gale blew out.

Trevaskis, abandoning a hopeless struggle, followed in the footsteps of many unlucky lovers and drowned his woes in drink. It was at the Kiddlywink in Monk's Cove that he did his drowning, and not at the Lamb and Flag, but as his farm lay about halfway between the two there was nothing remarkable in that.

What did cause amusement among the Covers, however, was the extraordinary small amount of liquor it required to lay him under the bench, and the volume of his snores when he was there.

Chapter XVI

1.

THE SOUTH-WESTERLY gale blown out, Ortho's business went forward with a rush. In the second week in January they landed a cargo a night to make up for lost time, and met with a minor accident, Jacky's George breaking a leg in saving a gig from being stove. This handicapped them somewhat. Anson was a capable boatman, but haphazard in organisation, and Ortho found he had to oversee the landings as well as lead the pack-train. Despite his efforts, there were hitches and bungles here and there; the cogs of the machinery did not mate as smoothly as they had done under the cock sparrow. Nevertheless, they got the cargoes through somehow, and there was not much to fear in the way of outside interruptions; the dragoons seemed to have settled to almost domestic felicity in Penzance, and the revenue cutter had holed her garboard strake taking a shortcut round the Manacles, and was docked at Falmouth. Ortho got so confident that he actually brought his horses home in plain daylight.

Then on the fourteenth of February, when all seemed so secure, the roof fell in.

Mr William Carmichael was the person who pulled the props away. Mr William Carmichael, despite his name, was an Irishman, seventeen years of age, and, as a newly-joined cornet of dragoons drawing eight shillings a day, occupied a position slightly less elevated than an earthworm. However, he was very far from this opinion. Mr Carmichael, being young and innocent, yearned to let blood, and he wasn't in the least particular whose. Captain Hambro and his two somewhat elderly Lieutenants, on the other hand, were experienced warriors, and consequently the most pacific of creatures. Nothing but a direct order from a superior would induce them to draw the sword—except to poke the fire. Mr Carmichael's martial spirit was in a constant state of effervescence; he hungered and thirsted for gore—but without avail. Hambro positively refused to let him run out and chop anybody. The Captain was a kindly man; his cornet's agitation distressed him, and be persuaded one of the dimpled Miss Jagos to initiate his subordinate in the gentler game of love (the boy would come into some sort of Kerry baronetcy when his sire finally bowed down to *delirium tremens*, and it was worth her while). But Mr Carmichael was built of sterner stuff. He was proof against her woman's wiles. Line of attack! At 'em! The Lieutenants, Messrs. Pilkington and Jope, were also gentle souls. Pilkington was a devotee of chess, Jope of sea fishing. Both sought to engage the fire-eater in their particular pastimes. It was useless; he disdained such trivialities. Death! Glory!

But Hambro, whose battle record was unimpeachable, knew that in civil police work, such as he was supposed to be doing, there is precious little transient glory to be picked up and much adhesive mud. He knew that, with the whole population against him, he stood small chance of laying the smugglers by the heels, and if he did the county families, who were as deeply implicated as any, would never rest until they had got him broken. He sat tight.

This did not suit the martial Carmichael at all. He fumed and fretted, did sword exercise in the privacy of his bedroom till his arm ached, and then gushed his heart out in letters to his mother, which had the sole effect of eliciting bottles of soothing syrup by return, the poor lady thinking his blood must be out of order.

But his time was to come.

On the eighth of February Pilkington was called away to Axminster to the bedside of his mother (at least, that is what he called her), and Carmichael was given his troop to annoy. On the morning of the fourteenth Hambro left on three days' leave to shoot partridges at Tehidy, Jope and Carmichael only remaining. Jope blundered in at five o'clock on the same afternoon, sneezing fit to split himself. He had been off Low Lee after pollack, and had got soaked through and through. He growled about the weather, which his boatman said was working up for a blow, drank a pint of hot rum bumbo, and sneezed himself up to bed, giving strict orders that he was not to be roused on any account.

Carmichael was left all alone.

To him, at seven of the clock, came Mr Richard Curral, riding officer, a conscientious but blighted man.

He asked for Hambro, Pilkington, and Jope in turn, and groaned resignedly when he heard they were unavailable.

'Anything I can do for you?' Carmichael inquired.

Curral considered, tapping his rabbit teeth with his whip handle. Carmichael was terribly young, the merest babe.

'N-o, I don't think so, thank you, sir. No, never mind. Pity they're away, though . . . seems a chance,' he murmured, talking to himself. 'Lot of stuff been run that way of late . . . ought to be stopped by rights. . . . Pity!' he sighed.

'What's a pity? What are you talking about?' said Mr Carmichael, his ears pricking. 'Take that whip out of your mouth!'

Mr Curral withdrew the whip; he was used to being hectored by military officers.

'Er—oh, . . . er—the Monk's Cove men are going to make a run tonight.' Mr Carmichael sat upright. 'Are they, b' God! How d' you know?'

'An informer has just come in. Gives no name, of course, but says he's from St Gwithian parish. Looks like a farmer. Wants no reward.'

'Then what's his motive?'

Mr Curral shrugged his shoulders. 'Some petty jealousy, I presume—it usually is among these people. I've known a man give his brother away because he got bested over some crab pots. This fellow says he overheard them making their plans in the inn there—lay under the table pretending to be drunk. Says that tall Penhale is the ringleader. I've suspected as much for some time. Of course, it may only be a false scent after all, but the informer seems genuine. What are you doing, sir?'

Mr Carmichael had danced across the room, opened the door, and was howling for his servant. His chance had come.

'Doing! . . . Why, going to turn a troop out and skewer the lot of 'em, of course. What d' you think?' shouted that gentleman, returning. 'I'd turn out the squadron, only half the nags are streaming with strangles. Toss me that map there. Now, where is this Monk's Cove?'

Mr Curral's eyes opened wide. He was not used to this keenness on the part of the military. One horse coughing slightly would have been sufficient excuse for Hambro to refuse to move, leave alone half a squadron sick with strangles. It promised to be a dirty night too. He had expected to meet with a diplomatic but nevertheless definite refusal. It was merely his three-cornered conscience that had driven him round to the billet at all, yet here was an officer so impatient to be off that he was attempting the impossible feat of pulling on his boots and buckling on his sword at the same time. Curral's eyes opened wider and wider.

'Ahem! Er—do you mean . . . er . . . are you in earnest, sir?'

'Earnest!' The cornet snorted, his face radiant. 'Damn my blood, but I am in very proper earnest, Mr What's-your-name—as these dastardly scoundrels shall discover 'ere we're many hours older. Earnest, b' gob!'

'But Mr Jope, sir. . . . Hadn't you better consult Mr Jope? . . . He . . .'

'Mr Jope be dam . . . Mr Jope has given orders that he's not to be disturbed on any account—on any account, sir. *I* am in command here at the moment, and if you will have the civility to show me where this plaguy Monk's Cove hides itself instead of standing there sucking your whip, you will greatly assist me in forming my plan of action.'

Curral bent over the map and pointed with his finger.

'Here you are, sir; the merest gully.'

'Then I shall charge down the gully,' said Mr Carmichael with that quick grasp of a situation displayed by all great commanders. The riding officer coughed. 'Then you'll have to charge at a walk, sir, and in single file; there's only a rough pack-track. Further, the track is picketed at the head. As soon as you pass a gun will be fired, and when you reach the Cove there won't be a cat stirring.'

Carmichael, like all great commanders, had his alternative. 'Then I shall charge 'em from the flank. Can I get up speed down this slope?'

Curral nodded. 'Yes, sir. You can ride from top to bottom in a moment of time.'

'How d'you mean?'

'It is practically a precipice, sir.'

'Humph! And this flank?'

'The same, sir.'

Carmichael scratched his ear and for the first time took thought. 'Look'ee,' he said presently. 'If I stop the pack-track here and there are precipices on either side, how can they get their horses out? I've got 'em bottled.'

Curral shook his head. 'I said *practically* precipices, sir. Precipices to go *down*, but not to come *up*. As you yourself have probably observed, sir, a horse can scramble up anything, but he is a fool going down. A horse falling uphill doesn't fall far, but a horse falling down a slope like that rolls to the bottom. A horse . . .'

'Man,' snapped the cornet, 'don't talk to me about horses. My father keeps twenty. I know.'

Curral coughed. 'I beg your pardon, sir. The informer tells me there are a dozen places on either side by which these fellows can get their beasts to the level. Remember it is their own valley; they are at home there, while we are strangers and in the dark.'

'I wish you could get out of this habit of propounding the obvious,' said Carmichael. He dabbed his finger down on the map. 'Look. Supposing we wait for them out here across their line of march?'

'They'd scatter all over the moor, sir. We'd be lucky if we caught a couple on a thick night like this.'

Carmichael plumped down on a chair and savagely rubbed his head.

'Well, Mr Riding Officer, I presume that in the face of these insurmountable difficulties you propose to sit down and do nothing—as usual. Let these damned ruffians run their gin, flaunt the law, do exactly as they like! Now let me tell you I'm of a different kidney, I . . .'

'You will pardon me, sir,' said Curral quietly, 'but I haven't as yet been given the opportunity of proposing anything.'

'What's your plan then?'

'How many men can you mount, sir?'

'Forty with luck. I'll have to beat the taverns for 'em.'

'Very good, sir. Send a small detachment to stop the head of the track; not to be there before ten o'clock. The rest, under yourself, with me for guide, will ride to the top of the cliff which overhangs the village from the east, and there leave the horses. The informer tells me there is a sheep track leading down from there and they picket the top of it—an old man, with a gun to fire if he hears anything. That picket will have to be silenced.'

'Who's going to do that?' the cornet inquired.

'I've got a man of my own I think can do it. He was a great poacher before he got religion.'

'And then?'

'Then we'll creep, single file, down the sheep track, muster behind the pilchard sheds, and rush the landing. The goods should be ashore by then. I trust that meets with your approval, sir?'

The cornet nodded, sobered. 'It does. You seem to be something of a tactician, Mr . . . er . . . Curral.'

'I served foreign with Lord Mark Kerr's regiment of Horse Guards, sir,' said the riding officer, picking up his whip.

Carmichael's jaw dropped. 'Horse Guards! . . . Abroad! . . . One of *us!* Dash my guts, man, why didn't you say so before?'

'You didn't ask me, sir,' said Curral, and sucked his whip.

2.

Uncle Billy Clemo sat behind a rock at the top of the sheep path and wished to Heaven the signal would go up. A lantern run three times to the truck of the flagpole was the signal that the horses were away and the pickets could come in. Then he would be rewarded with two shillings and a drop of hot toddy at the Kiddlywink—and so to bed.

He concentrated his thoughts on the hot toddy, imagined it tickling bewitchingly against his palate, wafting delicious fumes up his nostrils, gripping him by the throat, trickling, drop by drop, through his chilled system, warm and comforting, trickling down to his very toes. He would be happy then. He had been on duty since seven-thirty; it was now after ten, and perishing cold. The wind had gone round suddenly to the north-east and was gaining violence every minute. Before dawn it would be blowing a full gale. Uncle Billy was profoundly thankful he was not a horse-leader. While Penhale and company were buffeting their way over the moors he would be in bed, praise God! full of toddy. In the meanwhile it was bitter cold. He shifted his position somewhat so as to get more under the lee of the rock, and peered downwards to see how they were getting on. He could not see much. The valley was a pit of darkness. A few points of light marked the position of the hamlet, window lights only. The fisherfolk knew their own place as rats know their holes, and made no unnecessary show of lanterns. A stranger would have imagined the hamlet slept; in reality it was humming like a hive.

A dim half-moon of foam marked the in-curve of the cove; seaward was blank darkness again. Uncle Billy, knowing what to look for and where to look, made out a slightly darker blur against the outer murk—the lugger riding to moorings, main and mizzen set. She was plunging a goodish bit, even down there under shelter of the cliffs. Uncle Billy reckoned the boat's crews must be earning their money pulling in against wind and ebb, and once more gave thanks he was not as other men.

The wind came whimpering over the high land, bending the gorse-plumes before it, rattling the dead brambles, rustling the grass. Something stirred among the brambles, something living. He picked up his old Brown Bess. A whiff of scent crossed his nostrils, pungent, clinging. He put the Bess down again. Fox. He was bitter cold, especially as to the feet. He was a widower, and his daughter-in-law kept him short in the matter of socks. He stood up—which was against orders—and stamped the turf till he got some warmth back in his toes, sat down again, and thought about the hot toddy. The lugger was still there lunging at her moorings. They were a plaguy time landing a few kegs! Jacky's George would have finished long before—these boys! Whew! It was cold up there!

The gale's voice was rising to a steady scream; it broke against Uncle Billy's rock as though it had been a wave. Shreds of dead bracken and grass whirled over head. The outer darkness, which was the sea, showed momentary winks of grey breakers. When the wind lulled for a second a deep, melancholy bay, like that of some huge beast growling for meat, came rolling in from the south-west—the surf on the Twelve Apostles.

There were stirrings and snappings in the brambles. That plaguy fox again, thought Uncle Billy—or else rabbits. His fingers were numb now. He put the Bess down beside him, blew on his hands, thrust them well down in his pockets, and snuggled back against the rock. The lugger would slip moorings soon whether she had unloaded or not, and then toddy, scalding his throat, trickling down to his . . .

Something heavy dropped on him from the top of the rock, knocking him sideways away from the gun, pinning him to the ground; hands, big and strong as brass, took him round the throat, drove cruel thumbs into his jugular, strangling him.

'Got him, Joe,' said a voice. 'Bring rope and gag quick!'

He got no hot toddy that night.

3 .

'That the lot?' the lugger captain bellowed.

'Ay,' answered his mate.

'Cast oft that shore boat, then, and let go forrard soon's she'm clear.'

'Ay, ay. Pull clear, you; look lively!'

The *Game Cock's* crew jerked their oars into the pins and dragged the gig out of harm's way.

The mooring buoy splashed overboard, the lugger, her mainsail backed, came round before the wind and was gone.

'Give way,' said Anson, 'the wind's getting up a fright.' He turned to Ortho. 'You'll have a trip tonight . . . rather you nor me.'

Ortho spat clear of the gunwale. 'Have to go, I reckon; the stuff's wanted, blast it! Has that boat ahead unloaded yet?'

'She haven't signalled,' the bowman answered.

'No matter, pull in,' said Anson. 'We haven't no more than the leavings here; we can land this lil' lot ourselves. Give way all.'

Four blades bit the water with a will, but the rowers had to bend their backs to wrench the gig in against the wind and tide. It was a quarter of an hour before they grounded her nose on the base of the slip.

'Drag her up a bit, boys,' said Anson. 'Hell! What's that?'

From among the dark huddle of houses came a woman's scream—two—three—and then pandemonium, shouts, oaths, crashes, horses stamping, the noise of people rushing and struggling, and above all a boy's voice hysterically shouting 'Fire! Curse you! Fire!'

'Christ!' said Ortho. 'The Riders! Hey, push her off, for God's sake, push!'

The two bowmen standing in the water put their backs to the boat and hove; Ortho and Anson in the stem used their oars polewise.

'All together, he-ave!'

Slowly the gig began to make sternway.

'Heave!'

The gig made another foot. Feet clattered on the sliphead, and a voice cried: 'Here's a boat escaping! Halt, or I fire!'

'He-ave!' Ortho yelled. The gig made another foot and was afloat. There was a spurt of fire from the slip, and a bullet went droning overhead. The bowmen turned and dodged for safety among the rocks.

'Back water, back!' Anson exhorted.

There were more shouts from the shore, the boy's voice crowing shrill as a cockerel, a quick succession of flashes, and more bullets went wailing by. The pair in the boat dragged at their oars, teeth locked, terrified.

Wind and tide swept them up, darkness engulfed them. In a couple of minutes the shots ceased and they knew they were invisible. They lay on their oars panting.

'What now?' said Ortho. 'Go after the lugger? We can't go back.'

'Lugger's miles away, going like a stag,' said Anson. 'Best chance it across the bay to Porthleven.'

'Porthleven?'

'Where else? Wind's dead nor'-east. Lucky if we make that. Throw this stuff out; she's riding deep as a log.'

They lightened the gig of its entire load and stepped the mast. Anson was at the halyards hoisting the close-reefed mainsail. Ortho kept at the tiller until there was a spit of riven air across his cheek, and down came the sail on the run.

He called out, 'What's the matter?'

There was no answer for a minute, and then Anson said calmly from under the sail: 'Shot, I b'lieve.'

'What is? Halyards?'

'Me, b'lieve.'

'You! Shot! What d' you mean? Where?'

'In chest. Stray shot, I reckon; they can't hit nawthing when they aim. Thee'll have to take her thyself now. . . . O-ooh! . . .' He made a sudden surprised exclamation as if the pain had only just dawned on him and began to cough.

'Hoist sail . . . thou . . . fool. . . . A-ah!'

Ortho sprang forward and hoisted the sail. The gig leaped seawards. The coughing began again, mingled with groans. They stabbed Ortho to the heart. Instead of running away they should be putting back; it was a doctor they wanted. He would put back at once and get Anson attended to. That he himself would be arrested as the ringleader, tried, and either hung or transported did not occur to him. Half his happy boyhood had been spent with Anson. The one thing was to ease his agony.

'Going to put back,' he yelled to the prostrate man under the bow-thwart. 'Put back!'

'You can't,' came the reply . . . and more coughing.

Of course he couldn't. If he had thought for a moment he would have known it. Wind and tide would not let him put back. There was nothing for it but the twelve-mile thrash across the open bay to Porthleven. He prayed there might be a doctor there.

He luffed, sheeted home, rounded the great mass of Black Carn, braced as sharp as he dared, and met a thunderclap of wind and sea. It might have been waiting for him round the corner so surely did it pounce. It launched itself at him roaring, a ridge of crumbling white high overhead, a hill of water toppling over.

The loom and bellow of it stunned his senses, but habit is a strong master. His mind went blank, but his hand acted, automatically jamming the helm hard over. The gig had good way on; she spun as a horse spins on its hocks, and met the monster just in time. Stood on her stern, rose, see-sawed on the crest, three-quarters of her keel bare, white tatters flying over her, walloped down into the trough as though on a direct dive to the bottom, recovered, and rose to meet the next. The wild soar of the bows sent Anson slithering aft. Ortho heard him coughing under the stroke-thwart.

'She'll never do it,' he managed to articulate. 'Veer an' let . . . let . . . her drive.'

'Where for?' Ortho shouted. 'Where for? D' you hear me?'

'Scilly,' came the answer, broken by dreadful liquid chokings.

The waves broke with less violence for a minute or two, and Ortho managed to get the *Game Cock* away before the wind, though she took a couple of heavy dollops going about.

Scilly! A handful of rocks thirty miles away in the open Atlantic, pitch dark, no stars, no compass, the Runnelstone to pass, then the Wolf! At the pace they were going they would be on the islands long before dawn, and then it would be a case of exactly hitting either Crow Sound or St Mary's Sound or being smashed to splinters. Still, it was the only chance. He would hug the coast as near as he dared till past the Runnelstone — if he ever passed the Runnelstone — and then steer by the wind. It was all there was to steer by.

It was dead north-east at present, but if it shifted, where would he be then? It did not bear thinking on, and he put it from his mind. He must get past the Runnelstone first; after that . . .

He screwed up every nerve as tight as it would go, forced his senses to their acutest, set his teeth, swore to drive the boat to Scilly; but he had no hope of getting there, no hope at all.

The *Game Cock*, under the rag of canvas, ran like a hunted thing. It was as though all the crazy elements were pouring south-west, out to the open sea, and she went with them, a chip swept headlong in a torrent of clamorous wind and waters. On his right Ortho could just discern the loom of the coast. Breaker-stops broke hissing, astern, abeam, ahead. Spindrift blew in flat clouds, stinging like hail. Flurries of snow fell from time to time.

He was wet through, had lost all feeling in his feet, while his hands on the sheet and tiller were so numbed he doubted if he could loosen them.

On and on they drove into the blind turmoil. Anson lay in the water at the bottom, groaning and choking at every pitch.

Chapter XVII

THE MONK'S COVE raid was not an unmixed success. The bag was very slight, and the ringleader got clear away. Mr Carmichael's impetuosity was responsible for this. The riding officer was annoyed with him; he wished he would go home to Ireland and get drowned in a bog. Had any other officer been in charge of the soldiers they would have made a fine coup. At the same time, he reflected that had anyone else commanded the soldiers would not have been there at all. There were two sides to it. He consoled himself with the thought that, although the material results were small, the moral of the Monk's Cove free traders had suffered a severe jolt. At any rate, he hoped so. At the outset things had promised well. It was true that the cornet had only mustered thirty-one sabres instead of forty (and two of these managed to drop out between Penzance and Paul), but they had reached the clifftop not more than fifty minutes behind schedule, to find the picket trussed up like a boiled chicken and all clear.

Carmichael led the way down the sheep path—he insisted on it. 'An officer's place is at the head of his men,' he chanted. The sentiment is laudable, but he led altogether too fast. Seventeen, and carrying nothing but his sword, he gambolled down the craggy path with the agility of a chamois. His troopers, mainly elderly heroes, full of beer (they had been dragged, blaspheming, out of taverns just as they were settling down to a comfortable evening), and burdened with accoutrements, followed with all the caution due to their years and condition. The result was that Carmichael arrived at the base alone.

He crouched behind the corner of the pilchard shed and listened. The place was alive. It was inky dark; he could see nothing, but he could hear well enough.

'He-ave a! Up she goes! Stan' still, my beauty! Fast on that side, Jan? Lead on, you.'

'Bessie Kate, Bessie Kate, bring a hank o' rope; this pack's slippin'!'

'Whoa, mare, blast 'e! Come along wid that there lot, Zacky. Want to be here all night, do 'e?'

'Next horse! Pass the word for more horses. . . . Ahoy there! . . . Horses!'

Grunts of men struggling with heavy objects, subdued exhortations, complaints, oaths, laughter, women's chatter, hoofbeats, the shrill ki-yi of a trampled dog. The darkness ahead was boiling with invisible people, smugglers all, and engaged on their unlawful occupations.

Carmichael's hackles stood on end. He gripped his sword.

'Is that all?' a voice called, louder, more authoritative than the rest. 'Get them horses away then.'

The voice was referring to the boatload, but the cornet thought the whole run was through. In a minute the last horse would be off and he would lose the capture. Without looking to see how many of his men had collected behind him, he shouted 'Huzza!' and plunged into the thick of it. Death! Glory!

He plunged head first into Uncle Billy Clemo's daughter-in-law, butting her over backwards. She clutched out to save herself, clutched him round the neck, and took him with her. She lay on the ground, still grasping the cornet to her, and screamed her loudest. Mr Carmichael struggled frantically. Here was a pretty situation for a great military genius at the onset of his first battle! The women had the hug of a she bear, but his fury gave him the strength of ten. He broke her grip and plunged on, yelling to his men to fire. The only two who were present obeyed, but as he had neglected to tell them what to fire at, they very prudently fired into the air.

The cornet plunged on, plunged into somebody, shouted to the somebody to stop or be hewn limb from limb. The somebody fled, pursued by Carmichael, turned at bay opposite a lighted window, and he saw it was a woman. Another woman! Death and damnation! Were there nothing but damnation women in this damnation maze!

He spun about and galloped back, crashed into something solid—a man at last!—launched out at him. His sword met steel, a sturdy wrist-snapping counter, and flipped out his hand.

'S'render!' boomed the voice of his own servant. 'Stand, or I'll carve your heart out, you . . . oh, begging your pardon, sir, I'm sure!'

Carmichael cursed him, picked up his sword again, and rushed on. By the sound of their feet and breathing he knew there were people, scores of them, scurrying hither and thither about him in the blank darkness, but though he challenged and clutched and smote with the flat of his sword he met with nothing—nothing but thin air. It was like playing blind man's buff with ghosts. He heard two or three ragged volleys in the direction of the sea and galloped towards it, galloped into a cul-de-sac between two cottages, nearly splitting his head against a wall. He was three minutes fumbling his way out of that, blubbering with rage, but this time he came out on to the seafront.

Gunflashes on the sliphead showed him where his men were—firing at a boat or something—and he ran towards them cheering, tripped across a spar, and fell headlong over the cliff. It was only a miniature cliff, a bank of earth merely, not fifteen feet high, with mixed sand and boulders beneath.

The cornet landed wallop on the sand and lay there for some minutes thinking he was dead and wondering what style of monument (if any) his parents would erect to his memory: *"Hic jacet William Shine Carmichael, Cornet of His Majesty's Dragoons, killed while gallantly leading an attack on smugglers. Militavi non sine gloria. Aged 17."* Aged only seventeen! How sad! He shed a tear to think how young he was when he died, and then slowly came to the conclusion that perhaps he wasn't quite dead—only stunned—only half-stunned—hardly stunned at all.

A stray shot went wailing eerily out to sea. His men were in action; he must go to them. He tried to get up, but found his left leg was jammed between two boulders, and tug as he might he could not dislodge it. He shouted for help. Nobody took any notice. Again and again he shouted. No response. He laid his curly head down on the wet sand and with his tears wetted it still further. When at length (a couple of hours later) he was liberated it was by two of the smuggler ladies. They were most sympathetic, bandaged his sprained ankle, gave him a hot drink to revive his circulation, and vowed it was a shame to send pretty boys of his age out so late.

Poor Mr Carmichael!

Eli and Bohenna were the first to load, and consequently led the pack-train, which was strung out for a quarter of a mile up the valley waiting for Ortho. When they heard the shots go off in the Cove they remembered King Nick's standing orders, and scattered helter-skelter up the western slope. There were only three side tracks, and thirty-two horses to be got up. This caused jamming and delay.

The sergeant at the track-head heard the volleys as well, and, not having the least regard for Mr Carmichael's commandments, pushed on to see the fun. Fortunately, for the leaders, the chaotic state of the track prevented him from pushing fast. As it was, he very nearly blundered into the tail end of the train. A mule had jibbed and stuck in the bushes, refusing to move either way. Eli and two young Hernes tugged, pushed, and whacked at it. Suddenly, close beside, they heard the wild slither of iron on stone, a splash, and the voice of a man calling on Heaven to condemn various portions of his anatomy. It was the sergeant; his horse had slipped up, depositing him in a puddle. He remounted and floundered on with his squad, little knowing that in the bushes that actually brushed his knee was standing a loaded mule with three tense boys clinging to its ears, nose, and tail, to keep it quiet. It was a close call.

Eli took charge of the pack-train. He was terribly anxious about Ortho, but hanging about and letting the train be taken would only make bad worse, and Ortho had an uncanny knack of slipping out of trouble. He felt sure that if anybody was arrested it would not be his brother.

King Nick had thought of everything. In case of a raid by mounted men who could pursue, it would be folly to go on to St Just. They were to hide their goods at some pre-ordained spot, hasten home, and lie doggo.

The pre-ordained spot was the "Fogou," an ancient British dwelling hidden in a tangle of bracken a mile to the north-west, a subterranean passage roofed with massive slabs of granite, lined with moss and dripping with damp, the haunt of badgers, foxes, and bats. By midnight Eli had his cargo stowed away in that dark receptacle thoughtfully provided by the rude architects of the Stone Age, and by one o'clock he was at home in bed, prepared to prove he had never left it. But he did not sleep, tired as he was. Two horses had not materialised, and where was Ortho? If he had escaped he should have been home by now . . . long ago. The gale made a terrific noise, moaning and buffeting round the house; it must be awful at sea.

Where was Ortho?

Eli might just as well have taken his goods through to St Just for all the dragoons cared. Had the French landed that night, they would have made no protest. They would have drunk their very good healths.

When the sergeant and his detachment, the snow at their backs, finally stumbled into Monk's Cove, it was very far from a scene of battle and carnage that met their gaze. Homely would better describe it. The cottages were lit up, and in them lounged the troopers attended by the genial fisherfolk in artistic *déshabillé*, in the clothes in which they, at that moment, had arisen from bed (so they declared). The warriors toasted their spurs at the hearths and drank to everybody's everlasting prosperity.

The sergeant made inquiries. What luck?

None to speak of. Four-fifths of the train was up the valley when they broke in, and got away easily. That little whelp Carmichael had queered the show, charging and yapping. Where was he now? Oh, lying bleating under the cliff somewhere. Pshaw! Let him lie a bit and learn wisdom, plaguy little louse! Have a drink, God bless us!

They caught nothing, then?

Why, yes, certainly they had. Four prisoners and two horses. Two of the prisoners had since escaped; but no matter, the horses hadn't, and they carried the right old stuff—gin and brandy. That was what they were drinking now. Mixed, it was a lotion fit to purge the gullet of the Great Mogul. Have a drink, Lord love you!

The sergeant was agreeable.

It was not before dawn that these stalwarts would consent to be mustered. They clattered back to Penzance in high fettle, joking and singing. Some of the younger heads (recruits only) were beginning to ache, but the general verdict was that it had been a very pleasant outing.

Mr Carmichael rode at their head. His fettle was not high. His ankle was most painful, and so were his thoughts. Fancy being rescued by a pair of damnation girls! Moreover, two or three horses were going lame. What would Jope say to him when he returned — and Hambro? Brrh! Soldiering wasn't all it was cracked up to be.

Mr Curral rode at the tail of the column. He, too, was a dejected man. That silly little fool of a Carmichael had bungled the haul of the year; but he didn't expect the Collector would believe it; he was sure to get the blame. He and his poacher had captured two horses, to have them taken from them by the troopers, the tubs broached, and the horses let go. Dragoons! They had known what discipline was in the Horse Guards! It was too late to go to Bosula or the gypsy camp now; all tracks would have been covered up — no evidence. The prisoners had by this time dwindled to a solitary youth whom Curral suspected of being a halfwit, and who would most assuredly be acquitted by a Cornish jury. He sighed and sucked the head of his whip. It was a hard life.

* * *

Phineas Eva, parish clerk of St Gwithian, came to call on Teresa one afternoon shortly after the catastrophe. He was dressed in his best, which was not very good, but signified that it was a visit of importance.

He twittered some platitudes about the weather, local and foreign affairs — the American colonists were on the point of armed rebellion, he was creditably informed — tut, tut! But meeting with no encouragement from his hostess, be dwindled into silence and sat perched on the edge of the settle, blinking his pale eyes and twitching his hat in his rheumatic claws. Teresa seemed unaware of his presence. She crouched motionless in her chair, chin propped on knuckles, a sombre, brooding figure.

Phineas noted that her cheeks and eyelids were swollen, her raven hair hanging in untidy coils, and feared she had been roistering again.

If so, she would be in an evil mood. She was a big strong woman, he a small weak man. He trembled for his skin. Still, he must out with it somehow, come what might. There was his wife to face at the other end, and he was no less terrified of his wife. He must out with it. Of the two it is better to propitiate the devil you live with than the devil you don't. He hummed and hawed, squirmed on his perch, and then with a gulp and a splutter came out with it.

His daughter Tamsin was in trouble, and Ortho was the cause. He had to repeat himself twice before Teresa would take any notice, and then all she did was to nod her head.

Phineas took courage; she had neither sworn nor pounced at him. He spoke his piece. Of course. Ortho would do the right thing by Tamsin. She was a good girl, a very good girl, docile and domestic, would make him an excellent wife. Ortho was under a cloud at present, but that would blow over. King Nick had powerful influence and stood by his own. Parson Coverdale of St Just was always friendly to the free traders; he would marry them without question. He understood Ortho was in hiding among the St Just tinners; it would be most convenient. He . . . Teresa shook her head slowly.

Not at St Just? Then he had been blown over to Scilly after all. Oh well, as soon as he could get back Parson Coverdale would. . . . Again Teresa shook her head.

Not at Scilly! Then where was he? Up country?

Teresa rose out of her chair and looked Phineas full in the face, stood over him, hair hanging loose, puffy, obese, yet withal majestic, tragic beyond words. Something in her swollen eyes made him quail, but not for his own skin, not for himself.

'A Fowey Newfoundlander put into Newlyn Pool 's morning,' she said, and her voice had a husky burr. 'Ten leagues sou'-west of the Bishop they found the *Game Cock* of Monk's Cove—bottom up.'

Phineas gripped the edge of the settle and sagged forward. 'Then! . . .'

'Yes,' said Teresa, 'drowned. Go home and tell that to your daughter. An' tell her she 've got next to her heart the only lil' livin' spark of my lovely boy that 's left in this world. She 'm luckier nor I.'

Chapter XVIII

BUT ORTHO was not drowned. Dawn found the *Game Cock* still afloat, still scudding like a mad thing in the run of the seas. There was no definite dawn, no visible uprising of the sun; black night slowly changed into leaden day, that was all.

Ortho looked around him. There was nothing to be seen but a toss of waters, breakers rushing foam-lipped before, beside him, roaring in his wake. The boat might have been a hind racing among a pack of wild hounds intent on overwhelming her and dragging her under. There was nothing in sight. He had missed the Scillies altogether, as he had long suspected.

After passing the Runnelstone he had kept his eyes skinned for the coal-fire beacon on St Agnes (the sole light on the islands), but not a flicker of it had he seen. He must have passed the wrong side of the Wolf and have missed the mark by miles and miles. As far as he could get his direction by dawn, the wind had gone back, and he was running due south now. South—whither? He did not know, and cared little.

Anson was dead, sitting up, wedged in the angle of the bows. He had died about an hour before dawn, Ortho thought, after a dreadful paroxysm of choking. Ortho had cried out to him, but got no answer beyond a long-drawn sigh, a sigh of relief, the sigh of a man whose troubles are over. Anson was dead, leaving a widow and three young children. His old friend was dead, had died in agony, shot through the lungs, and left to choke his life out in an open boat in midwinter. Hatred surged through Ortho, hatred for the Preventive. If he ever got ashore again he'd search out the man that fired that shot and serve him likewise, and while he was choking he'd sit beside him and tell him about Anson in the open boat. As a matter of fact, the man who fired the shot was a recruit who let off his piece through sheer nerves and congratulated himself on having hit nobody. But Ortho did not know that.

All they had been trying to do was to make a little money—and then to come shooting and murdering people! . . . Smuggling was against the law, granted; but there should have been some sort of warning. For two winters they had been running cargoes, and not a soul seemed to care a fig. Then, all of a sudden, crash! The crash had come so suddenly that Ortho wondered for a fuddled moment if it had come, if this were not some ghastly nightmare and presently he would wake up and find himself in bed at Bosula and all well. A cold dollop of spray hit him in the middle of the back, drenching him; and there was Anson sitting up in the bows, the whole front of his smock deluged in blood, blood mingled with seawater washed about on the bottom of the boat. It was no dream. He didn't care where he was going or what happened. He was soaked to the skin, famished, numb body and soul, and utterly without hope, but mechanically he kept the boat scudding.

The clouds were down very low and heavy-bellied. One or two snow-squalls swept over. Towards noon a few pale shafts of sunshine penetrated the cloud-wrack, casting patches of silver on the dreary waters. They brought no warmth, but the very sight of them put a little heart into the castaway. He fumbled in the locker under his seat and found a few scraps of stinking fish intended for bait. These he ate, bones and all, and afterwards baled the boat out, hauled his sheet a trifle, and put his helm to starboard, with a hazy idea of hitting off the French coast somewhere about Brest, but the gig promptly shipped a sea so he had to let her away and bale again.

Anson was getting on his nerves. The dead man's jaw lolled in an idiotic grin, and his eyes were turned up so that they were fixed directly on Ortho. Every time he looked up there were the eyes on him. It was more than he could stand. He left the tiller with the intention of turning Anson over on his face, but the gig showed a tendency to gybe, and he had to spring back again. When he looked up the grin seemed more pronounced than ever.

'Grizzling because you're out of it and I ain't, eh?' he shouted, and was immediately ashamed of himself. He tried not to look at Anson, but there was a horrid magnetism about those eyes.

'I shall go light-headed soon,' he said to himself, and rummaging afresh in the locker found a couple of decayed sand eels and ate them.

The afternoon wore on. It would be sunset soon and then night again. He wondered where next morning would see him, if it would see him at all. He thought not.

'Can't go on for ever,' he muttered; 'must sleep soon. Then I'll be drowned or froze.' He didn't care. His sodden clothes would take him straight down, and he was too tired to fight. It would be all over in a minute, finished and done with. At home, at the Owls' House now, Wany would be bringing the cows in. Bohenna would be coming down the hill from work, driving the plough oxen before him. There would be a grand fire on the hearth and the black pot bubbling. He could see Martha fussing about like an old hen, getting supper ready, bent double with rheumatism—and Eli, Eli! . . . He wondered if the owls would hoot for him as they had for his father.

He didn't know why he'd kept the boat going; it was only prolonging the misery. Might as well let her broach and have done with it. Over with her—now! But his hand remained steadfast and the boat raced on.

The west was barred with a yellow strip—sunset. Presently it would be night, and under cover of night Fate was waiting for him, crouched like a footpad.

* * *

He did not see the vessel's approach till she was upon him. She must have been in sight for some time, but he had been keeping his eyes ahead and did not look round till she hailed.

She was right on him, coming up hand over fist. Ortho was so surprised he nearly jumped out of his clothes. He stood up in the sternsheets goggling at her foolishly. Was it a mirage? Had he gone light-headed already? He heard the creak of her yards and blocks as she yawed to starboard, the hiss of her cut-water shearing into a sea, and then a guttural voice shouting unintelligibly. She was real enough, and she was yawing to pick him up! A flood of joy went through him. He was going to live after all! Not for nothing had he kept the *Game Cock* running. She was on top of him. The short bowsprit and gilded beak stabbed past; then came shouts, the roar of sundered water, a rope hurtling out of reach, a thump, and over went the *Game Cock*, run down. Ortho gripped the gunnel, vaulted on to the boat side as it rolled under, and jumped.

The vessel was wallowing deep in a trough at the time. He caught the foremast chains with both hands and hung, trailing up to the knees in bubbling brine. Something bumped his knee. It was Anson. His leer seemed more pronounced than ever; then he went out of sight. Men in the channels gripped Ortho's wrists and hoisted him clear. He lay where they threw him, panting and shivering, water dribbling from his clothes to the deck.

Aft on the poop a couple of men, officers evidently, were staring at the *Game Cock* drifting astern, bottom up. They did not consider her worth the trouble of going after. A deckhand gave Ortho a kick with his bare foot, handed him a bowl of hot gruel and a crust of bread. Ortho gulped these and then dragged himself to his feet, leaned against the main bitts, and took stock of his surroundings.

It was quite a small vessel, rigged in a bastard fashion he had never seen before, square on the mainmast, exaggerated lugs on the fore and mizzen. She had low, sharp entry, but was built up aft with quarter-deck and poop; she was armed like a frigate, and swarming with men.

Ortho could not think where she housed them all. And such men! Brown, yellow, white and black, with and without beards. Some wore pointed red caps, some wisps of dirty linen wound about their scalps, and others were bareheaded and shorn to the skin but for a lock of oily hair. They wore loose garments of many colours—chocolate, saffron, salmon, and blue—but the majority were of a soiled white. They drew these close about their lean bodies and squatted, bare toes protruding, under the break of the quarter-deck, in the lee of scuttlebutts, boats, masts—anywhere out of the wind. They paid no attention to him whatever, but chatted and spat and laughed, their teeth gleaming white in their dark faces. One of them produced a crude two-stringed guitar and sang a melancholy dirge to the accompaniment of creaking blocks and hissing bow wave. The sunset was but a chink of yellow light between leaden cloud and leaden sea.

There was a flash away in the dusk to port, followed by the slam of a gun.

A gigantic old man came to the quarter-deck rail and bellowed across the decks. Ortho thought he looked like the pictures of Biblical patriarchs—Moses, for instance—with his long white beard and mantle blowing in the wind.

At his first roar every black and brown man on deck pulled his hood up and went down on his forehead, jabbering incoherently. They seemed to be making some sort of prayer towards the East. The old man's declamation finished off in a long-drawn wail; he returned whence he came, and the men sat up again. The guitar player picked up his instrument and sang on.

A boy, twirling a flaming piece of tow, ran up the ladders and lit the two poop lanterns.

Away to port other points of light twinkled, appearing and disappearing.

The deckhand who had given him the broth touched him on the shoulder; signed to him to follow, and led the way below. It was dark on the main-deck; all the light there was came from a single lantern swinging from a beam. But Ortho could see that it was also packed with men. They lay on mats beside the hatch-coamings, between the lashed carriage-guns, everywhere; it was difficult to walk without treading on them. Some of them appeared to be wounded.

The deckhand unhooked the lantern, let fall a rope ladder into the hold, and pushed Ortho towards it. He descended a few feet and found himself standing on the cargo, bales of mixed merchandise apparently. In the darkness around him he could hear voices conversing, calling out. The man dropped after him, and Ortho saw that the hold was full of people, Europeans from what he could see, lying on top of the cargo. They shouted to him, but he was too dazed to answer. His guide propelled him towards the after bulkhead and suddenly tripped him. He fell on his back on a bale and lay still while the deckhand shackled his feet together, picked up the lantern, and was gone.

'Englishman?' said a voice beside him.

'Ay.'

'Where did you drop from?'

'Picked up—I was blown offshore.'

'Alone?'

'Yes, all but my mate and he's dead. What craft is this?'

'The *Ghezala*, xebec of Salé.'

'Where are we bound for?'

'Salé, on the coast of Barbary, of course; to be sold as a slave among the heathen infidels. Where did you think you was bound for? Fortunate Isles with rings on your fingers to splice a golden queen—eh?'

'Barbary—infidels—slave.' Ortho repeated stupidly—no wonder Anson had leered as he went down.

He turned, sighing, over on his face. 'Slaves—infidels—Barb . . .' and was asleep.

Chapter XIX

HE WOKE up eighteen hours later, at about noon—or so his neighbour told him; it was impossible to distinguish night from day down there. The hold was shallow and three parts full; this brought them within a few feet of the deck beams and made the atmosphere so thick it was difficult to breathe, congested as they were. Added to which the rats and cockroaches were very active and the stale bilge water, washing to and fro under the floor, reeked abominably.

The other prisoners were not talkative. Now and again one would shout across to a friend and a short conversation would ensue, but most of the time they kept silence, as though steeped in melancholy. The majority sounded like foreigners.

Ortho sat up, tried to stretch his legs and found they were shackled to a chain running fore and aft over the cargo.

His left-hand neighbour spoke. 'Woke up, have you? Well, how d'you fancy it?'

Ortho grunted.

'Oh well, mayn't be so bad. You'm a likely lad, you'll fetch a good price, mayhap, and get a good master. 'Tain't the strong mule catches the whip, 'tis the old 'uns—y'understan'? Tomorrow's the best day for hard work over there and the climate's prime; better nor England by a long hawse and that's the Gospel truth, y'understan'?'

'How do you know?' Ortho enquired.

The man snorted. 'Know? Ain't I been there nine year?'

'In Salé?'

'No—Algiers . . . but it's the same, see what I mean? Nine years a slave with old Abd-el-Hamri in Sidi Okbar Street. Only exchanged last summer, and now, dang my tripes, if I ain't took again!'

'Where did they catch you?'

'Off Prawle Point on Tuesday in the *Harvest*, yawl of Brixham—I'm a Brixham man, y'understan'? Puddicombe by name. I did swore and vow once I was ashore I would never set foot afloat no more. Then my sister Johanna's George took sick with a flux and I went in his place just for a day—and now here we are again—hey, hey!'

'Who are all these foreigners?' asked Ortho.

'Hollanders, took off a Dutch East Indiaman. This be her freight we'm lyin' on now; see what I mean? They got it split up between the three on 'em. There's three on 'em, y'understan', was four, but the Hollander sank one before she was carried, so they say, and tore up t'other two cruel. The old *reis*—admiral that is—he's lost his mainmast. You can hear he banging away at night to keep his consorts close; scared, y'understan'? Howsombeit, they done well enough. Only been out two months and they've got the cream of an Indies freight, not to speak of three or four coasters and a couple of hundred poor sailors that should fetch from thirty to fifty ducats apiece in the *soko*. And then there's the ransoms too, see what I mean?'

'Ransoms?' Ortho echoed. Was that a way home? Was it possible to be ransomed? He had money.

'Ay, ransoms,' said Puddicombe. 'You can thank your God on bended knees, young man, you ain't nothin' but a poor fisher lad with no money at your back, see what I mean?'

'No, I don't—why?'

'Why—'cos the more they tortured you the more you'd squeal and the more your family would pay to get you out of it, y'understan'? There was a dozen fat Mynheer merchants took on that Indiaman, and if they poor souls knew what they're going through they'd take the first chance overboard—sharks is a sweet death to what these heathen serve you. I've seen some of it in Algiers city—see what I mean? Understan'?'

Ortho did not answer. He had suddenly realised that he had never told Eli where the money was hidden—over seven hundred pounds—and how was he ever going to tell him now? He lay back on the bales and abandoned himself to unprofitable regrets.

Mr Puddicombe, getting no response to his chatter, cracked his finger joints, his method of wiling away the time. The afternoon wore on, wore out. At sundown they were given a pittance of dry bread and stale water. Later on a man came down, knocked Ortho's shackles off and signed him to follow.

'You're to be questioned,' the ex-slave whispered. 'Be careful now, y'understan'.'

The Moors were at their evening meal, squatting, tight-packed round big pots, dipping for morsels with their bare hands, gobbling and gabbling. The galley was between decks, a brick structure built athwart-ship. As Ortho passed he caught a glimpse of the interior. It was a blaze of light from the fires, before which a couple of crewmen toiled, stripped to the waist, stirring at steaming cauldrons; the sweat glistened like varnish on their muscular bodies.

His guide led him to the upper deck. The night breeze blew in his face, deliciously chill after the foul air below. He filled his lungs with draughts of it. On the port quarter tossed a galaxy of twinkling lights—the Admiral and the third ship. Below in their rat-run holds were scores of people in no better plight than himself, Ortho reflected; in some cases worse, for many of the Dutchmen were wounded. A merry world!

His guide ran up the quarter-deck ladder. The officer of the watch, a dark silhouette lounging against a swivel mounting on the poop, snapped out a challenge in Arabic to which the guide replied. He opened the door of the poop cabin and thrust Ortho within.

It was a small place, with the exception of a couple of brass-bound chests, a table, and a chair, quite unfurnished, but it was luxurious after a fashion and, compared with the squalor of the hold, paradise.

Mattresses were laid on the floor all round the walls and on these were heaped a profusion of cushions, cushions of soft leather and of green and crimson velvet. The walls were draped with hangings worked with the same colours and a lamp of fretted brasswork, with six burners, hung by chains from the ceiling. The gigantic Moor, who had called the crew to prayers, sat on the cushions in a corner, his feet drawn up under him, a pyramid of snowy draperies. He was running a chain of beads through his fingers, his lips moved in silence. More than ever did he look like a Bible patriarch. On the port side a tall Berber lay outstretched, his face to the wall; a watchkeeper taking his rest. At the table, his back to the ornamented rudder-casing, sat a stout little man with a cropped head, scarlet face and bright blue eyes. Ortho saw, to his surprise, that he did not wear Moorish dress but the heavy blue seacoat of an English sailor, a canary muffler and knee breeches.

The little man's unflinching bright eyes ran all over him.

'Cornishman?' he enquired in perfect English.

'Yes, sir.'

'Fisherman?' appraising the boy's canvas smock, apron, and boots.

'Yes, sir.'

'Blown offshore—eh?'

'Yes, sir.'

'Where from? Isles of Scilly?'

'No, sir, Monk's Cove.'

'Where's that?'

'Sou'-west corner of Mount's Bay, sir, near Penzance.'

'Penzance—ah, ha! Penzance!' the captain repeated. 'Now, what do I know of Penzance?' He screwed his eyes up, rubbed the back of his head, puzzling. 'Penzance!'

Then he banged his fist on the table. 'Damme, of course!'

He turned to Ortho again. 'Got any property in this cove—houses, boats or belike?'

'No, sir.'

'Father? . . . brothers? . . . relations?'

'Only a widowed mother, sir, and a brother.'

'They got any property?'

'No, sir.'

'What does your brother do?'

'Works on a farm, sir.'

'Hum, yes, thought as much; couple of nets and an old boat stopped up with tar—huh! Never mind, you're healthy; you'll sell.'

He said something in Arabic to the old Moor, who wagged his flowing beard and went on with his beads.

'You can go,' said the captain, motioning to the guide. Then as Ortho neared the door he called out: 'Avast a minute!' Ortho turned about.

'You say you come from near Penzance. Well, did you run athwart a person by the name of Gish by any chance? Captain Jeremiah Gish? He was a Penzance man. I remember. Made a mint o' money shipping "blackbirds" to the Plate River, and retired home to Penzance, or so I've heard. Gish is the name—Jerry Gish.'

Ortho gaped. Gish, Captain Jerry; he should think he did know him. He had been one of Teresa's most ardent suitors at one time, and still hung after her, admired her gift of vituperation; had been in the Star Inn that night he had robbed her of the hundred pounds. Captain Jerry! They were always meeting at races and suchlike; had made several disastrous bets with him. Old Jerry Gish! It sounded strange to hear that familiar name here among all these wild infidels, gave him an acute twinge of homesickness.

'Well?' said the corsair captain. 'Never heard of him, I suppose?'

Ortho recovered himself. 'Indeed, sir, I know him very well.'

The captain sat up. 'You do?' Then with a snap, 'how?'

It flashed on Ortho that he must be careful. To disclose the circumstances under which he had hobnobbed with Jerry Gish would be to give himself away.

'How?'

Ortho licked his lips. 'He used to come to Cove a lot, sir. Was friendly like with the innkeeper there. Was very gentlemanly with his money of an evening.'

The captain sank back, his suspicions lulled. He laughed.

'Free with the drink, mean you? Ay, I warrant old Jerry would be that. Ha, ha!' He sat smiling at recollections, drumming his short fingers on the table.

Some flying spray-beads rattled on the stern windows. The brass lamp swung back and fore, its shadow swimming with it up and down the floor. The watchkeeper muttered in his sleep. Outside the wind moaned. The captain looked up. 'Used to be a shipmate of mine,

Jerry—when we were boys. Many a game we've played. Did y' ever hear him tell a story?'

'Often, sir.'

'You did, you did? Spins a good yarn, Jerry—none better. Ever hear him tell of what we did to that old black woman in Port o' Spain. McBride's my name—Ben McBride. Ever hear it?'

'Yes, I believe I did, sir.'

'That's a good yarn that, eh? My Ged, she screeched! Ha, ha!' Tears trickled out of his eyes at the memory.

'Told you a good few yarns, I expect?'

'Yes, sir, many.'

'Remember 'em?'

'I think so, sir.'

'Do you? Hum—hurr!' He looked at Ortho again, seemed to be considering.

'Do you? Ah, hem! Yes, very good. Well, you must go now. Time to snug down. Ahmed!'

The guide stood to attention, received some instructions in Arabic, and led Ortho away. At the galley door he stopped, went inside, and came out bearing a lump of meat and a small cake, which he thrust on Ortho, and made motions to show that it was by the captain's orders.

Three minutes later he was shackled down again.

'How did you fare?' the Brixham man grunted drowsily.

'Not so bad,' said Ortho.

He waited till the other had gone to sleep, and then ate his cake and meat; he was ravenous and didn't want to share it.

* * *

Black day succeeded black night down in the hold, changing places imperceptibly. Once every twenty-four hours the prisoners were taken on deck for a few minutes. In the morning and evening they were fed. Nothing else served to break the stifling monotony. It seemed to Ortho that he had been chained up in blank gloom for untold years, gloom peopled with disembodied voices that became loquacious only in sleep. Courage gagged their waking hours, but when they slept, and no longer had control of themselves, they talked, muttered, groaned, and cried aloud for lost places and lost loves. At night that hold was an inferno, a dark cavern filled with damned souls wailing. Two Biscainers did actually fight once, but they didn't fight for long — hadn't spirit enough. It was over a few crumbs of bread that they fell out. The man on Ortho's right, an old German seaman, never uttered a word. One morning, when they came round with food, he didn't put his hand out for his portion, and they found that he was dead — a fact the rats had discovered some hours before. The only person who was not depressed was Mr Puddicombe, late of Brixham and Algiers. He had the advantage of knowing what he was called upon to face combined with a strong strain of natural philosophy.

England viewed from Algiers had seemed a green land of plenty, of perennial beer and skittles. When he got home he found he had to work harder than ever he had done in Africa and, after nine years of subtropics, the northern winter had bitten him to the bone. Provided he did not become a Government slave (which he thought unlikely, being too old) he was not sure but that all was for the best. He was a good tailor and carpenter and generally useful about the house, a valuable possession in short. He would be well treated. He would try to get a letter through to his old master, he said, and see if an exchange could be worked. He had been quite happy in Sidi Okbar Street. The notary had treated him more as a friend than a servant; they used to play "The King's Game" (a form of chess) together of an evening. He thought Abd-el-Hamri, being a notary, a man of means, could easily effect the exchange and then, once comfortably settled down to slavery in Algiers, nothing on earth should tempt him to take any more silly chances with freedom, he assured Ortho. He also gave him a lot of advice concerning his future conduct.

'I've taken a fancy to you, my lad,' he said one evening, 'an' I'm givin' you advice others would pay ducats and golden pistoles to get; y'understan'?'

Ortho was duly grateful.

'Are you a professed Catholic by any chance?'

'No, Protestant.'

'Well, if you was a Catholic professed I should tell you to hold by it for a bit and see if the Redemptionist Fathers could help you, but if you be a Protestant nobody won't do nothin' for you, so you'd best turn *Renegado*, and turn sharp—like I done; see what I mean.'

'*Renegado?*'

'Turn Moslem. Sing out night and mornin' that there's only one Allah and nobody like him. After that they got to treat you kinder. If you'm a *Kafir*—Christian, so to speak—they're doin' this here Allah a favour by peltin' stones at you. If you're a Mohammedan you're one of Allah's own and they got to love you; see what I mean? Mind you, there's drawbacks. You ain't supposed to touch liquor, but that needn't lie on your mind. God knows when the corsairs came home full to the hatches and business was brisk there was mighty few of us *Renegados* in Algiers city went sober to bed, y'understan'? Then there's Ramadan. That means you got to close-reef your belt from sunrise to sunset for thirty mortal days. If they catch you as much as sucking a lemon they'll beat your innards out. I don't say it can't be done, but don't let 'em catch you; see what I mean? Leaving aside his views on liquor and this here Ramadan I ain't got nothin' against the Prophet.

'When you get as old and clever as me you'll find that religions is much like clo'es, wear what the others is wearin' and you can do what you like. You take my advice, my son, and as soon as you land holla out that there's only one Allah and keep on hollaing; understan'?'

Ortho understood and determined to do likewise; essentially an opportunist, he would have cheerfully subscribed to devil worship had it been fashionable.

One morning they were taken on deck and kept there till noon. Puddicombe said the officers were in the hold valuing the cargo; they were nearing the journey's end.

It was clear weather, full of sunshine. Packs of chubby cloud trailed across a sky of pale azure. The three ships were in close company, line ahead, the lame flagship leading, her lateens wing and wing. The gingerbread work on her high stem was one glitter of gilt and her quarters were carved with stars and crescent moons interwoven with Arabic scrolls. The ship astern was no less fancifully embellished. All three were decked out as for holiday, flying long coachwhip pennants from trucks and lateen peaks and each had a big green banner at a jackstaff on the poop.

No land was in sight, but there were signs of it. A multitude of gulls swooped and cried among the rippling pennants; a bundle of cut bamboos drifted by and a broken basket.

McBride, a telescope under his arm, a fur cap cocked on the back of his head, strutted the poop. Presently he came down the upper deck and walked along the line of prisoners, inspecting them closely. He gave Ortho no sign of recognition, but later on sent for him.

'Did Jerry Gish ever tell you the yarn of how him and me shaved that old junk dealer in Derry and then got him pressed?'

'No, sir.'

McBride related the story and Ortho laughed with great heartiness.

'Good yarn, ain't it?' said the captain.

Ortho vowed it was the best he had ever heard.

'Of course, you knowing old Jerry would appreciate it—these others—' The captain made the gesture of one whose pearls of reminiscence have been cast before swine.

Ortho took his courage in both hands and told a story of how Captain Gish had got hold of a gypsy's bear, dressed it up in a skirt, cloak and bonnet and let it loose in the Quaker's meeting house in Penzance. As a matter of fact it was not the inimitable Jerry who had done it at all but a party of young squires; however, it served Ortho's purpose to credit the exploit to Captain Gish. Captain Gish, as Ortho remembered him, was a dull old gentleman with theories of his own on the lost tribes of Israel which he was never tired of disclosing, but the Jerry Gish that McBride remembered and delighted in was evidently a very different person—a spark, a blood, a devil of a fellow. Jeremiah must be maintained in the latter role at all costs. Ever since his visit to the cabin Ortho had been thinking of all boisterous jests he had ever heard and tailoring them to fit Jerry, against such a chance as this. His repertoire was now extensive.

171

The captain laughed most heartily at the episode of "good old Jerry" and the bear. Ortho knew how to tell a story, he had caught the trick from Pyramus. Encouraged, he was on the point of relating another when there came a long-drawn cry from aloft. The effect on the Arab crew was magical.

'Moghreb!' they cried, 'Moghreb!' and dropping whatever they had in hand raced for the main ratlines. Captain McBride, however, was before them. He kicked one mariner in the stomach, planted his fist in the face of another, whacked yet another over the knuckles with his telescope, hoisted himself to the fife rail and from that eminence distributed scalding admonitions to all and sundry. That done, he went hand over fist in a dignified manner up to the topgallant yard.

The prisoners were sent below, but to the 'tween decks this time instead of the hold.

Land was in sight, the Brixham man informed Ortho. They had hit the mark off very neatly, at a town called Mehdya, a few miles above Salé, he understood. If they could catch the tide they should be in by evening. The Admiral was lacing bonnets on. The gun ports being closed, they could not see how they were progressing, but the Arabs were in a high state of elation; cheer after cheer rang out from overhead as they picked up familiar landmarks along the coast. Even the wounded men dragged themselves to the upper deck. The afternoon drew on. Puddicombe was of the opinion that they would miss the tide and anchor outside, in which case they were in for another night's pitching and rolling. Ortho devoutly trusted not; what with the vermin and rats in that hold, he was nearly eaten alive. He was just beginning to give up hope when there came a sadden bark of orders from above, the scamper of bare feet, the chant of men hauling on braces, and the creak of yards as they came over.

'She's come up,' said he of Brixham. 'They're stowing the square sails and going in under lateens. Whoop, there she goes! Over the bar.'

Crash-oom! went a gun. *Crash-oom!* went a second, a third, and a fourth.

'They're firing at us!' said Ortho.

Puddicombe snorted. 'Ay, powder! That's rejoicings, that is. You don't know these Arabs. When the cow calves they fire a gun; that's their way o' laughing. Why, I've seen the corsairs come home to Algiers with all the forts blazin' like as if there was a bombardment on. You wait; we'll open up in a minute. Ah! There you are!'

Crash-oom! bellowed the flagship ahead. *Zang! Zang!* thundered their own bow-chasers. *Crash-oom!* roared the ship astern, and the forts on either hand replied with deafening volleys. *Crack-wang! Crack-wang!* sang the little swivels. *Pop-pop-pop!* snapped the muskets ashore; in the lull came the noise of far cheering and the throb of drums, and then the stunning explosions of the guns again.

'They've dowsed the mizzen,' said Puddicombe. 'Foresail next and let go. We'm most there, son. See what I mean?'

They were taken off at dusk in a ferry-float. The three ships were moored head and stem in a small river with walled towns on either hand—a town built upon red cliffs to the south, a town built upon a flat shore to the north. To the east lay marshes and low hills beyond, with the full moon rising over them.

The xebecs were surrounded by a mob of skiffs full of natives, all yelling and laughing and occasionally letting off a musket. One grossly overloaded boat, suddenly feeling its burden too great to bear, sank with all hands.

Its occupants did not mind in the least; they splashed about, bubbling with laughter, baled the craft out, and climbed in again. The ferry deposited its freight of captives on the spit to the north, where they were joined by the prisoners from the other ships, including some women taken on the Dutch Indiaman. They were then marched over the sand flats towards the town, and all the way the native women alternately shrieked for joy or cursed them. They lined the track up to the town, shapeless bundles of white drapery, and hurled sand and abuse. One old hag left her long nail-marks down Ortho's cheek, another lifted her veil for a second and sprayed him with spittle.

'*Kafir-b-Illah was rasool!*' they screamed at the hated Christians; then '*Zahrit! Zahrit! Zahrit!*' would go the shrill joy-cries.

Small boys with shorn heads and pigtails gambolled alongside, poking them with canes and egging their curs on to bite them, and in front of the procession a naked wild man of the mountains went leaping, shaking his long hair, whooping and banging a goatskin tambourine.

They passed under a big horseshoe arch and were within the walls. Ortho got an impression of huddled, flat houses gleaming white under the moon, of men and women in flowing white, donkeys, camels, children, naked blacks and renegade seamen jostling together in clamorous alleys; or muskets popping, tom-toms thumping, pipes squealing; of laughter, singing, and screams; while in his nostrils two predominant scents struggled for mastery—dung and orange blossom.

Chapter XX

ORTHO AND his fellow prisoners spent the next thirty-nine hours in one of the town *matamoras*, a dungeon eighteen feet deep, its sole outlet a trapdoor in the ceiling. It was damp and dark as a vault, littered with filth, and crawling with every type of intimate pest. The omniscient Puddicombe told Ortho that such was the permanent lodging of Government slaves; they toiled all day on public works and were herded home at night to this sort of thing.

More than ever was Ortho determined to forswear his religion at the first opportunity. He asked if there were any chances of escape from Morocco. Puddicombe replied that there were none. Every man's hand was against one; besides, Sidi Mahomet I had swept the last Portuguese garrison (Mazagan) off the coast six years previously, so where was one to run? He went on to describe some of the tortures inflicted on recaptured slaves, such as having limbs rotted off in quicklime, being hung on hooks and sawn in half, and counselled Ortho most strongly, should any plan of escape present itself, not to divulge it to a soul. Nobody could be trusted. The slave gangs were sown thick with spies, and even those who were not employed as such turned informer in order to acquire merit with their masters.

'Dogs!' cried Ortho, blazing at such treachery.

'Not so quick with your "dogs,"' said Puddicombe quietly. 'You may find yourself doin' it some day—under the bastinado.'

Something in the old man's voice made the boy wonder if he were not speaking from experience, if he had not at some time in the throes of torture given a friend away.

On the second day they were taken to the market and auctioned. Before the sale took place the Basha picked out a fifth of the entire number, including all the best men, and ordered them to be marched away as the Sultan's perquisites. Ortho was one of the chosen in the first place, but a venerable Moor in a sky-blue jellab came to the rescue, bowing before the Governor, talking rapidly, and pointing to Ortho the while. The great man nodded, picked a Dutchman in his place, and passed on. The public auction then began, with much preliminary shouting and drumming. Prisoners were dragged out and minutely inspected by prospective buyers, had their chests thumped, muscles pinched, teeth inspected, were trotted up and down to expose their action, exactly like dumb beasts at a fair.

The simile does not apply to Mr Puddicombe; he was not dumb. He lifted up his voice and shouted some rigmarole in Arabic. Ortho asked him what he was saying.

'Tellin'' em what I can do, bless you! Think I want to be bought by a poor man and moil in the fields? No; I'm going to a house where they have couscous every day—y'understan'? See what I mean?'

'Ahoy there, lords!' he bawled. 'Behold me! Nine years was I in Algiers at the house of Abd-el-Hamri the lawyer in Sidi Okbar Street. No *Nesrani* dog am I, but a Moslem, a true believer. Moreover, I am skilled in sewing and carpentry and many kindred arts. Question me, lords, that ye may see I speak the truth. Ahoy there, behold me!'

His outcry brought the buyers flocking. The auctioneer, seeing his opportunity, enlarged on Mr Puddicombe's supposed merits. Positively the most accomplished slave Algiers had ever seen, diligent, gifted and of celebrated piety. Not as young as he had been perhaps, but what of it? What was age but maturity, the ripeness of wisdom, the fruit of experience? Here was no gadabout boy to be for ever sighing after the slave wenches, loitering beside the storytellers and forgetting his duty, but a man of sound sense whose sole interests would be those of his master. What offers for this union of all the virtues, this household treasure? Stimulated by the dual advertisement, the bidding became brisk, the clamour deafening, and Mr Puddicombe was knocked down body and soul for seventeen pounds thirteen shillings and fourpence (53 ducats) to a little hunchback with ophthalmia, but of extreme richness of apparel.

Prisoner after prisoner was sold off and led away by his purchaser, until only Ortho remained. He was puzzled at this and wondered what to do next, when the venerable Moor in the blue jellab finished some transaction with the auctioneer and twitched at his sleeve. As the guards showed no objection, or, indeed, any further interest in him, he followed the blue jellab. The blue jellab led the way westwards up a maze of crooked lanes until they reached the summit of the town, and there, under the shadow of the minaret, opened a door in an otherwise blank wall, passed up a gloomy tunnel, and brought Ortho out into a courtyard.

The court was small, stone-paved, with a single orange tree growing in the centre and arcades supported on fretted pillars running all round.

A couple of slave girls were sweeping the courtyard with palmetto brooms under the goadings of an immensely stout old Berber woman, and on the north side, out of the sun, reclining on a pile of cushions, sat Captain Benjamin McBride, the traditional picture of the seafarer ashore, his pipe in his mouth, his tankard within reach, both arms filled with girl. He had a slender, kindling Arab lass tucked in the crook of his right arm, his left arm encompassed two fair-skinned Moorish beauties. They were unveiled, bejewelled and tinted like ripe peaches, their haiks were of white silk, their big-sleeved undergarments of coloured satin, their toes were painted with henna and so were their fingers, they wore black ink beauty spots on their cheeks. Not one of the brilliant little birds of paradise could have passed her seventeenth year.

Captain McBride's cherry-hued countenance wore an expression of profound content.

He hailed Ortho with a shout, 'Come here, boy!' and the three little ladies sat up, stared at the newcomer and whispered to each other, tittering.

'I've bought you, d' y' see?' said McBride. 'An' a tidy penny you cost me. If the Basha wasn't my very good friend you'd ha' gone to the quarries and had your heart broken first and your back later, so you're lucky. Now bestir yourself round about and do what old Saheb (indicating the blue jellab) tells you, or to the quarries you go-see? What d' y' call yourself, heh?'

Ortho told him.

'Ortho Penhale, that'll never do.' He consulted the birds of paradise, who tried the outlandish words over but could not shape their tongues to them. They twittered and giggled and wrangled and patted McBride's cheerful countenance.

'Hark 'e,' said he at last. 'Tama wants to name you "Chitane" because you look wicked. Ayesha is for "Sejra" because you're tall, but Schems-ed-Dah here says you ought to be called "Säid" because you're lucky to be here.' He pressed the dark Arab girl to him. 'So Säid be it. Säid I baptise thee henceforth and forever more—see?'

Break-of-Dawn embraced her lord, Tama and Ayesha pouted. He presented them with a large knob of coloured sweetmeat apiece and they were all smiles again. Peace was restored and Ortho stepped back under his new name, Säid—the fortunate one.

From then began his life of servitude at the house on the hill, and it was not disagreeable. His duties were to tend the captain's horse and the household donkey, fetch wood and water and run errands. In the early morning McBride would mount his horse (a grossly overfed, cow-hocked chestnut), leave the town by the Bab Malka, ride hell for leather, every limb in convulsion, across the sands to the shipyards at the south-east corner of the town. Ortho, by cutting through the Jewish quarter and out of the Bab Mrisa as hard as he could run, usually managed to arrive within a few minutes of the captain and spent the rest of the morning walking the horse about while his master supervised the work in the yards. These were on the bend of the river under shelter of a long wall, a continuation of the town fortifications. Here the little xebecs were drawn up on ways and made ready for sea. Renegade craftsmen sent spars up and down, toiled like spiders in webs of rigging, splicing and parcelling; plugged shot holes, repaired splintered upperworks, painted and gilded the flamboyant beaks and sterns; while gangs of slaves hove on the huge shore capstans, bobbed like mechanical dolls in the sawpits, scraped the slender hulls and payed them over with boiling tallow. There were sailmakers to watch as well, gunsmiths and carvers; plenty to see and admire.

The heat of the day McBride spent on the shady side of his court in siesta among his ladies, and Ortho released the donkey from its tether among the olive trees outside the Bab Chaafa and fetched wood and water, getting the former from charcoal burners' women from the Forest of Marmora. He met many other European slaves similarly employed, Frenchmen, Spaniards, Italians, Dutchmen, Portuguese, Greeks and not a few British. They spoke Arabic together and a *lingua franca*, a compound of their several tongues, but Ortho was not attracted by any of them, they were either too reticent or too friendly. He remembered what Puddicombe had said about spies and kept his mouth shut except on the most trivial topics. Puddicombe he frequently encountered in the streets, but never at the wells or in the charcoal market; the menial hauling of wood and drawing of water were not for that astute gentleman, he had passed into a higher plane and was now steward with menials under him.

His master (whom he designated "Sore Eyes') was very amiable, when not suffering from any of his manifold infirmities, amiable, not to say indulgent. He had shares in every corsair in the port, fifteen cows and a large orchard. The slaves had couscous, fat mutton and chicken scrapings almost every day, butter galore and as much fruit as they could eat. He was teaching Sore Eyes the King's Game and getting into his good graces. But, purposely, not too deep. Did he make himself indispensable, Sore Eyes might refuse to part with him and he would not see Sidi Okbar Street again—a merchant had promised to get his letter through. Between his present master and the notary there was little to choose, but Salé was a mere rat-hole compared with Algiers. He enlarged on the city of his captivity, its white terraces climbing steeply from the blue harbour, its beauty, wealth and activity, with all the tremulous passion of an exile pining for home.

Many free renegades were there, also, about the town with whom Ortho was on terms of friendship—mutineers, murderers, ex-convicts, wanted criminals to a man. These gentry were almost entirely employed either as gunners and petty officers aboard the corsairs or as skilled labourers in the yards. They had their own grog shops and resorts, and when they had money lived riotously and invited everybody to join. Many a night did Ortho spend in the *renegado* taverns when the Rovers were in after a successful raid, watching them dicing for shares of plunder, and dancing their clattering hornpipes; listening to their melancholy and boastful songs, to their wild tales of battle and disaster, sudden affluence and debauch; tales of superstition and fabulous adventure, of phantom ships, ghost islands, white whales, sea-dragons, Jonahs, and mermaids; of the pleasant pirate havens in the Main; slave barracoons on the Guinea coast; orchid-poisoned forests in the Brazils; of Indian Moguls who rode on jewelled elephants beneath fans of peacocks' feathers, and the ice barriers to the north, where the bergs stood mountain-high and glittered like green glass.

Sometimes there were brawls when the long sheath knives came out and one or other of the combatants dropped, occasionally both. They were hauled outside by the heels, and the fun went on again. But these little unpleasantnesses were exceptional. The *mala casta* ashore were the essence of good-fellowship and of a royal liberality; they were especially generous to the Christian captives, far more kindly than the slaves were to each other.

The habitual feeling of restraint, of suspicion, vanished before the boisterous conviviality of these rascals. When the fleets came, banging and cheering, home over the bar into the Bou Regreg, and the *mala casta* were in town blowing their money in, the Europeans met together, spoke openly, drank, laughed, and were friends. When they were gone the cloud descended once more, the slaves looked at each other slantwise and walked apart.

But Ortho cared little for that; he was at home in the house on the hill and passably happy. It was only necessary for him to watch the Government slaves being herded to work in the quarries and salt pans, ill-clad, half-starved, battered along with sticks and gun butts, to make him content with his mild lot. Not for nothing had he been named Säid, the fortunate.

He had no longer any thought of escape. One morning, returning with wood, he met a rabble in the narrow Souika. They had a mule in their midst, and, dragging head down at the mule's tail, was what had once been a man. His hands were strapped behind him so that he could in no way protect himself, but bumped along the ruts and cobbles, twisting over and over. His features were gone, there was not a particle of skin left on him; and at this red abomination the women cursed, the beggars spat, the children threw stones, and the dogs tore.

It was a Christian, Ortho learnt, a slave who had killed his warder, escaped, and been recaptured.

The rabble went on, shouting and stoning, towards the Bab Fes, and Ortho drove his donkey home, shivering, determined that freedom was too dear at that risk. There was nothing in his life at the captain's establishment to make him anxious to run. The ample Mahma did not regard him with favour, but that served to enhance him in the eyes of Saheb the steward, between whom and the house-keeper there was certain rivalry and no love lost.

The two slave girls were merely lazy young animals with no thoughts beyond how much work they could avoid and how much food they could steal. Of the harem beauties he saw little except when McBride was present, and then they were fully occupied with their lord. McBride was amiability itself.

Captain McBride at sea, at the first sign of indiscipline, tricing his men to the main jeers and flogging them raw; Captain McBride, yardmaster of Salé, bellowing blasphemies at a rigger on a topmast truck, laying a caulker out with his own mallet for skimped work, was a totally different person from Ben McBride of the house on the hill. The moment he entered its portals he, as it were, resigned his commission and put on childish things. He would issue from the tunnel and stand in the courtyard clapping his hands and hallooing for his dears. With a flip-flap of embroidered slippers, a jingle of bangles, and twitters of welcome, they would be on him and he would disappear in a whirl of billowing haiks. The embraces over, he would disgorge his pockets of the masses of pink-and-white sweetmeats he purchased daily, and maybe produce a richly-worked belt for Ayesha, a necklace of scented beads for Tama, fretted gold hair ornaments for Schems-ed-Dah, and chase them round and round the orange tree, while the little things snatched at his flying coat-tails and squealed in mock terror.

What with overseeing the yards, where battered corsairs were constantly refitting, and supervising the pilots' school, where young Moors were taught the rudiments of navigation, McBride was kept busy during the day and his household saw little of him, but in the evenings he returned rejoicing to the bosom of his family, never abroad to stray, the soul of domesticity. He would lounge on the heaped cushions, his long pipe in his teeth, his tankard handy, Schems-ed-Dah nestling against one shoulder, Tama and Ayesha taking turns with the other, and call for his jester Säid.

'Hey, boy, tell us about ole Jerry and the bear.'

Then Ortho would squat and tell imaginary anecdotes of Jerry, and the captain would hoot and splutter and choke until the three little girls thumped him normal again.

'Rot me, but ain't that rich?' He would moan, tears brightening his scarlet cheeks. 'Ain't that jist like ole Jerry, the ole rip! He-he! Tell us another, Säid—that about the barber he shaved and painted like his own pole. Go on.'

Säid would tell the story. At first he had been at pains to invent new episodes for Captain Gish, that great hero of McBride's boyhood, but he soon found it quite unnecessary; the old would do as well—nay, better. It was like telling fairy stories to children, always the old favourites in the old words. His audience knew exactly what was coming, but that in no way served to dull their delight when it came. As Ortho (or Säid) approached a well-worn climax a tremor of delicious expectancy would run through Schems-ed-Dah (he was talking in Arabic now). Tama and Ayesha would clasp hands, and McBride sit up, eyes fixed on the speaker, mouth open like a terrier ready to snap a biscuit. Then the threadbare climax. McBride would cast himself backwards and beat the air with ecstatic legs, Schems-ed-Dah clap her hands and laugh like a ripple of fairy bells, Ayesha and Tama hug each other and swear their mirth would kill them.

When they recovered, the storyteller was rewarded with rum and tobacco from that staunch Moslem McBride, with sweetmeats and mint tea from the ladies. He enjoyed his evenings. During the winter they sat indoors before charcoal braziers in which burned sticks of aromatic wood, but on the hot summer nights they took to the roof to catch the sea breeze. Star-bright, languorous nights they were. Below them the white town, ghostly glimmering, sloped away to the coast and the flats. Above them the slender minaret, while on the lazy wind came the drone of breakers and the faint, sweet scent of spice gardens. Voluptuous, sea-murmurous nights, milk-warm, satin-soft under a tent of star-silvered purple.

Sometimes Schems-ed-Dah fingered a gounibri and sang plaintive desert songs of the Bedouin women, the two other girls, snuggling half-asleep against McBride's broad chest, crooning the refrains.

Sometimes Ayesha, stirred by moonlight, would dance, clicking her bracelets, tinkling tiny brass cymbals between her fingers, swaying her graceful body backwards and sideways, poising on her toes, arms outstretched, like a seabird drifting, stamping her heels and shuddering from head to toe.

Besides storytelling, Ortho occasionally lifted up his voice in song. He had experimented with his mother's guitar in times gone by, and found he could make some show with the gounibri.

He sang Romany ditties he had learnt on his travels, and these were approved of by the Moorish girls, being in many ways akin to their own. But mostly he sang sea songs for the benefit of McBride who liked to swell the chorus with his bull-bellow. They sang "Cawsand Bay," "Baltimore," "Lowlands Low," and "The Sailor's Bride," and made much cheerful noise about it, on one occasion calling down on themselves the reproof of the muezzin, who rebuked them from the summit of the minaret, swearing he could hardly hear himself shout.

Eleven months Ortho remained in congenial bondage in Salé.

Then one morning McBride sent for him. 'I'm goin' to set you free, Säid, my buck,' said he.

Ortho was aghast, asked what he had done amiss.

McBride waved his hand. 'I ain't got nothin' against you as yet, but, howsomdever, I reckon I'd best turn you loose. I'm goin' to sea again—as *reis*.'

'*Reis!*' Ortho exclaimed. 'What of Abdullah Benani?'

'Had his neck broken by the Sultan's orders in Mequinez three days ago, for losin' them three xebecs off Corunna. I'm to go in his place. I've settled about you with the Basha. You're to go to the Makhzen Horse as a free soldier. I'll find you a nag and gear; when you sack a rich kasbah you can pay me back. You'll make money if you're clever—and don't get shot first.'

'Can't I go with you?'

'No. We only take Christians with prices on their heads at home. They don't betray us then—you might.'

'Well, can't I stop here in Salé?'

'That you cannot. It has struck me that you've been castin' too free an eye on my girls. Mind you, I don't blame you. You're young and they're pretty, it's only natural. But it wouldn't be natural for me to go to sea and leave you here with a free run. Anyhow, I'm not doin' it.'

Ortho declared with warmth that McBride's suspicions were utterly unfounded, most unjust; he was incapable of such base disloyalty.

The captain wagged his bullet head. 'Maybe, but I'm not takin' any risks. Into the army you go—or the quarries.'

Ortho declared hastily for the army.

A fortnight later McBride led his fleet out over the bar between saluting forts, and Ortho, with less ceremony, took the road for Mequinez.

That phase of his existence was over. He had a sword, a long matchlock, and a passable Barb pony under him. Technically he was a free man, actually he was condemned to a servitude vastly more exacting than that which he had just left. A little money might come his way, bullets certainly, wounds probably, possibly death—and death was the only discharge.

He pulled up his horse at the entrance of the forest and looked back. His eye was caught by the distant shimmer of the sea—the Atlantic. He was going inland among the naked mountains and tawny plains of this alien continent, might never see it again.

The Atlantic! The same ocean that beat in blue, white, and emerald upon the shores of home, within the sound of whose surges he had been born. It was like saying goodbye to one's last remaining friend. He looked upon Salé. There lay the white town nestling in the bright arm of the Bou Regreg, patched with the deep green of fig and orange groves. There soared the minaret, its tiles a-wink in the sunshine. Below it, slightly to the right, he thought he could distinguish the roof of McBride's house—the roof of happy memories. He wondered if Schems-ed-Dah were standing on it looking after him. What cursed luck to be kicked out just as be was coming to an understanding with Schems-ed-Dah!

Chapter XI

ORTHO SAT on the bare hillside and watched his horses coming in. They came up the gully below him in a drove, limping from their hobbles, greys, chestnuts, bays, duns, and blacks—blacks predominating. It was his ambition to command a squadron of blacks, and he was chopping and changing to that end. They would look well on parade, he thought, a line of glossy black Doukkala stallions with scarlet trappings, bestridden by lancers in the uniform white burnous—black, white, and scarlet. Such a display should catch the Sultan's eye, and he would be made a Kaid Rahal.

He was a Kaid Mia already. Sheer luck had given him his first step.

When he first joined the Makhzen cavalry he found himself stablemates with an elderly Prussian named Fleischmann, who had served with Frederick the Great's dragoons at Rossbach, Liegnitz, and Torgau; a surly, drunken old *sabreur* with no personal ambition beyond the assimilation of loot, but possessed of experience and a tongue to disclose it. In his sober moments he held forth to Ortho on the proper employment of horse. He did not share the common admiration for the crack Askar lancers, but poured derision upon them. They were all bluster and bravado, he said; stage soldiers with no real discipline to control them in a tight corner. He admitted they were successful against rebel hordes, but did they ever meet a resolute force he prophesied red-hot disaster and prayed he might not be there.

His prayer was granted. Disaster came, and he was not there, having had his head severed from his shoulders a month previously while looting when drunk and meeting with a furious householder who was sober.

Ortho was in the forefront of the disaster. The black guards, the *boukhari*, were having one of their periodic mutinies, and had been drummed into the open by the artillery. The cavalry were ordered to charge. Instead of stampeding when they saw the horse sweeping on them, the guards lay down, opened a well-directed fire, and emptied saddles right and left.

A hundred yards from the enemy the lancers flinched and turned tail, and the *boukhari* brought down twice as many more. Ortho did not turn. In the first place he did not know the others had gone about until it was too late to follow them, and secondly his horse, a powerful entire, was crazy with excitement and had charge of him. He slammed clean through the *boukhari* like a thunderbolt, with nothing worse than the fright of his life and a slight flesh wound.

He had a confused impression of fire flashing all about him, bullets whirring and droning round his head, black giants springing up among the rocks, yells—and he was through. He galloped on for a bit, made a wide détour round the flank, and got back to what was left of his own ranks.

Returning, he had time to meditate, and the truth of the late (and unlamented) Fleischmann's words came back to him. That flesh wound had been picked up at the beginning of the charge. The nearer he had got the wilder the fire had become. The guards he had encountered flung themselves flat; he could have skewered them like pigs. If the whole line had gone on, all the blacks would have flung themselves flat and been skewered like pigs. A regiment of horse charges home with the impact of a deep-sea breaker, hundreds of tons.

The late Fleischmann had been right in every particular. The scene of the affair was littered with dead horses and white heaps like piles of crumpled linen—their riders. The *boukhari* had advanced and were busy among these, stripping the dead, stabbing the wounded, cheering derisively from time to time.

Ortho had no sooner rejoined his depleted ranks than a miralay approached and summoned him to the presence of Sidi Mahomet himself.

The puissant grandson of the mighty Muley Ismail was on a hillock where he could command the whole field, sitting on a carpet under a white umbrella, surrounded by his Generals, who were fingering their beards and looking exceedingly downcast, which was not unnatural seeing that at least half of them expected to be beheaded.

The Sultan's face was an unpleasant sight. He bit at the stem of his hookah, and his fingers twitched, but he was not ungracious to the renegade lancer who did obeisance before him.

'Stand up,' he growled. 'Thou of all my askars hast no need to grovel. How comes it that you alone went through?'

'Sidi,' said Ortho, 'the Sultan's enemies are mine—and it was not difficult. I know the way.'

Mahomet's delicate eyebrows arched. 'Thou knowest the way! Ha! Then thou art wiser than these . . . these'—he waved his beautiful hand towards the Generals—'these sorry camel-cows who deem themselves warriors. Tell these ass-mares thy secret. Speak up and fear not.'

Ortho spoke out. He said nothing about his horse having bolted with him, that so far from being heroic he was numb with fright. He spoke with the voice of Fleischmann deceased, expounded the Prussian's theory of discipline and tactics as applied to shock cavalry, and, having heard them *ad nauseam*, missed never a point. All the time the Sultan sucked at his great hookah and never took his ardent, glowering eyes from his face, and all the time in the background the artillery thumped and the muskets crackled.

He left the royal presence a Kaid Mia, commanding a squadron, a bag of one hundred ducats in his hand, and a month later the cavalry swept over the astonished *boukhari* as a flood sweeps a mudbank, steeled by the knowledge that a regiment of imperial infantry and three guns were in their rear with orders to mow them down did they waver. They thundered through to victory, and the Kaid Säid-el-Ingliz (which was another name for Ortho Penhale) rode, perforce, in the van, wishing to God he had not spoken, and took a pike thrust in the leg and a musket ball in his ribs, and was laid out of harm's way for months.

But that was past history, and now he was watching his horses come in. They were not looking any too well; he thought, tucked-up, hide-bound, scraggy—been campaigning overlong, travelling hard, feeding anyhow, standing out in all weathers. He was thoroughly glad this tax collecting tour was at a close and he could get them back into garrison. His men drove them up to their heel-pegs, made them fast for the night, tossed bundles of grass before them, and sought the campfires that twinkled cheerily in the twilight. A couple of stallions squealed, there was the thud of a shoe meeting cannon bone, and another squeal, followed by the curses of the horse guard. A man by the fires twanged an oud and sang an improvised ditty on a palm tree in his garden at Tafilet.

> 'A queen among palms,
> Very tall, very stately,
> The sun gilds her verdure
> With glittering kisses.
> And in the calm night time,
> Among her green tresses,
> The little stars tremble.'

Ortho drew the folds of his jellab closer about him—it was getting mighty cold—stopped to speak to a farrier on the subject of the shoe shortage, and sought the miserable tent which he shared with his Lieutenant, Osman Bâki, a Turkish adventurer from Rumeli Hissar.

Osman was just in from headquarters and had news. The engineers reported their mines laid, and the Sari was going to blow the town walls at moonrise—in an hour's time. The infantry were already mustering, but there were no orders for the horse. The Sari was in a vile temper, had commanded that all male rebels were to be killed on sight—women optional. Looting was open. Osman picked a mutton bone, chattering and shaking; the mountain cold had brought out his fever. He would not go storming that night, he said, not for the plunder of Vienna; slung the mutton bone out of doors, curled up on the ground, using his saddle for pillow, and pulled every available covering over himself.

Ortho ate his subordinate's share of the meagre repast, stripped himself to his richly-laced kaftan, stuck a knife in his sash, picked up a sword and a torch, and went out.

The General was short of cavalry, unwilling to risk his precious bodyguard, and had therefore not ordered them into the attack. Ortho was going, nevertheless. He was not in love with fighting, but he wanted money; he always wanted money.

He walked along the campfires, picked ten of the stoutest and most rascally of his rascals, climbed out of the gully, and came in view of the beleaguered kasbah. It was quite a small place, a square fortress of mud-plastered stone, standing in a gorge of the Middle Atlas, and filled with obdurate mountaineers who combined brigandage with a refusal to pay tribute. A five-day siege had in no wise weakened their resolve. Ortho could hear drums beating inside, while from the towers came defiant yells and splutters of musketry.

'If we can't get in soon the snow will drive us away—and they know it,' he said to the man beside him, and the man shivered and thought of warm Tafilet.

'Yes, lord,' said he, 'and there's naught of value in that *roua*. Had there been, the Sari would have not thrown the looting open. A sheep, a goat or so—paugh! It is not worth our trouble.'

'They must be taught a lesson, I suppose,' said Ortho.

The man shrugged. 'They will be dead when they learn it.'

A German sapper slouched by, whistling "Im Grünewald mein Lieb und Ich," stopped and spoke to Ortho. They had worked right up to the walls by means of trenches covered with fascines, he said, and were going to blow them in two places simultaneously and rush the breaches. The blacks were going in first. These mountaineers fought like devils, but he did not think there were more than two hundred of them and the infantry were vicious, half-starved, half-frozen, impatient to be home. Snow was coming, he thought, could smell it—whew!

A pale haze blanched the east; a snow peak gleamed with ghostly light; surrounding stars blinked as though blinded by a brighter glory, blinked and faded out. Moonrise. The German called '*Besslama!*' and hurried to his post. The ghost-light strengthened. Ortho could see ragged infantrymen creeping forward from rock to rock; some of them dragged improvised ladders. He heard sly chuckles, the chink of metal on stone, and the snarl of an officer, commanding silence.

In the village the drums went on, *thump, thump; thump, thump*—unconscious of impending doom.

'Dogs of the Sultan,' screamed a man on the gatetower, 'little dogs of a big dog, may Gehenna receive you, may your mothers be shamed and your fathers eat filth—a-he-yah!' His chance bullet hit the ground in front of Ortho, ricochetted and found the man from Tafilet. He rolled over, sighed one word, *nkel*—palm groves—and lay still.

His companions immediately rifled the body—war is war. A shining edge, a rim of silver coin showed over a saddle of the peaks. '*G mare!*' said the soldiers. 'The moon—ah, *now!*'

The whispers and laughter ceased, every tattered starveling lay tense, expectant.

In the village the drums went on—*thump, thump; thump, thump*. The moon climbed, up, up, dragged herself clear of the peaks, drenching the snow-fields with eerie light, drawing sparkles here, shadows there; a dead goddess rising out of frozen seas.

The watchers held their breath, slowly released it, breathed again.

'Wah! The mines have failed,' a man muttered. 'The powder was damp. I knew it.'

'It is the ladders now, or nothing,' growled another. 'Why did the Sari not bring cannon?'

'The Tobjyah say the camels could not carry them in these hills,' said a third.

'The Tobjyah tell great lies,' snapped the first. 'I know for certain that . . . hey!'

The north corner of the kasbah was suddenly enveloped in a fountain of flame, the ground under Ortho gave a kick, and there came such an appalling clap of thunder he thought his eardrums had been driven in. His men scrambled to their feet, cheering.

'Hold fast! Steady!' he roared. 'There is another yet . . . ah!' The second mine went up as the debris of the first came down—mud, splinters, stones and shreds of human flesh.

A lump of plaster smashed across his shoulders and an infantryman within a yard of him got his back broken by a falling beam. When Ortho lifted his head again, it was to hear the exultant whoops of the detachments as they charged for the breaches. In the village the drums had stopped, it was as dumb as a grave. He held his men back. He was not out for glory.

'Let the blacks and infantry meet the resistance,' he said. 'That man with a broken back had a ladder, eh? Bring it along.'

He led his party round to the eastern side, put his ladder up and got over without dispute. The tribesmen had recovered from their shock to a certain extent and were concentrating at the breaches, leaving the walls almost unguarded. A mountaineer came charging along the parapet, shot one of Ortho's men through the stomach as he himself was shot through the head and both fell writhing into a courtyard below.

The invaders passed from the wall to a flat roof and there were confronted by two more stalwarts whom they cut down with difficulty. There was a fearful pandemonium of firing, shrieks, curses and war whoops going on at the breaches, but the streets were more or less deserted. A young and ardent askar kaid trotted by, beating his tag-rag on with his sword-flat. He yelped that he had come over the wall and was going to take the defenders in the rear; he called to Ortho for support. Ortho promised to follow and turned the other way—plunder, plunder!

The alleys were like dry torrent-beds underfoot, not five feet wide, and dark as tunnels. Ortho lit his torch and looked for doors in the mud walls. In every case they were barred, but he battered them in with axes brought for that purpose—to find nothing worth the trouble.

Miserable hovels all, with perhaps a donkey and some sheep in the court, and a few leathery women and children squatting in the darkness wailing their death song. Ornaments they wore none—buried of course; there was the plunder of at least two rich Tamgrout caravans hidden somewhere in that village. His men tortured a few of the elder women to make them disclose the treasure, but though they screamed and moaned there was nothing to be got out of them. One withered hag did indeed offer to show them where her grandson hid his valuables, led them into a small room, suddenly jerked a koummya from the folds of her haik and laid about her foaming at the mouth.

The room was cramped, the men crowded and taken unawares, the old fury whirled and shrieked and chopped like a thing demented. She wounded three of them before they laid her out. One man had his arm nearly taken off at the elbow. Ortho bound it up as best he could and ordered him back to camp, but he never got there. He took the wrong turning, fell helpless among some other women and was disembowelled.

'Y'Allah, the Sultan wastes time and lives,' said an askar. 'The sons of such dams will never pay taxes.'

Ortho agreed. He had lost two men dead and three wounded and had got nothing for it but a few sheep, goats and donkeys. The racket at the breaches had died down, the soldiery were pouring in at every point; it would be as well to secure what little he had. He drove his blearing captures into a court, mounted his men on guard and went to the door to watch.

An infantryman staggered down the lane bent under a brass-bound coffer. Ortho kicked out his foot, man and box went headlong. The man sprang up and flew snarling at Ortho, who beat him in the eyes with his torch and followed up with menaces of his sword. The man fled and Ortho examined the box which the fall had burst open. It contained a brass tiara, some odds and ends of tarnished Fez silk, a bride's belt and slippers—that was all, value a few blankeels—faugh!

He left the stuff where it lay in the filth of the kennel, strolled aimlessly up the street, came opposite a splintered door and looked in.

The house was more substantial than those he had visited, of two storeys, with a travesty of a fountain bubbling in the court. The infantry had been there before him. Three women and an old man were lying dead beside the fountain, and in a patch of moonlight an imperturbable baby sat playing with a kitten.

An open stairway led aloft. Ortho went up, impelled by a sort of idle curiosity. There was a room at the top of the stair. He peered in. Ransacked. The sole furniture the room possessed, a bed, had been stripped of its coverings and overturned. He walked round the walls prodding with his sword at suspicious spats in the plaster in the hopes of finding treasure. Nothing.

At the far end of the gallery was another room. Mechanically he strolled towards it, thinking of other things, of his debts in Mequinez, of how to feed his starved horses on the morrow—these people must at least have some grain stored, in sealed pits probably. He entered the second room; it was the same as the first, but it had not been ransacked, it was not worth the trouble. A palmetto basket and an old jellab hung on one wall, a bed was pushed against the far wall, and there was a dead man. Ortho examined him by the flare of his torch. A low type of Chaouia foot soldier, fifty, diseased, and dressed in an incredible assortment of tatters. Both his hands were over his heart clenching fistfuls of bloody rags, and on his face was an expression of extreme surprise. It was as though death were the last person he had expected to meet. Ortho thought it comical.

'What else did you expect to find, jackal, at this trade?' he sneered, swept his torch round the room—and prickled.

In the shadow between the bed end and the wall he had seen something, somebody, move.

He stepped cautiously towards the bed and, sword point forwards, on guard. 'Who's there?'

No answer. He lowered his torch. It was a woman, crouched double, swathed in a soiled haik, nothing but her eyes showing. Ortho grunted. Another horse-faced mountain drudge, work-scarred, weather-coarsened!

'Stand up!' he ordered. She did not move. 'Do you hear?' he snapped, and made a prick at her with his sword.

She sprang up, and at the same moment flung her haik back. Ortho started, amazed. The girl before him was no more than eighteen, dark-skinned, slender, exquisitely formed. Her thick raven hair was bound with an orange scarf; across her forehead was a band of gold coins, and from her ears hung coral earrings. She wore two necklaces, one of fretted gold with fish-shaped pieces dangling from it, and a string of black beads such as are made of pounded musk and amber. Her wrists and ankles were loaded with heavy silver bangles. Intricate henna designs were traced halfway up her slim hands and feet, and from wrist to shoulder patterns had been scored with a razor and left to heal. Her face was finely chiselled, the nose narrow and curved, the mouth arrogant, the brows straight and stormy, and under them her great black eyes smouldered with dangerous fires.

Ortho sucked in his breath. This burning, lance-straight, scornful beauty came out of no hill village. An Arab this, daughter of whirl-wind horsemen, darling of some desert sheik, spoil of the Tamgrout caravans.

Well, she was his spoil now. The night's work would pay after all. All else aside, there was at least a hundred ducats of jewellery on her. He would strip it now, before the others came and demanded a share.

'Come here,' he said, dropping his sword.

The girl slouched slowly towards him, pouting, chin tilted, hands clasped behind her, insolently obedient, stopped within two feet of him and stabbed for his heart with all her might.

Had she struck less quickly and with more stealth she might have got home. Penhale's major asset was that, with him, thought and action were one. He saw an instantaneous flicker of steel and instan-taneously swerved. The knife pierced the sleeve of his kaftan below the left shoulder. He grabbed the girl by the wrist and wrenched it back till she dropped the knife, and as he did this with her free hand she very nearly had his own knife out of his sash and into him—very nearly. But that the handle caught in a fold he would have been done. He secured both her wrists and held her at arms' length. She ground her little sharp teeth at him, quivered with rage, blazed murder with her eyes.

'Soldier,' said Ortho to the dead man behind him, 'now I know why you look astonished. Neither you nor I expected to meet death in so pretty a guise.'

He spoke to the girl. 'Be quiet, Beauty, or I will shackle you with your own bangles. Will you be sensible?'

For answer the girl began to struggle, tugged at his grasp, wrenched this way and that, with the frantic abandon of a wild animal in a gin. She was as supple as an eel, and for all her slimness marvellously strong. Despite his superior weight and power, Ortho had all he could do to hold her. But her struggles were too wild to last and at length exhaustion calmed her. Ortho tied her hands with the orange scarf, and began to take her jewellery off and cram it in his pouch. While he was thus engaged she worked the scarf loose with her teeth and made a dive for his eyes with her long finger nails.

He tied her hands behind her this time and stooped to prise the anklets off. She caught him on the point of the jaw with her knee, knocking him momentarily dizzy. He tied her feet with a strip of haik. She leaned forward and bit his cheek, bit with all her strength, bit with teeth like needles, nor would she let go till he had well-nigh choked her. He cursed her savagely, being in considerable pain. She shook with laughter. He gagged her after that, worked the last ornament off, picked up his sword and prepared to go. His torch had spluttered out, but moonlight poured through the open door and he could see the girl sitting on the floor gagged and bound, murdering him with her splendid eyes.

'*Msa! kheir, lalla!*' said he, making a mock salaam. She snorted, defiant to the end. Ortho strode out and along the gallery. His cheek stung like fire, blood was trickling from the scratches, his jaw was stiff from the jolt it had received. What a she-devil, but by God, what spirit! He liked women of spirit, they kept one guessing. She reminded him somewhat of Schems-ed-Dah back in Salé, the same rapier tempering and blazing passion, desert women both. When tame they were wonderful, without peer—when tame. He hesitated, stopped and fingered his throbbing cheek.

'What that she-devil would like to do would be to cut me to pieces with a knife, slowly,' he muttered. He turned about, feeling his jaw. 'Cut me to pieces and throw 'em to the dogs.' He walked back. 'She would do it gladly, though they did the same to her afterwards. Tame that sort! Never—in life.' He stepped back into the room and picked the girl up in his arms. 'Wildcat, I'm going to attempt the impossible,' said he.

Even then she struggled.

The town was afire, darting tongued sheets of flame and jets of sparks at the placid moon. Soldiers were everywhere, shouting, smashing, pouring through the alleys over the bodies of the defenders. As Ortho descended the stairs a party of Sudanese broke into the courtyard, one of them took a wild shot at him.

'*Makhzeni!*' he shouted, and they stood back.

A giant petty officer with huge hoops of silver wire in his ears held a torch aloft. Blood from a scalp wound smeared his face with a crimson glare. At his belt dangled four fowls and a severed head.

'Hey, the Kaid Ingliz,' he said, and tapped the head. 'The rebel Basha, I slew him myself at the breach. The Sari should reward me handsomely, El Hamdou-lillah!' He smiled like a child expectant of sweetmeats. 'What have you there, Kaid?'

'A village wench merely.'

'Fair?'

'So-so.'

The big man spat. 'Bah! They are as ugly as their own goats, but'—he grinned, knowing Ortho's weakness—'she may fetch the price of a black horse, eh, Kaid?'

'She may,' said Ortho.

Chapter XXII

TWO DAYS later the force struck camp, leaving the town behind them a shell of blackened ruins, bearing on lances before them the heads of thirty prominent citizens as a sign that Caesar is not lightly denied his tribute.

They streamed north-east through the defiles, a tattered rabble, a swarm of locusts, eating up the land as they went. The wounded were jostled along in rough litters at the mercy of camp barbers and renegade quacks; the majority died on the way and were thankful to die. The infantry straggled for miles (half rode donkeys) and drove before them cattle, sheep, goats, and a few women prisoners. What with stopping to requisition and pillage, they progressed at an average of twelve miles a day. Only among the foot soldiers and the cavalry was there any semblance of march discipline, and then only because the General kept them close about him as protection against his other troops.

Beside Ortho rode the Arab girl, her feet strapped under the mule's belly. Twice she tried to escape—once by a blind bolt into the foothills, once by a surer, sharper road. She had wriggled across the tent and pulled a knife out of its sheath with her teeth. Osman had caught her just as she was on the point of rolling on it. Ortho had to tie her up at night and watch her all day long. Never had he encountered such implacable resolve. She was determined to foil him one way or the other, at no matter what cost to herself. He had always had his own way with women, and this failure irritated him. He would stick it as long as she, he swore—and longer.

Osman Bâki was entertained. He watched the contest with twinkling china-blue eyes. His mother had been a Georgian slave, and he was as fair as a Swede.

'She will leave you—somehow,' he warned.

'For whom? for what?' Ortho exclaimed. 'If she slips past me the infantry will catch her, or some farmer who will beat her life out.

Why does she object to me? I have treated her kindly—as kindly as she will allow.'

Osman twirled his little yellow moustache. 'Truly, but these people have no reason, only a mad pride. One cannot reason with madness, Kaid. Oh, I know them. When I was in the service of the Deys . . .'

He delivered an anecdote from his unexampled repertoire proving the futility of arguing with a certain class of Arab with anything more subtle than a bullet.

'Sell her in Morocco,' he advised. 'She is pretty, will fetch a good sum.'

'No, I'm going to try my hand first,' said Ortho stubbornly.

'You'll get it bitten,' said the Turk, eyeing the telltale marks on Ortho's face with amusement. 'For my part I prefer a quiet life—in the home.'

They straggled into Morocco city ten days later, to find the Sultan, in residence for the winter, building sanctuaries and schools with immense energy.

Ortho hoped for the governorship of an outlying post where he would be more or less his own master, get some pig hunting, and extort backsheesh from the countryfolk under his protection; but it was not to be. He was ordered to quarter his stalwarts in the kasbah and join the Imperial Guard. Having been in the Guard before at Mequinez, having influence in the household and getting a windfall in the way of eight months' back pay, he contrived to bribe himself into possession of a small house overlooking the Aguedal Gardens close to the Bab Ahmar.

There he installed the Arab girl and a huge housekeeper to look after her.

Then he set to and gave his unfortunate men the stiffening of their lives.

He formed his famous black horses into one troop, graded the others by colours, and drilled the whole all day long.

Furthermore, he instituted a system of grooming and arm-cleaning hitherto unknown in the Moroccan forces—all on the Fleischmann recipe. Did his men show sulks, he immediately upended and bastinadoed them. This did not make him popular, but Osman Bâki supported him with bewildered loyalty, and he kept the *mokadem* and the more desperate rascals on his side by a judicious distribution of favours and money. Nevertheless, he did not stroll abroad much after dark, and then never unattended.

They drilled in the Aguedal, on the bare ground opposite the Powder House, and acquired added precision from day to day. Ortho kept his eye on the roof of the Powder House.

For two months this continued, and Ortho grew anxious. What with household expenses and continued *douceurs* to the *mokadem*, his money was running out, and he was sailing too close to the wind to try tricks with his men's rations and pay at present.

Just when things were beginning to look desperate a party appeared on the roof of the Powder House, which served the parade ground as a grandstand.

Ortho, ever watchful, saw them the moment they arrived, brought his command into squadron column, black troop to the fore, and marched past underneath.

They made a gallant show, and Ortho knew it. Thanks to the grooming, his horses were looking fifty per cent better than any other animals in the Sherifian Army; the uniformity added another fifty. The men knew as well as he did who was looking down on them, and went by sitting stiff, every eye fixed ahead.

The lusty sun set the polished hides aglow, the burnished lance-heads aglitter. The horses, fretted by sharp stirrups, tossed their silky manes, whisked their streaming tails. The wind got into the burnouses and set them flapping and billowing in creamy clouds; everything was in his favour. Ortho wheeled the head of his column left about, formed squadron line on the right, and thundered past the magazine, his shop window troop nearest the spectators, shouting the imperial salute, '*Allah y barek Amer Sidi!* ' A good line, too, he congratulated himself; as good as any Makhzen cavalry would achieve in this world. If that didn't work, nothing would. It worked.

A slave came panting across the parade ground summoning him to the Powder House at once.

The Sultan was leaning against the parapet sucking a pomegranate and spitting the pips at his Grand Vizier, who pretended to enjoy it. The fringes of the royal jellab were rusty with brick dust from the ruins of Bel Abbas, which Mahomet was restoring. Ortho did obeisance and got a playful kick in the face; His Sublimity was in good humour.

He recognised Ortho immediately. 'Ha! The lancer who alone defied the *boukhari*, still alive! Young man, you must indeed be of Allah beloved!' He looked the soldier up and down with eyes humorous and restless. 'What is your rank?'

'Kaid Mia, Sidi.'

'Hum! Thou art Kaid Rahal now, then.' He turned on the Vizier. 'Tell El Mechouar to let him take what horses he chooses. He knows how to keep them. Go!'

He flung the fruit rind at Ortho by way of dismissal.

Ortho gave his long-suffering men a feast that night with the last ready money in his possession. They voted him a right good fellow; soldiers have short memories.

He was on his feet now. As Kaid Rahal, with nominally a thousand cut-throats at his beck and nod, he would be a fool indeed if he couldn't blackmail the civilians to some order. Also there was a handsome sum to be made by crafty manipulation of his men's pay and rations. El Mechouar would expect his commission out of this, naturally, and sundry humbler folk—"big fleas have little fleas"—but there would be plenty left. He was clear of the financial thicket. He went prancing home to his little house, laid aside his arms and burnous, took the key from the housekeeper, ran upstairs and unlocked the room in which the Arab girl, Ourida, was imprisoned. It was a pleasant prison with a window overlooking the Aguedal, its miles of pomegranate, orange, and olive trees. It was the best room in the house and he had furnished it as well as his thin purse would afford, but to the desert girl it might have been a tomb.

She sat all day staring out of the barred window, looking beyond the wide Haouz plain to where the snow peaks of the High Atlas rose, a sheer wall of sunlit silver—and beyond them even. She never smiled, she never spoke, she hardly touched her food. Ortho in all his experience had encountered nothing like her. He did his utmost to win her over, brought sweetmeats, laughed, joked, retailed the gossip of the palace and the souks, told her stories of romance and adventure which would have kept any other harem toy in shivers of bass, took his gounibri and sang Romany songs, Moorish songs, English ballads, flowery Ottoman *kasidas, ghazels and gûlistâns*, learned from Osman Bâki; cursed her, adored her.

All to no avail; he might have been dumb, she deaf. Driven desperate, he seized her in his arms; he had as well embraced so much ice. It was maddening. Osman Bâki who watched him in the lines of a morning raving at the men over trifles, twisted his yellow moustache and smiled. This evening, however, Ortho was too full of elation to be easily repulsed. He had worked hard and intrigued steadily for this promotion. Three years before he had landed in Morocco a chained slave, now he was the youngest of his rank in the first arm of the service. Another few years at this pace and what might he not achieve? He bounded upstairs like a lad home with a coveted prize, told the girl of his triumph, striding up and down the room, flushed, laughing, smacking his hands together, boyish to a degree. He looked his handsomest, a tall picturesque figure in plum-coloured breeches, soft riding boots, blue kaftan and scarlet tarboosh tilted rakishly on his black curls. The girl stole a glance at him from under her long lashes, but when he looked at her she was staring out of the window at the snow-wall of the Atlas, rose-flushed with sunset, and when he spoke to her she made no answer—he might as well have been talking to himself. But he was too full of his success to notice, and rattled on and on, pacing the little room up and down, four strides each way. He dropped beside her, put his arm about her shoulders, drew her cold cheek to his flushed one.

'Listen, my pearl,' he rhapsodised, 'I have money now and you shall have dresses like rainbows, a gold tiara and slave girls to wait on you, and when we move garrison you shall ride a white ambling mule with red trappings and lodge in a striped tent like the royal women. I am a Kaid Rahal now, do you hear? The youngest of any, and in the

Sultan's favour. I will contrive and scheme and in a few years . . . the Standard!—*ecschkoun-i-araf?* And then, my honey-sweet, you shall have a palace with a garden and fountains. Hey, look!'

He scooped in his voluminous breeches' pockets, brought out a handful of trinkets and tossed them into her lap. The girl stared at him, then at the treasures and drew a sharp breath. They were her own, the jewellery he had wrenched from her on that wild night of carnage three months before.

'You thought I had sold them—eh?' he laughed. 'No, no, my dear, it very nearly came to it, but not quite. They are safe now, and yours again—see?'

He seized her wrists and worked the bangles on, snapped the crude black necklace round her neck and hung the elaborate gold one over it, kissed her full on the quivering mouth. 'Yours again, for always.'

She ran the plump black beads through her fingers, her breathing quickened, she glanced at him sideways, shyly; there was an odd light in her eyes. She swayed a little towards him, then the corners of her mouth twitched and curved upwards in an adorable bow—she was smiling, smiling! He held out his arms to her and she toppled into them, burying her face in his bosom.

'My lord' said she.

The proud lady had surrendered at last!

'Osman, Osman Bâki, what now?' thought Ortho, and crushed her to him.

The girl made a faint pained exclamation and put her hand to her throat.

'Did I hurt you, my own?' said Ortho, contrite.

'No, my lord, but you have snapped my necklace,' she laughed. 'It is nothing.'

He picked up the black beads, wondering how he could have done it, and she put them down on the rug beside her.

'It is a poor thing, but a great saint has blessed it—my king, take me in your arms again.'

203

They sat close together while the rosy peaks faded out and the swift winter dusk filled the room, and he told her of the great things he would do. Elation swept him up, everything seemed possible now with this slim clinging beauty to solace and inspire him, he would trample on and on, scattering opposition like straw, carving his own road, a captain of destiny. She believed in his bravest boasts. Her lord had but to will a thing and it was done; who could withstand her lord? 'Not I, not I,' said she. 'Hearken, tall one. I said to my heart night and day, "Hate this Roumi askar, hate him, hate him!"—but my heart would not listen, it was wiser than I.'

She nestled luxuriously in his arms, crooning endearments, melting and passionate, sweeter than honey in the honeycomb. It grew dark and cold. He went to the door and called for the brazier.

'And tea,' Ourida added. 'I would serve you with tea, my heart's joy.'

The housekeeper brought both.

Ourida rubbed her head against his shoulder. 'Sweetmeats?' she cooed.

He jerked his last blankeels to the slave with the order.

Ourida squatted cross-legged on a pile of cushions and poured out the sweet mint tea, handed him his cup with a mock salaam. He did obeisance as before a Sultana, and she rippled with delight. They made long complimentary speeches to each other after the manner of the Court, played with each other's hands, were very childish and merry.

Ourida pressed a second cup of tea on him. He drank it off at a gulp and lay down at her side.

'Rest here and be comfortable,' said she, drawing his head to her. 'Tell me again about that battle with the *boukhari*.'

He told her in detail, omitting the salient fact that his horse had bolted with him, though, in truth, he had almost forgotten it himself by now.

'All alone you faced them! Small wonder Sidi Mahomet holds thee in high honour, my hero. And the fight in the Rif?'

He told her all about the guerrilla campaign among the rock fast-nesses of the Djebel Tizighene, of a single mountaineer with a knife crawling through the troop lines at night and sixty hamstrung horses in the morning.

Ourida was entranced. 'Go on, my lord, go on.'

Ortho went on. He didn't want to talk. He was most comfortable lying out on the cushions, his head on the girl's soft lap. Moreover, his heavy day in the sun and wind had made him extraordinarily drowsy, but he went on. He told her of massacres and burnt villages, of ambushes and escapes, of three hundred rebels rising out of a patch of cactus no bigger than a sheep pen and rushing in among the aston-ished lancers, screaming and slashing. The survivors of that affair had fled up the opposite hillside flat on their horses' necks, himself among the foremost, but he did not put it that way; he said he "organised the retreat."

'More,' breathed Ourida.

He began to tell her of five fanatics with several muskets and quantities of ammunition shut up in a saint's shrine and defying the entire Sherifian forces for two days, but before he had got halfway his voice tailed off into silence.

'You do not speak, light of my life?'

'I am sleepy—and comfortable, dearest.'

Ourida smoothed his cheek. 'Sleep, then, with thy slave for pillow.'

He felt her lips touch his forehead, her slim fingers running through his curls, through and through . . . through . . . and . . . thr ough . . .

'My lord sleeps?' came Ourida's voice from miles away, thrilling strangely.

'Um . . . ah! . . . almost,' Ortho mumbled. 'Where . . . you . . . going?' She had slipped from under him, he had an impulse to grasp her hand, then felt it was too much trouble.

'Listen, Säid-el-Ingliz,' said Ourida in his ear, enunciating with great clarity, 'you are going to sleep for *ever*, you swine!'

He forced his weighted lids apart. She was bending right over him. He could see her face by the glow of the brazier, transformed, exultant, her teeth were locked together and showing, her eyes glittered.

'For *ever*,' she hissed. 'Do you hear me?'

'Drugged, by God!' thought Ortho. 'Drugged, poisoned, fooled like a fat palace eunuch!'

Fury came upon him. He fought the drowse with all the power that was in him, sat up, fell back again.

The girl laughed shrilly.

He tried to shout for help, for the housekeeper, achieved a whisper.

'She has gone for sweetmeats and will loiter hours,' mocked the girl. 'Call louder, call up your thousand fine lancers. Oh, great Kaid Rahal, Standard Bearer to be!'

'Osman—they will crush you . . . between . . . stones . . . for . . . this,' he mumbled.

She shook her head. 'No, great one, they will not catch me. I have three more poisoned beads.' She held up the remnant of her black necklace.

So that was how it was done. In the tea. By restoring her the trinkets he had compassed his own end. His eyelids dropped, he was away, adrift again in that old dream he had had rocking in the smuggler's boat under Black Carn, floating through star-trembling space, among sombre continents of cloud, a wraith borne onwards, downwards, on streaming airways into everlasting darkness.

'Great lord of lances,' came a whisper out of nowhere, 'when thou art in Gehenna thou wilt remember me, thy slave.'

He fought back to consciousness, battled with smothering wraps of swansdown, through fogs of choking grey and yellow, through pouring waters of oblivion, came out sweating into the light, saw through a haze a shadow girl bending over him, the red glimmer of the brazier.

With an immense effort he lifted his foot into the coals, bit hard into his under lip. 'Not yet, not yet!'

The girl displayed amusement. 'Would'st burn before thy time? Burn on. Thou wilt take no more women of my race against their wish, Kaid, or any other women, though methinks thy lesson is learned over late.

'Why fight the sleep, *Roumi?* It will come, it will come. The Rif herb never fails.' On she went with her bitter raillery, on and on.

But Ortho was holding his own. He was his mother's son and had inherited all her marvellous vitality. The pain in his burnt foot was counteracting the drowse, sweat was pouring out of him. The crisis was past. Could he but crawl to the door? Not yet; in a minute or two. That housekeeper must be back soon. He bit into his bleeding lip again, closed his eyes. The girl bent forward eagerly.

'It is death, Kaid. Thou art dying, dying!'

'No, nor shall I,' he muttered, and instantly realised his mistake.

She drew back, startled, and swooped at him again.

'Open your eyes!' She forced his lids up.

'Failed!'

'Failed!' Ortho repeated.

'Bah! There are other means,' she snarled, jumped up, flitted round the room, stood transfixed in thought in the centre, both hands to her cheeks, laughed, tore off her orange scarf, and dropped on her knees beside him.

'Other means, Kaid.' She slipped the silk loop round his neck, knotted it and twisted.

She was going to strangle him, the time-hallowed practice of the East. He tried to stop her, lifted his heavy hands, but they were powerless, like so much dead wood. He swelled his neck muscles, but it was useless, the silk was cutting in all round, a red-hot wire. He had a flash picture of Osman Bâki, standing over his body, wagging his head regretfully, and saying, 'I said so,' Osman Bâki with the Owls' House for background. It was all over, the girl had waited and got him in the end. Even at that moment he admired her for it, she had spirit, never had he seen such spirit. Came a pang of intolerable pain, his eyeballs were starting out, his head was bursting open—and then the tension at his throat inexplicably relaxed.

Ortho rolled over panting and retching, and as he did so heard footsteps on the stairs.

A fist thumped on the door, a voice cried, 'Kaid! Kaid!' and there was Osman Bâki.

He peered into the room, holding a lantern before him. 'Kaid, are you there? Where are you? There is a riot of Draouia in the Jemaa el-Fnaa; two troops to go out. Oh, there you are — *Bismillah!* What is this?'

He sprang across to where Ortho lay and bent over him.

'What is the matter? Are you ill? What is it?'

'Nothing.' Ortho croaked. 'Trying hashish . . . took too much . . . nothing at all. See to troops yourself . . . go now.' He coughed and coughed.

'Hashish!' The Turk sniffed, stared at him suspiciously, glanced round the room, caught sight of the girl and held up the lantern.

'Ha, ha!'

The two stood rigid, eye to eye. The soldier with chin stuck forward, every hair bristling, like a mastiff about to spring, the girl unflinching, three beads of her black necklace in her teeth.

'Ha, ha!' Osman put the lantern deliberately on the ground beside him and stepped forward, crouched double, his hands outstretched like claws. 'You snake,' he muttered. 'You Arab viper, I'll . . . I'll . . .'

Ortho hoisted himself on his elbow. The girl was superb! So slight and yet so defiant. 'Osman,' he rasped. 'Osman, friend. Go! The riot! Go; it is an order!'

The Turk stopped, stood up, relaxed, turned slowly about, and picked up the lantern. He looked at Ortho, walked to the door, hesitated, shot a blazing glance at the girl, gave his moustache a vicious tug, and went out.

Silence but for the sputter of the brazier and the squeak of a mouse in the wall.

Then Ortho heard the soft *plud-plud* of bare feet crossing the room, and he knew the girl was standing over him.

'Well, sweet,' he sighed, 'come to complete your work? I am still in your hands.'

She tumbled on her knees beside him, clasped his head to her breast, and sobbed, sobbed, sobbed, as though she would never stop.

Chapter XXIII

ORTHO SPENT that winter in Morocco city, but in the spring was sent out with a force against the Zona Arabs south of the Figuig Oasis, which had been taken by Muley Ismail and was precariously held by his descendants. They spent a lot of time and trouble dragging cannon up, to find them utterly useless when they got there. The enemy did not rely on strong places—they had none—but on mobility. They played a game of sting and run very exasperating to their opponents. It was like fighting a cloud of deadly mosquitoes. The wastage among the Crown forces was alarming; two Generals were recalled and strangled, and when Ortho again saw the Koutoubia minaret rising like a spearshaft from the green palms of Morocco it was after an absence of ten months.

Ourida met him in transports of joy, a two-month baby in her arms. It was a son, the exact spit and image of him, she declared, a person of already incredible sagacity and ferocious strength. A few years and he, too, would be riding at the head of massed squadrons, bearing the green banner of the Prophet.

Ortho, burned black with Saharan suns, weak with privation, sick of the reek of festering battlefields, contemplated the tiny pink creature he had brought into the world and swore in his heart that this boy of his should follow peaceful ways.

Fighting men were, as a class, the salt of the earth, simple-hearted, courageous, dog-loyal, dupes of the cunning and cowardly. But apart from the companionship he had no illusions concerning the profession of arms as practised in the Sherifian Empire; it was one big bully maintaining himself in the name of God against a horde of lesser bullies (also invoking the Deity) by methods that would be deemed undignified in a pothouse brawl. He was in it for the good reason that he could not get out; but no son of his should be caught in the trap if he could help it. However, he said nothing of this to Ourida. He kissed her over and over and said the boy was magnificent and would doubtless make a fine soldier—but there was time to think about that.

He saw winter and summer through in Morocco with the exception of a short trip on the Sultan's bodyguard to Essaouira, which port Mahomet had established to offset fractious Agadir and taken under his special favour.

The sand-blown white town was built on the plans of an Avignon engineer named Cornut, with fortifications after the style of Vauban. This gave it a pronounced European flavour, which was emphasised by the number of foreign traders in its streets, drawn thither by the absence of custom. Also there was the Atlantic pounding on the island, a tang of brine in the air, and a sea wind blowing. Ortho had not seen the Atlantic since he left Salé. Homesickness gnawed at him.

He climbed the Harbour scala, and, sitting on a cannon cast for the third Philippe in 1595, watched the sun westering in gold and crimson, and dreamed of the Owls' House, the old Owls' House lapped in its secret valley, where a man could live his life out in fullness and peace — and his sons after him.

Walking back through the town, he met with a Bristol trader and turned into a wine shop. The Englishman treated him to a bottle of Jerez and the news of the world. Black bad it was. The tight little island had her back to the wall, fighting for bare life against three powerful nations at once. The American colonists were in full rebellion to boot, India was a cockpit, Ireland sharpening pikes. General Burgoyne had surrendered at Saratoga. Elliot was besieged in Gibraltar. French, American, and Spanish warships were thick as herring in the Channel; the Bristolian had only slipped through them by sheer luck and would only get back by a miracle.

Taxation at home was crippling, and every mother's son who had one leg to go upon and one arm to haul with was being pressed for service; they were even emptying the gaols into the navy. He congratulated Ortho on being out of the country and harm's way. Ortho had had a wild idea of getting a letter written and taken home to Eli by this man, but as he listened he reflected that it was no time now. Also, if he wanted to be bought out he would have to give minute instructions as to where the smuggling money was hidden. Letters were not inviolate; the bearer, and not Eli, might find that hidden money. And then there was Ourida and Säid II. Säid would become acclimatised, but England and Ourida were incompatible. He could not picture the ardent Bedouin girl—her bangles, silks, and exotic finery—in the grey north; she would shrivel up like a frostbitten lotus, pine, and die.

No, he was firmly anchored now. One couldn't have everything; he had much. He drank up his wine, wished the Bristolian luck with his venture, and rode back to the palace.

A week later he was home again in Morocco.

Added means had enabled him to furnish the Bab al-Ahmar house very comfortably, Moorish fashion, with embroidered *haitis* on the walls, inlaid tables, and plenty of well-cushioned lounges. The walls were thick; the rooms, though small, were high and airy, the oppressive heat of a Haouz summer did not unduly penetrate. Ourida bloomed, Säid the younger progressed from strength to strength, waxing daily in fat and audacity. He was the idol of the odd-job boy and the two slave-women (the household had increased with its master's rank), of Osman Bâki and Ortho's men. The latter brought him presents from time to time; fruit stolen from the Aguedal; camels, lions, and horses (chiefly horses) crudely carved and highly coloured, and, when he was a year old, a small shy monkey caught in the Rif, and later an old eagle with clipped wings and talons, which, the donor explained, would defend the little lord from snakes and such like. Concerning these living toys Säid II displayed a devouring curiosity and no fear at all. When the monkey clicked her teeth at him, he gurgled and pulled her tail till she escaped up the wisteria. He pursued the eagle on all fours, caught it sleeping one afternoon, and hung doggedly on till he had pulled a tail feather out. The bird looked dangerous. Säid II bubbled delightedly and grabbed for another feather, whereat the eagle retreated hastily to sulk among the orange-shrubs. Was the door left open for a minute, Säid II was out of it on voyages of high adventure.

Once he was arrested by the guard at the Bab Ahmar, plodding cheerfully on all fours for open country, and returned, kicking and raging, in the arms of a laughing petty officer.

Ortho himself caught the youngster emerging through the postern on to the royal parade ground.

'He fears nothing,' Ourida exulted. 'He will be a great warrior and slay a thousand infidels—the sword of Allah!—um-yum, my jewel.'

That battered soldier and turncoat infidel, his father, rubbed his chin uneasily. 'M'yes . . . perhaps. Time enough yet.'

But there was no gainsaying the fierce spirit of the Arab mother, daughter of a hundred fighting sheiks; her will was stronger than his. The baby's military education began at once. In the cool of the morning she brought Säid II to the parade ground, perched him on the parapet of the Dar-el-Heni, and taught him to clap his hands when the Horse went by.

Once she hoisted him to his father's saddle-bow. The fat creature twisted both hands in the black stallion's mane and kicked the glossy neck with his heels, gurgling with joy.

'See, see,' said Ourida, her eyes like stars for radiance. 'He grips, he rides. He will carry the standard in his day, *zahrit!*' The soldiers laughed and lifted their lances. 'Hail to the young Kaid!'

Ortho, gripping his infant son by the slack of his miniature jellab, felt sick. Ourida and these other simple-minded fanatics would beat him yet with their fool ideas of glory, urge this crowing baby of his into hardship, terror, pain, possibly agonising death.

Parenthood was making a thoughtful man of him. He was no longer the restless adventurer of two years ago, looking on any change as better than none. He grudged every moment away from the Bab al-Ahmar, dreaded the spring campaign, the separation it would entail, the chance bullet that might make it eternal.

His ambition dimmed. He no longer wanted power and vast wealth, only enough to live comfortably on with Ourida and young Säid just as he was. Promotion meant endless backstair intrigues; he had no taste left for them and had other uses for the money, and so fell out of the running.

A Spanish woman in the royal harem, taking advantage of her temporary popularity with Mahomet, worked her wretched little son into position over Penhale's head, and over him went a fat Moor,

Yakoub Ben Ahmed by name, advanced by the offices of a fair sister, also in the seraglio. Neither of these heroes had more than a smattering of military lore and no battle experience whatever, but Ortho did not greatly care. Promotion might be rapid in the Sherifian Army, but degradation was apt to be instantaneous — the matter of a sword-flash. He had risen as far as he could rise with moderate safety, and there he would stop. Security was his aim nowadays, a continuance of things as they were.

For life went by very happily in the little house by the Bab al-Ah-mar, pivoting on Säid II. But in the evening, when that potential conqueror had ceased the pursuit of monkey and eagle and lay locked in sleep, Ourida would veil herself, wind her haik about her, and go roaming into the city with Ortho. She loved the latticed souks with their displays of silks, jewellery, and leatherwork; the artificers with their long muskets, curved daggers, velvet scabbarded swords and pear-shaped powder flasks; the gorgeous horse-trappings at the saddlers, But these could be best seen in broad daylight; in the evening there were other attractions.

It was the Jemaa el-Fnaa that drew her, that great dusty clamorous fairground of Morocco where gather the storytellers, acrobats, and clowns; where feverish drums beat the sun down, assisted by the pipes of Aissawa snake charmers and the jingling ouds and cymbals of the Berber dancing boys; where the Sultan hung out the heads of transgressors that they might grin sardonically upon the revels. Ourida adored the Jemaa el-Fnaa. To the girl from the tent hamlet in the Sahara it was Life. She wept at the sad love stories, trembled at the snake charmers, shrieked at the crude buffoons, swayed in sympathy with the Berber dancers, besought Ortho for coin, and more coin, to reward the charming entertainers. She loved the varied crowds, the movement, the excitement, the din, but most of all she liked the heads. No evening on the Jemaa was complete unless she had inspected these grisly trophies of imperial power.

She said no word to Ortho, but nevertheless he knew perfectly well what was in her mind; in her mind she saw young Säid twenty years on, spattered with infidel blood, riding like a tornado, serving his enemies even as these.

Ferocious—she was the ultimate expression of ferocity—but knowing no mean, she was also ferocious in her love and loyalty; she would have given her life for husband or son gladly, rejoicing. Such people are difficult to deal with; Ortho sighed, but let her have her way.

Often of an evening Osman Bâki came to the house, and they would sit in the court drinking Malaga wine and yarning about old campaigns, while Ourida played with the little ape, and the old eagle watched for mice, pretending to be asleep.

Osman talked well. He told of his boyhood's home beside the Bosphorus, of Constantinople, Baghdad, and Damascus with its pearly domes bubbling out of vivid greenery. Jerusalem, Tunis, and Algiers he had seen also, and now the Moghreb, the "sunset land" of the first Saracen invaders. One thing more he wanted to see, and that was the Himalayas. He had heard old soldiers talk of them—propping the heavens. He would fill his eyes with the Himalayas and then go home to his garden in Rumeli Hissar and brood over his memories.

Sometimes he would take the gounibri and sing the love lyrics of his namesake, or of Nêdim, or "rose garden" songs he had picked up in Persia, which Ourida thought delicious. And sometimes Ortho trolled his green English ballads, also favourably received by her, simply because he sang them, for she did not understand their rhythm in the least. But more often they lounged, talking lazily, three very good friends together, Osman sucking at the hookah, punctuating the long silences, with shrewd comments on men and matters, Ortho lying at his ease watching the brilliant African stars, drawing breaths of blossom-scented air wafted from the Aguedal, Ourida nestling at his side, curled up like a sleepy kitten.

Summer passed and winter; came spring, and with it, to Ortho's joy, no prospect of a campaign for him. A desert marabout, all rags, filth, and fervour, preached a holy war in the Tissant country, gathering a few malcontents about him, and Yakoub Ben Ahmed was dispatched with a small force to put a stop to it. There were the usual rumours of unrest in the south, but nothing definite, merely young bucks talking big. Ortho looked forward to another year of peace.

He went in the Sultan's train to Essaouira for a fortnight in May, and at the end of June was sent to Taroudant, due east of Agadir. A trifling affair of despatches. He told Ourida he would be back in no time and rode off cheerfully.

His business in Taroudant done, he was on the point of turning home when he was joined by a Kaid Mia and ten picked men from Morocco bearing orders that he was to take them on to Tenduf, a further two hundred miles south, to collect overdue tribute.

Ortho well knew what that meant. Tenduf was on the verge of outbreak, the first signal of which would be his, the tax collector's, head on a charger. Had he been single he would not have gone to Tenduf, he would have made a dash for freedom, but now he had a wife in Morocco, a hostage for his fidelity.

Seeking a public scribe, he dictated a letter to Ourida and another to Osman Bâki, commending her to his care should the worst befall, and rode on.

The Basha of Tenduf received the Sultan's envoy with the elaborate courtesy that is inherent in a Moor and signifieth nothing. He was desolated that the tribute was behindhand, enlarged on the difficulty of collecting it in a land impoverished by drought (which it was not), but promised to set to work immediately. In the meantime Ortho lodged in the kasbah, ostensibly an honoured guest, actually a prisoner, aware that the Basha was the ringleader of the offenders, and that his own head might be removed at any moment. Hawk-faced sheiks, armed to the teeth, galloped in, conferred with the Basha, galloped away again. If they brought any tribute it was well concealed. Time went by; Ortho bit his lip, fuming inwardly, but outwardly his demeanour was of polite indifference. Whenever he could get hold of the Basha, he regaled him with instances of imperial wrath, of villages burned to the ground, towns taken and put to the sword, men, women, and children, lingering picturesquely on the tortures inflicted on unruly governors.

'But why did Sidi do that?' the Basha would exclaim, turning a shade paler at the thought of his peer of Khenifra having all his nails drawn out, and then being slowly sawn in half.

'Why?' Ortho would scratch his head and look puzzled. 'Why? Bless me if I know! Oh yes, I believe there was some little hitch with the taxes.'

'These walls make me laugh,' he remarked, walking on the Tenduf fortifications.

The Governor was annoyed. 'Why so? They are very good walls.'

'As walls go,' Ortho admitted. 'But what are walls nowadays? They take so long to build, so short a time to destroy. Why, our Turk gunners breached the Derunat walls in five places in an hour. The sole use for walls is to contain the defenders in a small space, then every bomb we throw inside does its work.'

'Hum!' the Basha stroked his brindled beard. 'Hum—but supposing the enemy harass you in the open?'

Ortho shrugged his shoulders. 'Then we kill them in the open, that is all. It takes longer, but they suffer more.'

'It took you a long time at Figuig,' the Basha observed maliciously.

'Not after we learned the way.'

'And what is the way?'

'We take possession of the wells and they die of thirst in the sands and save us powder. At Figuig there were many wells, it took time. Here'—he swept his hand over the burning champaign and snapped his fingers—'just that.'

'Hum,' said the Basha, and walked away deep in thought. Day after day came and went, and Ortho was not dead yet. He had an idea that he was getting the better of the bluffing match, that the Basha's nerve was shaking and he was passing it on.

There came a morning when the trails were hazy with the dust of horsemen hastening into Tenduf, and the envoy on the Kasha tower knew that the crisis had arrived.

It was over by evening. The tribute began to come in next day and continued to roll in for a week more.

The Basha accompanied Ortho ten miles on his return journey, regretting any slight misconstruction that might have arisen, and protesting his imperishable loyalty. He trusted that his dear friend, Säid-el-Inglez, would speak well of him to the Sultan, and presented him with two richly caparisoned horses and a bag of ducats as a souvenir of their charming relations.

Slowly went the train, the horses were heavy laden and the heat terrific. Ortho dozed in the saddle, impatient at the pace, powerless to mend it. He beguiled the tedious days mentally converting the Basha's ducats into silks and jewellery for Ourida. It was the end of August before he reached Taroudant. There he got word that the Court had moved to Rabat and he was to report there. Other news he got also, news that sent him riding alone to Morocco city, night and day as fast as driven horseflesh would carry him.

He went through the High Atlas passes to Goundafa, then north across the plains by Tagadirt and Aguergour. From Aguergour on, the road was crawling with refugees, men, women, children, horses, donkeys, camels loaded with household goods staggering up the Nifis valley, anywhere out of the pestilent city. They shouted warnings at the urgent horseman: 'The sickness, the sickness! Thou art riding to thy death, lord!'

Ortho nodded, he knew. It was late afternoon when he passed through Tameslouht and saw the Koutoubia minaret in the distance, standing serene, though all humanity rotted.

He was not desperately alarmed. Plagues bred in the beggars' kennels, not in palace gardens. It would have reached his end of the city last of all, giving his little family ample time to run. Osman Bâki would see to it that Ourida had every convenience. They were probably down at Dar El Beïda revelling in the clean sea breezes, or at Rabat with the Court. He told himself he was not really frightened, nevertheless he did the last six miles at a gallop, passed straight through the Bab Ksiba into the kasbah. There were a couple of indolent Sudanese on guard at the gate, and a few more sprawling in the shadow of the Drum Barracks, but the big Standard Square was empty and so were the two further courts.

He jumped off his horse at the postern and walked on. From the houses around came not a sound, not a move, in the street he was the only living thing. He knocked at his own door; no answer — good — they had gone!

The door swung open to his push, and he stepped in, half relieved, half fearful, went from room to room to find them stripped bare. Ourida had managed to take all her belongings with her, then. He wondered how she had found the transport. Osman Bâki contrived it, doubtless. A picture flashed before him of his famous black horse squadron trekking for the coast burdened with Ourida's furniture — a roll of *haitis* to this man, a cushion to that, a cauldron to another — and he laughed merrily.

Where had they gone, he wondered — Saff, Dar El Beïda, Essaouira, Rabat? The blacks at the barracks might know; Osman should have left a message. He stepped out of the kitchen into the court, and saw a man rooting the little orange trees out of their tubs.

'Hey!'

The man swung about, sought to escape, saw it was impossible and flung himself upon the ground, writhing, and sobbing for mercy.

It was a beggar who sat at the Bab Ahmar with his head hidden in the hood of his haik (he was popularly supposed to have no face), a supplicating claw protruding from a bundle of foul rags, and a muffled voice wailing for largesse. Ortho hated the loathly beast, but Ourida gave him money — 'In the name of God.'

'What are you doing here?'

'Great lord, have mercy, in the name of Sidi Ben Youssef the Blest, of Abd-el-Moumen, and Muley Idriss,' he slobbered. 'I did nothing, lord, nothing. I thought you had gone to the south and would not return to . . . to . . . this house. Spare me, O amiable prince.'

'And why should I not return to this house?' said Ortho.

The beggar hesitated. 'Mulay, I made sure . . . I thought . . . it was not customary, . . . young men do not linger in the places of lost love.'

'Dog,' said Ortho, suddenly cold about the heart. 'What do you mean?'

'Surely the Kaid knows?' There was a note of surprise in the mendicant's voice.

'I know nothing, I have been away . . . the lalla Ourida?'

The beggar locked both hands over his head and squirmed in the dust. 'Kaid, Kaid . . . the will of Allah.'

The little court reeled under Ortho's feet, a film like a heat wave rose up before his eyes, everything went blurred for a minute. Then he spoke quite calmly.

'Why did she not go away?'

'She had no time, lord. The little one, thy son, took the sickness first; she stayed to nurse him and herself was taken. But she was buried with honour, Kaid; the Turkish officer buried her with honour, in a colourful bier with tholbas chanting. I, miserable that I am, I followed also—afar. She was kind to the poor, the lalla Ourida.'

'But why, why didn't Osman get them both away before the plague struck the palace?' Ortho muttered fiercely, more to himself than otherwise, but the writhing rag heap heard him and answered.

'He had no time, Mulay. The kasbah was the first infected.'

'The first! How?'

'Yakoub Ben Ahmed brought many rebel heads from Tissant thinking to please Sidi. They stank and many soldiers fell sick, but Yakoub would not throw the heads away—it was his first command. They marched into the Kasha with drums beating, sick soldiers carrying offal.

Ortho laughed mirthlessly. So the dead had their revenge.

'Where is the Turk officer now?' he asked presently. 'Rabat?'

'No, Mulay—he too took the sickness, tending thy lancers.'

Ortho walked away. All over, all gone—wife, boy, faithful friend. Ourida would not see her son go by at the proud head of a regiment, nor Osman review his memories in his vineyard by the Bosphorus. All over, all gone, the best and truest.

Turning, he flung a coin at the beggar. 'Go . . . leave me.'

Dusk was flooding the little court, powder blue tinged with the rose-dust of sunset. A pair of grey pigeons perched on the parapet, made their love cooings and fluttered away again. From the Kasha minaret came the boom of the muezzin. High in the summer night drifted a white petal of a moon.

Ortho leaned against a pillar listening. The chink of anklets, the plud, plud of small bare feet.

'Säid, my beloved, is it you? Tired, my heart's dear? Rest your head here, lord, take thy ease. Thy fierce son is asleep at last; he has four teeth now and the strength of a lion. He will be a great captain of lances and do us honour when we are old. Your arm around me thus, tall one . . . äie, now am I content beyond all women . . .'

From twilight places came the voice of Osman Bâki and the subdued tinkle of the gounibri. 'Allah has been good to me. I have seen many wonders, rivers, seas, cities and plains, fair women, brave men and stout fighting, but I would yet see the Himalayas. After that I will go home where I was a boy. Listen while I sing you a song of my own country such as shepherds sing . . .'

Ortho's head sank in his hands. All over, now, all gone. . . . Something flapped in the shadows by the orange trees, flapped and hopped out into the central moonlight and posed there stretching its crippled wings.

It was the old eagle, disgustingly bloated.

That alone remained, that and the loathly beggar, left alone in the dead city to their carrion orgy. A shock of revulsion shook Ortho. Ugh!

He sprang up and, without looking round, strode out of the house and down the street to where his horse was standing.

A puff of hot wind followed him, a furnace blast, foul with the stench of half-buried corpses in the big Mussulman cemetery outside the walls. Ugh!

He kicked sharp stirrups into his horse and rode through the Bab Ksiba.

'Fleeing from the sickness—eh?' sneered a *mokadem* of Sudanese, who could not fly.

'No—ghosts,' said Ortho, and turned his beast on to the western road.

'The sea! The sea!'

Chapter XXIV

'PERISH ME! Rot and wither my soul and eyes if it ain't Säid!' exclaimed Captain Benjamin McBride, hopping across the court, his square hand extended. 'Säid, my bully, where d'you hail from?'

'I'm on the Bodyguard at Rabat. The Sultan's building there now. Scalas all round and seven new mosques are the order, I hear — we'll all be carrying bricks soon. I rode over to see you.'

'You ain't looking too proud,' said McBride, 'sort of wasted-like and God-ha'-mercy. Flux?'

Ortho shook his head. 'No, but I've had my troubles, and'—indicating the sailor's bandaged eye and his crutch — 'so have you, it seems.'

'Curse me, yes! Fell in with a fat Spanisher off Ortegal and mauled him down to a sheer hulk, when up romps a brace of American "thirties" and serves me cruel. If it hadn't been for nightfall and a shift of wind I should have been a holy angel by now. Bad times, boy, bad times. Too many warships about and all merchantmen sailing in convoy. I tell you I shall be glad when there's a bit of peace and goodwill on earth. Just now everybody's armed and its plaguy hard to pick up an honest living.'

'Governor here, aren't you?' Ortho inquired.

'Ay. Soft lie-abed shore berth till my wounds heal and we can get back to business. Fog in the river?'

'Thick, couldn't see across.'

'It's lying on the sea like a blanket,' said McBride; 'I've been watching it from my tower. Come along and see the girls. They're all here save Tama; she runned away with a Gharb sheik when I was cruising — deceitful slut! — but I've got three new ones.'

Ayesha and Schems-ed-Dah were most welcoming. They had grown somewhat matronly, but otherwise time seemed to have left them untouched. As ever they were gorgeously dressed, bejewelled and painted up with carmine, henna and kohl. Fluttering and twittering about their ex-slave they plied him with questions. He had been to the wars? Wounded? How many men had he killed? What was his rank? A kaid rahal of cavalry! . . . Ach! chut, chut! A great man! On the Bodyguard . . . ay-ee! Was it true the Sultan's favourite Circassians ate off pure gold? Was he married yet?

When he told them the recent plague in Morocco had killed both his wife and son, their liquid eyes brimmed over. No whit less sympathetic were the three new beauties; they wept in concert, though ten minutes earlier Ortho had been an utter stranger to them. Their hearts were very tender.

A black eunuch entered bearing the elaborate tea utensils As he turned to go, McBride called *aji*, pointing to the ground before him.

The slave threw up his hands in protest. 'Oh no, lord, please!'

'Kneel down,' the sailor commanded. 'I'll make you spring your ribs laughing, Säid, my bonny. Give me your hand, Mohar.'

'Lord, have mercy!'

'Mercy be damned! Your hand, quick!'

The piteous great creature extended a trembling hand, was grasped by the wrist and twisted on to his back.

'Now, my pearls, my rosebuds,' said McBride.

The five little birds of paradise tucked their robes about them and surrounded the prostrate slave, tittering and wriggling their forefingers at him. Even before he was touched he screamed, but when the tickling began in earnest he went mad, doubling, screwing, clawing the air with his toes, shrieking like a soul in torment—which indeed he was.

With the pearls and rosebuds it was evidently a favourite pastime; they tickled with diabolical cunning that could only come of experience, shaking with laughter and making sibilant noises the while—'Pish—pis-sh!' Finally, when the miserable victim was rolling up the whites of his eyes, mouthing foam, and seemed on the point of throwing a fit, McBride released him, and he escaped.

The captain wiped the happy tears from his remaining eye and turned on Ortho as one recounting an interesting scientific observation.

'Very thin-skinned for a black. D'you know, I believe he'd sooner take a four-bag at the gangway than a minute o' that. I do, so help me. I believe he'd sooner be flogged. *Vee-ry* curious. Come up and I'll show you my command.'

The Atlantic was invisible from the tower, sheeted under fog which, beneath a windless sky, stretched away to the horizon in woolly white billows. Ortho had an impression of a mammoth herd of tightly packed sheep.

'There's a three-knot tide under that, sweeping south, but it don't 'pear to move it much,' McBride observed. 'I'll warrant that bank ain't higher nor a first-rate's topgallant yard. I passed through the Western squadron once in a murk like that there. Off Dungeness it was. All their royals was sticking out, but my little hooker was trucks down, out o' sight.' He pointed to the north. 'Knitra's over there, bit of a kasbah like this. Er-rhossi has it, a sturdy fellow for a Greek, but my soul what a man to drink! Stayed here for a week, and 'pon my conscience he had me baled dry in two days—*me!* Back there's the forest, there's pig . . . What are you staring at?'

Ortho spun about guiltily. 'Me? Oh, nothing, nothing, nothing. What were you saying? The forest . . .'

He became suddenly engrossed in the view of the forest of Marmora.

'What's the matter? You look excited, like as if you'd seen something,' said McBride suspiciously.

'I've seen nothing,' Ortho replied. 'What should I see?'

'Blest if I know, only you looked startled.'

'I was thinking.'

'Oh was you? Well, as I was saying, there's a mort o' pigs in there, wild 'uns; and lions too, by report, but I ain't seen none. I'll get some sport as soon as my leg heals. This ain't much of a place though. Can't get no money out of charcoal-burners, not if you was to torture 'em for a year. As God is my witness, I've done my best, but the sooty vermin ain't got any!' He sighed. 'I shall be devilish glad when we can get back to our lawful business again. I've heard married men in England make moan about *their* "family responsibilities,' but what of me? I've got *three* separate families already, and two more on the way! What do you say to that—eh?'

Ortho sympathised with the much domesticated seaman and declared he must be going.

'You're in hell's own hurry all to a sudden.'

'I'm on the Bodyguard, you know.'

'Well, if you must that's an end on't, but I was hoping you'd stop for days and we'd have a chaw over old Jerry Gish. He, he! What a man! Say, would you have the maidens plague that eunuch once more before you go? Would you now? Give the word?'

Ortho declined the pleasure and asked if McBride could sell him a boat compass.

'I can sell you two or three, but what d'you want it for?'

'I'm warned for the Guinea caravan,' Ortho explained. 'A couple of *akkabaah* have been lost lately; the guides went astray in the sands. I want to keep some check on them.'

'I thought the Guinea force went out about Christmas.'

'No; this month.'

'Well, you know best, I suppose,' said the captain, and gave him a small compass, refusing payment.

'Come back and see us before you go,' he shouted as Ortho went out of the gate.

'Surely,' the latter replied, and rode southwards for Salé at top speed, knowing full well that, unless luck went hard against him, so far from seeing Ben McBride again, he would be out of the country before midnight.

While Ourida lived, life in Morocco had its compensations; with her death it had become insupportable. He had ridden down to the sea filled with a cold determination to seize the first opportunity of escape, and, if none occurred, to make one. Plans had been forming in his mind of working north to Tangier, there stealing a boat and running the blockade into beleaguered Gibraltar, some forty miles distant; a scheme risky to the point of foolhardiness. But remain he would not.

Now, unexpectedly, miraculously, an opportunity had come. Despite his denials, he *had* seen something from McBride's tower: the upper canvas of a ship protruding from the fog about a mile and a half out from the coast, by the cut and the long coachwhip pennant at the main an Englishman. Just a glimpse as the royals rose out of a trough of the fog billows; just the barest glimpse, but quite enough. Not for nothing had he spent his boyhood at the gates of the Channel watching the varied traffic passing up and down. And a few minutes earlier McBride had unwittingly supplied him with the knowledge he needed, the pace and direction of the tide. Ortho knew no arithmetic, but common sense told him that if he galloped he should reach Salé two hours ahead of that ship. She had no wind; she would only drift. He drove his good horse relentlessly, and as he went decided exactly what he would do.

It was dark when he reached the Bab Sebta, and over the low-lying town the fog lay like a coverlet.

He passed through the blind town, leaving the direction to his horse's instinct, and came out against the southern wall. Inquiring of an unseen pedestrian, he learnt he was close to the Bab Djedid; put his beast in a public stable near by, detached one stirrup, and, feeling his way through the gate, struck over the sandbanks towards the river. He came on it too far to the west, on the spit where it narrows opposite the Kasbah of the Udayas of Rabat, the noise of water breaking at the foot of the great fortress across the Bou Regreg told him as much.

Turning left-handed, he followed the river back till he brought up against the ferry boats. They were all drawn up for the night; the owners had gone, taking their oars with them. 'Damnation!' His idea had been to get a man to row him across, and knock him on the head in midstream; it was for that purpose that he had brought the heavy stirrup. There was nothing for it now but to rout a man out—all waste of precious time!

There was just a chance some careless boatman had left his oars behind. Quickly he felt in the skiffs. The first was empty, so was the second, the third and the fourth, but in the fifth he found what he sought. It was a light boat too, a private shallop and half afloat at that.

What colossal luck! He put his shoulder to the stem and hove—and up rose a man.

'Who's that? Is that you master?'

Ortho sprang back. Where had he heard that voice before? Then he remembered, it was Puddicombe's. Puddicombe had not returned to Algiers after all, but was here waiting to row Sore Eyes across to Rabat, to a banquet possibly.

'Who's that?'

Ortho blundered up against the stem, pretending to be mildly drunk, mumbling in Arabic that he was a sailor from a trading felucca looking for his boat.

'Well, this is not yours, friend,' said Puddicombe. 'Try down the beach. But if you take my advice you'll not go boating tonight; you might fall overboard and get a drink of water which, by the sound of you, is not what thou art accustomed to.' He laughed at his own delightful wit.

Ortho stumbled into the fog, paused, and thought matters over. To turn a ferryman out might take half an hour. Puddicombe had the only oars on the beach, therefore Puddicombe must give them up.

He lurched back again, steadied himself against the stem and asked the Devonian if he would put him oft to his felucca, getting a flat refusal. Hiccuping, he said there was no offence meant, and asked Puddicombe if he would like a sip of fig brandy. He said he had no unsurmountable objection, came forward to get it, and Ortho hit him over the head with the stirrup iron as hard as he could lay in. Puddicombe toppled face forwards out of the boat and lay on the sand without a sound or a twitch.

'I'm sorry I had to do it,' said Ortho, 'but you yourself warned me to trust nobody, above all a fellow *renegado*. I'm only following your own advice. You'll wake up before dawn. Goodbye.'

Pushing the boat off, he jumped aboard and pulled for the grumble of the bar.

He went aground on the sandspit, and rowing away from that very nearly stove the boat in on a jag of rock below the Kasbah of the Udayas. The corner past, steering was simple for a time, one had merely to keep the boat pointed to the rollers. Over the bar he went, slung high, swung low, tugged on to easy water, and striking a glow on his flint and steel examined the compass.

Thus, occasionally checking his course by the needle, he pulled due west. He was well ahead of the ship, he thought, and by getting two miles out to sea would be lying dead in her track. Before long the land breeze would be blowing sufficient to push the fog back, but not enough to give the vessel more than two or three knots; in that light shallop he could catch her easily, if she were within reasonable distance.

Reckoning he had got his offing he swung the boat's head due north and paddled gently against the run of the tide.

Time progressed. There was no sign of the ship or the land breeze that was to reveal her. For all he knew he might be four miles out to sea or one half only. He had no landmarks, no means of measuring how far he had come except by experience of how long it had taken him to pull a dinghy from point to point at home in Monk's Cove; yet somehow he felt he was about right.

Time went by. The fog pressed about him in walls of discoloured steam, clammy, dripping, heavy on the lungs. Occasionally it split, revealing dark corridors and halls, abysses of Stygian gloom, rolled together again. A hundred feet overhead it was clear night and starry. Where was that breeze?

More time passed. Ortho began to think he had failed, and made plans to cover the failure. It should not be difficult. He would land on the sands opposite the Bab Malka, overturn the boat, climb over the walls, and see the rest of the night out among the Mussulman graves. In the morning he could claim his horse and ride into camp as if nothing had happened. As a slave he had been over the walls time and again; there was a crack in the bricks by the Bordj-el-Kebir—he didn't suppose it was repaired, they never repaired anything. Puddicombe didn't know who had hit him; there was no earthly reason why he should be suspected. The boat would be found overturned, the unknown sailor presumed drowned. Quite simple. Remained the Tangier scheme.

By this time, being convinced that the ship had passed, he slewed the boat about and pulled in. The sooner he was ashore the better.

The fog appeared to be moving. It twisted into clumsy spirals which sagged in the middle, puffed out cheeks of vapour, bulged and writhed, drifting to meet the boat. The land breeze was coming at last—an hour too late! Ortho pulled on, an ear cocked for the growl of the bar. There was nothing to be heard as yet; he must have gone further than he thought, but fog gagged and distorted sound in the oddest way. The spirals nodded above him, like gigantic wraiths. Something passed overhead delivering an eerie screech. A seagull only, but it made him jump. Glancing at the compass he found that he was, at the moment, pulling due south. He got his direction again and pulled on. Goodness knew what the tide had been doing to him. There might be a westward stream from the river which had pushed him miles out to sea. Or possibly be was well south of his mark and would strike the coast below Rabat. Oh well, no matter, as long as he got ashore soon. Lying on his oars he listened again for the bar, but could hear no murmur of it. Undoubtedly he was to the southward. That ship was halfway to Fédala by now.

Then, quite clearly, behind a curtain of fog an English voice chanted: 'By the deep nine.'

Ortho stopped rowing, stood up and listened. Silence, not a sound, not a sign. Fichus and twisted columns of fog drifting towards him, that was all. But somewhere close at hand a voice was calling soundings. The ship was there. All his fine calculations were wrong, but he had blundered aright.

'Mark ten.'

The voice came again, seemingly from his left-hand side this time. Again silence. The fog alleys closed once more, muffling sound. The ship was there, within a few yards, yet this cursed mist with its fool tricks might make him lose her altogether. He hailed with all his might. No answer. He might have been flinging his shout against banks of cotton wool. Again and again he hailed.

Suddenly came the answer, from behind his back apparently.

'Ahoy there . . . who are you?'

228

' 'Scaped English prisoner! English prisoner escaped!'

There was a pause, then, 'Keep off there . . . none of your tricks.'

'No tricks . . . I am alone . . . *alone,*' Ortho bawled, pulling furiously. He could hear the vessel plainly now, the creak of her tackle as she felt the breeze.

'Keep off there, or I'll blow you to bits.'

'If you fire a gun you'll call the whole town out,' Ortho warned.

'What town?'

'Salé.'

'Christ!' the voice ejaculated and repeated his words. 'He says we're off Salé, sir.'

Ortho pulled on. He could see the vessel by this, a blurred shadow among the steamy wraiths of mist, a big three-master close-hauled on the port tack.

Said a second voice from aft: 'Knock his bottom out if he attempts to board . . . no chances.'

'Boat ahoy,' hailed the first voice. 'If you come alongside I'll sink you, you bloody pirate. Keep off.'

Ortho stopped rowing. They were going to leave him. Forty yards away was an English ship—England. He was missing England by forty yards, England and the Owls' House!

He jerked at his oars, tugged the shallop directly in the track of the ship and slipped overboard. They might be able to see his boat, but his head was too small a mark. If he missed what he was aiming at he was finished; he could never regain that boat. It was neck or nothing now, the last lap, the final round.

He struck to meet the vessel—only a few yards.

She swayed towards him, a chuckle of water at her cutwater, tall as a cliff she seemed, towering out of sight. The huge bow loomed over him, poised and crushed downwards as though to ride him under, trample him deep.

The sheer, toppling bulk, the hiss of riven water snapped his last shred of courage. It was too much. He gave up, awaited the instant stunning crash upon his head, saw the great bowsprit rush across a shining patch of stars, knew the end had come at last, thumped against the bows and found himself pinned by the weight of water, his head still up. His hands, his unfailing hands, had saved him again, he had hold of the bobstay!

The weight of water was not really great, the ship had little more than steerage way. Darkness had magnified his terrors. He got across the stay without much difficulty, worked along it to the dolphin-striker, thence by the martingale to the fo'c'sle.

The lookout were not aware of his arrival until he was amongst them, they were watching the tiny smudge that was his boat—he noticed that they had round shot ready to drop into it.

'Good God!' the mate exclaimed, 'who are you?'

'The man who hailed just now, sir.'

'But I thought . . . I thought you were in that boat.'

'I was, sir, but I swam off.'

'Good God!' said the mate again and hailed the poop: 'Here's this fellow come aboard after all, sir. He's quite alone.'

An astonished 'How the devil?'

'Swam, sir.'

'Pass him aft.'

Ortho was led aft. Boarding nettings were triced up and men lay between the upper deck guns, girded with sidearms. Shot were in the garlands and match-tubs filled all ready. A well-manned, well-appointed craft. He asked the man who accompanied him her name.

'*Elijah Impey*. East Indiaman.'

'Indiaman! Then where are we bound for?'

'Bombay.'

Ortho drew a deep breath. It was a long road home.

Chapter XXV

THE LITTLE Botallack man and Eli Penhale shook hands, tucked the slack of their wrestling jackets under their left armpits and, crouching, approached each other, right hands extended.

The three judges, ancient wrestlers, leaned on their ashplants and looked extremely knowing; they went by the title of "sticklers."

The wrestling ring was in a grass field almost under the shadow of St Gwithian church tower. To the north the ridge of tors rolled along the skyline, autumnal brown. Southward was the azure of the English Channel; west, over the end of land, the glint of the Atlantic with the Scilly Isles showing on the horizon, very faint, like small irregularities on a ruled blue line.

All St Gwithian was present, men and women, girls and boys, with a good sprinkling of visitors from the parishes round about. They formed a big ring of black and pink, dark clothes, and healthy countenances. A good-natured crowd, bandying interparochial chaff from side to side, rippling with laughter when some accepted wit brought off a sally, yelling encouragement to their district champions.

'Beware of 'en's feet, Jan, boy. The old toad is brear foxy.'

'Scat 'en, Ephraim, my pretty old beauty! Grip to an' scandalise 'en!'

'Move round, sticklers! Think us can see through 'e? Think you'm made of glass?'

'Up Gwithian!'

'Up St Levan!'

At the feet of the crowd lay the disengaged wrestlers, chewing blades of grass and watching the play. They were naked except for short drawers and on their white skins grip marks flared red, bruises and long scratches where fingers had slipped or the rough jacket edges cut in. Amiable young stalwarts, smiling at each other, grunting approvingly at smart pieces of work. One had a snapped collarbone, another a fractured forearm wrapped up in a handkerchief, but they kept their pains to themselves, it was all in the game.

Now Eli and the little Botallack man were out for the final.

Polwhele was not five feet six and tipped the beam at eleven stone, whereas Eli was five ten and weighed two stone the heavier. It looked as though he had only to fall on the miner to finish him, but such was far from the case. The sad-faced little tinner had already disposed of four bulky opponents in workmanlike fashion that afternoon—the collarbone was his doing.

'Watch his eyes,' Bohenna had warned.

That was all very well, but it was next to impossible to see his eyes for the thick bang of hair that dangled over them, like the forelock of a Shetland pony.

Polwhele clumsily sidled a few steps to the right. Eli followed him. Polwhele walked a few steps to the left; again Eli followed. Polwhele darted back to the right, Eli after him, stopped, slapped his right knee loudly and twisting left-handed grabbed the farmer round the waist and hove him into the air.

It was cleverly done—the flick of speed after the clumsy walk, the slap on the knee drawing the opponent's eye away—cleverly done but not quite quick enough. Eli got the miner's head in chancery as he was hoisted up and hooked his toes behind the other's knees.

Polwhele could launch himself and his burden neither forwards nor backwards, as the balance lay with Eli. The miner hugged at Eli's stomach with all his might, jerking cruelly. Eli wedged his free arm down and eased the pressure somewhat. It was painful but bearable.

'Lave 'en carry 'e so long as thou canst, son,' came the voice of Bohenna. 'Tire 'en out.'

Polwhele strained for a forwards throw, tried a backwards twist, but the pull behind the knees embarrassed him. He began to pant. Thirteen stone hanging like a millstone about one's neck at the end of the day was intolerable. He tried to work his head out of chancery, concluded it would only be at the price of his ears, and gave that up.

'Stay where 'e are,' shouted Bohenna to his protégé. 'T'eddn costin' *you* nawthin'.'

Eli stayed where he was. Polwhele's breathing became more laboured, sweat bubbled from every pore, a sinew in his left leg cracked under the strain. Once more he tried the forwards pitch, reeled, rocked, and came down sideways. He risked a dislocated shoulder in so doing, with the farmer's added weight, but got nothing worse than a heavy jar. It was no fall; the two men rolled apart and lay panting on their backs.

After a pause the sticklers intimated to them to go on. Once more they faced each other. The miner was plainly tired, the band hung over his eyes a sweat-soaked rag, his movements were sluggish. In response to the exhortations of his friends he shook his head, made gestures with his hands—finished.

Slowly he gave way before Eli, warding off grips with sweeps of his right forearm, refusing to come to a hold. St Gwithian jeered at him. Botallack implored one more flash. He shook his head; he was incapable of flashing. Four heavy men he had put away to come upon this great block of brawn at the day's end: it was too much.

Eli could not bring him to grips, grew impatient, and made the pace hotter, forcing the miner backwards right round the ring. It became a boxing match between the two right hands, the one clutching, the other parrying. Almost he had Polwhele; his fingers slipped on a fold of the canvas jacket. The spectators rose to a man, roaring.

Polwhele ran backwards out of a grip and stumbled. Eli launched out, saw the sad eyes glitter behind the draggles of hair, and went headlong, flying.

The next thing he knew he was lying full length, the breath jarred out of him and the miner on top, fixed like a stoat. The little man had dived under him, tipped his thigh with a shoulder, and turned him as he fell. It was a fair back, two shoulders and a hip down; he had lost the championship.

Polwhele, melancholy as ever, helped him to his feet.

'Nawthin' broke, Squire? That's fitty. You'll beat me next year; could of this, if you'd waited.' He put a blade of grass between his teeth and staggered off to join his vociferous friends, the least jubilant of any.

Bohenna came up with his master's clothes. '"Nother time you'm out against a quick man go slow—make 'en come to *you*. Eddn no sense in playin' tig with forked lightnin'. I shouted to 'e, but you was too furious to hear. Oh, well, 'tis done now, s'pose.'

He walked away to hobnob with the sticklers in the Lamb and Flag, to drink ale and wag their heads and lament on the decay of wrestling and manhood since they were young.

Eli pulled on his clothes. One or two Monk's Covers shouted 'Stout tussle, Squire,' but did not stop to talk; nor did he expect them to. He was respected in the parish, but had none of the graceful qualities that make for popularity.

His mother went by, immensely fat, yet sitting her carthorse firm as a rock.

'The little dog had 'e by the nose proper that time, my great soft bullock,' she jeered, and rode on laughing. She hated Eli; as master of Bosula he kept her short of money, even going to the length of publicly crying down her credit. Had he not done so, they would have been ruined long since instead of in a fair state of prosperity, but Teresa took no count of that. She was never tired of informing audiences—preferably in Eli's presence—that if her other son had been spared, her own precious boy Ortho, things would have been very different. *He* would not have seen her going in rags, without a penny piece to bless herself, not he. Time, in her memory, had washed away all the elder's faults, leaving only virtues exposed, and those grossly exaggerated. She would dilate for hours on his good looks, his wit, his courage, his loving consideration for herself, breaking into hot tears of rage when she related the fancied indignities she suffered at the hands of the paragon's unworthy brother.

She was delighted that Polwhele had bested Eli, and rode home jingling her winnings on the event. Eli went on dressing, unmoved by his mother's jibes. As a boy he had learnt to close his ears to the taunts of Rusty Rufus, and he found the accomplishment most useful. When Teresa became abusive he either walked out of the house or closed up like an oyster, and her tirades beat harmlessly against his spiritual shell. Words, words, nothing but words; his contempt for talk had not decreased as time went on.

He pulled his belt up, hustled into his best blue coat, and was knotting his neckcloth when somebody behind him said, 'Well wrastled, Eli.'

He turned and saw Mary Penaluna, with old Simeon close beside.

Eli shook his head. 'He was smaller than I, naught but a little man. I take shame not to have beaten 'en.'

But Mary would have none of it. 'I see no shame, then,' she said warmly. 'They miners do nothing but wrastle, wrastle all day between shifts, and underground too, so I've heard tell. But you've got other things to do, Eli; 'tis a wonder you stood up to 'en so long. And they're nothing but a passel o' tricksters; teddn what I call fitty wrastling at all.'

'Well. 'tis fair, anyhow,' said Eli. 'He beat me fair enough, and there's an end of it.'

' 'Ess, s'pose,' Mary admitted, 'but I do think you wrastled bravely, Eli, and so do father and all of the parish. Oh, look how the man knots his cloth—all twisted. You'm bad as father, I declare. Lave me put it to rights.' She reached up strong, capable hands, gave the neckerchief a pull and a pat, and stood back laughing. 'You men are no better than babies, for all your size and cursing and 'bacca. 'Tis proper now. Are 'e steppin' home along.'

Eli was. They crossed the field, and, turning their backs on the church tower, took the road towards the sea, old Simeon walking first, slightly bent with toil and rheumatism, long arms dangling inert; Mary and Eli followed side by side, speaking never a word. It was two miles to Roswarva, over upland country, bare of trees, but beautiful in its windswept nakedness. Patches of dead bracken glowed with the warm copper that is to be found in some women's hair; on grey boulders spots of orange lichen shone like splashes of gold paint. The brambles were dressed like harlequins, in ruby, green and yellow, and on nearly every hawthorn sat a pair of magpies, their black and white livery looking very smart against the scarlet berries.

Eli walked on to Roswarva, although it was out of his way. He liked the low house among the stunted sycamores, with the sun in its face all day, and the perpetual whisper of salt sea winds about it. He liked the bright display of flowers Mary seemed to keep going perennially in the little garden by the south door, the orderly kitchen with its sanded floor, clean whitewash, and burnished copper. Bosula was his home, but it was to Roswarva that he turned as to a haven in time of trouble, when he wanted advice about his farming, or when Teresa was particularly fractious. There was little said on these occasions—a few slow, considered words from Simeon, a welcoming smile from Mary, a cup of tea or a mug of cider, and then home again—but he had got what he needed.

He sat in the kitchen that afternoon twirling his hat in his powerful hands, staring out of the window and thinking that his worries were pretty nearly over. There was always Teresa to reckon with, but they were out of debt and Bosula was in good farming shape at last. What next? An idea was taking shape in his deliberate mind. He stared out of the window, but not at the farm boar wallowing blissfully in the mire of the lane, or at Simeon driving his sleek cows in for milking, or at the blue Channel beyond with a little collier brig bearing up for the Lizard, her grimy canvas transformed by the alchemy of sunshine. Eli Penhale was seeing visions, homely, comfortable visions.

Mary came in, rolling her sleeves back over firm rounded forearms, dimpled at the elbows. The once leggy girl was leggy no longer, but a ripe, upstanding, full-breasted woman with kindly brown eyes and an understanding smile.

'I'll give 'e a penny for thy dream, Eli—if 'tis a pretty one,' she laughed. 'Is it?'

The farmer grinned. 'Prettiest I ever had.'

'Queen of England take you for her boy?'

'Prettier than that.'

'My lor, it must be worth a brear bit o' money, then! More'n I can afford.'

'I don't think so.'

'Is it going cheap, or do you think I'm made of gold pieces?'

'It's not money I want.'

'You're not like most of us, then,' said Mary and started, 'there's father calling in the yard, must be goin' milkin'. Sit 'e down where 'e be and I'll be back quick as quick and we'll see if I can pay the price, whatever it is—sit 'e down and rest.'

But Eli had risen. 'Must be going, I believe.'

'Why?'

'Got to see to the horses. I've let Bohenna and Davy off for the day, 'count of wrestling.'

Mary pouted, but she was a farmer's daughter, a fellow bondslave of animals, she recognised the necessity.

'Anybody'd think it was your men had been wrestlin' and not you, you great soft-heart. Oh well, run along with 'e and come back when's done and take a bite of supper with us, will 'e? Father'd be proud and I've fit a lovely supper.'

Eli promised and betook himself homewards. Five strenuous bouts on top of six hours' work in the morning had tired him somewhat, bruises were stiffening, and his left shoulder gave him pain, but his heart, his heart was singing "Mary Penaluna—Mary Penhale, Mary Penaluna—Mary Penhale" all the way and his feet went wing-shod. Almost he had asked her in the kitchen, almost, almost—it had been tripping off his tongue when she mentioned her cows and in so doing reminded him of his horses. By blood, instinct and habit he was a farmer, the horses must be seen to first, his helpless, faithful servitors. His mother usually turned her mount into the stable without troubling to feed, unsaddle it, or even ease the girths. The horses must be seen to.

He would say the word that evening after supper when old Simeon fell asleep in his rocker, as was his invariable custom. That very evening.

Tregors had gone whistling down the wind long since; the unknown hind from Burdock Water had let it go to rack and ruin, a second mortgagee was not forthcoming, Carveth Donnithorne foreclosed and marched in. Tregors had gone, but Bosula remained, clear of debt and as good a place as any in the Hundred, enough for any one man. Eli felt he could make his claim, for even prosperous Simeon

Penaluna's daughter, with a clear conscience. He came to the rim of the valley, hoisted himself to the top of a bank, paused and sat down.

The valley, touched by the low rays of sunset, foamed with gold, with the pale gold of autumnal elms, the bright gold of ashes, the old gold of oaks.

Bosula among its enfolding woods! No Roman emperor behind his tall Praetorians had so steadfast, so splendid a guard as these. Shelter from the winter gales, great spluttering logs for the hearth, green shade in summer, and in autumn this magnificence. Holly for Christmas, apples and cider. The apples were falling now, falling with soft thuds all day and night and littering the orchard, sunk in the grass like rosy-faced children playing hide and seek.

Eli's eye ran up the opposite hillside, a patchwork quilt of trim fields, green pasture and brown ploughland, all good and all his.

His heart went out in gratitude to the house of his breed, to the sturdy men who had made it what it was, to the first poor ragged tinner wandering down the valley with his donkey, to his unknown father, that honest giant with the shattered face who had brought him into the world that he, in his turn, might take up this goodly heritage.

It should go on. He saw into the future, a brighter, better future. He saw flowers outside the Owls' House, perennially blooming; saw a whitewashed kitchen with burnished copper pans and a woman in it, smiling welcome at the day's end, her sleeves rolled up to show her dimpled elbows; saw a pack of brown-eyed, chubby little boys tumbling noisily in to supper—Penhales of Bosula. It should go on. He vaulted off the bank and strode whistling down to the Owls' House, bowed his head between Adam and Eve, and found Ortho sitting in the kitchen.

Chapter XXVI

THE RETURN of Ortho Penhale, nearly seven years after his supposed death, caused a sensation in West Cornwall. The smuggling affair at Monk's Cove was remembered and exaggerated out of all semblance to the truth. Millions of gallons had been run through by Ortho and his gang, culminating in a pitched battle with the dragoons. Nobody could say how many were killed in that affray, and it was affirmed that nobody ever would know. Midnight buryings were hinted at, hush money and so on; a dark, thrilling business altogether. Ortho was spoken of in the same breath as King Nick and other celebrities of the "Trade." His subsequent adventures lost nothing in the mouths of the gossips. He had landed in Barbary a slave, and in the space of two years become a general. The Sultan's favourite queen fell in love with him; on being discovered in her arms he had escaped by swimming four miles out to sea and intercepting an East Indiaman, in which vessel he had visited India and seen the Great Mogul.

Ortho discovered himself a personage. It was a most agreeable sensation. Men in every walk of life rushed to shake his hand. He found himself sitting in Penzance taverns in the exalted company of magistrates and other notables, telling the story of his adventures—with picturesque additions.

And the women. Even the fine ladies in Chapel Street turned their proud heads when he limped by. His limp was genuine to a point, but when he saw a pretty woman ahead he improved on it to draw sympathy and felt their softened eyes following him on his way, heard them whisper, 'Ortho Penhale, my dear . . . General in Barbary . . . twelve times wounded. . . . How pale he looks and how handsome!'

A most agreeable sensation.

To ensure that he should not pass unnoticed, he affected a slight eccentricity of attire. For him no more the buff breeches, the raffish black and silver coats; dressed thus he might have passed for any squire.

He wore instead the white trousers of a sailor, a marine's scarlet tunic he had picked up in a junk shop, a coloured kerchief loosely knotted about his throat, and on his bull curls the round fur cap of the sea. There was no mistaking him. Small boys followed him in packs, round-eyed, worshipful. Ortho Penhale, smuggler, Barbary lancer!

If he had been popular once, he was doubly popular now. The Monk's Cove incident was forgiven but not forgotten; it went to swell his credit in fact. To have arrested him on that old score would have been more than the Collector's life was worth. The Collector, prudent man, publicly shook Penhale by the hand and congratulated him on his miraculous escape.

Ortho found his hoard of six hundred and seventy pounds intact in the hollow ash by Tumble Down and spent it freely. He gave fifty pounds to Anson's widow (who had married a prosperous cousin some years before, forgotten poor Anson, and did not need it), and put a further fifty in his pockets to give to Tamsin Eva.

Bohenna told him the story as a joke, but Ortho was smitten with what he imagined was remorse.

He remembered Tamsin, a slim appealing little thing in blue, skin like milk, and a cascade of red-gold hair; he must make some honourable gesture—there were certain obligations attached to the role of local hero. It was undoubtedly somewhat late in the day; the Trevaskis lout had married the girl and accepted the paternity of the child (it was a boy, six years old now, Bohenna reported), but that made no difference, he must make his gesture. Fifty pounds was a lot of money to a struggling farmer; besides, he would like to see Tamsin again—that slender neck and marvellous hair! If Trevaskis wasn't treating her properly he'd take her away from him, boy and all, b'God he would!

He went up to the Trevaskis homestead one afternoon and saw a meagre woman standing at the back of a small house, washing clothes in a tub. Her thin forearms were red with work, her hair was screwed up anyhow on the top of her head and hung over her eyes in draggled rats-tails, her complexion had faded through long standing over kitchen fires, her apron was torn, and her thick wool socks were thrust into a pair of clumsy men's boots.

It was some seconds before he recognised her as Tamsin, Tamsin after seven years as a workingman's wife. A couple of dirty children of about four and five were making mud pies at her feet, and in the cottage a baby lifted its querulous voice.

She had other children, then, two, three, half a dozen perhaps—huh!

Ortho turned about and limped softly away, unnoticed, the fifty pounds still in his pockets.

Making amends to a pretty woman was one thing, but to a faded drudge with a school of Trevaskis bantlings quite another suit of clothes.

He gave the fifty pounds to his mother, took her to Penzance and bought her two flamboyant new dresses and a massive gold brooch. She adored him. The hard times, scratching a penny here and there out of Eli, were gone for ever. Her handsome, free-handed son was back again, master of Bosula, and darling of the district. She rode everywhere with him, to hurling matches, bull-baitings, races, and cockfights, big with pride, chanting his praises to all comers.

'That Eli would have seen me starve to death in a ditch,' she would say, buttonholing some old crony in a tavern. 'But Ortho's got respect for his old mother. He'd give me the coat off his back, or the heart out of his breast, he would, so help me!' (Hiccup.)

Mother and son rode together all over the Hundred: Teresa wreathed in fat, splendid in attire, still imposing in her virile bulk; Ortho in his scarlet tunic, laughing, gambling, dispensing free liquor, telling amazing stories. Eli stayed at home, working on the farm, bewildered, dumb, the look in his eyes of a suffering dog.

Christmas passed more merrily than ever before at the Owls' House that year. Half St Gwithian was present and two fiddlers. Some danced in the kitchen, the overflow danced in the barn, profusely decorated with evergreens for the occasion so that it had the appearance of a candlelit glade. Few of the men went to bed at all that night and, with the exception of Eli, none sober. Twelfth Night was celebrated with a similar outburst, and then people settled down to work again and Ortho found himself at a loose end. He could always ride into Penzance and pass the time of day with the idlers in the Star, but that was not to his taste. He drank little himself and disliked the company. Furthermore, he had told most of his tales and was in danger of repeating them. Ortho was wise enough to see that if he were not careful he would degenerate from the local hero into the local bore, and gave Penzance a rest. There appeared to be nothing for it but that he should get down to work on the farm; after his last eight years it was an anticlimax which presented few allurements.

Before long there would be no excuse for idleness. The Kiddlywink in Monk's Cove saw him most evenings, talking blood and thunder with Jacky's George. He lay abed late of a morning and limped about the cliffs on fine afternoons.

The Luddra Head was his favourite haunt; from its crest he could see from the Lizard Point to the Logan Rock, some twenty miles east and west, and keep an eye on the shipping. He would watch the Mount's Bay fishing fleets flocking out to their grounds; the Welsh collier brigs racing up-channel, jib-boom and jib-boom; mail packets crowding all sail for open sea; a big blue-water merchantman rolling home from the world's ends; or a smart frigate logging nine knots on a bowline, tossing the spray over her fo'c'sle in clouds. He would criticise their handling, their rigs, make guesses as to their destinations and business.

It was comfortable up on the Head, a slab of granite at one's back, a springy cushion of turf to sit upon, the winter sunshine warming the rocks, pouring all over one.

One afternoon he climbed the Head, to find a woman sitting in his particular spot. He cursed her under his breath, turned away, and then turned back again. Might as well see what sort of woman it was before he went; you never knew. He crawled up the rocks, came out upon the granite platform, pretending he had not noticed the intruder, executed a realistic start of surprise, and said, 'Good morning to you.'

'Good afternoon,' the girl replied.

Ortho accepted the correction and remarked that the weather was fine. The girl did not contest the obvious and went on with her work, which was knitting.

Ortho looked her all over, and was glad he had not turned back. A good-looking wench this, tall, yet well formed, with a strong white neck, a fresh complexion, and pleasant brown eyes. He wondered where she lived. St Gwithian parish? She had not come to his Christmas and Twelfth Night parties.

He sat down on a rock facing her. 'My leg,' he explained; 'must rest it.'

She made no remark, which he thought unkind; she might have shown some interest in his leg.

'Got wounded in the leg in Barbary.'

The girl looked up. 'What's that?'

Ortho reeled slightly. Was it possible there was anybody in England, in the wide world, who did not know where Barbary was?

'North coast of Africa, of course,' he retorted.

The girl nodded. 'Oh. 'ess. I believe I have heard father tell of it. Dutch colony. Isn't it?'

'No,' Ortho barked.

The girl went imperturbably on with her knitting; her shocking ignorance did not appear to worry her in the least. She did not ask Ortho for enlightenment, and he did not feel like starting the subject again. The conversation came to a full stop.

The girl was a ninny, Ortho decided, a feather-headed country ninny—yet remarkably good-looking for all that. He admired the fine shape of her shoulders under the blue cloak, the thick curls of glossy brown hair that escaped from her hood, and those fresh cheeks. One did not find complexions like that anywhere else but here in the wet south-west. He had an idea that a dimple would appear in one of those cheeks if she laughed, perhaps in both. He felt he must make the ninny dimple.

'Live about here?' he inquired.

She nodded.

'So do I.'

No reply. She was not interested in where he lived, drat her! He supplied the information. 'I live at Bosula in the valley. I'm Ortho Penhale.'

The girl did not receive this enthralling intelligence with proper emotion; she looked at him calmly and said: 'Penhale of Bosula, are 'e? Then I s'pose you'm connected with Eli?'

Once more Ortho staggered. That anyone in the Penwith Hundred should be in doubt as to who he was, the local hero! To be known only as Eli's brother! It was too much! But he bit his lip and explained his relationship to Eli in a level voice. The ninny was even a bigger fool than he had thought; but dimple she should. The conversation came to a second full stop.

Two hundred feet below them waves draped the Luddra ledges with shining foam-cloths, poured back the crannies dribbling as with milk—and launched themselves afresh. A subdued booming travelled upwards, died away in a long-drawn sigh, then the boom again. Great mile-long stripes and ribbons of foam outlined the coast, twisted by the tides into strange patterns and arabesques, creamy white upon dark blue. Jackdaws darted in and out of holes in the cliffside, and gulls swept and hovered on invisible air currents, crying mournfully. In a bed of campions just above the toss of the breakers a red dog-fox lay curled up asleep in the sun.

'Come up here often?' Ortho inquired, restarting the one-sided conversation.

'No.'

'Ahem! I do; I come up here to look at the ships.'

The girl glanced at him, a mischievous sparkle in her brown eyes. 'Then wouldn't you see the poor dears better if you was to turn and face 'em, Squire Penhale?'

She folded her knitting, stood up, and walked away without another word.

Ortho arose also. She had had him there. Not such a fool after all. And she had dimpled when she made that sally; just a wink of a dimple, but entrancing. He had a suspicion she had been laughing at him, knew who he was all the time, else why had she called him "Squire"?

By the Lord! Laughing at him, was she? That was a new sensation for the local hero. He flushed with anger. Blast the girl! But she was a damned handsome piece for all that. He watched her through a peephole in the rocks, watched her cross the neck of land, pass the earth ramparts of the Luddra's prehistoric inhabitants, and turn left-handed along the coast path. Then, when she was committed to her direction, he made after her as fast as he was capable. Despite his wound, he was capable of considerable speed, but the girl set him all the pace he needed.

She was no featherweight, but she skipped and ran along the craggy path as lightly as a hind. Ortho laboured in the rear grunting in admiration.

Catch her he could not; it was all he could do to keep her in sight. Where a small stream went down to the sea through a tangle of thorn and bramble she gave him the slip.

He missed the path altogether, went up to his knees in a boghole, and got his smart white trousers in a mess. Ten minutes it took him to work through that tangle, and when he came out on the far side there was no sign of the girl. He cursed her, damned himself for a fool, swore he was going back, and limped on. She must live close at hand. He'd try ahead for another mile and then give it up.

Within half a mile he came upon Roswarva standing among its stunted sycamores.

He limped up to the door and rapped it with his stick. Simeon Penaluna came out. Ortho greeted him with warmth. But lately back from foreign parts, he thought he really must come and see how his good neighbour was faring. Simeon was surprised; it was the first time the elder Penhale had been to the house. This sudden solicitude for his welfare was unlooked for.

He said he was not doing as badly as he might be, and asked the visitor in.

The visitor accepted; would just sit down for a moment or two and rest a bit. . . . His wounds, you know . . .

A moment or two extended to an hour. Ortho was convinced the girl was somewhere about; there were no other houses in the neighbourhood, and, now he came to remember, Penaluna had had a daughter in the old days, an awkward child, all legs like a foal. The same girl, doubtless. She would have to show up sooner or later. He talked, and talked, and talked himself into an invitation to supper. His persistency was rewarded; the girl he had met on the cliffs brought the supper in, and Simeon introduced her as his daughter Mary. Not by a flicker of an eyelash did she show that she had ever seen Ortho before, but curtsied to him as grave as a church image.

It was ten o'clock before Ortho took his way homewards. He had not done so badly, he thought. Mary Penaluna might pretend to take no interest in his travels, but he had managed to hold Simeon's ears fast enough.

The grim farmer had laughed, till the tears started, at Ortho's descriptions of the antics of the soldiers after the looting at Figuig, and the equatorial mummery on board the Indiaman.

Mary Penaluna might pretend not to be interested, but he knew better. Once or twice, watching her out of the tail of his eye, he had seen her lips twitch and part. He could tell a good story, and knew it. In soldier camps and on shipboard he had always held his sophisticated audiences at his tongue's tip; it would be surprising if he could not charm a simple farm girl.

More than ever he admired her, the soft glow on her brown hair as she sat sewing, her broad efficient hands, the bountiful curves of her. And ecod! In what excellent order she kept the house! That was the sort of wife for a farmer.

And he was a farmer now; why, yes, certainly. He would start work the very next day.

This wandering was all very well while one was young, but he was getting on for thirty, and holed all over with wounds, five to be precise. He'd marry that girl, settle down and prosper.

As he walked home, he planned it all out. His mother should stop at Bosula of course, but she'd have to understand that Mary was mistress. Not that that would disturb Teresa to any extent. She detested housekeeping and would be glad to have it off her hands. Then there was Eli, good old brother, best farmer in the Duchy. Eli was welcome to stop too and share all profits. Ortho hoped that he would stop, but he had noticed that Eli had been very silent and strange since his homecoming and was not sure of him, might be wanting to marry as well and branch out for himself. Tregors had gone, but there was over four hundred pounds of that smuggling money remaining, and if Eli wanted to set up for himself he should have every penny of it to start him, every blessed penny—it was not more than his due, dear old lad.

As soon as Mary accepted him—he didn't expect her to take more than a week in making up her mind—he'd hand the money over to Eli with his blessing. Before he reached home that night he had settled everybody's affairs to his own satisfaction and their advantage. Ortho was in a generous mood, being hotly in love again.

Chapter XXVII

TERESA RODE out of St Gwithian in a black temper. Three days before, in another fit of temper, she had packed the house-girl from Bosula, bag and baggage, and she was finding it difficult to get another. For two days she had been canvassing the farms in vain and now St Gwithian had proved a blank draw. She could not herself cook, and the Bosula household was living on cold odds and ends, a diet which set the men grumbling and filled her with disgust. She pined for the good times when Martha was alive and three smoking meals came up daily, as a matter of course.

Despite the fact that she offered the best wages in the neighbourhood, the girls would not look at her—saucy jades! Had she enquired she would have learnt that, as a mistress, she was reported too free with her tongue and fists.

St Gwithian fruitless, there was nothing for it but to try Mousehole. Teresa twisted her big horse about and set off forthwith for the fishing village in the hopes of picking up some crabber's wench who could handle a basting pan—it was still early in the morning. A cook she must get by hook or crook; Ortho was growling a great deal at his meals—her precious Ortho!

She was uneasy about her precious Ortho, his courtship of the Penaluna girl was not progressing favourably. He had not mentioned the affair, but to his doting mother all was plain as daylight. She knew perfectly well where he spent his evenings, and she knew as well as if he had told her that he was making no headway. Men successful in love do not flare like tinder at any tiny mishap, sigh and brood apart in corners, come stumbling to bed at night damning the door latches for not springing to meet their hands, the stairs for tripping them up; do not publicly, and apropos of nothing, curse all women—meaning one particular woman. Oh no, Ortho was beating up against a headwind.

Teresa was furious with the Penaluna hussy for presuming to withstand her son. She had looked higher for Ortho than a mere farmer's daughter; but, since the farmer's daughter did not instantly succumb, Teresa was determined Ortho should have her—the haughty baggage!

After all, Simeon owned the adjacent property and was undeniably well to do. The girl had looks of a sort (though the widow, being enormous herself, did not generally admire big women) and was reported a good housewife; that would solve the domestic difficulty. But the main thing was that Ortho wanted the chit, therefore he should have her.

Wondering how quickest this could be contrived she turned a corner of the lane and came upon the girl in question, walking into St Gwithian, a basket on her arm, her blue cloak blowing in the wind. Teresa jerked her horse up, growling 'Good morning.'

'Good morning,' Mary replied and walked past.

Teresa scowled after her and shouted, 'Hold fast a minute!'

Mary turned about. 'Well?'

'What whimsy tricks are you serving my boy Ortho?' said Teresa, who was nothing if not to the point.

Mary's eyebrows rose. 'What do 'e mean, "whimsy tricks"? I do serve 'en a fitty supper nigh every evening of his life and listen to his tales till . . .'

'Oh, you know what I mean well enough,' Teresa roared. 'Are 'e goin' to have him? That's what I want to know.'

'Have who?'

'My son.'

'Which son?' The two women faced each other for a moment, the black eyes wide with surprise, the brown sparkling with amusement, then Mary dropped a quick curtsey and disappeared round the corner.

Teresa sat still for some minutes glaring after her, mouth sagging with astonishment. Then she cursed sharply; then she laughed aloud; then, catching her horse a vicious smack with the rein, she rode on. The feather-headed fool preferred Eli to Ortho! Preferred that slow-brained hunk of brawn and solemnity to Ortho the handsome, the brilliant, the daring, the sum of manly virtues! It was too funny! Too utterly ridiculous! Eli, the clod, preferred to Ortho, the diamond! The girl was raving mad, raving! Eli had visited Roswarva a good deal at one time, but not since Ortho's return. Teresa hoped the girl was aware that Ortho was absolute owner of Bosula and that Eli had not a penny to his name—now. If she were not, Teresa determined she should not long go in ignorance.

At any rate, it could only be a question of time; Mary might still have some friendly feeling for Eli, but once she really began to know Ortho she would forget all about that. Half the women in the country would give their heads to get the romantic squire of Bosula; they went sighing after him in troops at fairs and public occasions. Yet something in the Penaluna girl's firm jaw and steady brown eyes told Teresa that she was not easily swayed hither and thither—she wished she could get Eli out of the way for a bit.

She rode over the hill and down the steep lane into Mousehole and there found an unwonted stir afoot.

The village was full of seamen armed with bludgeons and cutlasses, running up and down the narrow alleys in small parties, kicking the doors in and searching the houses.

The fisherwomen hung out of their windows and flung jeers and slops at them.

'Press gang,' Teresa was informed. They had landed from a frigate anchored just round the corner in Gwavas Lake and had so far caught one sound man, one epileptic, and the village idiot, who was vastly pleased at having someone take notice of him at last.

A boy, line fishing off Tavis Vor, had seen the gang rowing in, given the alarm, and by the time the sailors arrived all the men were a quarter of a mile inland. Very amusing, eh? Teresa agreed that it was indeed most humorous and added her shrewd taunts to those of the fishwives.

Then an idea sprang to her head. She went into the tavern and drank a pot of ale while thinking it over. When the smallest detail was complete, she set out to find the officer in command.

She found him without difficulty, an elderly and dejected midshipman, leaning over the slip rails, spitting into the murky waters of the harbour, and invited him very civilly to take a nip of brandy with her.

The officer accepted without question. A nip of brandy was a nip of brandy, and his stomach was out of order consequent on his having supped off rancid pork the night before. Teresa led him to a private room in the tavern, ordered the drinks and, when they arrived, locked the door.

'Look 'e, captain,' said she, 'do 'e want to make a couple of guineas?'

The midshipman's dull glance leapt to meet hers, agleam with sudden interest, as Teresa surmised it would. She knew the type, forty years old, without influence or hope of promotion, disillusioned, shabby, hanging body and soul together on thirty shillings a month; there was little this creature would not do for two pounds down.

'What is it?' he snapped.

'I'll give you two pounds and a good sound man—if you'll fetch 'en.'

The midshipman shook his tarred hat. 'Not inland, I won't go inland.' Press gangs were not safe inland in Cornwall, and he was not selling his life for forty shillings; it was a dirty life but he still had some small affection for it.

'Who said it was inland? To a small little cove just this side of Monk's Cove, you'll know it by the waterfall that do come down over cliff there. T'eddn more'n a two-mile pull from here, just round the point.'

'Is the man there?'

'Not yet, but I'll have 'en there by dusk. Do you pull your boat up on the little beach and step inside the old tinner's adit—kind of little cave on the east side—and wait there till he comes. He's a mighty strong man, I warn 'e, a notable wrestler in these parts, so be careful.'

'I'll take four of my best and sandbag him from behind,' said the midshipman, who was an expert in these matters. 'Stiffens 'em, but don't kill. Two pounds ain't enough, though.'

'It's all you'll get,' said Teresa.

'Four pound or nothing,' said the midshipman firmly.

They compromised at three pounds, and Teresa paid cash on the spot; Ortho, the free-handed, kept her in plenty of money—so different from Eli.

The midshipman walked out of the front door, Teresa slipped out of the back and rode away. She had little fear the midshipman would fail her. He had her money to be sure, but he would also get a bounty on Eli and partly save his face with his captain; he would be there right enough.

She continued her search for a cook in Paul and rode home slowly to gain time, turned her horse, as usual, all standing into the stable, and then went to look for her younger son.

She was not long in finding him, a noise of hammering disclosed his whereabouts.

She approached in a flutter of well simulated excitement.

'Here you, Eli, Eli,' she called.

'What is it?' he asked, never pausing in his work.

'I've just come round by the cliffs from Mousehole. There's a good ship's boat washed up in Zawn a Bal. Get you round there quick and take her into Monk's Cove, she'm worth five pounds if she'm worth a penny.'

Eli looked up. 'Hey! . . . What sort of boat?'

'Gig, I think—she'm lying on the sand by the side of the adit.'

Eli whistled. 'Gig—eh! All right, I'll get down there soon's I've finished this.'

Teresa stamped her foot. 'Some o' they Mousehole or covemen'll find her if you don't stir yourself!'

Eli nodded. 'All right, all right, I'm going. I'm not for throwing away a good boat any more'n you are. Just let me finish this gate. I shan't be a minute.'

Teresa turned away. He would go and there was over an hour to spare, he would go fast enough, go blindly to his fate. She turned up the valley with a feeling that she would like to be as far from the dark scene of action as possible. But it would not do Eli any harm, she told herself, he was not being murdered, he was going to serve in the navy for a little, as tens of thousands of men were doing. Every sailor was not killed, only a small percentage, no harm would come to him, good rather; he would see the world and enlarge his mind. In reality she was doing him a service.

Nevertheless her nerves were jumping uncomfortably. Eli was her own flesh and blood after all, John's son. What would John, in heaven, say to all this? She had grasped the marvellous opportunity of getting rid of Eli without thinking of the consequences; she was an opportunist by blood and training, could not help herself.

Well, it was done now, there was no going back—and it would clear the way for Ortho.

Yet she could not rid herself of a vision of the evil midshipman crouching in the adit with his four men, handlers and sandbags, waiting, waiting, and Eli striding towards them through the dusk, whistling, all unconscious. She began to blubber softly. But she did not go home; she waddled on up the valley, sniffling, blundering into trees, blinking the tears back, talking to herself, telling John in heaven that it was all for the best. She would not go back to Bosula till after dark, till it was all over.

*　*　*

Eli strapped the blankets on more firmly, kicked the straw up round the horse's belly, picked up the oil bottle, and stood back.

'Think he'll do now,' he said.

Bohenna nodded. ' 'Ess, but 'twas a mercy I catched you in time. Gived me a fair fright when I found 'en.'

'I'll get Ortho to speak to mother,' Eli said. ' 'Tisn't her fault the horse isn't dead. Here, take this bottle in with you.'

Bohenna departed.

Eli piled up some more straw and cleared the manger out. A shadow fell across the litter.

'Might mix a small mash for him,' he said without looking round.

'Mash for who?' a voice inquired. Eli turned about and saw, not Bohenna, but Simeon Penaluna, dressed in his best.

'Been to market,' Simeon explained. 'Looked in on the way back. What have 'e got here?'

'Horse down with colic. Mother turned him loose into the stable. Corn bin was open, he ate his fill, and then had a good drink at the trough. I've had a proper job with him.'

'All right now, eddn 'a?'

'Yes, I think so.'

Simeon shuffled his expansive feet. 'Don't see much of you up to Roswarva these days.'

'No.'

More shufflings. 'We do brearly miss 'e.'

'That so?'

Simeon cleared his throat. 'My maid asked 'e to supper some three months back . . . well, if you don't come up soon it'll be getting cold like.'

There was an uncomfortable pause, then Eli looked up steadily. 'I want you to understand, Sim, that things aren't the same with me as they were, now Ortho's come home. My father died too sudden; he didn't leave a thing to me. I'm nothing but a beggar now. Ortho . . .'

The gaunt slab of hair and wrinkles that was Simeon's face split into a smile.

'Here, for gracious' sake don't speak upon Ortho! He's pretty nigh talked me deaf and dumb night after night, of how he was a king in Barbary and whatnot and so forth . . . clunk, clunk, clunk! In the Lord's name do you come up and let's have a little sociable silence for a change!'

'Do you mean it?' Eli gasped.

'Mean it,' said Simeon, laying a hairy paw on his shoulder. 'Did you ever hear me or my maid say a word we didn't mean—son?'

Eli rushed across the yard and into the house to fetch his best coat.

Teresa was standing in front of the fire, hands outstretched, shivering despite the blaze. She reeled when her son went bounding past her, reeled as though she had seen a ghost.

'Eli! My God, Eli!' she cried. 'What—how—where you been?'

'In the stable physicking your horse,' he said, climbing the stairs. 'I sent Ortho after that boat.'

He did not hear the crash his mother made as she fell; he was in too much of a hurry.

* * *

Ortho climbed the forward ladder and came out on the upper deck. The ship was thrashing along under all plain sail, braced sharp up.

The sky was covered with torn fleeces of cloud, but blue patches gleamed through the rents, and the ship leapt forward lit by a beam of sunshine, white pinioned, a clean bone in her teeth. A rainstorm had just passed over, drenching her, and ever rope and spar was outlined with glittering beads, the wet deck shone like a plaque of silver. Cheerily sang the wind in the shrouds, the weather leeches quivered, the reefpoints pattered impatient fingers, and under Ortho's feet the frigate trembled like an eager horse reaching for its bit.

'She's snorting the water from her nostrils all right,' he said approvingly. 'Step on, lady.'

So he was aboard ship again. How he had come there he didn't know. He remembered nothing after reaching Zawn a Bal cove and trying to push that boat off. His head gave an uncomfortable throb. Ah, that was it! He had been knocked on the head—press gang.

Well, he had lost that damned girl, he supposed. No matter, there were plenty more, and being married to one rather hampered you with the others. Life on the farm would have been unutterably dull really. He was not yet thirty. A year or two more roving would do no harm. His head gave another throb, and he put his hand to his brow.

A man polishing the ship's bell noted the gesture and laughed. 'Feelin' sick, me bold farmer? How d'you think you'll like the sea?'

'Farmer!' Ortho snarled. 'Hell's bells! I was upper yard man of the *Elijah Impey*, pick of the East Indies fleet!'

'Was you, be God?' said the polisher, a note of respect in his voice.

'Ay, that I was. Say, mate, what packet is this?'

'*Triton*, frigate—Captain Charles Mulholland.'

'Good bully?'

'The best.'

'She seems to handle pretty kind,' said Ortho, glancing aloft.

'Kind!' said the main with enthusiasm. 'She'll eat out of your hand, she'll talk to you.'

'Aha! . . . Know where we're bound?'

'West Indies, I've heard.'

'West Indies!' Ortho had a picture of peacock islands basking in coral seas, of odorous green jungles, fruit-laden, festooned with ropes of flowers; of gaudy, painted parrots preening themselves among the tree-ferns; of black girls, heroically moulded, flashing their white teeth at him. . . .

West Indies! He drew a deep breath. Well, at all events that was something new.

CROSBIE GARSTIN
PENHALE

Also available from Literary Nation:

High Noon (Penhale 2)

St Lucia, 1782. Ortho Penhale, taken by press gang into the Navy, is fighting against the French at the Battle of the Saintes under Admiral Rodney.

Returning home wounded to Bosula, his farm in west Cornwall, Penhale finds his world has changed irrevocably.

First published in 1925, *High Noon* follows the continuing adventures of Ortho Penhale as he finds a new love and embarks on a disastrous career as a slave ship captain.

ISBN 978-0-9933131-1-0

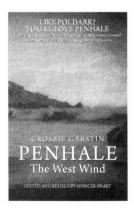

The West Wind (Penhale 3)

Cornwall, 1795. With Britain at war with France, Spain and Holland, Ortho Penhale is recruited to captain a privateer for his brother's friend Burnadick. After a disastrous assault on a Dutch man-o'-war, Penhale is imprisoned in Spain.

First published in 1926, *The West Wind* follows Ortho Penhale the fugitive as he travels across Spain heading for his beloved Cornwall. His past returns to haunt him as he embarks on his final triumphant act.

ISBN 978-0-9933131-2-7

LITERARY
NATION

Available from your local bookshop or buy online at www.literarynation.com

CROSBIE GARSTIN
PENHALE

The Witty Vagabond
by David Tovey

When news filtered down to West Cornwall during Easter Sunday in 1930 that Crosbie Garstin, then aged just 42, was missing, feared drowned, after a boating accident at Salcombe, a deep sense of shock affected the countless friends, acquaintances and admirers of this "beloved, gifted, famous author and poet", this "serious and conscientious artist", this "brave, laughing care-free soldier", and this "blithe and heroic spirit", who was "in every way a notable son of Cornwall". It seemed incredible that a fine sportsman and expert swimmer, who had experienced intrepid adventures all around the world, should drown in Salcombe estuary, that perceived haven of tranquillity. Whilst the initial disbelief was soon dispelled, as the facts became known, there are still those who contend that Crosbie did not drown but did a disappearing act, and it is a telling comment on human nature that, currently, there is more interest in this 'mystery', than there is in the widely diverse and hugely entertaining body of literature that he produced. The current neglect is all the more surprising as Crosbie's own life was one big adventure story in itself.

Comprehensively researched and written by David Tovey, a leading Cornish art historian, The Witty Vagabond offers a thorough and excellent insight into Crosbie Garstin's life and times.

Find out more information about this biography and order a copy from <ins>www.stivesart.info</ins>.

Printed in Great Britain
by Amazon